The PROTAGONISTS

By the same author:

ONE HALF OF THE WORLD

The PROTAGONISTS

BY JAMES BARLOW

Harper & Brothers   *Publishers*   *New York*

THE PROTAGONISTS

Copyright © 1956 by James Barlow

Printed in the United States of America

Library of Congress catalog card number: 57-11793

CONTENTS

v

PART ONE
VICTIM

I

THE man and the woman walk slowly, unwillingly, at a pace that is funereal. Tiredness contributes to the dragged movement of the woman, and the man, in kindness, in awe at her suffering, moves at her pace. He is taller than she, gaunt, a thing of structure and sinews, with a good, well-boned face, and a middle-aged body that is in almost athletic condition. He wears the black uniform of a bus-driver, but no hat: he is off duty. On the black sleeves are two diamond-shaped black patches of cloth. The uniform is not black enough to convey his mourning, so he has added the patches. The woman's attire is more obviously that of bereavement: all black and grey—gloves, shoes, stockings, handbag—everything. Older, in appearance, but not in fact, than the man, she has no need to wear black clothes; her middle-aged face, not trained or inclined to hide her feelings, shows the lined exhaustion and the stunned grief of some personal blow, some appalling loss. They are man and wife, these two; one sees that in their oneness; and one wonders in the slight impatience of the non-involved what, if they still have each other, they could lose that could hurt them so much.

Their background is quite startling. In a city they might not be conspicuous—for much of a city's background is black or dirty; but they are surrounded by green. Fields and trees stretch away to three horizons, ending in distance on two and Welsh mountains on a third; on the fourth is the sea, a cold, fast-moving sea despite the still air, green, choppy water flecked with white. There is not much cloud on this day and what there is spreads in two layers across itself in a pattern of extraordinary beauty. If one turns the head sideways, or even upside down, there is an incredible appearance of space and volume. The man and the woman are walking down a lane towards the sea and whichever way they stare is splendour; but they do not look; they do not see; the magnificence is merely distance to be overcome; the volume of salt air merely emphasizes the emptiness.

At a cross-road they turn right and walk along a main road (there is no pavement) parallel with the sea, which is half a mile away and about fifty feet lower. A few cars hurtle past: over-coiffured women yawn and stare (country bumpkins dressed in black: where on earth are they going?); someone throws out a cigarette stub from a saloon and it rolls near the man in an unintentional movement of contempt. The world passes by, anxious to be elsewhere: nothing special here: no town, no newspapers, the scenery flat, dreary and uninspiring, no good hotels, no music, no art, no petrol station, all looking rather too damp anyway; nothing but two people moving along the road. Should we give them a lift? No, better not; what have we to say to them? They do not even speak to each other. And that, indeed, is true. They have walked nearly two miles and scarcely said a word; it has all been said; there is nothing left to discuss.

The cemetery gates are unlocked, but there is no one else about. That is why the man and woman have come at this particular hour. There is a bus that they could have travelled in as far as the cross-roads. They must know the time of the bus, for the man himself drives it often. But they, wishing to be alone, visit the cemetery when they can expect to have it to themselves; the woman suffers the two-mile walk rather than endure the stares or even the sympathy of others; in the cemetery there is silence; no one says a word out of place.

The man approaches the small lodge where there is a tap and a watering-can. He then follows the woman, who is carrying chrysanthemums, to Grave 125. It has no stone; it is a recent grave; indeed, the whole cemetery is quite new and there is room for lots more dead. Several patches are marked out in anticipation (freehold or leasehold? one wonders). The woman bends to a small metal vase, removes some dead flowers, twists off the colander-like top of the vase, fills it with water and, having re-fastened the top, inserts the chrysanthemums one by one. The man stands near, watching her. The grave is tidied to the woman's satisfaction and they stand there, the ritual over, nothing to alleviate the suffering that brought them here; now they are face to face with it.

A shrieking noise attracts their attention, a scream of pure animality. Five or six seagulls—difficult to establish how many, for they hop about in busyness—have somehow forced a crow on to its back, and there is a frantic beating of wings now to accompany the shrieks, as the seagulls peck fiercely. It is a cruel, hard thing, unbearable to watch. Even the man flinches and turns away. It is too carnal—the killers and the victim, the shrieks of fear and satisfaction and the thing they fight about: a scrap of food. It is, for the couple, too reminiscent, and they make their way back with the watering-can towards the lodge.

The woman is tired now and moves to a seat by the tap. On an adjoining seat sits an old man. Because she does not recognize him the woman sits near—it is only friends and acquaintances she is afraid of and cannot bear to meet. The man on the seat is badly dressed, old, white-haired, and with a curious, spatial expression. He stares out to sea rather too evenly, and it occurs to the woman that something exceptional must be happening on the water. She looks, and on the horizon, eleven miles off, moves a boat. It is just an ordinary boat bound for the colliery farther up the coast, and the air is so still that behind the slow progress of the boat is a thin track of smoke. It stretches horizontally all the way along the horizon—a ribbon of smoke perhaps twenty or thirty miles in length. Remarkable. Very interesting; but not so extraordinary that it merits the prolonged, penetrating stare. The woman looks again at the man on the seat and she sees that he is blind. The first emotion beyond herself wells up in her throat and she feels pity. To be blind. The man on the seat has a small dog, and this animal now gets down and sniffs at the woman and her husband. He then jumps back on to the seat and licks the face of the man who is blind. The man's hands grope, fondle the dog in affection, and then proceed to a raincoat pocket to produce a rubber ball. This he throws to the ground and the dog jumps down eagerly to fetch it. The game continues until the dog, exploring too far, does not come back. The blind old man on the seat suddenly makes a noise —a screech of distorted, unhealthy sound that is far more abnormal than the shrieks of the crow or the satisfaction of the seagulls. After the first shock the woman realizes that the man is not peculiar, not mad or perverted in any way. It is just that he cannot speak. The strange, distorted cry is his communication, and the only one who understands it is a small dog, a mongrel with brown hair and watery brown eyes. It is so disturbing that the woman forgets her own tragedy and fetches the dog and the ball. She is glad that the old man cannot see her for she is crying. She thinks: There is always someone worse. To be blind and not able to speak; and yet he can offer love to a small animal. She weeps like a casualty —without awareness, as though she suffered from shell shock. And, in fact, she is a casualty; she and her husband are those

3

semi-participants, the next-of-kin. She is going to recover. At this moment she is being given shock treatment. She is confronted with another, more appalling casualty so that in the face of his disability she will again learn pity. The treatment will perhaps succeed: she cries now, not for her own flesh and blood, but for an old man who is blind and dumb and who sits (why?) on a cemetery seat with a dog.

If there is a battle—and that there exists a struggle of some description can hardly be disputed; we are not just animals who grow old; in our faces can be seen deteriorations that belong not only to age; in them can be discerned bitterness, pride, lust, greed, compassion, innocence, ignorance and the other things called qualities, relate these qualities to whatever you will—if there is a battle and it is, let us say, between good and evil, it is certain that these in the cemetery are casualties as well as next-of-kin. They are also participants. And in the grave they have visited lies another casualty. It is their daughter. The grave is only a few months old. This still, clean, cold day belongs to October and the daughter died in July. She, too, died in a battle, in part of the war between good and evil. Her sins and failures are well known. Her name, Olwen Rosemary Hughes, has been mouthed on the radio; it has been headlined; her picture has appeared in the newspapers; her defeats have been given all the publicity normally offered to a public interested in failure; she has been accorded the attention once allowed (before it became widespread, boring) to the fornication of a film star. Nobody has mentioned her victories; that is why her parents suffer so badly; and perhaps nobody ever will, for her last defeat was irrevocable, permanent. She was murdered.

In the war between good and evil the interest of the spectator—himself a casualty—is almost invariably directed towards the victories of evil. It is the same with that part of the struggle labelled crime—as though it were a separate part. The worst crime of all merits the greatest attention. A murderer is a rarity, a man apart, and it is natural that any focus of attention should be upon him. For anyone can be a victim: murder falls upon the innocent and the guilty, the rich and the poor, the normal and the abnormal, with the impartiality of an air raid. The killer, committing his deed without premeditation as he 'normally' does, in the uproar of the moment leaves a trail behind him. It is always interesting to see this trail pursued by authority, and then to hear the unhappy, normal words about love, unfairness, jealousy, the children, the other woman or man, the broken intentions, the meetings, the

4

hammer or knife that happened to be available—to hear about it and to realize that it might have been oneself.

When a young woman is murdered, no matter how innocent she may be, there is a tendency by the onlookers—the newspaper readers, the people in court, the man in the bar, even, perhaps, the police—to presume that she was killed with justification. And the justification is often said—at a comfortable, theoretical distance—to be that she involved the killer in a love affair; she drew him away from his family, wove a complicated net around him and finally made it necessary for him to commit violence to cut his way out of it. And if someone were to protest, 'It was not like that at all,' the same onlookers, the non-involved, the apathetic, would say, 'Well, what difference does it make? The pathologist said that the girl was not innocent. What d'you take us for? Mugs? We know all about it. We know a thing or two' (because we, too, are no longer innocent). They would shrug it all away; the truth does not matter all that much; let the parents suffer; let it all go down on record slightly inaccurate; what does it matter about the degree of guilt or who seduced whom? Waiting themselves for death in a more spectacular form, they find it easy to labour under the delusion that big explosions are the great sin of the world. Like many of us, while they wait to be destroyed, they do not believe the original sins matter so much. A dead body; a destroyed virginity; some lies; some unfaithfulness; some blasphemy; some person-to-person cruelty; some thefts—what do they matter if whole towns can be destroyed in the twinkling of an eye? But that sin is so big and obvious that even the atheists can see it. We have become enmeshed in our own complexity, and perhaps we should struggle back to the realization that the small, personal, individually-decided sins are the ones that hurt God the most. . . .

Olwen Hughes was born in a village called Coed Bell (Blue Wood) on the west coast of Wales, not far from the large seaside town and holiday resort of Bar Quay. The inhabitants of the village worked hard and lived frugally and righteously. If a woman put out washing on a Sunday they regarded it as sinful. If a boy took a girl over the hill against which the village leaned, it was almost certainly a sin; at any rate, explanations were demanded and both parents informed by witnesses. In theory these tendencies should have made Olwen suspicious of the behaviour of others; but in fact she was not inclined to be suspicious. It may be that among all the other incidents and accidents which led her to death was the accident of birthplace. If she had grown up in the town it is possible that the over-emphasized approaches of the holiday-makers along the promenade and in the cheap dance halls would have taught her to identify those men whose desires were for bodily satisfaction from the few who really loved her (although the man called Harrison had deceived others, more astute than she). For in the village was genuine quietness and peace. All the inhabitants spoke Welsh more easily than English. A few widows took in English visitors for the summer and were forgiven for it; but the main local occupations were dairy farming and quarrying. Olwen's visual memories during her first seventeen years were on a backcloth of green fields. In childish eagerness she watched the first lambs of February stand on their mothers' backs; the long, solemn processions of swollen cattle through the mud each after-noon; the patient response of the sheepdog to his master's whistle and the silly meanderings of sheep through gates and across rail-way lines: the activities of an equal innocence. She cycled to school in the cold gusts of October, through the dank smell of hedges, past the squashed dead toads and the mutilated hedgehogs, buffeted by winds at every corner, sometimes with friends, sometimes alone, never afraid, because she was where she belonged. And always at the end of the lane there was the sea to watch: cold and empty and eternal in winter, a hot, blue bath for visitors in summer. While the civilized world seemed to be drawing to a close, and sophisticated talk became sour with the inevitability of destruc-tion, here was absolute peace. In the same hot summer afternoons when the vapour trails over London and the faint crackle of cordite and cupro-nickel decided the first victory of those who did not really believe in glory, a hundred and a half miles away the twelve-year-old Olwen was not participating. She was to die in another, older war, and in that splendid summer she lay in the long grass and dreamed, or gathered flowers, or climbed through the gorse to the top of the hill to see the horizons spread around her. The sounds she heard were not hostile: the wind through the corn; the crash of the incoming waves; the sleepy lowing of cattle and the futile conversations of sheep; the faraway bark of a dog; the once-an-hour bus; the caw of the slow, flapping crows, black and manœuvrable as Heinkel bombers, although the distant thump was not a bomb, but work proceeding in the quarry. Talk, her own contribution to sound, was of school, of friends, of parents, of God; never of war or art or sin. When she met the man Harrison, Olwen was ashamed of her own lack of certain types of knowledge.

6

He talked so intimately of the theatre and books and of the indoor things that she was embarrassed, because these seemed more real than the reality they imitated. Yet despite her discomfort, she never disowned the reality; it was her wish to take the man Harrison 'when they were married' to share with him the value of silence and nature.

The Hughes family lived in a small old house surrounded by an untidy garden and a crumbling brick wall, beyond which was the lane that sloped down to the village. One street-lamp shone at night a quarter of a mile down the lane; there was no electricity or gas in the house, and water came from a pump. From her bedroom window Olwen could see the lane where it emerged beyond the trees, church spire and cottages of the village and wound several times in its mile and a half to the sea. Olwen and her brother Tom, two years older, would watch the lane to see a small bus which came along the coast road five miles from Bar Quay and then turned at right angles away from the shore and travelled into the village. The bus, a small vehicle that held twenty passengers, was driven by their own father, William Hughes, who also acted as conductor. His wife Nancy took in washing. The whole family led decent, quiet lives, worked hard, went regularly to chapel, and read their Bible without being self-conscious or ashamed about it.

Olwen's colouring, unlike her brother's sallow skin and dark hair of the typical Welshman, was unusual as well as beautiful. She had auburn hair of fine colour and texture, blue eyes and the excellent complexion that sometimes accompanies them. For a Welsh girl she was unusual in that she was quite tall. As a woman she had a wonderful body, with fine shoulders, long arms and legs covered with enough flesh to make her sensuous without being heavy. Her only awareness of her own beauty was instinctive, and showed in her rather clumsy gait, the typical walk of the shy girl, which is usually overcome or replaced after the teens. The cynic might well feel that such a girl was only created for physical love, but Olwen merited kinder attention than that. She had temper and physical courage, laughter and compassion; the willingness to work hard; she was devoted to her parents and brother, and later, as a nurse, to patients who were neither beautiful nor pleasant. In the face of other nurses' apathy she retained religious belief. She was the sort of girl who would sacrifice her life for a child, as, in a way, she did. Her faults, which were not serious, included the usual female ones of indifference to the arguments of the mind, to politics; the unawareness that sin is not something you only talk about in church; it has to be recognized and fought when it is encountered; and recognition is not always easy. Sin does not come to a young woman in the form of obvious ugliness; it comes in a sports car, is well clothed, has good taste, talks quite intelligently, and persuades until she has convinced herself that any sacrifice for love is a good choice, and probably a right and beautiful one.

As a child Olwen made friends easily. She was affectionate, energetic and full of conversation. She walked over the fields and hills and along the shore with her girl friends, played tig with her particular friend Peggy around the rambling, white-washed farm where Peggy lived with three sisters and her parents; learned there to love animals; on Saturdays would travel round in a milk float delivering milk with Peggy or her sisters; and on Sundays the same young girls would meet at and after Sunday School to ramble along the hillside picking flowers. After some years at the village national school Olwen proceeded to the county school at Bar Quay, which Tom already attended. She was always better on the playing fields than in the classroom. In school she was attentive, but some subjects, particularly algebra, trigonometry and Latin, she could scarcely understand at all. She was better at geography, history, art, the Scriptures and botany—things which depended on common sense and memory rather than progressive deduction. She could be thrown quite easily into a panic by sarcasm or anger from the teachers, a panic in which she could only stand silently, going scarlet and trying not to cry.

If the onlookers could have approached Olwen's vicar they might have expressed a different opinion about her (for that it was only an opinion, and an opinion by implication at that, is obvious; the girl was dead and therefore not available for cross-examination by newspaper reporters or the police). But the vicar, old even when Olwen was a child, was dead years before the man called Harrison encountered Olwen. Whatever may have been her behaviour towards the end of her life, Olwen took her religious beliefs seriously when she was a child and a teen-aged girl. She accepted God emotionally, which is to accept Him always. Never did she make the pseudo-scientific discovery that He could not exist. On the contrary, she was always quite positive of His existence. Sometimes, when she had committed a small wrong, she would feel an enormous fear and unhappiness, as though He were there, waiting for an explanation. She would even look fearfully over her shoulder . . .

II

OLWEN ROSEMARY HUGHES, thirteen years and ten months, four foot eight inches, six stone two pounds, blue eyes, auburn hair, occupation schoolgirl, moles on left arm and right shoulder, Protestant, single, nationality Welsh—Olwen, precocious, with a zest for life, in excellent health, aware that there was a mystery ahead that she would have to solve, probably alone, returned from the village school to find her brother talking to another boy at their own gate. It meant nothing; it had happened before; but this time Tom's friend stared at Olwen. He was about Tom's age, fifteen, pale and thin, sad in appearance, defeated perhaps, or aware of defeats in the world, and in his encountered eyes she saw astonishment, wonder, reverence and embarrassment all confused together. Her own heart thumped in curious, unexpected excitement, she blushed as much as the boy did, and hurried with hanging head into the house. From her bedroom window she peered cautiously to watch the boy and her brother, and with inexplicable disappointment saw him cycle away.

At tea she said, 'Who was your friend?'

Tom, deep in food, said, 'Oh, that was Leslie. Why?'

Not knowing the reason for her evasion, scarcely aware that it was only a half-answer, Olwen said, 'What a funny face he has. Sad.'

Tom gave the matter his momentary consideration. 'You've got a face like a pudding,' he said. A long half-minute later he delighted her by adding, 'Although he didn't think so.'

'What did he think?'

'What does that matter to you, since he has a funny face?'

'Was he rude about me?' she asked, indirect still in her first feminine subtleties.

'No,' said Tom. 'He seemed to like you.' Another pause, while he negotiated bread and jam, and then his explanation: 'He's a fool, anyway.'

'Why is he?'

'He reads poetry.'

Olwen thought: Another six months and I shall be at the county school, able to see him. She was prepared to wait, to carry the thought of him about with her in tenderness, and, if necessary, pain, for six months, perhaps to have it destroyed at the end. Her love belonged to the other, more tender side of puberty. It belonged to the most painful of all, and the most harshly dealt with; that which has to fit in with the whimsical plans of older people; which is laughed at, scorned as juvenile, and ended arbitrarily by the plans of parents. Yet which is infinitely more tender than anything that follows. It became unnecessary for Olwen to wait. Ten days later the boy came on a Saturday afternoon. He brought a great number of photographs of aeroplanes cut from magazines—perhaps he had no need for them any more—and since it was a rainy day the two boys spent the afternoon with the pictures spread on the floor of the front room. This was the one room of the house regarded as especially valuable. It contained faded, framed photographs of Olwen's grandparents; cabinets that lent the room part of its stuffy smell; plates along the frieze; plush, heavy furniture; an old gramophone; and a completely valueless, dark, heavily framed oil painting of a great-grandparent. Such was the naïve regard in which this painting was held that Olwen was brought up to understand that it was like 'one of Rembrandt's' in a tone that implied that it was without doubt the work of one of his contemporaries.

It was difficult to obtain an excuse to enter this room, but Olwen did so once or twice. The boy Leslie stared at her in obvious regard, but Tom ignored her altogether and had clearly forgotten, if he had ever known, the implications of the previous tea-time dialogue. The boy stayed to tea, but did not eat well. This was so unusual in either Tom or his friends that Olwen concluded jubilantly that Leslie's lack of appetite had some association with her own presence. In her delight she became boisterous, even facetious, until Tom in irritation asked, 'What's the matter with you? You're like a damn' wasp buzzing about.'

'Now, Tom,' his mother scolded at once. 'No bad words. Olwen can talk if she wishes.'

'Well, she talks tripe,' growled Tom.

'Not everybody wants to talk about silly aeroplanes,' Olwen said. The boy Leslie blushed and Olwen, realizing that she had included him in this criticism, rushed on, 'I'm sure Leslie's sick of hearing you talk about them.'

During the whole long, exasperating afternoon and evening there did not seem to be a single moment for Leslie and Olwen to talk to each other. He was so overcome that even in the general conversation at table he did not address her directly. Because the evening was wet and cold, the two boys stayed in the rear room of the house with Olwen and her mother; Mr. Hughes being at work. A few occasions arrived in which Olwen and Leslie were alone, but they seemed unable to use them; each time a suffocating silence spread between them so that the return of others was a relief. Just before he departed Leslie, in a moment together, said with visible effort, 'I go for a ride on my bike along the shore on Sunday mornings.'

Olwen said, in the depression of the evening, 'Do you?' and the dialogue withered altogether.

Later, in the warm, comforting wishful-thinking of near-sleep Olwen thought with tenderness of the boy who had in silence conveyed such a lot to her. She analysed his every gesture and blush, and in the morning asked permission to go to chapel later in the day.

Outside the house it was bitterly cold and her tenderness seemed foolish. She could scarcely recall what Leslie looked like; she might bicycle along the shore for miles and see nobody; she could miss him by being too early or too late; and if she met him he might conclude that she had wished to see him; and this, although true, did not seem at all desirable. Nevertheless, she rode the mile to the shore, and since Leslie went to the school at Bar Quay she rode on the hard sand towards the pier on a horizon some miles off. The sky and the sea were grey; the strong wind was in her face; the sand blew grittily about; her eyes and nose moistened; she had to bend her head, and would not have seen Leslie at all if she had not heard his bicycle bell.

In the cold Leslie looked paler than before; his nose and eyes watered too; he was not altogether attractive, but Olwen liked him. It was the gentleness, his sadness, that stirred her. She did not know why he was awed by the sight of her, although he evidently was, treating her with something near to reverence.

They did not know what to say to each other. They desired to speak the truth, and were unaware that love has to have ordinary moments; it is prolonged and sustained by the usual lies and hypocrisy, the tedious, everyday conversations about time and place.

'Shall we go somewhere?' Leslie asked, happier with something to do.

'Let's visit the lighthouse,' Olwen suggested. It was in fact the only place to go unless they were to remain on the featureless shore in what amounted to a small-scale sandstorm. They cycled about three miles to the lighthouse, which was not really a lighthouse, but an observation tower erected during a previous war.

Inside, away from the wind, they glowed. 'It's *warm*,' said Olwen in astonishment.

'We could always come here,' said Leslie. 'Until the summer,' he qualified; for in the summer the lighthouse was surrounded by visitors, children, dogs, caravans and other, more furtive lovers.

They stayed for half an hour, not talking much, half-silent in awe of each other. The touch of sleeves was like a physical contact, a kiss of clothes, almost unbearable. It did not take long to examine the tower, its entrance, the stone steps and the observation room; there were empty cigarette packets, some old newspapers, and the rest was dust and cobwebs. They stared out of the narrowed windows. Sandhills for miles each way; nobody about; the grey sea crashing itself into foam; seagulls poised in the face of the wind, eyes and heads turning, observing too, to swerve away gracefully.

As they walked down the stone steps Leslie said, 'You have dust on your coat.'

'Will you brush it off?'

But to do that would be like striking her. Leslie could not do it. 'What's the matter?' Olwen asked. She was as nervous and fidgety as the boy; like all new lovers, they were so much in apprehension of each other and that thing they had found, that it was not until about to depart that they ventured to share it.

'Nothing,' said Leslie. 'I like you,' he added. It was an explanation.

'But I mustn't go home with my coat dirty,' Olwen said.

It was her excuse for the same event. He dusted the whitewash from her shoulders and then touched her auburn hair. They kissed clumsily and softly, and in that contact was born the love and compassion that led Olwen to her death.

They met many times that spring, always on the shore. Leslie never came to the house again, for Tom, having obtained the photographs, ended the friendship in that careless, capricious way that schoolboys do. Olwen waited with longing for the summer which she could share with him—they would walk through the hills, leaving the shore for the visitors—and for the end of the summer when she would be a younger pupil at the same school.

It ended as it began, in tenderness, with a dream-like quality of sadness. He met her one Saturday afternoon and his mouth was down-turned in genuine gloom. 'I've got to leave,' he said. 'To London.'

'How exciting!' said Olwen.

'I mean for good,' Leslie complained. 'I shan't see you again.'

'Not even to-morrow?'

'No. It's my father. His job. They haven't said a word about it to me before. They say I have to pack to-morrow, and to see aunts and things.' He concluded in dejection, 'We leave on Monday.'

There was not much to say. She knew he would never come back; even in love one does not make visits when one is fifteen; one accepts the arbitration of parents.

'Will you write to me?'

'Of course I will.'

'It's such a pity. I'm going to the county school in September.'

They cycled to the lighthouse, heavy-hearted, and found two older lovers inside, tightly pressed against each other in silence. The entire day was prejudiced against young lovers, for it began to rain. They rode the whole way to Bar Quay and sat in a shelter. They could only hold hands, for in the wet afternoon of early summer old ladies, having ventured out without umbrellas, now sat and stared with hostile curiosity at the young. The rain became heavier, and there arrived a moment when there was nothing to do but go home. Leslie, without a raincoat, cycled all the way with Olwen to the village. Half-way up the lane, in the darkness of the rain and trees, they separated in tender misery. At the last moment he gave her a small packet. 'Open it when I've gone,' he asked. In the quietness of her bedroom, with the rain still hissing outside, and tears still possible and imminent, Olwen opened the package and found inside a brooch made in the shape of a lighthouse.

Olwen received a few letters from Leslie, but she never saw him again. He influenced her life in that his love did not have time to deteriorate; it was not sapped away in any quarrels or indifference; she was left with a tender, uncomplicated view of love; it was as if he was a casualty in the war that was raging. Without their more permanent pain, she was like the young war widows who would never know the ordinariness of marriage, but would move through the remainder of their lives knowing that something perfect had gone out of them. Sneered at and despised as semi-spinsters, as they grew older they would look back to the brittle glory of the 1940s: to the departures at railway stations, the dancing while the bombs shook the tables and glasses, to the films and plays, to his guarded confessions, to the passion; in the midst of drabness they could look behind, never knowing that perfection might have faltered and grown old and ordinary. Olwen was only a child, and recovery for her was quick and at times pleasant; to say that she had a boy in London made the lads at school seem suburban.

Autumn, 1943. The bombers stream out both times round the clock—wedges of destruction a hundred miles long and two or three deep and wide. Across and under the Mediterranean there thumps explosion after explosion. Petrol flames and men die horribly. Beside the statistical destruction emerges slowly the probability that we are going to win.

By the school gates the leaves fell from the plane trees. The rounded clouds were pushed quickly across the sky. There was little traffic, for the visitors had gone home. It was a delicious quiet, a peace that was broken only by the sound of children's voices. There was no sign of war, but nevertheless an assault was forming; for the million-millionth time the oldest battle of all commenced.

Each afternoon the sixth-form boy stood at the school gates watching Olwen through the smoke as it issued from the pipe he had. The glance was different; it was significant; it was adult and unnerving, and in some way she knew why it was more serious than the innocent admiration of those third-, fourth- and fifth-form boys which had preceded it. It was because it held no awe, perhaps no respect; it approached her beauty on equal, even superior terms.

Olwen, in the fifth form, was beginning the last three terms of her school life. She was plump now, with a wide, beautiful face, incredibly smooth and rounded in this, her sixteenth year, and with a body that was as ripe as a woman's. She had become aware of her face and body, conscious that men stared at her legs and figure, and, although scarcely aware of the full vulgarity of these stares, was embarrassed by them—embarrassed and yet pleased. She was torn between a desire to wear attractive clothes and stockings and look desirable, and the shy necessity of wearing woollen stockings and presenting as flat a chest as possible. She longed to be a woman, a person with rights and freedoms, but saw that it would have its disadvantages. She would blush easily and even unnecessarily, and did not altogether enjoy visiting the town of Bar Quay except in the safety of winter. There were crowds of soldiers there from the wartime camp; there were drunks in the afternoon and fights in the evening; it was unsafe to sit in a cinema unless friends were contiguous; women with bold faces and clothes promenaded with arrogant confidence; not knowing why, Olwen was afraid of them. The soldiers looked at her boldly and suggestively; some whistled and a few even spoke to her; all of them whispered to each other and her face would go hot in fear and unaccountable shame. It was a relief to cycle home to the village. She would pass soldiers out walking with town girls, but they never penetrated as far as the village: five miles was too far for girls with high heels.

Each afternoon she would chatter at the school gates, unnerved and yet attracted by that unwavering examination by the sixth-form boy. She averted her gaze, smiled to show that she was busily engaged, and made loud and adult remarks about Beethoven, the war, marriage, the peculiarities of the teachers—anything that entered her head. She talked eagerly, for to stop would reveal that she was not popular, or was not gay, or was ignorant—it might convey any unfavourable impression the older boy cared to form.

The sixth-form boy, whose name was Bond, was tall, cumber-somely built, as big as a man and appearing old enough to be one. His Christian name, rarely used because he was not liked much, was Paul. Like the soldiers, he had noticed Olwen's adult body, her smooth, long legs, her pulchritude; otherwise he would not have bothered to pursue her, being already involved with waitresses, girls at the fun fairs and shopgirls. Olwen was flattered as well as perturbed by the attentions of an older boy, particularly one who was going soon to the university; and she acted in a very grown-up manner until Bond actually spoke to her. Then she stammered, answered in monosyllables, and conveyed a true impression of innocence and inexperience.

She listened attentively to Bond's talk about himself, about books, the war, love and life in general. It was the most sophisti-cated talk she had heard, and the compliments that went with it were different to those that had preceded them. They did not plead or falter in reverence: we both know about this beauty, they said, it is ours and we must share it. Olwen admired Bond when he smoked his pipe; liked the way he handled people less nervously than did her own father; and went with him willingly and shyly into cafés and the theatres of the town. If his kisses were different —exploring inside her mouth: it made her rather giddy and faint— and if one arm and hand hugged her below instead of around the waist, it did not seem important enough to dispute. She liked him very much because it gave her an importance to be the friend of a sixth-form boy.

When Bond suggested a swim in the sea, Olwen accompanied him with the anticipation of a pleasant Saturday afternoon and evening: tea in a café to follow the swim, then a visit to a theatre or cinema, and finally, before her bus left, a walk in the dusk and his words and the probing tongue. . . . It was still warm and as bright as summer on the shore, and after the swim she and Bond lay on the sand in the sunlight. The beach was crowded with holiday-makers, and when Bond desired to kiss her she presumed she understood perfectly his plea for the privacy of a beach hut. But inside the hut Bond's kisses, having probed her mouth to induce the pleasurable excitement, soon moved from the mouth to her shoulders. At the same time the hands that had been embracing her—the one, as before, much too low; how low explained perfectly well by the pressure of her wet bathing costume against her skin—the hands began to stroke her bare arms and back. It seemed to be the approach that had been whispered and joked about, in theory, at school, and Olwen was too alarmed to move. Bond took this for consent and began slowly to peel off her swim suit. Olwen now struggled, and Bond soon found his efforts ludicrous, if not impossible. He explained that this was very adult; she must not be afraid; this was love; there was nothing wrong. But Olwen's virtue was not an accident, and, in any case, the ugliness in his eyes was not adult or beautiful; it was animal. She resisted the words as well as the gestures.

'What's the matter, Olwen?' Bond asked, polite with difficulty. Couldn't the fool see her own ripeness and how necessary it was to burst it? 'I thought you liked me.'

'I don't like that.'

Bond smiled in superiority. 'You don't know about it. You can't be a kid for ever,' he said. It was an explanation, not an apology; it seemed he pitied her. 'No use being a smasher if you don't have fun.' The smile was confident, mature—Bond was one of those who think the act of sex is the cleverest thing in the world; he could not stop admiring himself for being as accomplished as the animals. 'Perhaps you don't know how to have fun.' He would demonstrate, the fading smile said, and forgive her ignorance. Had Bond learned to have fun? Well, yes, he had. Bond had a certain talent for that kind of thing. Then one was not individual or remarkable to Bond? Well, no, except for the red hair; you see, as Bond understood it, love could be dished out wholesale; there was no necessity for a retail trade. . . . Olwen found such an approach too carnal, too emotionless. More than a decade later she was a woman, but still a virgin, and even the man called Harrison, more experienced and subtle than Bond, had to explain and promise much about love and marriage before

16

attempting any physical relationship. None of this was mentioned in the newspapers when Olwen died. The child Olwen clutched her wet costume and protested, 'Stop it, Paul.'

'Come on, angel,' Bond said. 'Don't start going weepy. I'll make you feel good. Nothing else, I promise.'

'I'm sorry,' Olwen said. 'I want to go.'

'What's the matter with you?'

'You've spoilt it. I liked you as you were.'

'You're scared,' he mocked. 'You're only a kid.'

'I'm not scared,' Olwen said, 'but I don't want to be touched. We're both still wet.'

'I'm almost dry,' Bond said. He grabbed a towel and started to dry Olwen's back, which was still flecked with spots of water.

'I want to get dry in my own hut,' Olwen said. Her voice trembled, and she knew that he would regard it, with her behaviour, as childish. But it was obviously not love that actuated him—love does not plead so hard against the wishes of the loved one—Bond sought his own pleasure, not hers. He wanted what the soldiers joked about in the semi-respect of whispers: the fine shoulders and the firm stomach, the graceful legs and the untouched, woman's breasts. Olwen walked to the door, but Bond, abandoning his limited measures of charm and politeness, began to struggle with her. She was too full of panic to fight back, but she pulled his hair and made it too painful for him to overcome her. He had to desist and stood there, lust replaced by anger. 'Scram,' he sneered. 'You're not that wonderful. I can get someone better than you any day—someone who knows the tricks. You stay with fifth-form kids—you'll be safer with them.'

Olwen said nothing and left quickly in relief. Outside, the sun glared, the sand was hot under her feet and children laughed. She dressed quickly and cycled home. On the way she began to tremble and cry, and was forced to stop to be sick. But she was loyal to whatever had existed between herself and Bond in that she said nothing to her parents or Tom, all of whom would have acted quickly on her behalf.

Six weeks later her friend Peggy asked her to accompany her to a dance in the town—not a school dance, for Peggy had left school a year before, but a dance in a hall packed with soldiers, older girls and the hard-eyed women who sprang from nowhere and seemed to have endless leisure. Peggy, a tall, heavy girl with a great deal of physical energy and a tendency to become bored quickly if she was not using it, was a year older than Olwen. She spent her time now driving her father's lorry about recklessly—from the farm to the railway station and back with milk churns, to Bar Quay for seeds and chemical manures. Although she did not share Olwen's reluctance—she collected soldier friends as other girls collected stamps—she understood it, and with this invitation she offered explanations.

'You see,' she said, 'Harry's got a friend who's only about eighteen. He's not like Harry. I mean,' she added quickly, 'that he's shy, quiet and that. Harry said that if I knew someone——'

'It does sound a bit casual,' Olwen said.

'I *know*,' Peggy said. 'But, I mean, you can't have the usual formalities in a war. I'd bring you back in the lorry. They're quite nice dances, and we'd come home before twelve.'

'I'll ask Mama,' Olwen said.

She put the decision in the hands of another, and was quite surprised when her mother gave her consent. 'What time will you be back?' Mrs. Hughes asked Peggy. 'I'll bring her back in the lorry at twelve, honestly. The dances don't end until two, but we'll leave before then,' said Peggy piously. 'No drinking, mind you,' Olwen's mother said. 'And I'll wait up for you,' she added, with a smile that nevertheless did not deny the intention.

It was a cold October Saturday evening when Peggy came to collect Olwen. She had a scarf round her head, was overpainted and was smoking. To Olwen the paint and the cigarette savoured faintly of sin; it was in any case her first venture into a completely adult world—the world at war—and she was full of misgivings.

The dance hall had been some kind of civic institution. It had now a definitely military aspect—the walls were scratched; the furniture was damaged; paint flaked off the tall entrance columns; notices about boxing matches flapped on its outside walls; in the men's lavatories obscene drawings and jokes were pencilled on the walls. Inside the large main hall etiolated cherubims and the paintings of bearded aldermen looked down with disapproval on the occasion. There were many people already dancing: soldiers in battle-dress, all· of whom had obtained black shoes from somewhere; women whom Olwen recognized as having been girls in the fifth form when she had been in the third; other women whose sardonic stares made her uncomfortable; a few girls who stayed with the one soldier they had obviously met in their own homes; a few civilian youths who had, incredibly, come for the music. There was a crowd round the makeshift bar, including men who were doing some steady drinking and some women whose encouraging laughs were just a little too shrill and prompt. The noise made by the already sweating band was deafening. Olwen did not like the look of any of it. These were the men who would bring victory for the most sacred of causes, but she found difficulty in associating them with it.

A broad soldier with bright blue eyes and very fuzzy hair approached across the dance floor. He was not especially tall, but deep in the chest, and with hips that swayed as he walked.

'Hello, Peg o' my heart,' he said. It was obvious that he was one of those people who take over the responsibility for things when others are hovering, and decide what everybody shall do. He had a small black moustache that bobbed up and down as he talked, and was so cheerful that it gave Olwen confidence.

'Watcha, Harry,' said Peggy. 'Where's your friend?'

Harry's friend, like Olwen, was hanging back shyly. He was a boy, quite thin and small with a young, nervous face from which the Army had scarcely removed the pallor of the city. There was that about him that still told of hard work in the bad atmosphere of a factory, of too much smoking in too many cinemas and billiard halls, of not enough sleep and not quite the right kinds of food, and of energy frittered away in the masturbations of innocence. His courage and his shyness and his integrity were all he would ever have, but because he did not know it he did not in resentment burn out his energy, as many of his friends did, in fights and fornication and insolence. . . .

Harry swung round. 'Here he is. Did y'think you'd escaped, Joe?'

Joe blushed uneasily. 'How d'y'do?' said Peggy. 'This is Olwen.'

'That's a nice name,' said Harry. 'Got nice hair, hasn't she?' He paused, on the edge of a dirty joke, but instead of it said, 'Like a pint of wallop, it looks.'

'Hello,' said Olwen.

'Hello, Olwen,' Joe said faintly. He blushed outright now, his mouth hung open slightly, and he found Olwen so beautiful as to be unbearable to look upon. Each time he had to summon courage to dart quick glances at the extraordinary, glowing child's face.

'Well, what are we all having?' roared Harry.

'I'll have an 'alf,' said Joe.

'Gin and tonic,' said Peggy promptly.

'I'd like a lemonade,' said Olwen.

Harry looked at her, grinned, seemed to regard this as a deplorable choice in liquid refreshment, and then said, 'Okay, so be it.'

He was back with the drinks in scarcely any time, being one of those men who can cut straight through a crowd, give an order in a loud, friendly voice and be served with it at once.

They stood about, talking and sipping their drinks, except for Harry, who downed his pint quickly and went in search of another. When the music recommenced its noisy, uneven thump Harry shouted, 'Let's dance!' He grabbed Peggy by her hips and seemed to launch her into the crowd in a waltz.

Joe and Olwen stood about, arms hanging awkwardly, too aware that they had been brought for each other's company, until Joe said, 'Would you like to?'

It reassured Olwen to find that he was nervous; after all, he was a soldier. They danced like sadness, slowly and silently down the edges of the ballroom.

'Do you come here often?' Joe asked.

'I've never been before.'

'Nor me. Harry talked me into it. I can't really dance.'

'You're all right to-night.'

'Do you really go to school?'

'Yes,' she said, but added immediately, 'I'm leaving before long.'

'I'm only eighteen,' Joe said, 'but school seems a long time ago. I've been working since I was fourteen.'

'What at?'

'Oh, all sorts. In a shop and then in a factory. They were glad to have me 'cause of the war.'

'How long have you been a soldier?'

'Six months. I'm not very good at it yet.'

'Are soldiers really as rough as they seem? It's awful the way they stare.'

'Some of 'em,' said Joe. 'Harry's a case. He's all right, you know. He's decent to me—I get on with him.'

'He seems—jolly.'

'He's a good 'un. He never tries to get me on a line like some of 'em.'

'On a line?'

Joe was suddenly bothered; his hand sweated in hers. He explained quickly, 'Some of 'em think you're pansy if you don't go with women.'

Olwen was amazed at his innocence; he was as untouched as she, surrounded by a lot of Bonds, clever with their words and sneers and persuasions. She looked at his face in its seriousness and liked what she saw.

About an hour later, when the atmosphere was thick, the place packed and the foreheads of the soldiers were filmed with sweat, Olwen said, 'I feel a bit sick. Could we go outside?'

'Okay,' said Joe. 'Would you like another drink?'

Olwen refused and they wandered outside as others had been doing. The cold salt air struck and refreshed them. There was no moon, but the blacked-out wartime night was relieved by the stars. 'Let's just walk to the sea and back,' said Olwen. 'I'll feel all right then.'

It was the first time she had been in Bar Quay at night. Despite the absence of light, it was as crowded as during the day. The sound of high-heeled shoes and the heavier, accompanying boots seemed to fill the town, but little could be seen. Olwen sensed others nearby, more silent, in shop doorways, but identified nothing. As they neared the shore it became lighter. The approaching tide could be discerned, and on the sands dark shapes walked together. Other people were strolling along the promenade, hugged close together; identified as human by the flavour of their trails of cigarette smoke and as masculine and feminine by their voices. Nobody was separate, alone, and Olwen did not protest when Joe held her hand. They walked cautiously about, two innocents who were uncomfortably aware of others, far less separate, who sat close together on wooden seats or half sprawled without words in the corners of the beach shelters. In the silence following each crash of the incoming tide could be heard significant giggles and shrills from the direction of the sand. Joe and Olwen proceeded a few hundred yards beyond the end of the promenade until they felt themselves to be alone.

'I like being here,' Joe said. 'I hadn't seen the sea before.'

'I don't like the town,' said Olwen.

'Don't you live in the town?'

She described it to him: the hill which he could see on the horizon each day as he paraded, marched and did physical training was where she lived.

'It must be good there,' said Joe. 'I hope I see it before I leave here.'

Olwen remembered the warnings about soldiers; the girls who had had to leave the district; others who had married in a hurry; small wonder that the village was hostile and anxious to retain its isolation; but Joe was as innocent as she. 'I hope so too,' she said in honesty.

He kissed her suddenly, nervously, half as though it was expected of him. 'Have you got a boy?' he asked.

Olwen said quickly, 'Not at the moment.'

'Well,' said Joe, still nervous and half defiant, 'you've got one now if you want.'

Just before midnight Joe took Olwen to the car park and they waited in tenderness for the other two. As they were arranging the details of where they should next meet, Peggy and Harry staggered in together. They were slightly drunk, friendly drunk, and the goodbyes were prolonged because of it.

On the way back to the village in the lorry Peggy said, 'What a mouldy hole that place was. Thank God I'm getting out of it.'

'Are you getting married?'

Peggy swerved in her laughter. 'Oh, that's a good one. *Me* getting married. I don't need to—I can get it wholesale.'

'Well, what are you doing, then?' Olwen asked, disliking this coarseness.

'I'm going to do a bit more for the soldiers,' said Peggy. 'I am about to become a nurse.'

The idea appealed straight away to that compassion of which Olwen was capable. 'What a good idea. Are you going to Cardiff?'

'No fear,' said Peggy. 'Too many damn' relations there. I'm going to Birlchester.'

It was in England, a hundred miles away, a huge city, remote from any experience of Olwen's. 'That's a long way from home,' Olwen commented.

Too apprehensive of the village to meet Joe there—for eyes peered from behind net curtains; postmen talked; nothing was secret or sacred—Olwen walked the mile to the shore and on the following Saturday waited for him at the cross-roads near the new cemetery. He arrived in the small bus and at the sight of him all the misgivings collected during the previous seven days were forgotten; she hadn't made a mistake.

They greeted each other nervously; without the presence of the talkative Harry and Peggy, they tended to be silent.

Olwen said, 'That was my father who drove the bus.'

'He was talking to me.'

'What about?'

'All about the camp and that.'

'Not about me?'

'No, only about where I was going.'

'What did you say?'

'To meet my girl.'

These were the words Olwen wanted to hear, and she hung her

head in shyness. She took him a walk along the shore to the light-house. It was a long time since she had been, and she found with shame that it had grown ugly during the years since Leslie. But if he noticed the ugliness Joe said nothing about it, and he was grateful for the privacy of the tower in which to kiss. Afterwards they travelled to Bar Quay on another bus service, ate fish and chips in a café, and at seven o'clock made their way to the dance hall.

A week later they gazed on the world from the top of the hill above the village. Above the trees and gorse Joe gasped at the view. Down below moved the tiny woollen dots which were sheep. The fields stretched away in a patchwork of innumerable greens to the small sore on the horizon which was the town. A toy train moved along the coast—it was so toy-like that Joe laughed. On another horizon was the dark purple outline of a different range of hills. Out at sea, unseen on the horizon at sea-level, a convoy of ships proceeded. The harsh roar of a military aeroplane filled the bowl of land below them, and Joe saw with astonishment that it flew at a lower level than themselves. Olwen could see that the boy was deeply affected by it all, even troubled.

'The world's a big place,' Joe said awkwardly. 'In a city you think there's not enough room. I mean, this is worth dying for.'

'Aren't there things in the city worth dying for?'

Joe said, 'In the city you've got nowhere to go with a girl. All those thousands—it isn't fair. You have to go to the pictures.'

'I like the pictures,' Olwen said.

'Yes, but they're not real, see?'

'They're not meant to be. They're only—well, pictures.'

Joe said, 'I mean, people want to be alone, to talk and that.'

Olwen asked in curiosity, 'What do you do in a city to be alone with a girl?'

'You have to go in the parks and boozers,' Joe said. 'Never really alone, see? Not like this.'

Olwen smiled. 'Round here if a boy comes up the hill with a girl they say it's—you know, sinful. . . .'

Joe laughed briefly. 'Whatever you do it's wrong. Too many regulations,' he said. He held her rather clumsily. His face was pink and his eyes abject; he had something important to say. 'You know what? You're something worth dying for.'

'I wouldn't ask anyone to die for me.'

'You're a nice girl,' Joe said. 'I don't just like you. You understan'? You're not just another girl.'

'I am.'

'I don't mean that,' he pleaded. 'Oh, Christ, don't you see? I mean I love you.'

She touched the roughness of his greatcoat and then his face and hair. 'I'm glad,' she said.

An hour later they came down into a mist. Under the darkness of the trees they trod on the slippery, damp leaves and breathed the trapped, autumnal air into each other's faces. 'Are you sure your folks want to see me?' Joe asked.

He found tea with Olwen's parents and brother something of an ordeal. When she exclaimed to Joe, 'You don't eat a lot for a growing lad,' Mrs. Hughes meant it kindly, but the boy-soldier was covered with confusion.

At the sink, as they washed up afterwards, her mother said to Olwen, 'He's a nice lad, but isn't he shy? Not like a soldier at all.' After the washing up Olwen found herself in the other room with Joe, among the heavy furniture, plates and the dark painting, a fire lit mysteriously and nobody interrupting. Without hesitation she turned off the lamp and relaxed before the firelight with Joe until it was time for him to leave. While Joe was out of sight, putting on his coat, Tom whispered, 'He's all right. I like him.' Her father's approval came last of all, the next morning. 'He's a good lad. Bring him here as often as you like.'

She did. All through that autumn and winter Olwen met Joe as often as school hours and his duties permitted. Her home was a home for him, too, because her parents accepted it as right and natural that, after a walk with Olwen, he should come in for tea and supper. He even spent a short leave there.

One Saturday in the spring he failed to keep a rendezvous. Olwen spent a worried week-end wondering what had happened, and was only partially relieved when a letter arrived on the Monday morning postmarked Bar Quay. When she opened it and read the first few words of the rounded, childish script, she knew that everything was all right: her world was still intact. It was just that he would soon be leaving for a camp in England. Full of yearning for him, Olwen hoped that he would come to her, dramatically, in the middle of the night even, with prolonged moments to speak of his love before he went back to the camp and on to the other part of Britain. She wrote a long letter in return, begging him to do so.

He came three days later. Olwen cycled home from school and there he was, standing awkwardly as he always did, the boots too big and the coat too heavy for him, waiting at her own doorway.

They embraced without this time bothering about privacy.

'I've only got two hours,' Joe said.

'Let's go somewhere quiet.'

'You'd better have your tea first.'

'I don't want any tea.'

'You'd better tell your mama then.'

Olwen did this and then they walked, as they had often done, out of the village, over several stiles and up a path into the green thickness of the woods.

'It's cold in the trees,' Joe said. 'Let's get into the sun where it's warm.'

They sat by a bush in a shaft of sunlight. It was so warm that they took off their coats, and so quiet that the world at war seemed unreal.

But it wasn't.

'When are you leaving?' Olwen asked.

'To-night. They haven't said much.'

'Where are you going?'

'I can't tell you.'

She was shocked. 'You can tell *me*.'

He was palpably nervous and she could not understand why. Because it was their last meeting perhaps?

Joe said, 'It's somewhere in Wiltshire.'

She understood suddenly: he was frightened and the fright belonged to something bigger than either of them. 'It's the invasion,' she said.

'It will be.'

'You'll be all right. I'll pray for you.'

'I'm not complaining,' Joe said. 'The war brought me to you. It may take me away.' He smiled. 'But I'll be back.'

'Let's forget about it,' Olwen said. 'Why does it have to take you away now? I'm leaving school in six weeks. I could have seen you often.'

She leaned heavily against him, and he lost his anxiety in her kisses, in the quietness and the warmth. White flowers on a may tree waved in front of his eyes; there was a drone of insects; the warm softness of Olwen drew him towards drowsiness, but he became too conscious of it to sleep. It was too feminine and real to be ignored. Joe whispered, 'Let me touch you,' and his left hand, hoping for acceptance and ignoring rejection, had felt into her blouse before Olwen in shock (but not fear: he was no Bond) pleaded, 'Joe, you *are* afraid.'

25

He said, almost in tears, 'I'm not afraid, and, if I am, it's only of myself.'

'You don't think you'll come back to me and you want——'

'You feel so soft. I only wanted to touch. Nothing more. It was because I was nearly asleep and I forgot——'

In the warmth and the tenderness, her body had relaxed so that it pleaded with her to surrender, and more than surrender, to participate. A tingling shot out pleasurably from the contact of his hand through her breasts and stomach even to her legs. It sought to envelop her. He was going away to risk his life, and he loved her. It was one of war's temptations to persuade one that a small sin would not be noticed, and was even permissible inside the chaos of the greater one. She groaned because she saw this, but did not want to hurt Joe. 'A boy at school tried to touch me,' she said. 'I wouldn't let him. Why should I let you, Joe?'

'I've never touched anyone before. I don't know what made me——'

With the hand that had arrested him, she pulled his hand down on to her left breast, and nearly fainted in the cold-hot ecstasy that resulted. Joe, misunderstanding her gesture, began to circulate his hand. He sweated as he kissed her passionately and attempted gently to stroke her legs; but Olwen said, 'No, my dear,' and hugged the one hand to her breast as if she wanted it to touch her heart. Everything else she resisted, and at length Joe calmed down, understood the gesture and accepted her control. He longed to do with her the things he had never done at all, but loved her enough to wait. People married when they were twenty these days and that, for him, was only eighteen months away.

Later Olwen murmured, 'What's the time?'

'Time to leave,' said Joe. 'I'll have to run.'

They tidied themselves urgently and went quickly to the bus stop in the village. The bus came into sight as they reached it. 'I'll write,' Joe said. He seemed to think of something else. 'Here. Have this.' It was his cap badge. He kissed her hard on the mouth, said, 'And thank you, Olwen, thank you,' the bus came and he was gone. 'Oh, God,' Olwen whispered, 'take care of him.'

A few days later she received her second letter from him and answered at once eagerly. Two weeks later the invasion of Normandy commenced, but still his letters came from that other part of Britain. Then no letters came for two weeks and Olwen knew he had left England. Letters began to arrive in strange, military envelopes from abroad. They worried and pleased her. There were times when she could feel the fear in his words, and she longed for just one more similar day of warmth and love in which to comfort him. One day she had one of her own letters back, and had to go to school with all the agonies of a kind of widowhood. She tried to imagine Joe had found another girl; one whose hands did not arrest his eagerness—she even hoped that that had happened. She tried to believe that he had moved elsewhere and that his letters had gone astray; tried, as a last resort, to see him as a prisoner. But she had seen the agony in his eyes that day, and knew what his gratitude had been for. 'And thank you, Olwen, thank you.' (Thank you for granting me months of tenderness, with tender passion at its end; thank you for granting me a particle of beautiful past that I can hug secretly in the hammer blows of the future.) She knew only too well that he was dead, and weeks later a letter came from Harry telling her how he had died.

Olwen was numbed with despair. She had left school: there was nothing to do but walk about, and her every step took her where he had been. And in these places she would have foolish moments, forgetting he had gone, when her eyes would see him; she would move forward to speak and then weep bitterly in the face of reality. Her body, too, ached with longing, and she wished that she had surrendered; for perhaps he had known he was going to die. She would lie in bed, unable to sleep, and in shame (for she knew he had been as innocent as she) she would feel sensuous and would picture his eager eyes above her. Then she would fall asleep and see him die in the most realistic, terrible, smashed postures. She would approach his apparently sleeping body only to find bluebottles crawling round his eyes. She would awake sweating, thanking God it hadn't happened, only to realize that he was dead and perhaps it had. She lost some of that lovely child's roundness and colour. She took to staying in her bedroom, writing letters to him and alternating this with bouts of tears. Everywhere she looked was happiness perverted into unhappiness. She knew then that hell may easily be a beautiful place. She longed to go somewhere miles away, as Tom had done by joining the Army, where there was nothing that could remind her and no one even to sympathize. The notion of moving became an obsession and eventually took a form and shape. Olwen went to her mother. 'Mama,' she pleaded. 'I'm not happy here without him. I want to go away. I want to help in the war. Let me become a nurse.'

III

HER decision seemed less inevitable as she stood on the railway platform at Bar Quay with her parents and Tom. Even with Peggy waiting at the other, unfamiliar end of the journey, Olwen's eagerness faded and the decision seemed foolish, even wrong. She was trembling when her mother embraced her. The train was packed with khaki, kitbags, rifles and ruddy faces who stared at her in frank admiration. She recognized that it was a sad world, frantically busy with its own destruction; she had left peace behind: the train pulled away and Olwen watched the pier and the promenade recede. It was only a small town really—just a promenade, a pattern of a few score roads, some hotels, the pier and a military camp. . . . The train thundered along the coast, passed the lighthouse in a flash and the hills in a few minutes. Olwen was on her way to become a nurse in a sanatorium. . . .

It took Olwen a long time to become used to the city of Birlchester. She was only seventeen and had never before seen a big city. There was so much traffic, such a noise; there was one bus service that took over an hour to circle the outer suburbs. For months Peggy had to guide her about whenever they went outside the sanatorium. The atmosphere of Birlchester was hardly suitable for convalescence: dusty and airless, it swirled papers about in the feeble breezes of summer. The rain became filth at a touch. All the buildings were dirty outside and a struggle to keep clean inside. Dead cats and dogs lay in the gutters, killed by the dozen each day. Some suburbs were devoted entirely to gas-works. Smelling of gas, they were surrounded by railway yards, cranes, coal, dirty houses, and above all, dominating the horizon and destroying it, the skeletons of framework which held the huge cylinders, looking like the structure of a defeated, crashed squadron of dirigibles. The people looked pale and ill. They moved about in huge, alarming crowds, not knowing of their own illness. She understood now the sudden, appalling emotion that had perturbed Joe that afternoon on the hill. When Olwen went to church she found it empty; not believing what she saw, she went to another, then another, but found them all the same: a small choir, a few old ladies and gentlemen, and long rows of empty seats. England seemed very much a foreign country. She wrote home, telling them all about it. On her leaves she was welcomed with love to tell it all again; it was more astonishing than the war. . . .

The nurses were older than Olwen, but no one seemed to take notice of ages, only of ranks; it was like being in an army. The matron was a small, kindly woman who treated Olwen with kindness whenever she encountered her. There were several sisters, a surprising number of them from Wales and even speaking Welsh. They were strict, but it was no worse than school. The hours were longer, but there was normally one long break during the day. At first the behaviour of the English and Irish nurses seemed dreadful. They would smoke at the slightest opportunity, their language was appalling, and their talk about patients unbelievably callous. They yawned and spat and talked about sex. At the staff dances and parties they seemed to drink quite heavily and kiss anyone. On Sundays only the Catholics would go to church. If the others were off duty they would miss breakfast and stay in bed until twelve. But after the first shock of it Olwen realized that their behaviour was not as bad as it seemed. None of them took advantage of the nearness of male patients. If they went out drinking, they at least did it together and came back together. If they swore and quarrelled it was because they were really exhausted, and for the same reason they ate ravenously. (The English ate such terrible food: no wonder they were ill: chips and sausages, cod, macaroni, and beef as tough as leather.) In about a year Olwen's behaviour became something similar, except that she continued to go to church. A cigarette after a long spell of duty was a sort of ritual; she could not avoid it and eventually enjoyed it. Fish and chips in a café, followed by a cinema visit and a drink in a pub, made a change from the institutional life they all led.

Olwen had never been to work before and did not protest at having to scrub floors and empty cans of sputum and blood. There were a number of operations, but not so much of the blood and mess of an ordinary hospital. Most of the patients had their lungs collapsed by air through a needle. It was months before Olwen saw anyone have a surgical operation. When she did she found the spectacle extremely brutal: the hours-long struggle of the sweating surgeon, as he cut ribs away, as terrible to witness as the patient himself. Olwen did not faint, but at the end went away to be sick. Routine work was more pleasant: temperature-taking, bed-making, preparing foods and assisting in the medical blocks. The patients had a habit of doing the things that they shouldn't. All of them had been cajoled into coming into the sanatorium for a rest. Having arrived, every single one of them would have hallucinatory moods when he decided he was cured; they didn't appreciate the long time a lung takes to heal; after the first cough and terror had worn off, they would claim they were being held as prisoners to keep the staff in employment. It was one of the nurses' jobs to persuade them to stay, and while they were staying, to co-operate.

Olwen Hughes was now in the same city as the man who called himself Harrison, but it was unlikely that they would have met if Olwen had not encountered, first Stephen Taylor and, later, Mrs. Dawson. If she had met Mrs. Dawson before she met Taylor she would not have seen Harrison, but unfortunately it occurred the other way round.

She had been at the sanatorium about four years when Taylor arrived as a patient. He came one Monday afternoon with two other men at a time when Olwen was on day duty on a male block of the hospital. Patients always arrived on a Monday; the beds had to be emptied, one way or the other, on the previous Friday; the rooms were sterilized, and by Monday afternoon the lockers, beds and linen would be available.

The three new patients, nervous and made slightly out of breath by the weight of cases and bags, had been directed along stone corridors to the duty room in which Olwen was preparing tea trays.

'Sit down, please,' she said.

The three men sat on hard chairs while Olwen wrote down their names. When she considered their pulses would be as near normal as possible, she held each of three wrists in turn and afterwards took temperatures. The men were then weighed. Taylor was slightly over nine stone and had a frame which indicated that he should have been two stone heavier. The weighing completed, Olwen smiled and said, 'I'll show you to your chalets. When the bell rings at half-past four, Mr. Smith and Mr. Wilde will follow the other men down to tea. Mr. Taylor, you'll have your tea in bed.'

'Why?'

The tone was rude and Olwen looked quickly at the white face, the cheap clothes and haircut. Taylor was about twenty-seven years old, and beneath the taut pallor of illness had a good face.

'It's the regulation,' she said. 'You have a slight temperature.'

'Bloody silly if you ask me,' Taylor said.

'I didn't ask you,' Olwen said. 'And it's another requirement of the hospital that patients do not use bad language—in front of the staff, anyway,' she concluded, her smile still there.

30

She could see that for some reason he was absolutely furious, his pallor glowing into a deep pink. 'I didn't ask for a stuck-up tart for a nurse either,' he said.

'If you'll follow me, I'll show you where to go,' said Olwen, addressing all three. She was angry, but let her anger pass. He was ill; he would learn and adjust himself; if he wouldn't, he would die; she willingly accepted a little of his unhappiness. Although he protested slightly, she made certain that it was his case she carried; it was a small demonstration that as far as she was concerned he was part of her work and she would not be altered by words. Nevertheless, when another nurse took over at five-thirty and asked about the new patients, Olwen, answering, said, 'All right. The one in 17 is bad-tempered.'

He certainly seemed bad-tempered. She was making his bed next morning when a doctor came round with a sister, making the usual morning visit to all the bed patients. The doctor was young and determinedly cheerful. 'Hello,' he said. 'You're Taylor, are you? How are you?'

'How the hell do I know?' the patient said. 'Aren't you the doctor?'

The sister was so near to having palpitations that Olwen turned away to hide a smile. The doctor said, 'I don't know yet. You'll be examined in half an hour.'

When he and the sister had left, Olwen said, 'You shouldn't talk like that. You know what he meant. He's a good doctor and you may be glad of it.'

Taylor said in an even tone, 'I didn't ask to come here. They made me. I can get rid of this lot without a pack of nurses and doctors. I'm not scared of anything.'

Olwen paused before leaving. 'Nobody said you were. Nobody's scared of you either.'

She had no occasion to think of him until a week later, when shortly before supper a male patient approached her. 'You know that soldier in 17?'

'I didn't know he was a soldier.'

'He isn't now,' the patient said. 'Anyway, he's shut himself in. Someone said he was crying.'

Olwen had become a little hardened to patients' behaviour; she had to in order to survive herself; but she was startled now and even trembled slightly. '*Crying?*' she said, and gave a brief laugh. 'I don't believe it. That one's made of cement.'

She had been strolling about, talking to the bed patients and those others who were sitting about in long wicker chairs. Very few of the male patients had ever attempted to take advantage of this or any other association with the nurses. Sometimes men tried to kiss Olwen in the duty room; a few had suggested walks to the bushier parts of the grounds after dark; one or two had tried to feel her legs as she stood on a chair reaching for jars of medicine. But in the face of her cheerful refusals they soon desisted and Olwen was never frightened by this or by impertinence. Being in an institution where interruption was always likely gave her comparative safety. She talked now to several patients, and when she approached Taylor's chalet, along the stone corridors outside it, above lawns, a rockery and more distant pine trees, she found the windows closed and the curtains drawn. Olwen went to the other side and entered from the inside corridor without knocking.

In the artificial gloom it was some time before she saw Taylor. He was lying on his side, facing away from Olwen and the remainder of his room towards the wall by his bed.

Olwen said, 'Have you got a headache?'

Taylor seemed surprised by her presence, despite the noise of her entry. There was a pause and then he said, 'No.'

'You should leave the windows open, you know.'

'I just wanted to be alone.'

'But you are alone in here.'

'I mean really alone where I can do my own thinking; where none of these b——s can come in and do it for me.' His voice became derisive. 'Billiards. The hospital committee. I'm the men's captain—you can rely on me. Are you dead yet? Give three reasons to convince us that you're not. Would you like to read an improving book about an artist and his mistress? You can have free soap and writing paper 'cause you're ex-Service. A penny a day and you can have tea after we've taken your early-morning temperature. Not before, of course, because your temperature would read at 175 degrees Fahrenheit, and that would mislead the nurses, who know it's impossible to survive under such conditions. They might have to bury you, and then you'd have died with dignity, which is the last thing they want.' He paused, badly out of breath. 'Sometimes they're not real.'

Blushing in the darkness of his room because she'd never spoken such words before, Olwen said, 'Surely that's the reason for their existence—to lessen the reality. Can you meet reality all the time face to face?'

He was surprised by her words into a long silence. When he

spoke again it was without the rancid flavour. 'You're a nice person, nurse,' he said. 'But listen. Just before we went to Poland the Flying Fortresses came over. On their way to Marienburg, I think. It was the first time we'd seen anything since 1940, although we'd heard them at night. We couldn't believe it. They made a noise like the end of the world. We knew then that we were going to win. The blokes all came out to cheer and the Jerries were furious. We took no notice—so they shot a few. They shot my mate Bert, who'd been with me for three years. They got a Fort down and they shot *them* too. . . . That is reality, not messing about with semolina pudding and blood tests.'

The quiet, off-hand tone conveyed the picture better than gesticulations and hysterics could have done. Olwen felt inclined to say something trite or stupid—'I'm sorry,' or 'It must have been awful.' But instead she said calmly, 'That was real enough, but it belongs to the 1940s, not to this year. Reality for you, Mr. Taylor, is to eat a lot of food, rest with calmness, and open the windows.'

'That's only for survival.'

'Don't you want to survive?'

'Yes, but all that stuff——'

'One thing at a time,' said Olwen. 'This disease is supposed to give a lunatic elation.' She laughed. 'You had to be different even in that.' She drew the curtains back and opened the windows. 'Just because you had a tough time in the Army doesn't make you any better than those factory lads out there.'

He laughed outright and she felt extremely pleased, as if it was a personal victory over pain. 'You're a hell of a funny nurse,' Taylor said. 'You think I'm a dead loss, but you're going to cure me because I'm on your conscience.'

'What do you want for supper?' Olwen asked.

'I don't feel hungry.'

'Would you like a drink of beer?'

'What are you trying to do now? Kill me?'

'We have a bottle left over from a party. I could put it in a beaker and pretend it's tea if Sister comes.'

'Isn't beer forbidden?'

'Yes.'

'Then why should you give me any?'

Olwen couldn't answer that, because she wasn't sure herself. It was some association of ideas. Joe had been a soldier, but had died: Taylor was one and might die. She would prevent it. He was depressed: she would cheer him up. 'It might give you an appetite,' she said.

'Okay,' said Taylor. 'Bring on the beer.'

Three weeks later Olwen went on leave. When she returned from Wales to the sanatorium she brought some eggs. Half a dozen of these she took to Taylor. 'Want some eggs?' she asked nervously.

'I haven't seen you for a couple of weeks.'

'I've been on holiday.'

'I see. Had a good time?'

'It was a change.'

'How much are the eggs?'

'You can have them.'

'But why give them to *me*?'

'Don't you want them?'

'It's very nice of——'

'Then have them,' said Olwen, and left hurriedly.

A few days later he said to her, 'You've got small hands, nurse. Look at mine.'

His hands were not much larger when they compared them. Taylor made no attempt to hold her hand, and Olwen wondered at his remarks. 'I'm leaving next week,' she said.

He seemed disturbed. 'You can't leave yet.'

'Why can't I leave?'

'Where are you going?'

'On the women's section.'

'You're not leaving altogether?'

'Oh, no. I'll be back,' Olwen said. 'It's only for six months.'

'I'm hoping to be out of here in six months,' Taylor said. 'I'll go mad if I'm not.'

Olwen had been on the women's section a fortnight when Peggy brought her a brown-paper parcel. 'What goes on between you and Taylor?' she asked.

'Nothing. Why?'

'He's asked me to give you this.'

Inside the parcel Olwen found a pair of knitted gloves. They were in Fair Isle wool, the pattern was complicated and beautiful, and, of course, the fit was perfect. 'How is he?' she asked.

'Two hours up and no temperature.' Peggy snorted. 'Just so long as you've been here.'

Olwen made a point of passing through the men's section between two and four in the afternoon, between which hours she knew Taylor would be up. He was talking to a group of men;

she knew he wouldn't wish to be interrupted, and returned when he was back in bed eating his tea.

He was nervous. 'Hello.'

'You've been up,' Olwen said. 'I heard about it. I'm glad. Thank you for those gloves.'

'Occupational therapy,' he said with some of the bitterness. 'You gave me the eggs.'

'The gloves fit perfectly.'

'So did the eggs.' Taylor paused and then said, 'It was really an apology. I was very rude to you when I came.'

'Everybody is,' Olwen said. 'You should hear the women. It must be a symptom.'

He smiled at her. 'Then I'm getting better.'

She saw him occasionally during the months she was on the women's section. Always he said, 'Hello,' but never went further with any talk. When she returned to duty on the male section, Olwen found that he was still there; he was up for six hours each day and looked quite well.

Olwen was preparing tea trays one afternoon when she found that her list included Taylor's name. She carried his tea tray and tried to be cheerful when she entered his chalet. 'So you're back in bed,' she said. 'Is the weather too cold for you?'

Taylor looked sullen and white again. 'I don't want any tea.'

'Aren't you hungry?'

'What's the good of it?'

'Don't forget you're on my conscience if you don't eat,' Olwen said. 'We had an agreement about it.'

'Don't flannel me,' he said loudly. 'I don't have to eat.'

'What's the matter?'

'Nothing, except that I'm cheesed off.'

'Have you got a temperature? Why are you back in bed?'

'I've got fluid on the other lung. The quack's going to ease up on the collapsed one. I have news for you, nurse. You'll be fascinated. I'm afraid. They've worn me down at last. Not the Germans—oh, no, that would have been too obvious—it had to be Sister Jones, a pack of nurses and a doctor who is brave about other people's deaths. . . .'

'You'll get better.'

'Don't give me that crap,' he said. 'I'm going to die. How long have I got, nurse?'

'It's silly to ask questions like that.' Olwen smiled faintly. 'I'm not an insurance company.'

'You'd lie to me if you were,' Taylor said. 'You have to lie, anyway. It's very nice of you to lie to me, nurse. Do you pray for me too?'

His tone was derisive, and Olwen blushed as she answered, 'Yes.'

He was a little surprised by her 'Yes', and said, 'I'm sorry. I didn't know or imagine—— It's just that I've been here for months. I've seen the others. I know too much for a patient.'

'Everyone has setbacks.'

'Dirty, stinking hospitals,' Taylor said. 'They sap the guts out of you for months. . . . Why can't they do it clean and quick?' He lowered his voice and said, almost to himself, 'Why didn't it happen in France, Germany or Poland? I'd have laughed. . . .'

By the next day his mood had changed; he became calmer, cheerful, and made no mention of death. He ate all the food he was given. His fluid was extracted—a long needle was used to remove it; it was painful and alarming, but he said nothing. A week later there was fluid in both lungs. It was removed and more came. Yet still Taylor did not complain. It was not the frontal assault of pain he minded, but the prolonged wait for it; the trick pain had of waiting until he imagined he was on the way to cure before it struck again. He came to be regarded with respect as one of those patients who stay in sanatoria for years, whose recovery or death becomes an event in the whole busy hospital. He was called Stephen by the nurses and doctors, and gradually began to accept the role. He learned by its absence to forget the outside world (for him it was as far back as 1940) and his longing for it; to regard the institutional life as the normal one, and temperatures and fluids as the trials of the day.

In the succeeding days he began to take an interest in the occupational therapy and to become very expert at it. He made toys and handbags, insisting on giving Olwen one of the latter. He talked to her incessantly when she was near; it was always she who was asked to do any small task outside the hospital. Olwen posted his letters, bought magazines and cigarettes—even beer if he persisted. He watched her as she moved round his chalet to dust or wash or simply came in to talk, but she never suspected that he could be in love with her. He was a patient who was ill; he had been there a long time without falling in love with her; why should he start now? That was the way she might have reasoned, and not knowing that he was in love with her, she hurt him as often as she delighted.

36

Taylor knew how foolish and painful it might be to fall in love when he was ill, but he could not help himself. He knew her footsteps so well; he listened to her singing; he waited to hear about her every innocent activity; he watched the tossing of her auburn hair and the roundness of her face as she moved through the silence of his room, that prison he knew in every detail. She was so lovely in face and body, and so unaware of it that he longed to be the one to tell her. He ached to be as well as she, to be on equal terms; and in his bitter moments he wanted her to be ill, for the same reason. When he heard her laughter in the open air he hated the patients who could walk about; they meant no more to her than he, but they could chatter to her and be accepted. They could crowd her into a corner and seize a kiss if they willed. They could, if she were agreeable, meet her at night in or beyond the grounds. She seemed so innocent, but how could he know what she did? And how could any nurse be completely innocent?

He did not see her during all of one day, and wondered what had become of her. There was nobody he could ask without betraying himself. When he had given up hope for that day he heard her well-known footsteps in the dusk and waited impatiently until she would come to visit him.

She came in the dark at about ten o'clock and shone a torch on him. 'Hello, Stephen,' she said. 'Are you all right?'

'Are you on nights?'

'Only while Peggy's away. Have you had your drink?'

'Yes,' Taylor said. 'I'm waiting now for my good-night kiss.'

The words were trite and he knew it, but one cannot whisper beautiful phrases from a sick bed unless one is Proust.

'You're all very cheeky,' Olwen said, and the words gave him an agonized conception of what the other patients might be attempting to do. Perhaps they loved her too. One always had the foolish notion that one's discovery of something beautiful was individual, whereas in reality the whole world stared. 'I shan't dare answer any bell during the night.'

'Why won't you kiss me?' he asked sullenly. 'I'm a special patient.'

'You're not that special.'

He said in the bitterness of disappointment, 'You're afraid to.'

'You don't trap me that way,' she laughed.

'You might catch something,' he said angrily.

Olwen walked out without a reply, wounded by his words, but still not knowing the reason for them. Two hours later she tiptoed round the chalets to see that all the patients were asleep. Taylor had remained awake, knowing that she must come and waiting for her to do so. He made a slight movement and whispered sleepily, 'Who's that?'

'Go to sleep, Stephen.'

'I'm sorry for what I said.'

'Surely that hasn't kept you awake?'

'I had to apologize.'

'Go to sleep and don't worry. I had forgotten it.'

'Kiss me, then.'

'What for?'

'Does there have to be a reason?'

Olwen touched his head. 'I don't understand you,' she said. 'You didn't need to be unkind.' She kissed him. 'Why were you so angry?'

'Olwen,' he whispered. 'Surely you understand?'

She trembled at the force of his words. 'How did you know my name? Oh, Stephen, but I don't love you. I like you, but——'

'Don't say it twice,' he pleaded. 'Lie to me. Tell me anything you like. It won't matter. I'm going to die.'

In astonishment, he felt the splash of her instantaneous tears on his face. 'You're not going to die,' Olwen said. 'I won't let you. I pray for you. It wouldn't be fair.'

'It doesn't have to be fair,' he said. 'It's more complicated than that. If it was fair, life wouldn't be what it is. It would be that heaven you believe in.'

'Oh, how hurt you are,' she said, and kissed him fiercely in tremendous pity. 'Don't say angry things to me again. I will kiss you whenever you want me to. It will be easy to love you—— I just hadn't thought of it.'

He touched her soft, glabrous face. 'You're not used to untruths, are you?'

'I've only just started to love you. The words don't come easily yet.'

'I've never met anyone like you,' Taylor said. 'You're gentle and yet you're full of life. You sing children's songs. . . .'

'I was unaware——'

'I've heard you doing it.'

'You shouldn't have told me. Now I shan't be able——'

'Will you come a walk with me?'

She touched his face and hair. 'Of course I'll come a walk with you.'

'When will you come?'

'I'll come twelve months to-day.'

He winced. 'Is it as bad as that?'

Olwen whispered frantically, 'Twelve months isn't long, Stephen. You have to accept the time it takes to heal. And I'll be here all the time. Oh, my dear, learn to wait. . . .'

'I wish I was all right now,' he said. 'I'd like to walk beyond those pine trees with you.'

'That's what we'll do at the start. But you must be patient. What makes you so angry?'

He sighed. 'I don't know.'

'The war's been over for five years.'

'Not for me.'

'It's too late to be angry. We know it was cruel and unjust, but that's exactly why nobody wants another.'

'You talk like a politician,' said Taylor. 'I was captured in France. They marched us along the road to Luxembourg, collecting other parties on the way. It was boiling hot and they gave us no food. Blokes would drop out and the Nazis would bash 'em with their rifle butts. Some of them died. In one place they put us in a field where there was a mad bull. It killed two blokes. At the first halt I got dysentery. I used to faint all the time in the food queues. They gimme straw to fill my pants with. That was the start of five years. . . .'

'And now this,' said Olwen.

Taylor had taken hold of her hands. 'Your hands are very cold,' he said. 'I've been giving you the old hard-luck story and all the time you're freezing.'

'I'm not cold,' said Olwen. 'Only my hands. I must go to see the others. Shall I come back?'

'If you want to.'

'Would you like a drink of coffee?'

'If you'll have one.'

'All right. I'll be back.'

But when she returned with a jug of coffee Taylor was asleep, his mouth open and one arm limp across the bed. Olwen covered it and tiptoed away.

On the next evening and the five following it Olwen was again on duty. Taylor would not go to sleep until she had kissed him; and when she had kissed him he couldn't. 'It doesn't matter,' he said when Olwen found him awake at one o'clock on the sixth morning. 'I can sleep to-morrow when you're not here.'

She said with difficulty, 'I shan't be here for a long time.'

'Why not?'

'I've been instructed to go again on the women's section.'

There was an uncomfortable silence and then Taylor said with angry unhappiness, 'Did you have difficulty arranging it? Who's coming in your place? Someone very ugly, I hope.'

'Do you believe that of *me*? Do you think I want to go?'

'What am I to believe?'

'I must go on the women's section because I've been told to. That's all there is to it.'

'Why can't you say you won't?'

'What reason could I give? That I'm fond of one of the men? They'd keep me on the women's section all of the time if they thought it.'

'Will you come to see me?'

'As often as I can manage.'

'Don't bother if you don't want to.'

'Oh, you fool,' Olwen protested. 'Remember I'm at work, will you? I will take every risk I can for you.'

'Oh, God,' Taylor sighed. 'I know you will. Try to see my side, though. You're the only thing I value in the whole damn' world. . . .'

'You can write to me,' Olwen said. 'Haven't you any faith in me at all? And I will try to come to see you—because I want to— but it can only be for brief moments when I'm passing through.'

While Olwen was working on the women's section she talked to Mrs. Dawson. Mrs. Dawson was not particularly ill. 'The doctor says I can leave in six weeks if there's no setback. "Take it quietly," he says to me. "Potter about in the garden. Have a sleep in the afternoon. Let your kids look after you." I can see 'em doing it!' Mrs. Dawson shook with merriment. 'You're a good girl,' she said to Olwen. 'Don't you ever think of the world outside?'

Olwen shrugged. 'Not really.'

'Listen, my dear. Haven't you thought of what lovely hair you have?'

'Not since I was twelve.'

'I'm not joking,' explained Mrs. Dawson. 'Listen, kid, I've got a sister who'd like to see your hair.'

'Like to see my hair?' echoed Olwen.

'She's a hairdresser,' said Mrs. Dawson. 'Five quid a week she pays her girls to start with, and the ones she's got are lazy. Why don't you let me ask her?'

40

'It's nice of you to think of me,' Olwen said, 'but I'm needed here.'

'Well, see her, anyway,' Mrs. Dawson suggested. 'I know there's a vacancy. There's no harm in seeing her. She'll be here on Sunday.'

Olwen tried to keep out of the way of Mrs. Dawson and her visitor on the Sunday afternoon, but Mrs. Dawson eventually insisted on her presence.

'Olga,' she said, making the introduction, 'this is the girl I was telling you about. Nurse, this is my sister, Mrs. Harper.'

Olga Harper was a middle-aged, dyed blonde, with a tired, painted face and a small, unhappy mouth. She dressed well but unavailingly. It was all too evident that she lived for business and the money that business brought; everything else had been forgotten deliberately. 'You've got nice hair, nurse,' she said. 'If you ever want a job in this business, let Doris know and we'll get in touch. I've got three cubicles and the girls get at least five quid a week, plus tips.'

'Thank you very much,' Olwen said. 'I'll let you know.'

A starting wage of five pounds seemed quite a lot, but she was not interested while Stephen Taylor needed her pity. The decision was made for her. About three weeks after this conversation Peggy said at lunch, 'Listen, Olwen. Just how fond of that soldier are you?'

Olwen trembled in apprehension and glanced at the other nurses and the sisters, certain that they were listening to every word. 'I like him very much,' she said. With an effort she asked, 'Why?'

'I think he's dying.'

Olwen could not eat and abandoned any attempt to continue doing so. She saw the other nurses eating heartily. It was fantastic. The knives cut into meat, the forks moved in air selecting and then stabbed arbitrarily at little pieces of meat, potato and cabbage. The warm food rose upwards, tiny globules of gravy shaken off, and feminine mouths, slightly lipsticked, opened wide and then closed, the food inside. The trap. 'I think he's dying.' The logical conclusion. The inevitability of nothing. He has to solve it all by himself. It's a very big problem and no one other person has solved it, but he has to try. He must not be helped. There must be no cheating. I was going to help, but perhaps that would have been cheating of a kind. Oh God—if there is a God, and if You are not busy elsewhere this day, and if You love me, and if You love him—let's cheat a little. Let him stay alive so that I can show him, by love or by compassion or something—that the world is not what he believes. Let him have some happiness—I do feel that he deserves it. I know happiness is not a quality, and he really ought to manage without it—he should welcome the pain for someone else is spared it—but let's make an exception. Let's cheat for a little time, any-way—a few days perhaps. Let him live so that I may try to free him of the bitterness and convince him of his own immortality. Don't let him be embittered, please, because——

'I must see him,' she said. 'I'll ask permission.'

Peggy said, 'Do you think anyone would give it to you? And suppose they refused it? You've *got* to see him, haven't you? It can't wait, can it? And perhaps it shouldn't. Come at about three o'clock, when a lot of them will be having blood tests.'

Olwen sought an excuse to leave her own section at three o'clock, and then looked in the duty room of the male block to see if Peggy was there. Peggy said, 'You've got about ten minutes.'

Inside chalet No. 17 Stephen Taylor lay very still. His face was emaciated and quite white; the eyes had an unreality in them; it was impossible to doubt that he would soon be dead. He sat up-right, leaning on three pillows; his pale lips moved and he spoke slowly. 'You've come to see me?'

The anger did not seem to be in his face; nor any fear; nor any problem; he might have been playing chess or thinking about the problems others play with: how to make the first million; how to marry the boss's daughter; how to fly to the moon; what to do with the Jews or the Negroes; it was quite an interesting planet: rather dirty perhaps but otherwise fascinating: surely he did not *want* to leave it? He is not embittered, Olwen thought; my prayer has been answered.

She held his bony hands—in a short time he had become a skele-ton: an interesting skeleton with the right to vote: a skeleton that Goya should have been introduced to: still, only a skeleton: he would soon be out of the way, unable to complain; and this girl would have to find someone else to adjust her overcompensated generosity upon. It was nothing important really: not an im-portant case, even statistically, certainly not classical and completely without complications: just the usual human animal moaning be-cause the one was leaving his case of pain and the other had a streak of sadness. It was doubtful if it would be reported any-where beyond the doctor's exercise book. The intellectual weeklies wouldn't touch it with a barge-pole: too sentimental: too small: there was such a lot of big stuff to thrash the brains on. Probably some fool would have to be dug up to pay for the funeral. Olwen Rosemary Hughes said, not knowing of the ordinariness, the lack of intellectual merit, 'Stephen, I would have waited for you. I will——'

She stared at his lank hair, the sweat on his pillow, the pattern of his pyjamas and, inside them, a grey rim of dirt on a vest that would not be changed again. (It had a small interest: something unusual after all: the skeleton was animal enough to smell. Now surely that was statistical enough to justify comment?) His skin was dead—so dead that it proclaimed itself. The bones protruded in finality. In the cadaver face the lips were pale, the bones more real than the flesh, the hair lank, the skin sallow beyond sallow; only the eyes remained Stephen's: they still desired, they understood, they even pleaded still. Every word counted; everything he said must be significant; there was not much time, not much breath, the world waited for him to go: there were plenty more soldiers. Don't pray; there is scarcely time for that. What would he say? Please God, let it be real, let it be *him*, let me not be afraid, let him understand and let me——

He smiled—at a distance certainly, but not outside reality. (He is smiling at *me*. Does he think I am funny? Do I look feminine and concerned?) He said—the words just audible despite an absolute silence—'I know, I know. And thank you.' A long pause. Is he still here? 'They wanted me to see a priest,' he said. Another smile. He isn't attempting to cheat either. 'I told them that someone else said my prayers for me. Listen!'

She was listening intently: they were in the target area: the smallest sound could throw the earth off its axis. 'Yes, Stephen?'

'Tell me what it's all about. You know, don't you? I thought that because you hadn't been anywhere and I had, that I knew better. But it's not like that, is it? Why should I value anything in the world besides yourself? What's the point of it all?'

There was nothing to show what the point was except the light behind the eyes. It was still there: the light of the world: the thing that had loved her. Love would be the last thing to die. Oh God— if there is a God, and if You have not in disgust diverted Your love to another, more worthy planet, and if You are concerned about this particular case, and if You think I am a worth-while instrument, give me the words to use. I have the time and I think he has the time and the understanding, but I need the words. Was it too late for the words? Did he need them anyway? I know nothing about him, Olwen thought, except for his life here. She said, 'I don't really know. I don't think we are *meant* to know. It would give us an unfair advantage. Perhaps it's a sort of trick, Stephen—

a very complicated trick, quite beyond us, and not necessarily hostile.' Her eyes glistened and it needed a tremendous effort not to weep. 'You could only try, my dear. Perhaps that's what we have to do. And you were angry at the right things.'

A trickle ran down from Taylor's mouth. There was the smell of death in the room despite the open windows. Taylor seemed to accept her words. 'Will you think about me?' he asked. It was his last plea: there would be no one else to think of him, but that would not matter now.

'I'll think about you,' Olwen said; the tears could not be checked; they flowed in silence.

Taylor had turned with effort to look out of a window. Beyond the confines of the brick buildings and the perimeter fence was the world. The buses moved past too noisily and dirtily. The passengers stared out without humour or pity. Dust and grit blew newspapers about. There were ugly houses and lamp-posts to be seen in the hygienic glare of the sun. Unseen were the other, more disturbing things: the dive-bombers and the pulped meat of the recently killed; the fights for pig-swill in the prison compound; the ugly sound of rifle butts on flesh; some girls at Le Havre who had given a disgusting exhibition of perverted and abandoned femininity; the raping of young people and the killing of old by men believed to be comrades; the relations who were afraid to visit this hospital; the long needle drawing the liquid and the doctor yawning at its ordinariness. . . . It had been a bad world for him—no one believing in pity—but he did not wish to leave it. This nurse who was a child and a woman would never know what she had done. To tell her would necessitate revealing the other, ugly half of the world. Why inflict it on her? She had a wise innocence; it did not need horror and pain to persuade her that she was right. Someone had come out of the medical block and was crossing the lawn.

'Sister's coming,' he said.

'Then I must go,' said Olwen.

'Yes,' he said, looking back to the starched apron, the rolled-up sleeves and the two gold safety pins in the uniform, the rounded face and the startling hair. If one can believe in human beings one can believe in God; it had been the first step which he'd found so difficult. He was grateful for her tears. 'I've got to go soon myself.'

'Goodbye, my dear,' Olwen said, and touching him briefly, she fled.

He died in the night; someone else was with him; Olwen felt it as an act of unfaithfulness; she lay awake, knowing that death

44

must be near to him, but at one o'clock in the morning she fell asleep. She did not hear the plea of his bell in the duty room and the trot of feet along those stone corridors; the frantic summoning of the doctor and the last, useless choking struggle. Many of the patients awoke: it was like a prison at 9 a.m. on the morning of an execution: everyone was in some way aware. They heard the feet and the urgent discussions, the screams of animals in the darkness of the grounds, but nothing of Taylor. Yet they knew that he, too, had died.

Olwen came on duty, tired, afraid, exhausted already, to be greeted by someone who did not know about Stephen's love with the comment that he was dead, out of his misery, and wasn't it a good thing really, as there'd never been much hope? Olwen wept without explanation. Afterwards a revulsion set in. She knew a great longing to be free of sickness and fear. The war was long over, anyway, and the casualties buried. She thought about it for days, but once the idealism had been injured it became inevitable that she would leave. She was twenty-two years old and eager to live a normal life. Peggy was quite realistic about it. 'Five quid a week!' she said. 'Grab it as quickly as you can.' And once Olwen had set inquiries in motion Mrs. Dawson could not make the arrangements quickly enough for her. They were made with all the urgency of a funeral.

IV

THE bell rang, allowing cold, unsweetened spring air to flood into the hot sickliness of the shop. A few things trembled: flowers swayed in a vase, smiling faces on paper wavered like reflections in a distorted mirror, and one of these coiffured advertisements fell to the floor. There was no sound of voices—of course, Olwen realized, Mrs. Harper is out. There were no appointments due; expecting the caller to be some woman who desired to arrange one, Olwen stepped out of a cubicle to see who had called. The visitor was a man. He carried a briefcase of good leather— five guineas, she thought; it must have cost at least that. The man was very well dressed: good shoes (another five guineas), a heavy overcoat (thirty guineas), a tweed suit, bottle-green trilby, gloves —why, she thought with a flicker of internal amusement, he must be worth a hundred pounds as he stands. It was then that she noticed that he was a youngish man, not the usual middle-aged traveller, and that in his military face was an equally analytical gleam. The man was standing there in a rather poised attitude and staring at Olwen as she approached. There was a very slight alteration in his expression as she neared him—a variation in the type of analysis—but it was too instantaneous for her to define what the alteration had been. She blushed slightly because her white overall was in use now for the third day and was a little shabby; furthermore, a strand of hair had fallen over her forehead. But as she reached him she could see that he regarded her with polite approval, though even this made her slightly uncomfortable.

'Good morning,' the man said. 'Is the proprietress in?'

The stare did not falter and even though it was polite it contained an intensity. The man was thirty-five, possibly less, had a fresh, boyish complexion, darkish, and large, sentimental brown eyes. Olwen said, 'I'm sorry, but Mrs. Harper is out until this afternoon.'

'I'm from the Perfecta Soap Company,' the man said. 'We're considering extending——'

'I think you'd better see Mrs. Harper,' Olwen said. 'Would it be any trouble to call again this afternoon?'

'It will be a pleasure,' he said.

Olwen blushed mildly again and looked away. 'I can't guarantee that Mrs. Harper will be——'

'That's quite all right,' the man said. He paused. 'I'll have some lunch while I wait. Can you suggest somewhere?'

'There are a few cafés along the main road,' Olwen said. She smiled. 'They're rather full of ladies. Are you in a car?'

'Yes.'

'Well, there's the Dragon,' Olwen explained. 'It's about three miles along the main road towards Almond Vale.'

'Is that where you go?'

She blushed now in sheer embarrassment. 'No.'

'Would you care to?'

'I don't think so.'

'I'm sorry. That was an impertinence.'

The words eased her embarrassment slightly. 'It's not that,' she said, although it was. 'I only have an hour.'

'But if you went by car?'

He had tricked her with words, but she wriggled still. 'I go with a friend,' she said untruthfully.

'Bring your friend with you,' he suggested. 'I have to come back here, haven't I?'

'I don't think I should,' Olwen said. 'I mean, I don't know you.'

'My name's Harrison,' he said. 'Roy Harrison. I don't know you either, of course, but how else can I ever know you? But I understand how you feel—indeed, I admire you for it. . . . I don't know what made me ask—it's not a thing I've done before. . . .' He smiled with a stiff sort of affability. 'I'll ask you some other day.'

'You make me seem mean,' Olwen said. 'I don't wish to be——'

'Well, why not come?' he said. 'You know my name and company. It's broad daylight. I shan't eat you. You don't need to come again.'

Olwen laughed outright. 'All right,' she said. 'But I shan't be able to meet you before one.'

'Where shall I meet you? Here?'

'No,' said Olwen. 'Not here.'

'At the corner?'

'All right. By the lights.'

'Couldn't I know your name?'

'It's Hughes.'

'Please don't think I make a habit of taking attractive customers to lunch, Miss Hughes. It's just that——' But he did not specify what it was. 'I think you understand.'

'I don't really,' Olwen said. 'But you can explain it to me at lunch. You mustn't think I go to lunch with representatives either. . . .'

'I'm sure you don't,' Harrison said. 'That was a reason why I asked you.' He began to withdraw, resting a gloved hand on the door handle. 'I hope I'll see you at one o'clock.'

Olwen went back into the cubicle, where an impatient customer flicked the pages of *Vogue*. She was slightly astonished at her own behaviour. Yet there was a certain amount of truth in what Harrison had said. There was no other way of meeting him. She hoped that she had made her refusals sufficiently strong and numerous to counter any implication that she was being 'picked up'. But then, he was surely not that sort of man; there had been quite a distinguished calm about him, no impertinence. She felt a pang of apprehension at the idea of lunching at the Dragon. It was a hotel outside which large cars parked, where there were held expensive dances and other functions; where the women were more likely to be models than shop assistants and ex-nurses. It was not her world at all. It was not even a world she wished to enter.

The man called Harrison was sitting in a small red sports car when Olwen approached the cross-roads at one o'clock. He tooted the horn as Olwen neared. 'Hello, Miss Hughes. I'm glad you decided to come after all.'

'I very nearly didn't.'

'I'd have understood,' he said, and smiled the controlled smile again. 'But I'm so pleased that you did. I think we're both a little surprised at our behaviour, but there's no reason why two people shouldn't lunch together, is there?'

'Of course not,' Olwen said. The explanations and apologies embarrassed her because she still felt some misgivings. She changed the subject. 'What a nice little car.'

'Not a bad little bus, is she?' Harrison said. 'Does over seventy. Hop in, Miss Hughes.'

As there was no door, there could be no careful way of climbing in. She noticed that he glanced quickly at her legs as they were revealed; he did not stare, but after the quick glance looked completely away. It was a long time since she had been in a car, and the ride for that reason was enjoyable.

Inside the assembly room of the Dragon were a score of people seated at about a dozen tables. Most were middle-aged businessmen, but a few thirty-ish women were present, dressed with humiliating smartness. A handful of people were gathered at the bar, laughing among themselves. Harrison purchased Olwen a sherry without asking. 'I know you'll refuse to drink if I ask you,' he said, 'so I took the liberty of not asking. It's a very good sherry. Straight from the laboratory,' he concluded, and Olwen had to laugh with him.

They ate slowly and talked in embarrassed gusts. Olwen was troubled now because, looking across the table at his attentive face, it was impossible to doubt that Harrison was married. Why, then, did he want to bring her to lunch? Was he a man who liked to be surrounded and admired by girls? She put nearly the whole thought into words: 'Mr. Harrison, you are married, aren't you?'

His complete poise seemed slightly penetrated. 'What a curious question. How did you know?'

'Oh, I didn't,' Olwen said. 'It was just that you seemed the sort of man who would be.'

'I think I know what you wondered,' he said. A long pause while he seemed to collect words. 'You see, my wife is extremely ill.' Olwen was unable to keep the concern from her face; if she acknowledged that one should stand by the marriage vows, perhaps even more did she believe that one should not desert the sick or ugly. Harrison seemed to understand this, for he explained at once, 'Mentally ill, Miss Hughes.' His large brown eyes stared mistily at a vase of flowers: always send flowers, perhaps he thought: or did he think of the dignity of wreaths? 'I hoped for a long time that she would recover, but I was fooling myself. She's a complete stranger, Miss Hughes, a madwoman, ugly in every way. She will never recover. But I've stood by the past that we shared until the moment I met you.'

'I'm so sorry,' Olwen said.

Harrison paused for some time and then continued. 'They give her another year. It was an injury, you see. I don't like to talk about it. . . . Look, Miss Hughes, we've known each other for an hour and a half, but I like you and I can't disguise that. I saw you in that shop and for the first time in two years the agony ended. Evelyn went out of my mind—I don't think I've really *seen* anyone for those two years. You see, in this way you have helped me. But let's talk about you now. How did you come to be in a hairdresser's shop?' His tone and question implied that it was the wrong place to be: she did not belong: she should have been in an office or a library or parading in front of a camera: it was flattering, but snobbish. . . .

'I was a nurse,' Olwen said. 'About four years ago I nursed a man I liked. He died and a sort of revulsion set in. I had an offer—because of my hair, you see—and so when Stephen died——'

'And that's why you haven't married?'

Olwen looked away, not able to meet his eye. 'I've met others since then, but never anyone——'

'You see,' Harrison explained, 'I thought the same thing about you: that you seemed the sort of girl who would be. Naturally, although not entitled to, I wanted to know.'

Olwen smiled. 'Well, now you know everything.'

'Oh, no, not everything,' he said persuasively. 'I don't know your Christian name.'

'You're not really entitled to know it.' She added shyly, 'It's Olwen.'

'What an unusual name,' Harrison said. 'Names always are appropriate, don't you agree? They always fit. My wife was beautiful, too. Her name is Evelyn.'

'It is a nice name.'

'It fitted her so well. But not now. . . . You must come from Wales, Miss Hughes.'

'My parents are still there.'

'Then you live alone?'

'No,' said Olwen. 'With another girl, Hazel. She shares a room with me.'

'Is she a hairdresser?'

'No. She's a bus conductress. Rooms are very expensive, you see, so I agreed to share one.'

'Besides,' said Harrison, 'it's company. I know what loneliness is like.'

When they left the hotel a quarter of an hour later, he said to her: 'Miss Hughes, I have enjoyed your company. May I meet you again? I'll accept any terms you wish to make.'

'I don't know,' said Olwen. 'Do you really want to?'

'I do,' Harrison said. 'There's nothing frivolous about me. Look, tell me what you've decided when I come to see your employer this afternoon.'

'I can't do that,' Olwen said. 'Mrs. Harper would be angry if she knew that I had come here with you.'

'Do you think I should call on her at all? Would it embarrass you?'

'Perhaps you'd better not.'

'Do you have a half-day?'

'Yes. On Tuesdays.'

'Then may I take you to lunch again on Tuesday? We can discuss—all of this—again at lunch; and if you decide in my favour we could perhaps drive somewhere else afterwards or see a show....'

'All right,' said Olwen. 'I'd agree to that. And I've enjoyed myself to-day, thank you.'

'One more request,' said Harrison. 'May I call you Olwen?'

She nodded—for it was difficult to refuse without seeming churlish—and he went on, 'Will you call me Roy? That would give me an equal pleasure.'

At five-thirty Olwen, rather tired after the work, but still pleasurably excited and perturbed about her meeting with Harrison, walked home to her rooms. She lived now in an old, three-storied house with a widow and the other guest, Hazel. The house was in an Edwardian district, and was one of a straight, long line of nearly two hundred. It was respectable but dreary, with a very small front garden, scarcely two yards to the pavement, a long, dark hall and rather spacious, musty rooms. These were full of old, faded photographs, furniture bought at sales, heavily-framed pictures of cows in fields, bulky, second-hand wardrobes upstairs; even the wallpaper was dark. Olwen did not mind it at all. Mrs. Wilson, the widow, was very cheerful, laughing uproariously at the slightest opportunity. She was very nearly affectionate, certainly vitally interested in anything the two girls had to say. Hazel was five years younger than Olwen. She also was affectionate, admiring Olwen for her beauty, sincerity and seriousness. She confessed all her own misbehaviour to Olwen, more or less throwing herself on Olwen's mercy. She would explain all the events that had led to her getting drunk with her bus-driver, a married man, and permitting slight impropriety afterwards, and would expect Olwen to comfort her conscience. She listened to what Olwen had to say about the customers at work, her past experiences at hospital, her feelings about Joe and Stephen. The two girls' duty hours tended to overlap, but whenever this did not happen and they could share their leisure hours, they did so, going shopping or to the cinema.

As Olwen came beyond the porch into the long, tiled hall Mrs. Wilson greeted her. 'Here's Olwen,' she said. 'Are you tired? Hazel's in, and there's a letter from Wales for you.'

'My feet hurt,' Olwen said. 'Is the letter upstairs, Mrs. Wilson?'

'I gave it to Hazel. Are you going out to-night?'

'We might go to the pictures.'

Olwen climbed the stairs to the large front room, complete with bed and gas-ring, which was her home. Inside, on a bed, a girl was leaning against the pillows, reading a magazine. She was plump, dark-haired, pretty, but with an exhausted pallor, had large brown eyes and a rather naïve expression. She jumped as Olwen opened the door and entered.

'My God,' she said. 'You did give me a start. I was reading.'

'So I see. What's for tea?'

'Herrings. I've had mine.'

'Let's go out to-night. I feel restless.'

'Okay. I'd like that. What are you doing?'

'I'm writing in my diary.'

'But the day isn't over yet,' Hazel complained. 'Aren't we going out?'

'The day's over for me.'

'Are you tired or something?'

'It's not that. Something's happened.'

'You've met a man!' said Hazel. 'Tell me how it happened.'

'Wouldn't it be better if I didn't?' Olwen queried. 'It might be unlucky to talk about it. I'll tell you something—it may be serious.'

'How wonderful,' said Hazel in genuine happiness. 'Look, let's break all your rules to-night. It's St. Patrick's Day and you've met a man. Come and have a drink after the flicks.'

'All right,' said Olwen. 'But only one—I know you! And let's take Mrs. Wilson with us. Don't say anything to her, will you?'

On the following Tuesday at one o'clock, Olwen was more prepared for her second meeting with Harrison. There was no strand of hair over her forehead this time; she wore the only costume she had, her best shoes and one of her two pairs of nylon stockings.

He was waiting for her by his car in exactly the same place as before, and was visibly pleased to see her. Olwen's own heart fluttered at his appearance. He was theatrically good-looking, tall and slim, well-dressed in another tweed suit, the heavy tweed overcoat, brown shoes, and he carried his gloves in one hand. She realized with how much pleasure she had anticipated this next meeting and how much she desired to be relieved of that scruple, that faint hesitation promoted by the remembrance that it was he who had asked her out, quite boldly despite the politeness, and it was she who had inquired about the wife, not he who had offered the information. Yet she could not be perturbed at the way either of these things had taken place; they hadn't been obvious enough in either case to be categorized as wrong in any way; in any case, when questioned about the wife he had not lied to her. What was she worrying about? She could not herself define it. His large sentimental eyes smiled at her in obvious pleasure. He looks like an ex-officer, she thought.

'I'm so glad you came, Olwen,' he said. 'Once again I was afraid you might not.'

Olwen stared straight into his eyes and noted the dark, sallow face with its slightly taut hollows at each side. 'I know how you feel,' she said. 'I was the same. Let's not keep apologizing because we met in a shop.'

'Hear, hear!' Harrison said. 'Let's have lunch instead. I say, I've got one call to make afterwards. Do you mind? You could come with me.'

'I haven't decided about that yet,' Olwen said.

'Well, I hope you do.'

She had two sherries before her lunch and in consequence felt more confident—in fact, quite gay. Harrison's own conversation was witty and interesting. He made few attempts to flatter her, but instead talked earnestly and, when Olwen was talking, listened with all his attention.

'Listen, Roy,' she said towards the end of the meal. 'I've been thinking during the last few days—playing a sort of guessing game. Tell me if I made the correct conclusions. You're over thirty?'

'Thirty-five,' said Harrison.

'You were an Army officer?'

'Nearly right. I was R.A.F.'

'You were a pilot?'

'Bombers,' he said. His eyes misted over. Perhaps he was in the clouds, searching for the target indicators, thinking in terms of flak, photographs. Or was it that he made a study of inscrutability —or perhaps Yogi? He certainly seemed to become lost quickly in thought, and gazed unseeing at the end of the room. 'I was at Little Over.'

'Where's that?'

'It was a bomber station. Rather special. Dropped mines in the Kiel Canal—that was one of our shows. Only four of we originals left. I did sixty-four ops from there.'

'Sixty-four!'

'It's a lot,' Harrison admitted. 'I was very lucky. I'd already flown on fifty in the Middle East. Lost my first crew out there.'

'I knew you were something—reckless.'

He lowered his gaze modestly. 'All over now, Olwen.'

'I'm glad.'

'I'm flattered that you should be.'

'Then I guessed rather wildly that you'd been to Oxford or Cambridge. . . .'

'Woman's intuition!' he laughed. 'It was Oxford. I studied chemistry there——'

'I thought chemistry was studied at Cambridge,' Olwen said, remembering Bond.

'Oh, there's no hard-and-fast rule,' Roy said, waving his hands vaguely. 'I wasn't limited to chemistry. There was literature and rugger and beer-drinking as well. Splendid days. All gone now, of course—everything for money now. . . .'

'I also worked out that you are a representative because you can't stand the office sort of life.'

'Quite right,' he said. 'A fellow I knew in the R.A.F. was a district manager. . . . Matter of fact, they wanted to send me to Pakistan. English representative, you know. Very good job—house, servants, cars and what not. Interesting country too. But this terrible business happened to Evelyn . . . Can't go abroad now, of course. Not yet, anyway. . . .'

Harrison paused to look intently across the table at Olwen. 'I've been thinking, too, about all this. . . . Oh, don't blush, Olwen. I've been thinking about you very seriously. I want to do the right thing by you. . . . I don't suppose you like it much, coming with me when my wife's alive—if you can call that alive.' He shuddered. 'I had to speak to you when I saw you, Olwen. Couldn't leave it twelve months or you might have gone. . . . I saw the doctor on Sunday—that's the visiting day—and he says it may be less than twelve months. A merciful release. Or a miracle. But I don't believe in miracles.'

'I suppose,' said Olwen, 'that there's no harm in our just knowing each other.'

'That's how I felt,' Harrison said. 'But I can't pretend that it's a platonic kind of feeling. I admire you, Olwen. You're unbelievably beautiful.'

Olwen's blush deepened, but her concern faded slowly. He cared for her, but wanted to do the right thing by everybody. She couldn't ask for more, and looking at him in her relief she knew that she admired him tremendously. He was in love with her, but still capable of doing the moral thing. It indicated that he was a good man with a strong character. Mama and Dada and Tom would be excited when she told them. But when would that be? It would have to be after the twelve months Roy had mentioned. Any other way would worry them, for at that distance they wouldn't understand about the wife.

'I've been guessing too,' Roy said. 'You're twenty-two?'

'Nearly twenty-six,' Olwen said.

'Are you?' he said in surprise, and then smiled. 'You're a well-preserved old woman. Your family had a bad time in the war. Hence your working at an unfamiliar job in a strange city. . . .'

'I came here because I wanted to nurse,' she explained. 'A friend worked at a Birlchester hospital, so I followed her.'

'You send money away every week to your grey-haired granny?'

Olwen wondered what he was driving at. Was he trying to establish what was her social status? She felt for the first time a feeling of shame because her father was a bus-driver. She couldn't admit it to Roy; it might cancel everything when it had scarcely begun. 'My people are farmers,' she said, 'but I do send a pound or so each week to help Mama.'

'You have no brothers or sisters?'

'I have a brother.'

'He's at home on the farm?'

She hesitated. 'Yes.'

Roy looked straight at her with the large, sentimental eyes. 'You've been in love three or four times,' he guessed, 'always tenderly, and you've never made a fool of yourself?'

It sounded a little like an inquiry about her virginity, but Olwen answered truthfully, 'Something like that.'

'And now,' he said, 'you'd like a cup of coffee?'

'Absolutely right,' said Olwen.

When they left the hotel they found that the weather had deteriorated and it was raining heavily. Roy had left the hood of his car down and he fixed it now urgently, wiped the seats with a cloth, and ushered Olwen into the vehicle. 'Now you'll have to come with me,' he said. 'You couldn't wait about at bus stops in this.'

'All right,' said Olwen. 'My decision is made for me.'

The rain drummed on the canvas and there was a smell of oil, but she felt more a part of Roy's world because of it. The windscreen wiper on her side was not working, but when Roy stopped the car she could see that he was outside Birrell's, the shop at which she and Hazel obtained their groceries. Roy came back to the car elated. 'Got a good order there. A hundred and fifty gross.'

'Is that a lot?'

'It's not bad,' he said. 'I say, we can't very well go far in this rain, can we?'

'It's set in for the day,' Olwen said.

'What do you suggest?'

'I don't mind what we do,' Olwen said. She pointed back along the main road. 'Let's go to the cinema.'

Inside the darkness of the cinema Roy gave her a box of chocolates. After some time had elapsed he held her hand; he did not hold it for long, but before releasing it he gave an affectionate squeeze. Olwen returned this. After the show Roy took Olwen to a Tudor sort of café, full of old ladies, young mothers with their children, with horse-brasses and watercolours on the dark wooden walls.

'What did you think of the film?' he asked over the cakes and tea-cups.

It had been a film concerned with spies and the wartime Resistance Movement in France. 'It was exciting,' Olwen said. 'Did you like it?'

'Amusing,' he said, 'but not like the real thing.'

'It seemed real to me. I was biting my nails.'

Roy laughed. 'A good job you never became a spy,' he said.

'Well, you weren't either,' Olwen commented, slightly piqued. 'You were a pilot.'

'Up to 1944 certainly,' he said. 'Then I had slight eyestrain and

55

had to be taken off. I speak French, and so . . .' He waved his hands, palms upwards, to indicate without words the parachute droppings, the secret meetings and messages, the Gestapo. . . .

'You seem to have done everything.'

'Oh, no,' Roy said. 'Not everything. I've never kissed a red-haired girl.'

Olwen blushed scarlet instantly, but at an uncomfortable thought which somehow entered her mind. If redheads were the only women he had not kissed, did this not imply an abundance of blondes and brunettes? 'You should write a book about the things you've done,' she said.

He did not seem to notice her confusion, but commented, 'Some of the stuff's still secret. Where shall we go this evening? Dancing or a ride?'

'Is it raining?'

'I think it's stopped.'

'Then let's ride,' Olwen suggested, because she wanted to be near him in the car, to talk and to listen for hours yet to his talk. Dancing meant an impersonal crowd. . . .

'I know,' Roy said. 'We'll drive round and then have dinner at the Castle at Brownhill. It's a smart little place I discovered on my travels,' he explained. 'One gets a first-class meal there.'

'You've travelled a lot.'

'I cover the whole county.'

'Do you meet a lot of women?'

'Oh, Olwen,' he pleaded. 'You're still not at ease about this. You mustn't think on those lines. Two years ago Evelyn was as well as you. Since she—since then there's been nothing but work and the pain of waiting. I feel very guilty as it is. Don't make it too difficult for us to associate at all.'

'I'm sorry,' Olwen said. 'I wasn't being serious, anyway. Don't feel unhappy, Roy, because I would wait willingly for those twelve months to pass.'

'You mean——'

'I mean that I like you.'

She could see that he was tremendously elated, and because there could only be one reason for that, she was pleased too. She wanted him to fall in love with her; and it seemed that he would; she was very nearly in love with him; so long as they could retain some kind of integrity towards the unknown Evelyn, then Olwen was willing to love him patiently now, in tenderness, without passion, while they waited until they could legally and morally

56

become passionate. It did not seem to be too early to think on these lines, because he was serious, and this was the course of action that she intended.

He drove the sports car through the spring evening, rather pointlessly, as the darkness soon came. At the Castle, a small inn with many beams and unnecessary steps, they received a personal sort of welcome. Already she was beginning to collect memories, and this was one of place. . . . Olwen had several sherries and an excellent meal. Roy plied her with more sherry before they left, but she refused it. 'No, thanks, Roy. I'm nearly asleep as it is. Anyway, it's getting late.'

In the country lanes on the way back Roy drove slowly and eventually turned into one in total darkness to stop. With the engine stopped, it was so quiet that it was almost embarrassing. One could almost hear thoughts. 'Let's stop and talk,' Roy suggested, having already done so. 'Like a cigarette?'

He had now turned off the lights of the car, and she knew in a mixture of pleasure and alarm that he intended to kiss her. Olwen had not the power to deny the moment with cigarettes, and replied, 'No, thank you.'

'Do you want me to pretend?' he asked.

'Pretend?'

'Pretend that I don't love you. I do, you see, and it seemed pointless to hide that. . . .'

'I don't mind if you love me,' Olwen said—and if her voice trembled it surely could not be conscience—'as long as we can love with clear consciences.'

'You put it perfectly,' Roy said. 'We must do the right thing.'

He caressed her gently, her hair and face, even her ears, and then turned her face upwards. She closed her eyes as if to pretend she did not know she was being kissed: it was just something theoretical that was happening: something she wanted in thought. His kisses were quite gentle at first, but became longer and more passionate as the minutes went by. He did not seem to be in any hurry, even though it was late: it would take a long time to satisfy him. Olwen's head swam a little because of the sherry; her heart thudded as he kissed round her neck; she recognized that they had already passed the point of a mere tender, passionless relationship; it was his fault as well as hers, but she understood his eagerness and forgave him. There was a wife somewhere who was not legally or physically dead; yet neither was she legally nor physically alive. . . . Roy whispered her name and Olwen opened her eyes. In the feeble light she could see the taut hollows in his cheeks and a vein that ticked at the side of his eyebrow. There was no doubting the truth of his admiration; he was very excited; his very breathing was too heavy to be faithful; in his pleasure he had obviously forgotten his previous unhappiness, the accident and the beautiful wife who had gone mad and ugly. . . . 'Don't be too happy,' Olwen pleaded. 'We have a long time to endure.'

'You're so good,' he said, 'but so beautiful too. You must behave for the two of us.'

'The three of us,' she corrected.

He had changed his position slightly. His one hand was under her thighs, pulling her body across and into his embrace. She lay limp and soft and at ease in this position, knowing that he could take her physically and that apart from screams she would be powerless, but trusting him. Because of his kisses and crushing weight, she was moved further and further over the two seats. His hand trapped under a stockinged thigh touched flesh; she wriggled slightly so that he could free it, and moved into complete discomfort with the metal back of a seat jabbing into her. 'Roy,' she pleaded, laughing slightly. 'I'm getting all tangled up and the seat's hurting me.'

He stopped embracing her at once, freeing the hand as he lifted her to a sitting position. 'I'm so sorry,' he said. 'I was quite carried away.'

She began to re-smudge her lips with lipstick, indicating without words that they should stop. 'You certainly were,' she said. 'My stockings were torn across your gears.'

'What a pity,' he said. 'I'll get you some more. Size ten?'

'Yes. But how did you know?'

'You're about as tall as Evelyn.'

'You were touching my legs,' Olwen said. 'That was very naughty when I thought you were hugging me. . . . A good job I didn't have the other two sherries.'

'Darling,' Roy said, 'how absurd and charming you are. It was the way you collapsed across me.'

Olwen didn't allow him to drive her all the way to the Edwardian house. 'Listen, Roy,' she explained. 'I'm only a working girl and my rooms aren't in a very nice quarter.'

'As if I mind,' he protested.

'I know you don't, but I'd still prefer that you didn't see them. Let's pretend that I'm Cinderella.'

'Just as you wish,' Roy said.

He stopped the car at the same corner as they had started from. They clung together inside the car for over five minutes before they could bear to separate. This time his emotions were held in restraint; she felt he understood their need to be tender, not passionate, if they were to be loyal to Evelyn at all.

It was after eleven o'clock when Olwen entered her room. Hazel, in pyjamas, was listening to the small radio set they shared. She snapped it off in excitement and begged Olwen to tell her all about the afternoon and evening.

'I'm so excited I must talk to someone,' Olwen said. 'Oh, Hazel, he's nice and he loves me. I love him too. If you could only see him.'

'I did see him.'

'What?' said Olwen. 'Where?'

'I saw you both in the cinema.'

'Why didn't you speak?'

'What for?' Hazel said. 'You didn't seem short of conversation.'

'What did you think of him?'

'He's a good-looker,' said Hazel. 'He seems well provided for. I should grab him if you can.'

'He's terribly intense.'

'Intense?'

'You know—emotional. I thought he was going to get a bit hot.'

'Would you have let him?'

'Don't be silly,' said Olwen. 'He's not like that any more than I am, so the question doesn't arise.'

'Perhaps it will.'

'Oh, you and your mind, Hazel! He's been to Oxford and he was an officer. He's done the most exciting things, but he's glad to settle down now.'

'Sounds as though he mentioned marriage.'

'He's already married.'

'*What?*' cried Hazel.

'It's terrible for him,' said Olwen. 'His wife was involved in an accident and she's been insane for a long time.'

'Then he'll have to get a divorce,' said Hazel. 'It sounds quite romantic.'

'No,' said Olwen. 'It's not at all. She's very ill and will die. He feels extremely guilty coming with me at all. But what can he do?'

'I don't know,' said Hazel. 'I should wait and see what he wants to do.'

V

Some Extracts from Olwen Hughes's Diary

THURSDAY, March 17th. Something extraordinary happened to-day. I met R. He is a traveller who called when Mrs. H. was out this morning. After some conversation, he persuaded me to accompany him to lunch at the Dragon along Almond Vale Road. I didn't altogether wish to go, although I believe his invitation was spontaneous and he to be as embarrassed as myself. We both kept admitting this, although I don't think either of us regret the meeting, and we intend to meet again next Tuesday to sort of discuss it. The thing is, he's married. That would normally stop any association as far as I'm concerned, but R.'s wife was in an accident some time ago and is now not only insane, but fatally ill. (Ugly in every way, he said.) He did not explain about the accident, and I did not ask, assuming that in some way he was involved too—perhaps in his car. His explaining about it at all indicated that he is as serious about loyalties as I am. He was very polite and in control of himself; I would call him a gentleman if the word didn't seem to date back to the Ark.

Tuesday, March 22nd. A quiet morning at work. Met R. at one o'clock and he again drove me to the Dragon in his little red car. Afterwards R. called at Birrell's and obtained an order for a hundred and fifty gross—no wonder with that smile. It was raining, so we went to the flicks. (Hazel saw us there. She likes the look of R.) Then R. took me to tea at the Priory place. I'd never been there before because it's snobby and expensive. R. was one of the pilots who dropped mines in the Kiel Canal on some famous raid, and was a spy in the next year. We discussed whether we should meet again, but it is obvious that we must. In the evening R. drove all over the place, ending at a small inn in Brownhill. I had a lot of sherry—too much perhaps, I became so sleepy—and another lovely meal. In the car later R. became tender, even beyond tender. He admires me and told me so. I could see even in darkness that he does. He was very emotional. I think he must have been very unhappy during the last two years and found love quite strange and exciting in this renewal. He was quite lost in his eagerness; I had to explain to him that while we are as we are it is important that we do not venture beyond tenderness. He's terribly intense. I don't know what would happen if I let myself go—I'd be lost with him, I suppose.

Tuesday, March 29th. I thought about it all the week, not really believing that everything would be the same. R. took me to another place, the Queen's in the city. I had some more sherry—I am becoming quite blasé about sherry. No more beer with the nurses, although that was happiness of a sort at the time. R. bought me two pairs of nylons. One to replace those torn in his car the last time (his own fault—I was kicking a bit when I lost balance) and the other for what he called an un-birthday present. Have a feeling I shall receive several of those, but he really needn't. I love him already; there's no need for presents or persuasion for that very reason. This time, after tea, we went dancing. I haven't danced for ages; in fact I've led a very vegetable existence for years! I remember now that evening when I met Joe. How tender we both were. This was different. R. is a marvellous dancer, far better than I. He was tender again in the car and would have become passionate if I hadn't slowed things down a bit.

Haven't told Mama even now, because she wouldn't understand a bit about his being married. I will explain it all when I have my next holiday. I know it's all right, but I can see how it would appear to the village. I don't like to think of E. dying, and yet, as R. has said at least twice, if he hadn't spoken to me, but had waited for *that*, then by the time it had happened I might have gone away. (He meant married someone else, I think.)

Tuesday, April 5th. Tuesday is now definitely the most—in fact, the only wonderful day of each week. It was fine this afternoon and we drove miles. The buds are beginning to burst and colours to show. Dear God, I thank You for the spring. To be in love in the spring! I go about sighing and smiling to myself; I have to lower my gaze in buses and pretend to take an interest in hair-styles for fat ladies. But all the time I think of him. Oh, I remember Leslie and Joe and Stephen, but I recall them with pity. There was a note of unhappiness all the time with these others—someone always going away. R. isn't going away—he's come to stay. And he's not a boy; he's a man; we're both grown-up and know our obligations and limitations as well as our perfections. It will be wonderful if I can ever take R. to Wales. I know he's been to several distant parts of the world; he's complicated and intelligent, but I'd like to show him the simplicity and value of silence and trees and the sea. I believe that in many things—certainly in love and courage and religion—simplicity, not complicatedness, is the heart. Too much dashing about, either physically or mentally, leads to frustration or quarrels: a degree of apathy towards everything. R. is most tender, but almost vibrates with intensity. He even talks poetry. To-night we went to the city to the theatre. R. got seats in the circle—he does everything like that and I can't help liking it. Don't know why I've always been suspicious of the people with money—it must have been ignorance or jealousy. I should not think of marriage, I know, or I may be hurt and disappointed, but I do. He makes it so obvious that marriage is his intention. R. says he has a house, but lives in rooms while E. is ill. Perhaps we wouldn't live in that house because the memories of her would be too strong. I envy and pity her all in one breath! I wouldn't mind how or where we lived so long as we did.

Tuesday, April 12th. We had another day that belongs to us alone. Days like to-day are perfect because they can be relived in every detail: one can enjoy them twice or thirty times: no wonder old people live on their memories. And yet, now I wish to put it down on paper, what am I to write so that in years to come I may be reminded of every detail? What happened? We went to the Dragon, for a drive, to tea, a dance and then another short drive for a drink. (Have a suspicion that R. likes to drink, but he's not one of those men who soak themselves in beer. It's the glitter of the places and the conversations that he seems to enjoy. And sherry does make me chatter, too.)

It's the words I remember, and I laugh when I think of to-night. I had to slap R.'s face! Hazel was almost right—his passion overcame him. There's no doubt that we've moved slightly beyond the bounds of tenderness. We can't help it because I love him as personally as he loves me; it's so hard to keep love distant, impersonal. In the confined space of the car we cling close together. He starts in tenderness as I do, but in a quarter of an hour we're locked in an embrace so tight that every knot and bit of metal in my clothing is leaving an imprint on my body. It's as if he can't be near enough to me. I suppose, without realizing it, he longs to possess me, but, controlling himself, hugs me tightly instead. He only wanted to touch my skin, and I was in such a state that I nearly let him. I'm almost twenty-six and sometimes I've thought about physical love; I've thought about it with him in mind and wanted him to go on where dear Joe left off. How can I help it?

I shall wait, of course, but I'm a woman and healthy, and once or twice when I've stopped men I've wondered what would have happened if I'd let them do the things they wished to my body. And loving R. so much, my woman's body has its own arguments with my mind and I become my own enemy. But my beliefs control me. Nurses used to ask me, 'Why do you believe in God?' and my answers never convinced them. They wanted practical, physical, almost scientific explanations of every little difficulty, when if ever there was a thing that belonged to the heart. . . . R. knows my feelings about my faith; he respects them, although not sharing them; he also respects himself and me, and that emotion we share. . . . Dear R. I know he intended to be good. His love for me burst beyond its confines a little, that's all, and he tried to touch my skin, wanting to know my arms and shoulders and breasts. He was very tender, I'll admit, and I longed to allow him. 'I am touching your skin,' he said, 'when I stroke your face, shake hands or kiss; but you do not say that is a sin.' I tried again to explain my beliefs, but he said something about how the war and Evelyn's illness had finished all his. (I will try to do something about that.) So I said, 'You see, you're in need of that kind of love and you're just making me a substitute for your wife.' He was quite upset. 'I couldn't help wanting to know you,' he said, 'and, knowing you, I couldn't help wishing to love you.'

Tuesday, April 19th. R.'s car was out of order to-day, so we took a train to Almond Vale. We were like a couple of kids on the train—I think R. has forgotten what a simple thing like travelling on a train can be like. Almond Vale is a perfect little town. Its name is appropriate, for in the main street—not the shopping centre, but the one by the grass lawns and the river—the almond trees were so pink that it seemed like an illustration from a child's book. We had late lunch at an olde worlde place and then went on the river. R. rowed two or three miles; I watched his arms in their movement. How strong he is! . . . He talked about the future and more or less said he wanted to marry me. (First time he's really said it so definitely.)

He bought a bottle of sherry and as we had the compartment to ourselves coming back we both got slightly merry. (A first-class compartment—I think he did it on purpose, the rogue!) R. was very tender again, despite being merry, and I couldn't keep him off altogether. He pleaded so hard to touch and rather ignored my words of reply. In his fervour, he refused to accept them and it almost seemed as if he used his superior physical strength. At any rate, I had the feeling that I would have had to quarrel to stop him. Once he did touch me he became very gentle and it was I who felt slightly sick with ecstasy. Even without standing, I could feel my legs trembling; I became like liquid, only able to move downwards; and when his cool hand reached my breasts I knew how terribly much a woman and a desiring human I am. Oh, God, how strange You are to make us as we are—sin and creation in the same urge, all a question of degree and who's with whom. I looked in the mirror at home and saw what a woman I am. All the same, I'm glad I managed to limit him to the touches, for in the excitement of the moment he wanted to go beyond. (There would have been time and we were in a non-corridor train. It's a marvel I wasn't scared, but, then, despite his eagerness, I trust him.)

Sunday, April 24th. I went to church in the morning despite the flawless weather. Have been a little conscience-stricken since Tuesday. There's such a long time to wait and already we're in danger of losing our integrity and control. In the afternoon R. met me for an hour before going to visit his wife at the hospital. (What a terrifying experience that must be.) He tried to be naughty again in the car, but I became a bit mad. . . . After all, on a Sunday. He apologized and then brought out a small basket of strawberries from the rear of the car. He was most tender when we separated.

Tuesday, April 26th. R. had to go to Bristol to-day, so I was unable to see him. Hazel was on duty in the afternoon, so there was nothing to do and nobody to talk to. I went to the pictures because of the rain. It was a bitterly sad film, quite unreal actually, but I wept. I think it did me good! I've been too happy lately. Oh, I missed R. very much, but it gave me time to think. The trouble is that now I've thought I'm so undecided. I'd had the thought recently that I shouldn't see R. until the twelve months were past; we are drifting towards a happiness in which we shall be too selfish to care about others. And then I'm worried because he longs to possess me and is even showing slight impatience at my arguments. We have reached the stage in which he is allowed to touch me. I don't think I can stop him doing that a second and a third time; it is going to be hard to stop him possessing me further; and to possess me further means to possess me altogether. It's not as if I was impartial myself; I love him and my body trembles for him;

64

since that day on the train I have become liquid in my thoughts and dreams. . . .

Tuesday, May 3rd. Just before I left for work, Mrs. W. handed me a letter, and it was from him. It was a beautiful letter and I shall carry it everywhere with me. There was no address—R. is funny—he makes me use typed addressed envelopes because his landlady would open any handwritten letters and if she found that one was from a girl would be delighted to make trouble. (Who with, since the wife is mad?) Don't know why he doesn't leave, because money seems no object. Anyway, the letter wasn't about that. It was to tell me that he would be late, but would bring a picnic basket at two-thirty. There was some naughty poetry in the letter, something about 'Your breasts, like ivory globes circled with blue. A pair of maiden worlds unconquered.'

It was hard to resist the poetry, because R. makes love seem something beautiful, not nasty or shocking. When he wrote the letter he meant that, despite what had taken place on the train, I am still innocent. Oh, I wish I could still claim that, but I can't. I wish it and yet would hardly take back to-day for all the universe. A thing so lovely can't be wrong (which is what R. said), and yet now, hours later, the nerves and body quietened, my mind tells me coldly and logically that it is. My mind explains to me that it is not lovely, but exciting; that I was aware before it happened that it was exciting; that it's all a thudding desire of the flesh and little to do with the heart at all. And yet the heart must be a part of it, for I wouldn't have loved in that way with anyone unless I loved that person the way I love R. and had my love returned in the patient, sensitive way that R. has always given it. (I have known him about six weeks, but it seems right to talk about always.)

It wouldn't have happened at all but for the weather. I suppose life and death and the other things hang on threads like the weather, a word, a glance, which end of the street the postman starts at, whom Providence places as your neighbours and friends. . . . To-day the weather was perfect: a complete blue sky, and out of the breeze, the sun as warm as summer. I do not know where we went to—although we are now able to label a few places as belonging to us. We were quite alone in a field that sloped, from the top of which we could see the lane winding back to the small red car and, miles away, a railway train.

R. had asked me to bring cups and plates. Everything else he brought: there were sandwiches, cakes, cherries, strawberries, two flasks of tea and ice-cream in a third; finally, a bottle of sherry for when the sun went down and the chilly evening came. I don't know how R. crammed it all into the car. We just talked in the sunshine and then R. loved me. We were in a hollow as warm as an oven. He whispered such gentle explanations and love to me that I began to forget everything slowly—everything in the world except him. But even when the other things had gone—awareness, memory and much of conscience—and there was only his face and eyes and pleading words I tried to refuse. 'But we're going to be married, aren't we?' R. asked. 'Must we wait for a bit of paper before we're sure that your God approves of our love? Olwen, we've so long to wait.' I tried to be calm. 'Do you mean you want to marry me?' His hands were already exploring and I, becoming clay for his hands to mould in whatever way they willed, knew that I wanted all of him. Calmness and logic were impossible and to refuse his love insulting. I've refused for so long and he has been so patient. Perhaps all men really do it. Perhaps Tom does despite his anger. R. said, 'Of course I intend and long to marry you.' (Oh, such words!) 'So what's the harm?' And I just looked at him, made a quick prayer and let myself go; he knew it and whispered, 'Darling, I knew you would!' He was a little violent (he bit my shoulder), but I was in such a state I didn't mind any pain. Poor Evelyn, and yet she must have known it once. . . . Oh, God, don't be angry with me because I love him. I love You too. . . .

Tuesday, June 28th. It was stifling in the shop to-day. I was glad to have the afternoon off because of that, apart from the agony of meeting R. We were very busy this morning and I had a curious dizzy spell; I thought I was going to faint. Mrs. H. made me sit down for a while; she was quite apologetic and told me to slow down a bit. As if hairdressing was half as strenuous as nursing! It must have been the heat. All this wonderful weather will lead up to the most terrific storm. I only hope it doesn't come on a day when I meet R.

He had another un-birthday present to-day—some black stockings. Insisted that I put them on straight away, although they didn't match my costume at all; I had to go to the Ladies' in the Dragon; did feel a fool. The agony, I wrote accidentally, but it is true: a kind of frenzy. We are like the weather—the gentleness of spring has gone and the hot blast of summer is too much for me sometimes: I want the spring back. I would never have thought that

66

anyone could get me into such a state. R. delights in loving me until I'm slightly insane with longing—longing and dejection. For how sensual he is. Doesn't he love my heart any more? Do your hair this way, he says; then do it that way. Wear silk stockings. Wear nylons. Wear net stockings. Wear black undies, blue undies, green undies. . . . Oh, Roy, can't you reach the zenith of sensuality and pass beyond it to the real me? I sometimes cry, but heaven knows what about. I'm sure love could never have been like this for E., who, R. tells me, was always nervous and thin. Is that why he delights so much in the physical part of our love? Not that I don't share it; I am a healthy beast; God forgive me for it. I think I see now why there has to be pain in the world, and wait for mine in despairing enjoyment.

I am happy, but not at all satisfied. Everyone seems different when one's in love: not nicer, but slightly hostile. Perhaps it's because I have to lie. I can't even tell dear Hazel all of it, and sometimes when I evade her more direct questions she looks at me in something like resentment. It's the same with the two girls at work. They seem jealous because I'm so obviously in a world of my own. Perhaps people resent genuine happiness because there is so little of it. It makes me feel so absolutely alone. Perhaps I'm not so happy as I thought. There is not one single person who knows all about us. I've been home to Wales twice since I met him, but it was subtly different. I had to be on guard against those who, loving me possessively, wanted to hear about my every activity. I must write to Peggy and tell *her* all about it. She's the one person who would understand.

Friday, July 1st. I wrote to Peggy and she came to-night. It had been months since her last visit, and I was so pleased to see her. But not for long. She said the change in me was startling— I was fatter, rosier, and have a certain look in my eye. I told her what had caused it, and instead of sharing my joy Peggy was angry. I burst into tears, but she was relentless. Why should she criticize me after the things she's done? We drank our bottles of beer and smoked our cigarettes and were almost silent. Then she tried to lecture me: a bit of fun's a bit of fun, but what you're doing is dangerous, etc. I told her it wasn't just amusing to us and questioned her own behaviour. She waved that aside—it didn't matter! —and pleaded with me. It was awful. When she left I had to beg her not to write to Mama. She just looked at me and said, 'Doesn't that prove exactly what I've been saying?' It was hopeless—she just

67

didn't want to understand. I shall cry myself to sleep. Now R. and I are absolutely alone.

Tuesday, July 5th. Just as I thought. The storm broke to-day, almost at the moment I left the shop. We had to go to the pictures, the first time for weeks. It was rather nice really just to sit and hold hands. He loved on my original terms of tenderness for a few hours. The rain was still heavy when we came out, but the thunder had stopped. I was glad, because I'm scared of it. In the evening R. drove for miles and miles. I'm sure he was looking for somewhere dry, but there was nowhere. In the dusk he turned into a lane and we stayed in the car. Then we lived on his terms, despite the discomfort, until we were both tired. There was a leak in the hood, but he took no notice. He never does.

Tuesday, July 12th. I was ill again this morning. There can be no doubt now. I could scarcely breathe I was so afraid. I wish I had someone to talk to. And I wish so much that I had told Mama about R. How am I going to do it now and convince her that it's beautiful? She will be unhappy, and Dada and Tom will be angry.

What I am really afraid of is losing R. I do not mind the baby. I shall love it because it's the fruit of our love. But I can't imagine R. being anything at all except gallant and passionate. He loves me (and love itself) so much that he might be angry at the possibility of a third part of our lives. He despises the humdrum, everyday things. And even if E. died to-day—she's terribly ill, R. says; he has that worry already—our marriage would be uncomfortably soon after her funeral.

Tuesday, July 19th. I intended to tell R. last week, but didn't; I wanted to again to-day but did not dare. He was so full of things in opposition to the ordinary. I am reluctant to take the chance of losing or even altering my happiness. But now there's no doubt and he will have to be told. I wonder why I'm so scared as well as so worried? Perhaps he will be delighted. It would be what we intended after our marriage, so why not before? At least the world doesn't pour scorn on people like us to-day. We are bound to make a few people unhappy, and because they are unhappy we are sure to be affected and upset too, no matter how enormous our love is.

We went to that little spot on which we made love for the first time that day in the spring. In the same hollow the sun was

warmer than before—my legs are brown. I asked R. to be gentle
—it was impossible to stop him altogether—and he was slow and
tender. Because I was not in such a state as usual I was detached
and able to watch R. in his happiness. How he looks at me in his
excitement! That was when I should have told him. Funny the
way that little vein throbs at the side of his head. The excitement,
I suppose.

Monday, July 25th. To-morrow we are going to Almond Vale
and I must tell R. It is every day now and I should leave work.
I think I will give Mrs. H. notice to-morrow, and if, when I've
told him, R. is angry, then I can leave the week's money and go
straight home. I don't know why I should even imagine he might
be angry and refuse his responsibility—my health makes me slightly
odd, I suppose—but if he did I want the relief of going home to
Wales. They would forgive me in their love. Oh, God, forgive
me too. Don't be angry. Don't take him away altogether. I know
that what I've done is terribly wrong, because it's an enjoyable sin
and the most tempting (and knowing that it is adds to my guilt).
But I haven't hurt anybody, and I won't give my baby away.
Not even for him. . . .

VI

TUESDAY, the twenty-sixth day of July, was, in Birlchester,
one of those cloud-covered, sultry, exhausting days on which
world wars commence, violent quarrels flare up and even the
mildest of people have irritable headaches. At the seaside the same
temperature applied, but its humidity was absent and the heat was
relieved by a sea breeze. Old ladies were able to have a light breakfast, move to the promenade in coats and with small dogs, and
even complain of the cold chill in the air. Younger ladies, without coats, indeed without much clothing at all, were able, after
a refreshing sleep, to contemplate the violent activities of tennis
and swimming. In the lifeless air of the industrial city things were
different. There was no breeze, for there was no atmosphere; nobody had slept well: in the moist, oppressive glare of morning
even the nicest girls found that they were sweating, and contem-
plated a day's work at a typewriter with solemn irritation. It was
a day on which one was defeated before one began; it was yet
another indictment of the industrial way of life.

Olwen Hughes, twenty-six years and six weeks old, five foot six inches tall, nine stone seven pounds in weight, blue eyes, auburn hair, medium build, I.Q. adequate, emotional Protestant, trained sanatoria nurse, trained hair-stylist, moles on left arm and right shoulder, unmarried, more than two months pregnant, had slept badly and in short patches during the steamy night. She had dropped off to sleep several times, only to awake sweating and to kick off the blankets and sheet; falling asleep again each time without their cover, she had reawakened later shivering. She stepped out of bed, slightly miserable, as usual burdened with the unhappiness of her particular sin, aware that this was not going to be a pleasant day. Work in the sweet, overpowering, sickly atmosphere of the hairdressing saloon had to be followed by an explanation to Roy that he was going to be a father. Inevitably there was going to be unhappiness in the day. The time of happiness was passing; that of responsibility and perhaps punishment approaching. Olwen drank some cold water and fought off the desire to be sick. Hazel, whose day sometimes started as early as five-thirty, had already left. Olwen ate a small breakfast of corn flakes in milk, some bread and butter, drank two cups of tea and then trod downstairs. A letter had arrived for her from Wales. She read it, sitting on the stairs in slight dizziness, scanning the innocent, unaware words of her mother. That was another agony to be endured and inflicted. Her mother had not heard from Olwen for two weeks; she was not complaining, only pleading to hear. Olwen was moved to the first emotion of the day beyond the slight grip of horror in which she had awakened. At that moment she felt absolutely no emotion towards the man called Roy Harrison; she knew she would later in the day and in his presence, but at the moment she was filled with a longing for the love without complications of her mother: it could be relied on to forgive, even to plead with others to forgive.

Mrs. Wilson appeared along the tiled hall. 'Hello, Olwen, dear. The post has come?'

'A letter from my mother.'

'Nothing for me?'

'No, Mrs. Wilson.'

'Ah, well, no bills either. It's going to be hot again.'

'I didn't sleep well.'

'Nor me. You look a bit pale.'

'I'm a little miserable to-day,' Olwen said. 'Something in the letter. And I didn't sleep much.'

'Conscience, I expect,' said Mrs. Wilson.

70

Olwen stared at her. 'That and the heat,' she agreed, and walked slowly to the door. 'I wish I could go to Wales to-day, Mrs. Wilson, if you'll forgive me saying so.'

'You'll go for the Bank Holiday.'

'Yes. Perhaps before. G'bye, Mrs. Wilson, dear.'

Olwen walked the half-mile to Olga Harper's shop at a leisurely pace. The air was already warm and dusty; bus tickets and scraps of paper swirled in the gutters at the passing of each vehicle. Men stared at Olwen as she walked, slowly and deep in thought, along the pavements: stared at the auburn hair, the gentle face and the swelling breasts, and then turned again to the headlines of their papers. It had been a quiet twenty-four hours; not much had happened to upset them. A famous person had died of senility. Someone (in America, of course) had married someone else who possessed sixty billion dollars. A film was being made of another pornographic novel. A Communist had escaped to become a Catholic; a Catholic had decided to become a Buddhist; a famous politician had gone right over to the opposite Party. A jet fighter had blown up and its pilot had been killed. A man with a piece of wood had struck at a leather ball all day to the exasperation of at least half a county. A famous person had said that the times were difficult. An actor had been accused of homosexuality with another actor. An actress with three children had in the Divorce Court admitted adultery with four men. Rain with thunder was expected in London and the southern counties. In the Midlands it would continue close, possibly with thunder during the night.

At ten-thirty, between two hairdressing appointments, Olwen said to Mrs. Harper, 'May I speak to you?'

'Speak on,' said Mrs. Harper. She lighted a cigarette and puffed smoke furiously. 'My God, what an airless sort of day.'

'Privately,' Olwen requested, blushing slightly.

There were two girls standing near, sipping drinks of tea rapidly. They stared curiously as Olwen made her request. They did not know or understand Olwen very well: she was not talkative; she was interested but not excited by films; she set an example of hard work which they reluctantly had to follow; altogether, it seemed to them, she fancied herself to be a cut above them.

'All right,' said Mrs. Harper, and led the way into a small partitioned part—the office. As she closed the door behind them she asked, 'What's up?'

'Mrs. Harper, I want to leave.'

'Oh, God, no, not you, Olwen.'

'I'm sorry,' said Olwen.

'But *why?*' asked Mrs. Harper. The first suspicion entered her mind. 'You've had a better offer? You're going into the city centre?'

'No. I just want to go home.'

'Who doesn't?' protested Mrs. Harper. 'I'd like to go to bed for a week. Got family trouble or something?'

Olwen blushed deeply, at first misunderstanding her question. 'Something like that.'

'It's a bit bloody rough on me,' complained Mrs. Harper. 'Those two sluts won't do a stroke if I'm not here. Can't you wait a few weeks until I get somebody?'

Olwen shook her head. 'No.'

'You'll stay until the holiday?' It was ten days off.

'Of course.'

Mrs. Harper had been thinking, which meant thinking about herself. 'You'll have to do this afternoon. You can't have that if I've got to go and look all over the place——'

'I can't stay this afternoon.'

The gash mouth twisted. 'You want it all your own way, don't you?'

'I would,' Olwen said, 'but I have something terribly important to do this afternoon.'

'Important!' sneered Mrs. Harper. 'Well, don't come asking for references, that's all. If anyone lets me down——'

'I don't want any references,' Olwen said. She began to move to the door.

'Wait a minute!' Mrs. Harper said. She was obviously angry. It was because she saw that she was unable to hurt Olwen; and this indicated how unimportant the job at Olga's had been to Olwen; it implied a snub at Mrs. Harper herself. For a moment Mrs. Harper had seen her importance in another's perspective. She picked up an exercise book, flicked its pages and then said loudly, 'I can do your appointments for the next week. I don't want anyone here who doesn't want to be here. How do I know what you'd whisper in customers' ears?'

'Mrs. Harper, you know——'

'Spare me the righteous indignation,' Mrs. Harper rasped, exultant at the sudden blush and the glistening in Olwen's eyes. 'I'm a business woman. Here's a week's money. Goodbye, Miss Hughes. See if you can get six ten a week elsewhere.'

Olwen was very red in the face, but too tremulous and near to sickness to be angry. She walked quickly past the cubicles, said

'Goodbye' with difficulty to the two faces that stared out in curiosity, and almost at once found herself on the kerb, not knowing what to do. Calming down, she laughed dryly, feeling free. She had been at the shop several years and had always worked hard—harder than Mrs. Harper herself. Now she was dumped without references or reward. But there had been one reward Mrs. Harper had not known about. A desire came to Olwen to settle everything; not to wait until one o'clock, but to telephone Roy now and tell him about the baby. The branch office of a travel agency mocked her with advertisements of holidays in Corsica, ten days at the Riviera, boat trips to Norway. Idle, half-naked women sprawled in isolated selfishness on burning sand: no mention of children or of work or of God: the handsome men waited in the background, bronzed, alone, equally without responsibility: happiness was possible if you didn't care and if you could pay. Olwen stared at it, not seeing the insult, untouched by that sort of envy, and thought: If he despises me I'll buy a ticket there and go home to-day. I could catch the three o'clock train. She had a depressing apprehension of failure: it was a bad day all right.

In a telephone booth Olwen looked for the number of the Perfecta Soap Company (the name had been spoken to her once, but she had remembered it in love all these months), but when she dialled it a female voice announced, 'Rejuvenated Oil.'

'Is that Central 9999?'

'Rejuvenated Oil at your service.'

'I wanted Perfecta Soap.' (I sound unwashed, she thought.) 'I must have dialled——'

'Just a moment,' said the voice. There were clicking noises and then another female voice said, 'Are you calling?'

'Put this through to 172,' the first voice said.

There was complete silence during which Olwen, looking up, encountered with a shock her own anxious face in a mirror. The silence ended and a deep male voice, so important that one could almost smell the cigar smoke and see the pot belly, said, 'Bushell here.'

'Is that Perfecta Soap?'

'Yes. Bushell here.'

'I want to speak to Mr. Harrison.'

'We have several Mr. Harrisons, madam.'

'He's a traveller.'

'The travellers only come in on Fridays, madam. Harrison's in Sheffield.'

'But he can't be. I'm going to——' Olwen, sweating suddenly, chopped her sentence in half and said instead, 'Oh, I didn't think. . . .'

'Did you wish to place an order?'

'I just wanted—to ask him something.'

'That's not Mrs. Harrison?'

'Of course not,' Olwen said. 'She's ill—in hospital. I thought you knew——'

'I'm sorry to hear it,' said the deep voice. 'Very sorry. But she never was strong. Are you a friend of the family?'

'Something like that.'

'Give her my regards,' instructed the deep voice. 'I'm so busy these days—the name's Bushell. Which hospital is she in?'

'I don't—I've forgotten. I must ring off. Goodbye.'

Olwen put the receiver down immediately. I nearly got Roy into trouble then, she thought. How naughty of him not to go to Sheffield so that he can see me! I wonder why that man asked if I was a friend of the family? A family sort of implies children. Perhaps he meant Roy's parents. I'm incapable of thought to-day. I feel like a stewed prune. I'll have a drink of coffee.

She entered a restaurant and lingered there for a quarter of an hour. Afterwards she wandered vaguely along the main road. She passed the gates of a small, dry, dusty park and then turned back, deciding to enter. Purchasing a newspaper, Olwen sat on a park seat for what seemed a very long time. She scanned the newspaper, although the words were meaningless and her thoughts insisted on intrusion. Occasionally, feeling conspicuous, she glanced up to see if anyone was watching her. But the old men on another seat were deep in talk among themselves; the children afar off carried on playing shrilly; the few mothers who passed wheeling prams did not look at her. There was nothing in the park to gaze at in respect: just a few quarrelling sparrows splashing dust; dry, baked grass, some feeble trees, a small splash of colour from the flowers, the ornate green gentlemen's lavatory and the ladies' wrapped more respectfully in rhododendron bushes. It was a very small park.

When she concluded it must be nearly one o'clock Olwen hurried out, back on to the main road. But the clock above the model liner and the sepia nudes informed her that it was only twelve-fifteen. Not believing it, she walked quickly towards the place of appointment, but another clock pointed at twelve-twenty and she slowed down to an amble.

74

In the window of a chemist's shop stood a collection of cameras. Olwen would have walked on, but her attention was caught by one priced at four pounds. An idea entered her mind, and once there could not be resisted. She would take a photograph of Roy before she told him about the baby. Then, if he despised her, and the whole happiness ended in bitterness and separation, then at least she would possess a photograph to remind her that it had existed at all. Alone and sneered at, she would be able to read through her diary and capture events which might otherwise have been forgotten, and the photograph would be there as a confirmation, a kind of proof. Olwen entered the shop and inquired about the particular camera.

'Not a bad job,' said the old man behind the counter. 'Useful. Good on views especially.'

'Doesn't it take a portrait?'

'No.' The old man laughed at Olwen's ignorance. 'You'd want the Mark IX model for that. It's twelve guineas.' He considered Olwen: perhaps she had twelve guineas. 'Mind you, it's worth the money.'

'I haven't got twelve guineas,' Olwen admitted. 'Can't I get people at all with this one?'

'Oh, yes, but you said portraits . . .'

'Well, I meant——'

'Listen,' the man said. 'Give 'em about twelve feet, put 'em in the viewfinder nice and square, with plenty of margin for error, and you'll have a picture as clear as sunshine. It'll blow up a treat.'

'Blow up?'

'Enlarge.'

'I'll take it,' Olwen decided. 'Will you put a film in, please?'

The man did this. 'How about a case?' he asked.

'Perhaps it will go in my handbag.'

'Shouldn't put it in there,' said the man. 'Might get scratched.' He bent down, searched among tins and cardboard boxes, and brought out a cloth satchel. 'Shop-soiled, five bob. How about it?'

'Sorry,' said Olwen. 'I haven't much money on me.'

A bell rang as another customer entered the shop. 'Here you are,' the man said quickly. 'I'll give you the case.'

'That is nice of you,' said Olwen. The day is improving, she thought. 'Thank you very much.'

It was by now twelve-forty and she walked towards the cross-roads where Roy was to meet her. He arrived at twelve-fifty. Olwen ran across the road and climbed into the car, all the minor troubles of the day disappearing. Roy seemed so much himself: happiness returned to her. 'Oh, darling, I *am* glad to see you.'

'Well,' said Roy slowly, looking at her, 'that does sound nice.'

'I've had a horrible morning,' Olwen said.

Roy started to drive. 'It's over now,' he said, and then, as a quick afterthought, 'Anything happened?'

'I more or less had the sack.'

'The sack! What had you done?'

'It wasn't exactly the sack,' Olwen explained. 'I gave notice and Mrs. Harper became unpleasant.'

'You gave notice!' said Roy.

'Yes,' said Olwen. She longed to tell him; he seemed so safe compared with Mrs. Harper; but she remembered her desire to take a picture before his expression could be altered into unhappiness or disappointment or disgust. . . . 'Roy, I'm going back to Wales to wait for you. We're having too much happiness.'

He took it with considerable calm, with unexpected, even disappointing reasonableness. 'Olwen, perhaps you're right. You always did the behaving for both of us. I don't want you to go, but we've months to wait. . . .' A pause and then he asked, 'Do your parents know about us?'

'No,' Olwen said. 'It's all so difficult, you see, because they're part of the village, and the village wouldn't understand. . . .'

'You're going to tell them?'

'Yes.'

'Everything?'

'Yes, Roy, everything.'

'And I'll come to see them.'

She was delighted. 'Roy, Roy, that would be marvellous. Then they'd understand. . . .'

'We shall be able to write,' Roy said. 'It will be a new kind of love.'

'Part of the same one,' Olwen said. 'I don't want it damaged.'

They had turned into the car park of the Dragon. There was no one about; the few other cars in the park were empty. Roy kissed Olwen fiercely, bending her backwards on to the seats of his car. 'Is to-day our last day?' he asked.

'It will have to be. I've no money except my train fare home.'

Another kiss, prolonged and probing into her mouth. Roy's hand pulled open her green blouse roughly and explored quickly inside, despite Olwen's protests. She could not sit up and was forced to endure his hand. 'And this afternoon?' Roy said. 'The last time?'

'No,' Olwen said, almost angry. 'Let me sit up, Roy.' He did so, sensing the anger. 'We mustn't do anything again,' Olwen said. 'There are reasons. It would only make the separation harder.'

Roy said nothing further about it. There was constraint between them at lunch, not lessened when Olwen pleaded with Roy. Afterwards, sitting in the car in the sunshine, Olwen in a burst of affection put her hand on his on the steering-wheel. 'I'm sorry, Roy.'

He smiled at once and became his old, charming self. I must get the picture, she thought, before I have to resist him again with the real reasons, and destroy the original us.

They left the Dragon at about two-fifteen and were in Almond Vale well before three. Roy parked the car at the back of a cinema —this was a technique of his to avoid the payments demanded at official car parks.

It was warm and quiet. Great slabs of cumulus clouds moved across the sky, but even in their shadow it was warm. The hazy, distant horizons were illuminated in patches by wide bars of gold. 'It will rain to-morrow,' Olwen said, 'but we shall be left alone to-day.'

They strolled along the river bank. Not many people were about and those who passed did so at wide distances. The only person to speak to them was a boatman, a young man dressed in a vaguely maritime costume and peaked hat who stared rudely at Olwen's legs and breasts as she approached. 'Want a boat, mister?' he asked.

'Do you?' Roy asked.

'No,' Olwen said. 'I'd prefer to walk.'

The man spat and sat down on an oil-drum as Olwen and Roy walked on. About a mile further away from the town the path along the river bank ended. 'Let's just go a bit further,' said Roy, and Olwen knew with misgiving why he said it. They stepped over alder branches and on to the hard, caked earth which for most of the year was the mud of the river's edge. It was absolutely quiet now and they had not seen anyone, even at a distance, for nearly half an hour.

Roy found a hollow and examined it; it was surrounded by bushes and the grass was hot to sit upon. Very suitable. 'It's quite dry,' he said. 'No ants to bite you,' he added, smiling. He sat down.

'Stay where you are!' commanded Olwen.

'Good heavens!' said Roy. 'Is that thing a camera? I thought it was food.'

'How far away am I?'

'About fifteen feet.'

Olwen advanced a few steps. 'Now smile,' she said.

He already was smiling, and she pressed the lever. 'Now I must wind on,' she said, doing so.

Roy stood up and approached her. 'Now let me take one of you,' he said. 'In the appropriate position,' he added, bending her body backwards so that he might kiss her. Olwen lost balance and, despite clutching his arms, fell slowly to the grass. 'Perfect,' said Roy. He had his memories, too, which he wanted on bromide paper, and they were as much of the legs as the rounded face and the auburn hair. 'Stay just as you are.'

'What do you think I am?' Olwen said. She sat with her legs tucked under her and smiled. 'Now take one.'

Reluctantly, he did so. Then, collapsing on the grass beside her, he said, 'Now you've had your way, let me have mine.' The second kiss was fiercer than the first and he unfolded Olwen's body backwards. 'Be gentle, my dear,' Olwen pleaded. 'You must be gentle. No naughtiness to-day. I mean it.' She thought quite tenderly of the life within her. For answer, Roy bit deeply into her throat. His hands, ignoring her pleas, were exploring inside her clothes. She could see the vein throbbing at the side of his head. The look in his eyes was the same as it had been before lunch when he had pinioned her down in the car. She knew with shock that he was not proposing to stop for words of hers. Her own body began to sweat in fright, despite the cool air on her thighs. 'Roy, Roy,' she cried. 'When are we going to be married?'

'Another year,' he said.

'But you said——'

'What difference does it make?' In his frenzy he was curt. There was only one way to stop him, although she knew it would mean a quarrel; he never was very tender until exhausted. She touched his bare arm. 'Roy, dearest, I'm going to have a baby.'

It stopped him. He looked at her angrily. 'You bloody little fool!'

Olwen said desperately, 'Please don't be cross. I couldn't bear it if you were cross. You're part of it too, you know. I don't mind, Roy, I don't mind. It's part of what should——'

'You don't mind!' he sneered—she winced before the sneer: he had never sneered at her before. 'Are you stupid or something? My God, what a sentimental fool you must be.'

'But we shall have a baby eventually,' Olwen said. 'Why——'

'Who said we'd have a baby?'

'Everyone does when they get married,' Olwen said. 'Don't be so worried, Roy. I can go away to my parents. I can wait. Nobody here will know.'

'I don't want babies,' he said. 'We had one and it died, thank goodness.'

'Roy!' Olwen protested, stunned with shock at his callousness. 'You can't be selfish all your life; and think, it may be a little boy who looks like you. You'll think differently when we're married.'

He had rolled slightly away and was biting his nails. It was an incredible gesture from one whose every previous action had seemed so mature and courteous. The look on his face was something she had never seen before; it was a punishment to look at it. 'We're not getting married,' he said.

His sour mood was so obviously real that she could not touch him with words; she did not even wish to touch him physically; he was so patently not interested in tenderness; he was so clearly a man whose plans have gone astray. An anguish was filling Olwen's whole being; a terrible knowledge that there was something here that needed more than apology, needed explanation; a chilly apprehension that his love—that love which she had believed as tender, emotional and far-reaching as her own—was perhaps only lust. Things poured out from the store of memory like flashbacks in a film: little events and words that had led to her physical surrender. She knew the terror of one who has fallen into a trap.

She refused to believe them yet. 'But you said you *wanted* to be married,' she said. It was true: he had said it several times and now it was her only hope.

He made a gesture of dismissal with his hands, and without a word revealed that what he said was not necessarily what he meant. Words were what one used on fools to obtain what you desired: should his integrity be higher than the politicians'? 'You don't think I'm going to marry a mouse of a thing who gets herself caught, do you?' he said. 'You'll have to get rid of it. I'll give you twenty quid to help.'

Olwen turned very pale and swayed in weakness. It was the end. This ugly Roy was as real as the tender one; was part of him; her love died in crucifixion with his murderous words; the diary and the picture would never mean anything now. . . . She struggled to her feet, feeling an immense urge to run from the presence of this naked cruelty. 'I'm not getting rid of the baby. To me that's murder.'

He gave a brief, derisive laugh. 'Oh, stop talking crap. If you've got a mother fixation, I don't see why I should pay for it.'

Olwen had begun to cry. 'I don't think you ever did love me.'

'Oh, stop snivelling,' Roy shouted. 'I can't stand snivelling women. I'm not good for any more than twenty quid, anyway. You've cost me a packet.'

'I don't want your twenty pounds.'

'Well, you needn't file any order against me,' he said with another harsh laugh. 'I've never seen you before, young lady.'

'I know where you work,' Olwen said. 'I shall go to see them. I know your Mr. Bushell. Perhaps he'd like to hear what sort of a traveller he has. . . .' Another terrible memory came to her and she gasped, 'Your name isn't Harrison at all, is it?'

He was alarmed at once. He sprang to his feet, grabbed her by the shoulders and then twisted one of her arms. 'How do you know about Bushell?'

'Let go of my arm,' she cried. 'Roy, what's happened to you? Don't I mean anything at all?'

Roy twisted her arm more and saw the colour fade completely from her face; she slumped against him in a slight faint. 'What about Bushell?'

'I telephoned this morning.'

'What about?'

'Please leave go of my arm.' He released it for a moment. 'About you.'

'Are you mad? What about me?'

'Only to ask if you were there. I wanted to tell you.'

He twisted the arm again. 'Tell me what?'

'About having the sack and about the baby.'

'Did you tell *him*?'

'No.'

'And you'd better not.'

'I shall,' said Olwen, weeping bitterly. 'You can twist my arm off. You don't think I have that kind of courage, do you? I shall tell him.'

'You've got no proof.'

'I have a letter here that talks about marriage,' Olwen said.

She trembled as she saw his terrible face. 'You've got it here, have you?' he said with malicious satisfaction. 'Let's have it.'

'It's at home.'

'No, it's not,' Roy said. 'I know where it is.'

He released her and they both ran the few yards to where Olwen's handbag lay on the grass. Olwen reached the spot first, caught the bag and would have run on, but he caught her ankle and she fell on her face.

Roy was on top of her at once and his hands went round her

throat to control her wriggling. There was no thought in his head but to prevent Olwen getting away. It was not only the letter. They would know there was some truth in her words without any letter; there were blood tests; there were people she could fetch as witnesses. His large hands pressed and pressed.

Olwen could not believe that it was happening. He only wanted to frighten her. It couldn't happen to her. After all, he was a normal person. She wanted nothing from him now and would say so. But the hands pressed on past the point of normality and she struggled madly, sweating profusely all the time. She tried to scream, to protest, even to look at him so that he might know what he was doing and desist. She half-turned and in her agony saw the vein at the side of his head pulsating furiously. Her lips moved and silently formed the words, 'Roy, the baby. . . .'

PART TWO

CRIMINAL

I

IT is four forty-five of the afternoon of July 27th. Without awareness I draw my car slowly towards the gutter and bring it to a stop. I do not at this moment quite know where I am. Instinct has made me stop at this time and place before I drive home to weak tea and a boiled egg. That part of the planet on which the four wheels of my car rest is revolving at about nine hundred miles an hour. The planet itself is gyrating round a star at several thousand miles an hour. The star is ninety-six million miles distant and is one in a constellation sixty million light years across. The constellation is one of many. Somewhere, the fools say, there is a God who cares about love and the hairs of our heads and whether one possesses a piece of paper before one loves a woman.

It is Wednesday afternoon and in the absence of noise from the car I can hear the other movements: people walking along the pavement, dogs barking, shop doors opening and closing, buses passing by, other cars; in a temporary lull I hear far overhead the thin scream of a jet plane. Some of the people all of the time. I am a human being; I do not like other human beings, but I seek my pleasures through them. People are ugly. Look at those who pass by now. The harassed, middle-aged crowd wait in livid silence, hating the possibility of another's supremacy, at a bus stop. A twice-swollen fool pushes a pram and drags a brat from shop to shop. Love is the world, the poets say. But not if you're caught. Oh, no. The woman is elbowed out of the way by anyone who comes near. They see she is no longer beautiful, so they do not care that she is tired or ill or in pain. Some bricklayers walk towards a cheap café. They are powerfully built and have cheerful faces, but no brains. Animals. They talk cricket. They look at a girl who passes by. She is shapely, but with a face of incredible stupidity. Another animal. She smirks at the men. They whistle back. Somewhere, the fools say, there is a beautiful God who made man in His image. But man is not beautiful. The world is full of people who are ugly or ill or stupid: the world shoves them around, and they pay, willingly and even eagerly, in money and pain and time, not knowing that it could be different, righteously indignant if someone tries to make it different. These are the fools who have not the courage of their convictions because they have no convictions. Because life kicks them in the face, they shrug and say it is a struggle. Because they have to marry someone whose beauty soon fades into the usual appearance of approaching death, they romanticize themselves: they say that love has the quality of sadness. But that is not the considered opinion of the world. All the literature of the world, as far back as it reaches and in all places, excludes mention of marriage. Love without rules, love without being trapped by rent and age and children and gas bills—how can anyone consider it in any other way? Yet they do. They rush madly at the biological trap, ignoring the great gift of freedom which science and the rubber industry has given them.

A newsboy shouts about murder. A body has been found. The bricklayers buy a paper. They yawn. It is a warm afternoon after the rain. They do not know that in the red car thirty feet away sits the man who has committed murder. In the bright glitter of this afternoon is my moment in the world. Some of the people all of the time—yes, I've always managed that. Now I have a secret and must fool all of the people all of the time. The circumstances are such that I believe I will. Nevertheless, I have my moment of terror. I feel I must put on my dark spectacles, but I resist the urge and instead walk with deliberate slowness to the newsboy and back. Then, when I have read the words, I think: It is my moment, but they will never know unless I tell them: I must write it down. And now, two hours later, I am doing that. It is my intention to put this manuscript into the strong, indifferent arms of my bank, the trustee department. To be opened after my death at, I hope, a ripe old age.

In the newspaper the victim's name was not mentioned. It merely stated in the Stop Press that a Miss Jacqueline Best and a Mr. Reginald Meredith (I struggle hard to picture them, but cannot), out walking last evening, found the body of a young woman in a copse near the bank of the River Pigeon, about a mile from the small town of Almond Vale, Middleshire. Apparently Miss Best had to receive attention for shock. I bet it put Mr. Meredith off his stroke too. They won't trot round the mulberry bushes again: they'll buy a double bed and get married at once! In slight irritation and apprehension, I wish that they had postponed their walk a few hours, for then the torrential rain of this morning would

84

have filled up the river and covered those hard, sun-baked banks on which Mr. Meredith and Miss Best were able to walk not many hours after I did. Then the victim might not have been found for another twelve months.

Her name was Olwen Hughes. I didn't want or intend to kill her, of course, although in the surrounding circumstances it was perhaps inevitable. I believe in life and love, both of them at high pressure; and I persuaded her to my way of thinking, although she was always a bit mushy. They all are to a certain extent; it's in their nature; I have to persuade every woman that she is the one thing I live for—as, of course, she is at the time. It shows how badly we are in need of a bodily freedom that we both have to feign everlasting love for the few months we're together. In the face of such a lie, one partner is bound to be hurt or angered, and not having the freedom I have, being too deep in the mire of sentiment or religion, it has always been the female. Even in the cases of those women who have no emotional or religious scruples there is vanity: they are annoyed with me because I admit love is not going to last for ever, not even their special brand. This Olwen Hughes was twenty-six and, being a product of her times, naturally wanted the make-believe to turn into wedded bliss and all that stuff. I offered her fifty quid to get out, but it was useless. She just didn't understand anything beyond the orthodox sentimentality. As well as God she acknowledged society and believed we owed it a duty. It seemed to me—and for a long time, while we were in love, she agreed—that the framework of society is raving mad. No one can say with certainty, politically and socially, why we are alive. Heaven knows, they are all trying: the ether and print are full of their remedies and exhortations. But all without result. The whole thing, surely, is based on the chance of birth, inclination and circumstance. In these, I admit, I've been very lucky. Poor Olwen! She wanted everyone to work their guts out, from the schoolroom to the grave, for absolutely no reason whatsoever. Whatever was dreary was right! Society, I suggest, prefers the Olwen Hugheses of the world to those like myself because they're easier to handle. They fill in the forms willingly; they fight the wars; they pay the bills; they acknowledge the God; they suffer the work and illness and squalor; they stay allied to their dreary partners; they acknowledge the rules and even believe in them. But I am not fooled by society or God or even Freud. I realize that we're on our own—look at what ugly things most humans are or become: are they immortal, and, if so, what the hell for?—

and, apprehending we're on our own, I appreciate that there is nothing we need refrain from. The great sin is being found out. I did not intend or wish to kill Olwen Hughes, but since I have done and the thing was brought on by herself, I see no reason to be sorry. Conscience and lack of courage are the things that make people sorry. Conscience, as I've explained, is a lot of twaddle. Courage—well, if, when these words are read, World War II means anything at all, then our squadron's attack on the Kiel Canal—laying mines at deck level in a ten-tenth's concentration of flak—will explain what sort of a man I am.

Extraordinary to think that as I write the Middleshire Police may still be searching round that copse. The rain has stopped—there'll be the curious there too: the tourists! I presume that by to-morrow the police, having found Olwen's handbag and laundry-marks, will have switched their attentions to the city of Birlchester. Olwen lived and worked on the south-west side of the city—the opposite side to mine—and this was, I suppose, the reason why we drove to the small riverside town of Almond Vale, on the main road to Bristol and Wales.

I'm a representative of the Perfecta Soap Company and I called at a hairdresser's shop some time in March. It had recently been repainted, which was what drew it to my attention. Olwen can attribute her own death to so many tins of paint; also to the absence of the proprietress.

What am I to say about her? I remember well the impression she made. A rather tall girl, with a hefty, plastic body; underneath the white apron was the puppy fat of the schoolroom; it wobbled in delicious outrage as she moved. A wide, heart-shaped face with a good mouth, and eyes that looked at you with frankness. She was unaware of herself. Possibly that was her first attraction for me: this creamy girl with the long, excellent bones covered by sufficient flesh to make her extremely desirable did not know she was beautiful; she had never been aroused. In addition there was her auburn hair. I had never loved a redhead. Although I knew she was the sort who remained innocent by choice, and although I never become involved with customers unless they themselves half-suggest it, nevertheless I knew I had to possess her. It was unbearable to think of that face and body belonging to some hum-drum clerk or shop assistant with dirty hands, beery breath and unseeing eyes. This, I thought, has to be mine first. That wide, credulous face must be excited until it pleaded surrender. The hundreds of thousands of auburn hairs, the millions of pores that breathed, the soft flesh that creased and folded in unbearable sensuality under the protection of wool and silk and nylon, the perfect integration of blood, flesh and bone must tremble, reveal and abandon itself, as others had done before it, for me. Love was a battle in words and time, and I had the advantage in so far as my words were more adequate than hers. She had the advantage of her beauty, but I was not like other men, in awe of it. I did not want it permanently and therefore had no need to beseech and plead. If it became necessary, I would use the ace card and talk of marriage, but I wanted to avoid that if possible. The danger of Olwen's serious, virtuous type is that they take love so seriously. When, at the end, you explain to them that it was a game and that the game, very enjoyable while it lasted, is over, they protest. They demand an umpire—one prejudiced in their favour at that! I intended to have and provide a good time before I dumped her: before either of us could be bored by the other, I would have gone.

She advanced demurely across the shop, and in spite of her innocence I could see that she was favouring me with the eye. She even blushed. Nobody can deny that she came out with me quickly enough and willingly.

When I had explained the reason for my call, Olwen said, in a mellifluous voice free from any Welsh accent, 'You'll have to come back this afternoon, sir, if you don't mind, when the proprietress will have returned.'

'About what time?'

'At about three.'

'Then I'd better have lunch,' I said. 'Can you recommend anywhere?'

'There's the Dragon,' she said. 'It's about three miles along the main road. They tell me it's very good, although I've never been.'

She gave me one of her frank, piercing, all-woman stares, and I said, 'Would you care to lunch with me?'

But, like all of her type, Olwen did not want the onus of responsibility should anything happen in the future. She always wished to be in the position of enjoying herself and yet, should the person or the circumstances not suit her, able to withdraw saying, 'Not my fault. You persuaded me to come here. If I'd known——' It's part of the female dialogue in the game, of course, so I was not at all discouraged when she answered, 'But I don't know you.'

'Equally, I don't know you,' I said. 'Let's get to know each other over lunch.'

Olwen hesitated. 'I can't come until one,' she said.

'I can wait.'

'And you mustn't come here,' Olwen said. She didn't want the proprietress to learn that she'd made a friend of a customer. This was why I never met the proprietress and retained the advantage of anonymity.

'Where shall I meet you?'

'By the cross-roads,' she said. 'Is that your car?'

She was looking through the shop window at my red sports. I said, 'Yes. I'll be parked near the traffic lights at one o'clock.'

I was turning away when she said, 'What's your name?'

'Roy Harrison.'

'I'm Olwen Hughes,' she said.

Perhaps she was surprised at her own impertinence, for when she arrived at the car at one o'clock the first thing she said was, 'Please don't think I've done this before, Mr. Harrison.'

'I'm sure you don't do it at all,' I said. I saw already that she was a girl who had a conscience, and anticipated that exciting day when it was overcome. 'That was one reason why I asked you.'

She nipped into the car then, unable to avoid showing her nylons and a splash of thigh. It was as I'd guessed: she had long legs that tapered from thighs white and rounded and soft. (Inexplicable the way the back of the female thigh never hardens into muscle as does the male; this despite the fact that women do many of the standing-up jobs; Olwen's thighs were flexible enough to wobble in incredible sensuality.) She sat there, not knowing what she had aroused, certain of her safety, and rightly so. This century, so disastrous for men, has been very fortunate for women. The beautiful ones enjoy something more than an equality: they have the advantage of a prejudice in their favour. The same law that allows them to flout their sensuality is severe upon those who assault it without permission! Fortunately, one has the advantage of brains and words, and they have the disadvantage of their natures, which plead alongside myself for their surrenders.

We drove to this Dragon Hotel. I use many of the hotels in the county, but had not previously visited this one. It was a great barn of a place, full of business gentlemen and their tarts stuffing themselves with chicken and suet pudding.

Olwen had a sherry before lunch and seemed to like it: I made a mental note of the fact. During the meal she looked up from her shyness and stared at me with a quizzical gaze, her large eyes as steady and innocent as fruit drops, and said, 'Mr. Harrison, you are married, aren't you?'

88

I was startled into an admission that I was. I presumed she'd seen me somewhere previously with a woman. But I worried and admitted unnecessarily: my one mistake perhaps. For it was only the demure Olwen with the scruples who had asked. Demure girls who don't know the game are always possessive: obviously, not believing in freedom, they are bound to be: it's why they believe so strongly in the institution of marriage. She wished to ascertain if I was married so that, if I was not, she could set her traps accordingly, and if I was, and if it was an unfortunate marriage, then she could brood about divorce. . . . I was able to set her conscience at rest. 'I am married,' I said. Her conscience blushed all over her face, and I explained, 'My wife is ill.' This didn't seem to ease her discomfort so I explained further, 'Mentally ill. You see, Miss Hughes, she was involved in an accident.'

She wanted to know all the gory details, but I said instead, 'They give her a year, Miss Hughes. . . . She's a complete, ugly stranger, fatally ill in body and mind.'

She still hummed and hawed, so I carried on, 'But until this moment I'd remained true to the past Evelyn and I had shared.'

Olwen felt a little better then. 'I don't suppose,' she said, 'it matters if we just know each other.' Her very words belied her belief in platonic friendship, for if simply meeting her was all that was involved, why had she haggled in the first place? She knew damn' well it was never a question of platonic friendship. 'Evelyn is a nice name,' she commented.

'Names always fit, don't they?' I said. 'But not now. Not now. . . . Why aren't you married, Miss Hughes?'

She said quickly, 'What do you mean?'

'You see,' I said, 'I felt exactly the same about you: that you were the sort of person who would be.'

'Oh, no,' she said, trotting out her story. 'I was a nurse and the boy I was in love with died. I couldn't stomach nursing after that and, because of my hair, obtained a job in a hairdressing establishment quite easily.'

I was amused at that dump being called an establishment, but said, 'I'm sure you did. Your hair is the most perfect shade of auburn I have ever seen.'

Her face coloured auburn, too, at this, but she said, demurely enough, 'I shall have to return to work now. It must be near two o'clock.'

Outside the boozer I said, using all the charm indigestion allowed

89

me, 'I have enjoyed your company. . . . It's years since I talked to a girl so pleasant.'

'It was a very enjoyable lunch,' Olwen said. 'Thank you very much. I hope I shall come here again.'

'I'd like to bring you,' I said, seizing the hint. 'Do you have a half-day?'

'On Tuesdays,' she said.

'Then may I meet you next Tuesday?' I said. 'Perhaps after luncheon we could drive somewhere or go dancing.'

'I'd like that very much.'

'Will you do me a favour?'

'What is it?'

'Will you grant me the pleasure of being called Roy?'

'Of course!' she said. 'And you must call me Olwen.'

On the following Tuesday at one o'clock I met her for the second time. To do so meant commencing work earlier, moving round more quickly, and shortening my conversations; but that's not difficult and I've done it for other women. I cover the county of Middleshire, including the city of Birlchester, and I've been at it for so long that it's largely automatic: a question of collecting the orders.

Olwen was dressed very simply in a bottle-green costume that contrasted well with the auburn hair. Her blouse was paler green— she died in another, similar one. She was quite startling in her beauty; not especially sensual in her face, but certainly in her body and legs and the awkward, shy way she moved.

I began straight away to relieve her conscience. 'I'm so glad you came, Olwen,' I said—inserting the 'Olwen' to remind her of her permission to use it: I didn't intend losing the ground I'd gained. 'I was afraid once again that you might not.'

She was surprisingly agreeable about it. 'I know how you feel,' she said, securely convinced that she did. 'Let's not keep apologizing because we met in a shop.'

This time she had two sherries before the lunch and in consequence lost some of her seriousness. We were quite conversational until I felt that perhaps, after all, it might be the usual walkover. Then in her own way she started to probe with questions and I knew I had to guard my answers. 'Listen, Roy,' she said— she was willing to call me Roy. 'I've been playing a guessing game during the last week. Tell me if I guessed correctly. You're over thirty?'

'Thirty-five,' I said.

'You were a naval officer in the war?'

'Almost right,' I said. 'I was in the R.A.F. at Little Over.'

'Wasn't that a bomber station?' she said. 'The one from where they set out to drop mines in the Kiel Canal?'

I blushed modestly, and she gave a little gasp. 'You mean you went with them?'

It seemed time to gaze into space: into the distant, historical past: beyond the bottles and the bar to the roar of Merlin engines on that well-known raid. I was a pilot at the famous Little Over for a time. On that Kiel day I saw the way casualties were going and afterwards wangled my way out of operations on to training. However, women like the modest admissions of a few heroisms, and Olwen, regarding my silence as confirmation of all sorts of other heroisms, said, 'I read about it at school.'

'All over now, Olwen.'

'I'm glad,' she said.

'I'm pleased that you are.'

She reddened a bit. 'Then I guessed that you'd had a good education—one that included Oxford or Cambridge. . . .'

'Oxford,' I said untruthfully, catering to her sense of snobbery. She could not be bothered with education herself, or the arts and politics, but expected to marry someone who had. Oh, Olwen, you were just the same as the others really! A typical British woman! You didn't know what went on in the world, yet you had the impertinence to expect it to behave on your terms! I said, 'I've been thinking about you, too, Olwen, during the last few days—thinking too much about you. . . .' She blushed in delight, although it would have been a shock if she'd known the content of those thoughts! I pressed on: 'I saw the doctor on Sunday. He says it will be a merciful release, and that it may come in less than twelve months.'

'Poor Evelyn,' said Olwen.

We looked at each other and I could see she didn't give a damn about Evelyn. As long as her own conscience was in the clear, Evelyn could be in pain or mad or dead. . . .

'What have you been guessing?' Olwen asked.

'That you're about twenty-one or two.' I really thought she was.

'Nearly twenty-six,' she admitted.

'You carry your old age well,' I said. She laughed, her lips moving into a sensuous crescent, and said eagerly, 'Go on!'

'I deduced that your parents had a bad time in the war; and therefore you send money home to help your mother.'

'Something like that,' she said.

'You've been fond of several people,' I said, looking into the large blue eyes, 'but never in love passionately.'

She liked it; I could see that. Perhaps she'd never had a line shot at her before. Perhaps all the men who'd been with her previously had been awed by that red beauty into silence and obedience. 'I don't think that's any business of yours,' she said, but added to soften the impertinence, 'Not yet.'

It was pouring with rain when we left the Dragon, and we decided to go to the flicks. We sat through some ghastly film about the war; the hero sacrificing himself for some obscure cause, probably to do with chewing-gum. I held Olwen's hand for a short while, squeezed it and had the squeeze returned. She filled her lovely body with chocolates as fast as I could provide them. After the film we went to some Tudor café and loafed about over tea. Olwen discussed the film and I had to tell her a few things about real war. 'You seem to have done everything,' she said.

'Oh, no,' I said. 'I've never kissed a red-haired girl.'

She blushed scarlet in delight, unaware of the thought I'd really had. 'You should write a book,' she said.

'I don't believe in boasting about the war,' I said, and this pleased her too. 'War's ugly and shouldn't be dramatized into any form of art or emotionalism which could further its existence. . . .' She did not seem to know what I was talking about, so I went on, 'Where shall we go this evening? Dancing or a ride in my car?'

For all her demureness, Olwen wished to proceed with the squeezing without wasting time and energy dancing. She said, 'I'd like to go for a drive.'

I suggested a ride out into the country and dinner at the Castle in Brownhill. It's a perfect place to take a woman, although I've only been with one or two. Only people with cars can reach it—which excluded the risk of any of Olwen's friends. I suppose a few country yokels go in the bars, but the dining-room is for people like us, who want a private alcove.

Olwen said, 'Is this where you used to bring Evelyn?'

'No,' I explained. 'I've merely had lunch here sometimes. . . . Don't make it too difficult for us to associate at all, Olwen.'

'Don't be unhappy,' Olwen said, touching my hand. 'If we've twelve months to wait we might as well pass them without unhappiness.'

'You mean——?'

'I mean that I like you,' she said.

It could only mean that she loved me—women don't *like* men—and I was tremendously pleased. I even became too confident. After the meal and some sherry—not enough to coke her up, unfortunately—we carried on driving. By now it was dark and there was no point in the movement. I turned into a lane, doused the lights and said, 'Let's talk. Cigarette?'

'No, thanks,' Olwen said, her voice uneven in nervousness.

She was in such a hurry to be kissed that she couldn't pause to have a smoke! She was too nervous to talk much in the silence, so I commenced to kiss, slowly at first and with whispers. Olwen closed her eyes and lapped it up. Her face was hot and she moved about restlessly at the beginning, no doubt bothered because she was with a married man. But my whispers explained all that away satisfactorily—kisses did not harm, we were friends, my wife was not really alive. . . . Olwen had a large mouth, firmer than it looked, which was a frenetic ache to kiss. 'Don't make me too happy, Roy,' she pleaded. 'I've got to endure for twelve months.' She wants it, I thought; the large, healthy body is itself screaming for satisfaction. She was limp across me in the confined space, so abandoned that I was certain she wanted me; if my one available hand could find its way beneath the silk I would soon make her body sick with need. But it was trapped by her weight on top of it. 'You're so good,' I whispered, 'but too beautiful to remain unloved. . . . You must behave for the both of us.' We were both thoroughly excited now; no previous woman had been able to draw away from such a proximity to ecstasy; my one hand, now free, had wandered quite a way up; and then the fool remembered her parents and her God and that it was marriage she must hold out for. She wriggled about, protested, 'No, no,' and at last resumed the demure role: 'Please, please!' and then the excuse: 'The seat's hurting me.' There is no second wave in an attack like that, and I knew that it was all over for that one day.

I resumed my own role, releasing her at once. It was true that she was lowered across the metal seats, but nothing was hurting her. However, although I could have ignored her plea, I did things her way because I enjoy the game for itself as well as the final result. I don't plead with women: they surrender and plead with *me*. I will have a lot of fun with you, I thought in anger, before I laugh in your face and dump you.

'I've torn my stockings on your gears,' she complained.

'I'm sorry,' I said. 'I'll buy you some more.'

'Will you?' Olwen said. 'I'd be grateful. Size ten.'

She was quite perky because she'd had her own way, full of
confidence because she believed she could control me, and happy
because we really had had a good time, I'd whispered the usual
line, and her body had glistened in excitement without putting
any weight on her conscience. I didn't mind. I'd enjoyed it too.
If they want to play the game slowly, I can do it like that. They
won't talk me into marriage in that fashion. I knew it was the
last battle that counted, in love as well as war.

II

JULY 28th. After writing for over two hours last night I went
to the tennis club for the first time in six weeks. It was too late
to begin playing, of course, but there was an amusing crowd at
the bar. It included a girl of about nineteen, all chest and bottom,
anxious to be admired by a man of the world instead of the usual
teen-age lout. I shall have to be careful, because a few years ago
I had an affair with a married woman there; when she was dumped
she talked and her talk reached my wife; that was what caused
Evelyn's breakdown. . . . However, there's often a bit of jiggery-
pokery at the club: drinking and a kiss in the changing-rooms
with someone else's wife: and with patience Brenda—that's the
busty girl—could be the next one. She herself is impatient to be
beyond the talking, but I must seem reluctant; I must be dragged
into the affair so that, when it ends, her pitiful little brains must
not comprehend who was really the victim.

However, you wish to know about Olwen. There was quite
a splash in the local papers to-day. I'm beginning these words in
a perfectly respectable café, a pot of tea in front of me; some old,
too-rich, tedious ladies are sitting at other tables. Just then I happened to look up and in the startled, encountered eyes of a young
woman, sitting with another young wife and several assorted, well-
behaved children, all talking in the usual nasal middle-class
unknowing confidence—in her eyes I remarked that doe-like embarrassment and enjoyment that reveals when a woman comprehends
she's being mentally stripped. This one doesn't mind it. She keeps
looking, her friend facing away from me is unaware of the combat
of eyes. She thinks I'm making reports or something. Well, in a
way I am, but what a shock doe-eyes would have if she could
read this. She spoke then to the waitress. In her crystal-clear

station-announcer's voice she said, like part of an elocution lesson, 'Have you any cakes, please?' Delicious irony! The two children —hers, I think—are called Angela and Peter.

It came as quite a shock to see the headline and there, beneath it, as spotted as a Seurat painting, a smiling, uniformed Olwen. I hadn't a photograph of her, so I cut this out to keep. Perhaps, as the case moves on into lack of solution, the weekly magazines may take an interest and I can obtain some clearer, glossier photographs. Heaven forbid that I should forget the girl! That would be inexcusable! The *Birlchester Gazette* said EX-NURSE SLAIN. Why ex-nurse, I wonder? Of course, with the *Gazette*, which concentrates its limited mental powers on to local sport, one can expect anything. Perhaps they weren't sober. Ah, no, of course, it was the photograph. Where did they get it? From the Chief Constable of Middleshire? And where did *he* get it? Things are moving. They've visited someone who has a photograph of Olwen. Well, why worry? They were bound to do that. Perhaps, on second thoughts, 'hairdresser's assistant' was too long and difficult for the *Gazette's* compositors. They completely forgot to put 'redhead', which is always good for a profound thought or two. Let me quote their precious style: 'The Middleshire Police are investigating the death of Olwen Hughes, a twenty-six-years-old ex-nurse, whose body was found on Tuesday evening in a copse on the river bank near Almond Vale. Early this morning (they mean yesterday—it's Thursday now) police resumed their search of the area, despite pouring rain and occasional thunder. Detective-Inspector Maddocks of the Middleshire County Police, Almond Vale, examined the scene last night at dusk and again early to-day, this time accompanied by other senior officers. The Chief Constable of Middleshire and a pathologist also visited the scene. The girl's attire was disarranged and assault must be suspected. The investigations are being continued over a wide area.'

Doe-eyes is leaving. She has gathered her children, handbag, shopping basket and friend into a tidy pattern, left a sixpenny tip, and is now disputing politely with her friend about who shall pay the bill. She took a last quick glance over this way, but blushed into haughtiness when I offered a slight smile. Afraid her friend might see, I suppose. Standing up, she's not quite so good-looking. The child-bearing has widened her hips a little too much, and it emphasizes that her legs aren't really long enough. Middle age is about to turn her into the usual dumpiness. She'll walk home now, talking politely to her friend about nothing, and will, perhaps with

95

the aid of a servant, commence to prepare the evening meal for her husband. He will be a civil servant, well paid, polite, intelligent, perhaps intellectual, probably going bald, a member of a club or two, very serious about his political party, and as dull and lifeless as a cold rice pudding. They will have the children put to bed, rather sweetly, and will perhaps proceed to a concert. Or perhaps they'll crane forward in their theatre seats, anxious not to miss the dialogue in some adultery play. Doe-eyes (who has never committed adultery) will applaud politely at the end, certain that it was very intelligent and that somewhere a significant point was made to cancel out the remainder, which seemed rather naughty. At about eleven doe-eyes and her husband will go to bed, still talking politely, and they may decide to make love. She will manœuvre him into it, perhaps, for she's feeling restless today. The light will be out as it always is, originally because of shyness, but now because she doesn't wish her husband to see her eagerness. He might be shocked. And when she's hugging him terribly tightly so that he's nearly complaining (it was a heavy day at the office; there's another to-morrow; why not wait for the week-end?) she'll think about me. . . .

'The investigations are being continued.' . . . I'm sure they are. What fun they'll be having! I know the police. They're not much cop, if you'll excuse the pun. The average constable's on the look-out for a bit of skirt or a put-up, or both. A put-up is a place where he can have a crafty smoke or a cup of tea while on his beat. Providing the put-up is in a 'strategical position' (i.e. where he can see out of the window when he raises himself off the chair!), his senior officers don't mind. The plain-clothes men have almost complete freedom; they play like little boys, thoroughly enjoying themselves. They work their own hours and get boozed up with their 'clients'. They receive about fifteen quid a week, but some of it is handed on to 'information received'. In one way and another they have their rake-off from the prostitutes also. Oh, the plain-clothes are competent enough if it's offences in lavatories and parks, old half-witted lags, street betting or the pros. Same goes for the C.I.D. men. The *modus operandi* tells them which habitual burglar to look for. They take him to the station and back-hand him a few, and there you are. The fool is probably glad to get some good prison food once more. Of course, the police are not daft in the head, and no doubt this Maddocks will try hard. But they rely on habits. In his case he'll do it in reverse: Which of Miss Hughes's friends and acquaintances did anything unusual or out of routine on that day? Why? And so on. But none of Olwen's friends have seen me or my car—the poor fool didn't want me to see her lodgings because she was ashamed of them. What a comfort that is to me now! The scientists can tell the coppers a lot, but only what kind of thing happened and when. There has to be somebody to give a name before they can use the scientific deductions. Nobody has seen me. And my routine is my own—I'm a traveller and account to no one for my movements.

As long as the police merely suspect assault they'll confine their searches to madmen and vagrants. This will make it very difficult for them, because with assault of that kind it is, obviously, a person not previously known to the victim. I wonder what led them to this early conclusion? The untidiness, I suppose. Things were scattered about as if we had been fighting. . . . When they get tired of looking for madmen the police will start to dig out Olwen's male acquaintances. I don't think there were many before me, and certainly none at the same time. Which is a pity, for it would complicate things. However, because I intended to possess Olwen and then depart without leaving any forwarding address, what information I gave her was largely false. The one dangerous thing she had was the name of my employers. She threatened to see Bushell, my district manager. Bushell is an old friend from R.A.F. days, but because of the age of his friendship he knows bits about my past. The friendship has not included recent years, thank goodness, but a word from Olwen would have meant trouble.

It took a long time to force Olwen to succumb. She was determined to marry me and in the end that was the line I had to take. She held out for about six weeks, until the beginning of May. Perhaps, being practical as women are, she had been waiting for the warmer weather! For we had nowhere we could meet. She lived in one room with another girl—Hazel, I believe her name was. Hazel, a bus conductress, never encountered me; nor did Olwen's landlady. We could only meet on the Tuesday afternoons anyway because Olwen had to work all day on the Saturdays. We did manage a few Sunday afternoon meetings, but not often, because that was when I had to see Evelyn. I told Olwen that my landlady had a habit of opening handwritten letters. Therefore, when she wrote to me it was in typed, addressed envelopes I provided, and the letters came to the Company's office. There was always the risk that someone, not noticing my district number on the letter, might have opened it, but it was a risk that had to be taken. She wrote three mushy letters which I've destroyed (they weren't worth keeping: too sentimental—I'd sooner retain the photo). I only wrote one letter to her—there was no need to write at all really, but she was determined to have one, and it helped in the seduction. I had the sense to leave out my address, and my signature was merely 'R.' That hardly seems to damn me, but with the knowledge of what sort of a person (i.e. a traveller) killed Olwen, and what sort of a car he had (i.e. a red sports), it would have been easy enough for the police to show the handwriting in the newspapers and ask for information. If Olwen had left that letter at home, if in fact she had not treasured it so much that she carried it everywhere with her, then I might not have got it back and might well have been under interrogation by this Maddocks.

We both became very fond of each other—admittedly for different reasons—and that in itself induces a slight carelessness in the so-called moral code. She was completely infatuated by me, and easily overawed by good hotels, first nights at the theatre, dances, gifts of clothes, my conversation. . . . She was quite satisfied that her kisses were an equal bargain; that in return she had only to talk about our love, and if our love became a little giddy, then to give brief lectures about God—she was satisfied and certain that I was. The appetite of her healthy body would only show itself via her mouth in her ferocious kisses. I could feel her whole person aching in tension as she clung to me. Sometimes I pleaded that I might know the smoothness of her shoulders and arms and breasts: nothing beyond that, I assured her: I must be loyal to my wife even if she wasn't really a wife any more: I would, with Olwen, wait the twelve months and more until Evelyn's death allowed us to be married. Only we should have to wait months beyond for respectability's sake. Did she think the mere touch of my hands would be much more than the embraces we already indulged in? Unfortunately, she did! I waited and sweated for the day when she'd find it unbearable and would be able to explain the touches to the God she was always bringing into the car. In the end I had to mention marriage more directly. I'd hinted at it quite a lot, and once it came out into the open Olwen was able to abandon everything—her parents, her job, her ethics, her God—everything went overboard for romance. She suddenly found herself able to lie and be hypocritical before her friends and parents and inside her church just as easily as anybody else; so easily that she might have been accustomed to it, at the very least waiting to do it for love; and she scarcely mentioned Evelyn's name once she'd appropriated her possession. In short, she began to enjoy herself.

On one of the last Tuesdays in April, my car being out of order, we made the first of our two visits to this Almond Vale place. In the compartment of the train some country people stared at us and smiled: I suppose we did look like two lovers: in her shyness Olwen sat rigidly, not touching my hands, pointing out of the window at the different types of trees and soil and the patterns of ploughing. Similarly, as we walked about the quiet pavements of Almond Vale, she named the plants and trees which were beginning to pullulate. She had the quality of gentility and it was impossible not to be affected by it: the sad, wise face and the lissom, untouched body contradicted each other.

I remember Almond Vale that day: a pleasant little town, pink with almond blossom. Baskets of flowers hung on the lamp-posts, the local gentry walked about with thoroughbred dogs or hovered outside bookshops. A band played in a park some way off; nearer there was the hiss of water from a fountain; on the river people propelled punts lazily, and there was a small steamer that tooted up- and down-stream every half-hour. Not being yet holiday time, it was very quiet—sufficiently so to make us conspicuous; but then, nobody is going to remember as far back as April. The weather was lazy, too, warm and still, so we decided to go on the river.

Olwen trailed her hand through the water and smiled sheepishly while I rowed about three miles downstream. When we were quite clear of other people, and screened by bushes and weeping willows, I pulled towards an island, ostensibly to pause.

I sat by her side and shared a few chocolates with her. Then in the warmth of the sun and half-covered by raincoats we lay in each other's embrace, not talking very much, so drowsy that we could have slept. I looked at her hair and the smooth perfection of her face, her closed eyes and her white throat. My hand rested on her stomach; down beyond the throat, inside the blouse, I could see the beginnings of her large breasts. Sagging to the side to which she leaned, they rose gently at each breath, and, wanting her unbearably, I thought: We cannot enjoy the natural fruition of our sentimental love because of the words in a book. Nobody has seen this God who was between us; it's all words and print and is disputed by science and other religions. I leaned her head back and kissed her on the mouth as it opened in surprise. 'Olwen,' I said, 'it's unbearable to love you so much.'

'Am I stopping you loving me?' she said.

'Yes,' I said simply.

She knew that I meant physical love and smiled with the pleasure of being wanted; not aroused herself, she didn't really comprehend what I endured. 'We must wait,' she said. 'You won't lose me.'

'When we get married,' I said, 'will you make up for the years we didn't know each other?'

She said, 'Darling,' embraced me, and for the time being that was the end of that.

On the train back the compartment was empty. It was a first-class compartment without corridors. I'd brought a flask of sherry, not only because we both liked it, but to coke her up. We drank some of the sherry, sat on the seats, and finding them awkward, eventually had to sprawl. It was an all-stations train and each quarter of an hour, at every stop, Olwen went to the window and looked along the platform, not wishing our privacy intruded upon any more than I did. Dusk soon came and after my direct mention of marriage she was eager to talk about it close to me. When we were both out of breath, and she was making faint protests, 'My hair's an awful mess,' I said, 'Never mind your hair—it's dark now, anyway. Do you really love me?'

'More than anything,' she said.

'Will you always, I wonder?'

'Why should you doubt it?'

I did not explain my doubts, which were invented to make her prove her love. Instead I said, 'What wonderful things we could do.'

'When, darling, when do you mean?'

'After we're married.'

'Oh, God, Roy,' she whispered—she even mouthed her endearments in His name. 'Then you meant it. Oh, yes, we'll be wonderful. There won't be anybody quite like us.'

'I'm sure now,' I said.

'I didn't know you'd ever doubted,' Olwen said. 'Was it because I'd never——'

She was about to plunge into one of those long, feminine analyses, but I smothered it. Coming away from her, my hand 'caught' in her blouse in an apparent accident for which neither of us could be held responsible. The five buttons—glass or pearl or whatever they were: I forget now—jumped open without any suggestion of force; the whole movement seemed a natural continuation of the smothering kiss, and could be enjoyed because it had not been sought. I kissed again and my hands explored. Her one hand made a gesture of resistance, which I overruled, and then she was lost with me in waves of pleasure. 'Oh, God,' Olwen pleaded, 'can't

I have both of you?' Her agony was obvious; she trembled terribly, her whole body shivered and her breath came quickly. It was the moment when she passed from her world to mine. The tactile love was an unbearable delight: I was lost to time and place: I had won, and when she gasped, 'Not now, Roy,' I knew she meant because there was not time. The train began to slow, and, getting to her feet, Olwen fastened her clothes quickly and then combed her hair. And sure enough some fool of a man climbed in at the next station, and since we were late and there was nowhere to go on arrival, the victory was not consummated for another week.

On the following Tuesday the weather was again fine, and my car being in order I took her for a picnic. I took a lot of stuff: strawberries and cakes and flasks of tea: I have a certain talent for that kind of thing.

I was by no means certain that she would come. There was that look of agony in her eyes when she did. She knew she could not retreat from the tactile love: we could only advance farther into love. Olwen put up a pretence of resisting, of course, and when it had been overcome—when we had again reached tactile love she cried, 'Oh, Roy, Roy, it can't be wrong, can it, if we're going to be married?' Her voice was full of conscience, and later, when it was all over and I lay there, able to think in detachment that it would be a long time before I was satiated, she was so quiet and still that I wondered if she was ill. Then I saw that tears were trickling silently down her face; they had reached her ear on one side. In tenderness and gratitude—she had overcome a lot for me—I stroked her hair and asked, 'What's the matter?'

'Nothing, my dearest.'
'Are you sorry?'
'I don't think so.'
'I didn't hurt you?'
'No.'
'Then why are you crying?'
'Because I love you.'

(Later.) It would be tedious to catalogue either the women I've known, the technique of dealing with them, or their self-deception and protestations. Many were willing and therefore unworthy victims; there are not so many Olwens in the world. Yet there is a curious parallel between Olwen and another woman I once knew. It was a long time ago, but I never forget her. How could I? She was intelligent, complicated, religious, extraordinarily beautiful, she was married, and she, too, is dead. Any fool can pick up the easy stuff: the waitresses and bus conductresses and Service girls: but Myrel had been a model: her photograph could be found now in the back numbers of the glossy female magazines.

I wouldn't have met her if I had done well at school, and I would have been a better scholar if it hadn't been for Ruby. Ruby was the first one of all. At school—I experienced the distresses of puberty at Birlchester High—I was something of a stinker. I admit it. I was a big, bumptious, spotted, conceited youth. Before I thought about girls, I used to take the mickey out of other boys with my pal, a horrible youth called Moore. I remember well working all the complexes and repressions out of my system with Moore: knocking the pansy kids about at the back of the boys' bogs, prodding them in class with compass points, crowding them off their bicycles into the gutters, and most startling of all, forcing them to enter toy-shops to steal. I was never popular, of course, being even then too individual. My only popularity was one term during which I affected a stammer during Scripture lessons. It was a part of each lesson that a boy or girl should read the passages aloud. When my turn came I used to stammer. When the old master shouted, 'Stop laughing! The boy can't help his impediment,' the laughter increased to uproar.

In my teens I grew beyond all this and began to think about girls. Soon after I went out with my first one I asked to see what she wore under her tunic, and I had to twist her arms off before she'd show me. Some of my cousins—they haven't spoken to me for years!—used to find my games disconcerting too. I had to smash their toys or pour scorn on their childishness until they wept; even then they resisted—and quite rightly so in the face of my awful technique! I used to watch the girls doing physical training in the school hall, but I never could persuade one to do anything. They were too young and too close to discipline to feel the urge.

Ruby came to our place as a maid during my last term at school. She was an attractive guttersnipe, brought up on margarine and chips, who soon noticed that I stared at the bulges which wobbled under her apron and at her black silk legginess as she climbed the stairs. She was a dirty little thing, and would go straight from love-making in the bushes of a park to the nearest pub or fish and chip shop. In her crudity she taught me without inhibitions the things it would have taken years to learn within the refined, apologetic petting of my own middle class. I went with her on her night off every week that summer, sometimes on the Sunday as well. I used to copy my homework frantically in the school quad-rangle next morning. My parents never made any association between the fact that on the one night each week Ruby went out I used to say, 'I've finished my homework early to-day. Can I go out?' My mother used to say, 'Yes. Some fresh air will do you good. I think it's wicked the way these schools expect pupils to stay indoors hour after hour on summer evenings.'

When I sat for the School Certificate examinations I found everything so difficult that a kind of hopeless apathy took hold of me. It did me some small good, at least preventing me from being nervous. Other kids, who had worked hard for months, now panicked, felt sick and did not do as well as they might.

I prepared the ground for failure. 'They were stiff exams this year,' I said to my mother. 'Honestly, I doubt if a quarter of the chaps will pass.'

She didn't take the hint because, of course, she didn't want to. 'You'll pass,' she said. 'I know you. You're a clever boy. Your father doesn't think so, but I realize that you're different from other boys.' I said, 'You're a special kind of mother,' and in my embrace I could feel her heart thudding in pleasure as heavily as Ruby's had done.

When failure arrived in an envelope at the breakfast table it didn't leave me with much to say. 'Moore failed too,' I commented. 'Honestly, if *he* failed they must have been the worst exams for years.' My old man, sitting at the table glowering at *The Times* (Hitler spoke and his digestion was ruined), lowered the paper and said in his usual voice of gloom, 'You have to have a School Certificate to get into *my* office, Roy. You'd better start looking for a job.' His 'you' was plural.

My mother said nothing. She'd built my reputation so high that for once she didn't even attempt to have her own way with the old man. About once in a decade he gets courageous and obstinate, and this was one of those occasions.

We found a suitable job in a travel agency—a 'shipping office', my mother called it, and sure enough there was a scale model of a passenger liner in the window. Apart from an occasional panic when I had to appeal to the more approachable of the senior clerks, I found the work quite interesting: one met adult members of the public and, of course, there was no homework.

In the office I made a friend with mutual tastes. This was Blake, slightly older than myself, as blond as I was dark, the randiest thing on wheels. Knocking around with Blake opened my eyes about girls; I discovered that the possession of a car proves a great help in a seduction. Better-class girls were prepared to do all that Ruby had done, and so the time came to dump her. A few suggestions to my mother and within a week we had no maid in the house. Blake was reckless—he died in air combat in 1941. Together we went swimming; to the speedways; to air displays; to motor races; to dances; and everywhere found girls eager to come with us and provide excitement on the way back. (I wonder what happened to these sort of girls. Did they go into the Services when war came? Do they sit by the fire now with children and watch the television? I can scarcely recall a single name, and in all my journeys nowadays I never see one of those half-remembered faces.) Our Saturday night's pub-crawl almost invariably ended with two girls picked up at a dance or in a bar and taken in Blake's indispensable small car to what amounted to the nearest field. As I grew out of the spots and bumptiousness I noticed that when we picked up two who were together the prettier always made for me. Blake became a little jealous. On the back seats one night the girl I'd picked was resisting too vociferously and I literally threw her out. She was too drunk to be hurt, but Blake didn't like it. He said, 'One of these days some girl is going to cause you trouble.' It didn't seem unlikely so I parried, 'Or I'm going to get *her* into trouble.' But when I did he didn't hear all about it because he had entered the R.A.F.

Mrs. Burgess, as at first I had to call her, came to the travel agency in October, 1939. Her husband was understood to be a major who had been called to duty with the Territorial Army the month before. She had been a model until a few years previously, and I was able to dig out photographs of her from magazines—very interesting they were, too—long before I knew her. She was thirty-three, but looked ten years younger. Her arrival created a minor sensation, but within two weeks she was accepted by those clerks who had not yet been called up.

I awaited my call-up with indifference, certainly not with enthusiasm. Six feet tall, twenty years old but looking more, full of confidence but able to hide it, I had yet to seduce a married woman. Marriage seemed to me automatically to turn a woman ugly, but, looking at Myrel Burgess, I knew that the only thing to hold me back would be fear of any consequences. My confidence evaporated somewhat when she took not the slightest notice of me; indeed, she took not the smallest notice of anyone beyond what her work required. She was tall, slim, and dressed in quiet perfection. To some she might even appear thin, and she did nothing with her clothes to show a sensual appearance, yet I knew from the photographs that her shoulders were perfect, and although her breasts were small she had long, heavy thighs. Her face was the most beautiful I have ever seen: it was the pride in the face that one wanted to humiliate. She had a gracefully-shaped head; she could wear ear-rings effectively; her hair was black, and even the spectacle of the back of her head excited me. She appeared sculptured, indifferent and slightly arrogant: it was impossible to imagine her being silly or prosaic or crude: I wanted her in something akin to anger: she was a challenge.

Mrs. Burgess read a lot and one day I commented on a book. 'Oh, you'd like it,' she told me. 'It's just the thing for a young man.'

'What's it about?'

'The war.'

'Oh,' I said, 'the war.'

'You don't feel strongly about the war?'

'I'm afraid I don't.'

'My husband's in the Army,' Mrs. Burgess said. 'I have to feel strongly about it.'

'I suppose you think I ought to be in the Army.'

'No.'

'But if your husband ought to be . . .'

'I didn't say that.'

'You implied it.'

'I didn't imply it.'

'I'm sorry,' I said. 'I'm saying the wrong things.'

'You're not.'

'Well, I don't feel I dare say any more.'

'I know you daren't,' she said. 'You mean that the only other possible implication is that I don't want my husband home. Well, I don't. . . .'

'Then I have said the wrong thing.'

'Not at all,' Mrs. Burgess said. 'I'm sure you won't shout it round the office. We're not very happy. It's quite a common experience, I believe. You really must read the novel,' she concluded, dropping the subject.

I did—that same day; and I would have commented on it during the following day, but in the morning a naval officer entered the agency and asked to see Mrs. Burgess. After a rapid consultation with the manager, Mrs. Burgess left the office with the officer and did not return that day.

The next day I asked her to lunch.

She did not bat an eyelid, and neither refused nor accepted. 'Where do you go?' she asked.

I told her and she inquired, 'Is the food good?'

'It's quite passable,' I said.

'Then I'll come,' she said. 'Shall I meet you outside?'

I said evenly, 'We can go further afield if you prefer.'

'We haven't the time,' she said. 'Besides, why should we?'

There was no answer to that without some admission of my motives; and I had to learn more about her before I could speak of those.

And in the middle of lunch she seemed to have read my mind, for she said abruptly, 'What are your motives?'

I was shaken. 'What do you mean?'

'I mean, what do you live for?'

I wanted to give an answer which would please her, but, looking into her calm blue eyes, I could not fathom the workings of her mind. 'I live for the sake of living,' I said truthfully.

'Are you happy that way?'

'Yes. Why not?'

'I don't think I've been happy since I was a child,' she said.

'But you have everything. . . .'

She sighed. 'Oh, yes, everything. . . .'

'You don't have to be modest,' I said, 'and I know you're not a fool. You must know you're beautiful. You seem to have money. You're not ill, are you?'

'I don't know,' she said, shaking her head. 'Perhaps if I had less. Surely there's something.'

'Something?'

'Some point in all this—life.'

'Whatever it is, I don't expect anyone's found it,' I said, and laughed with all the charm I could. 'There's a war on. Seize the life and squeeze the pleasure out of it before it's knocked out of your hand.'

'Is that what you do, Roy?'

I turned on the modesty, the shyness, the boyishness. 'I'm afraid I do. You know, don't you, that I'm only twenty?'

'And I'm thirty-three,' she said. 'I wonder why I tell you that?'

'You know that I like you,' I said candidly.

Mrs. Burgess moistened her lips. 'I'm a serious sort of person, Roy,' she said. 'I'm not a flirt or anything like that.'

'I know,' I said, and then smiled again. 'You know, you had me badly frightened with that naval officer of yours.'

She laughed. 'Oh, Alex. He's my brother.'

Outside on the pavement, before we separated, she touched my hand. 'Don't get called up too soon, will you, Roy?' she said. 'I wouldn't want that.'

'No,' I said. 'I wouldn't want it either. Mrs. Burgess, what's your name?'

'It's Myrel,' she said, and touched my hand again, this time in caution. 'But not in the office. . . .'

I took her to the restaurant on the next day, but she was distant, cold, barely civil; she ended by paying for her own lunch. She remained the same for several days until I asked over lunch, 'Myrel, what's the matter? Would you like me to leave you alone?'

'No,' she said, smiling tenderly. 'That's the difficulty. I'm having conscience trouble, that's all. It's not doing my digestion much good.'

'You still love your husband?'

'No,' she said. 'I'm quite fond of Basil, but I don't love him.'

'Then what is it?'

She said with difficulty, 'Well, I still believe in marriage.'

'Why not?' I smiled. 'It's an admirable institution.'

'It's *part* of an admirable institution,' she said slowly. At the time I didn't know what she meant, but it must have been all this religious stuff. 'Roy, there's a rather special dance at the Regal Hotel to-morrow night,' she went on quickly. 'It's in aid of something. Will you take me?'

I gasped. 'I'd love to.'

'Well, that's settled then,' she said. 'No reason why two people shouldn't dance, is there?'

And, of course, there isn't. But in the middle of the evening Myrel said, 'Oh, God, Roy, I feel miserable. Take me home.'

'I'll get a taxi,' I said.

In the taxi I held her hand and then caressed her because she was weeping. It was touching to see such a flawless, calm, beautiful woman trembling, but I knew my victory might be near: hysteria in women presages surrender or a quarrel. In tenderness I asked about her health, the possibility of a chill or a headache, and explored all other avenues until it was obvious her trouble was merely love or conscience or both. 'I think you're the most beautiful woman I've ever seen,' I said. 'Like a model.'

She was tender after her tears and in the face of the compliment:

after all, she was thirty-three. 'Do you?' she whispered—it occurred to me that she was merely nervous in anticipation. 'How far have you been looking for beautiful women? Wigan? Exeter? Monte Carlo? Day returns to Colwyn Bay? Didn't you know I'd been a model?'

'What made you give it up?' I asked, and she smiled at the 'unintentional' compliment.

She lived in an impressive block of flats. 'How cold it is,' she said inside. 'Turn the gas-fire on, Roy, while I make a drink.' When she returned from a kitchen she said, 'Guess what this is?' I stared at the drinks and she answered herself: 'It's cocoa. No drunken orgies in *my* flat.'

Myrel had a small bottle in one hand. She shook out two tablets on to the palm of the other.

'What are those?' I asked.

'My good-night pills.'

I took them from her quickly. 'Please don't take them yet,' I insisted.

She stared at me plaintively: impossible to know what thoughts were behind the pointed face. 'You mean you want to stay the night?'

I actually blushed. 'I can't stay all night. You know I'm only twenty. My parents——'

'Never mind about your parents,' Myrel said. 'What about you? I can't understand you. . . .'

I attempted to embrace her, but she resisted. 'I love you,' I said.

She stared into my eyes so that I had to turn away. 'Does anybody really love anyone else at your age except themselves?' she asked. 'It takes years of practice to forget self.' (She always talked like this; she read too many books for an ex-model; she was an odd mixture of sex appeal and blue-stocking.) 'You're too confident,' she explained. 'You act as if you're quite used to entering flats with married women while their husbands are away in the Army.' Her bitterness was unjustified, for the invitation had been hers.

'I'm not a love-sick school-kid,' I said. 'Why shouldn't I enter your flat, anyway? You asked me, didn't you? We're having a cup of cocoa, aren't we?'

Her laughter was out of proportion to my humour. I seized her by the shoulders and found that she was trembling. 'What do you bother me for?' she said. 'You don't care about me. You admire yourself.'

'I do love you,' I said. 'I'm dizzy with it. I couldn't be drunk on cocoa, could I?'

'I don't believe it.'

'Myrel, it's true,' I pleaded. 'What do I have to do to prove it?'

'I don't know,' she said, and seemed suddenly to collapse in surrender. 'Don't take any notice of me. My husband says I'm neurotic.'

'Then he doesn't love you.'

'Then, can I drop my obligations?' she asked, more to herself than me.

'What are you talking about?'

'Oh, you fool,' she said. 'You've no wisdom at all. You're going to learn it at the end, not the beginning. I'm talking about my conscience and the institution of marriage.'

But when I carried her limp body into a bedroom I found a gas-fire already burning.

I left two hours later and walked along the cold pavements in the utter darkness thinking about her. Never had I known anyone like her. What I had previously enjoyed as a game, a bit of fun you could, with persuasion, inflict on fools in the back of a car, Myrel promoted into a turbulence of such intensity that I was exhausted. I saw that with application it was a new way for me to enjoy the game. But one must remain slightly detached, aware of the silly incongruities that occur before and after passion; one must never become emotionally involved, like Myrel, or one was lost in surrender to one person. To induce that utter abandonment has since then given me the main pleasure; and when one induces it in a creature of inhibitions and credulities like Olwen then one approaches ecstasy.

Myrel had given me a key. 'Come at any time,' she said. When I explained that to be away from home overnight would be difficult she said, 'Then come on Sunday mornings. It's not as if we go to church any more, is it?'

I climbed the steps to her flat one bright Saturday, carrying a suitcase, ready to repeat for the fourth time a manœuvre which had succeeded thrice before. This was simply to inform my parents that I had gone to see Blake in Wiltshire; apprise Blake of the manœuvre; obtain the train fare from my parents, and then walk two miles and spend the week-end with Myrel!

Inside the hall of the flat I recoiled at the sight of a khaki greatcoat which was hanging there. I was on my way out when a man's voice boomed, 'Why, come in, my good fellow. I was half-expecting you.'

It was, of course, Basil—the first and only time a husband ever caught me! 'How do you do?' I said. 'I just called because I thought Mrs. Burgess might care to accompany me to a dance.'

Basil was a tall, beefy Army officer, thirty-fivish, who looked much too unpleasant to be the husband of someone like Myrel.

'Come in, Roy,' Myrel's voice called. Then, as we came into the flat, she continued, calmly enough, 'No dancing, I'm afraid, Roy. Basil's only forty-eight hours.'

'Unexpectedly,' said Basil. 'An unexpected forty-eight hours.'

'This is Roy,' said Myrel. 'We work together.'

'Quite,' said Basil. 'I appreciated that instantly.'

'Where are you stationed?' I asked.

The attempt at civil conversation had to be made. The man could not possibly know what had been going on for the last five months. He might suspect a few cinema shows, a kiss under the mistletoe at the office party, but nothing more. Nobody, I felt sure, looking at the quiet, poised Myrel, could imagine the agonies she was capable of—perhaps not even this man.

'Oh, I can't tell you that,' said Basil. 'You might be the enemy. Somewhere in England. I may be going abroad soon; ski-ing, they tell me.'

'How nice for you,' drawled Myrel. 'You always were good at that.'

'Ski-ing?' I queried. 'Why?'

'God knows why,' said Basil. 'You mean where, don't you? Don't you read the papers?'

'Oh, you mean Finland.'

'I mean Norway,' said Basil. 'How deeply you must be in love. I know exactly how you feel. She's beautiful, isn't she? So poised on all occasions.'

'Oh, don't be ridiculous,' said Myrel.

'I expect you want to know where you stand,' said Basil.

'I don't know what you're talking about,' I said.

'I'm an Army officer,' said Basil. 'Know the facts of life. You wish to marry Myrel, don't you?'

'Basil, don't be tiresome,' said Myrel.

'If you want to marry her, that's all right,' said Basil. 'Won't stand in your way. Wait a little while and I may be killed. You can do it honourably then. . . .'

'Oh, God,' said Myrel. 'All this repertory because we have lunch together.'

'We haven't much time,' said Basil. 'I've only forty-eight hours.

Let's skip the preliminary lies and get down to cases. Suitcases, in fact. Be so good as to open the suitcase, will you?'

'What for?' I asked.

'If it doesn't contain what I think it does then this is ridiculous.'

'It contains pyjamas,' I said. 'After the dance I'm staying at an hotel.'

'Sorry,' said Basil. He turned to Myrel. 'I really am sorry. I would like to have been ridiculous. Now, where shall we go?'

'What for?' I asked.

His pose of cynical disinterest dropped. 'What the hell d'you think? I'm going to knock your smug face in. . . .'

He was jumping to conclusions without proofs, so I prolonged the bluff to the very end. I pretended to appeal to Myrel: 'Tell him he's mistaken.'

'God!' said Basil. 'A coward too. Myrel, you're an awful fool.'

She was weeping. 'I tried very hard,' she said between sobs. 'I didn't want to. Don't hurt him, Basil.'

I said, 'We'll soon see who's the coward.' I was taller, but the officer was heavier. It was a brief, humiliating fight which took place in the hall out of Myrel's sight. I was only a kid and I thought officers were gentlemen; but Basil's first blow was well below the belt and I was in agony. After that Basil could do as he liked. Quite early in the mêlée I forgot where I was. I could hear Basil grunting and cursing, but was conscious mainly of the pain. I staggered slowly to a corner and refused to fight: it was the only thing to do: he might have injured me permanently. He felt a real hero, shouted, 'Get out!' and, swallowing blood, I found myself crawling down to the street.

Hours later, after I'd cleaned up at the railway station, and had a few drinks, Myrel came to our house. Fortunately, I answered the door. She stood in the hall, pale, beautiful, and, for the only time that I knew of, untidy. We did not touch each other, but stood like strangers a few feet apart.

Myrel said, 'He's gone back.'

'What's he going to do?'

'He says he's finished. When he has a longer leave he will see a solicitor.'

'A divorce!' I said. 'What do you want *me* to do?'

In a tired voice, devoid of all sophistication, Myrel asked, 'What do you *want* to do?'

'I don't know,' I said. (I didn't—I hadn't had time to think of the implications.) 'I don't want to upset my parents.'

I was about to suggest marriage when I was twenty-one, but Myrel chipped in. 'He was right,' she said. 'You are a coward. Oh, Roy, how damnably right he was. Why is Basil always right? He believes in nothing, cares about nothing. . . .'

'I still love you,' I said.

She wasn't having it. 'No,' she said. 'You never loved me. I always doubted it. The first bit of trouble and you bale out.' She began to walk rapidly across the hall to the front door. 'Goodbye, Roy.'

'What are you going to do?'

'I'm going to somewhere in England,' she said tersely. 'If he'll have me back I'll never do it again. If not—if not I shall pray very hard and then kill myself.'

There was no part for me in this neurosis and I said, 'Don't let me stop you.' She left at once. 'Closet,' I said as she closed the door, for I never believed she would.

Two days later Myrel was dead. I heard later about what happened. She went to somewhere in England, but Basil, the officer and gentleman (when it suited him), could not forgive her one adultery. Myrel wept and pleaded, but the scene eventually embarrassed him: other officers were nearby; a barracks is a different place to a flat, and he could not forgive her for becoming emotional inside it. Myrel was found dead in an all-night train as it brought her body back to Birlchester. She had taken thirty of those sleeping tablets. The office sent a lovely wreath, to which I contributed handsomely.

III

JULY 29th. There's a man from Scotland Yard there now. He's been at Almond Vale since Wednesday morning apparently, but the dear old *Gazette* didn't notice. Olwen's picture is in the London dailies to-day; but precious little else; my moment in the world is still my own secret. There's a photograph of the Yard man in the *Gazette*: he's a big, fat slob, scowling all over his face. The usual suet-pudding belly these men have, the inevitable bowler hat and belted raincoat: he looks like a plumber: a very good plumber, but nevertheless a plumber. However, let me not underestimate him: he solved the quarry murder last year. The Middleshire Police can't be up to scratch if they've dragged in Whitehall. I bet this Inspector Maddocks has had a rocket from the Chief Constable for calling a Yard man in, and *he'll* be scratching his head in a few days when the information he has peters out or proves to be false. This Superintendent MacIndoe sat by the Chief Constable of Middleshire at the inquest, where a coroner decided that Olwen had been murdered. It gave me a frightened moment to read the words in print, but the moment passed.

I had a busy day to-day. I didn't see Brenda last night because I developed a sudden utter tiredness. Delayed exhaustion, I suppose. I telephoned her, saying that unexpected business had to be attended to, and fixed a date for to-morrow afternoon. She was disappointed about the postponement of our game of tennis, but obviously delighted at the idea of an afternoon with me. After the match to-morrow—we're both in a sort of tournament—she's agreed to come for a ride in the car and have a drink outside the club. 'I love riding in cars,' she said. 'I'm too lazy to ride a horse.' I think she mentioned that for its snobbery effect. I don't see why sitting on a horse should prove tiring to anyone but the horse; heaven knows, Brenda's backside appears comfortable enough to withstand the jog of a camel.

I slept like a log in the night, for which sleep I was grateful to-day. On Friday of each week I have to report to Head Office in town, and it is then I must see Bushell. I was just afraid he might have had something to say about Olwen's telephone call on Tuesday morning, even though the call was made to a 'Mr. Harrison'. If she had given her address and asked for the traveller I would have needed to account for myself. It was a great relief when Bushell said nothing; just made the usual remarks and jokes and let me depart.

In my relief I decided to deal with the one other thing which Superintendent MacIndoe will try to find out. I drove my sports car into a dealer's and part-exchanged it for a saloon. The saloon was second-hand and actually I lost on the deal—I could see the chap grinning all over his face at making fifty quid out of another 'mug'. But the point is this. The dealer does not know I'm a traveller. It is just possible that Olwen's friends, although they didn't see my car, know that it was a red sports and that the man who drove it is a representative.

Last night I sat down and, after writing, spent the balance of the evening reading because I was so tired. Read the most frightfully amusing book. It was all about a man rather like myself. Women ran after him like wasps after jam. He treated them like dirt, being completely callous and indifferent; if they pleaded very hard he would perhaps condescend to live with them for a while; but only on his terms, which were very odd terms indeed. He does the wicked uncle on a girl of breeding, gives her a child and then leaves her. At the end he reappears, insults her parents, and says in effect, 'Are you coming? I'll give you five minutes to pack.' He makes it quite clear that he has no intention of marrying her and has no use for babies. The girl drops everything—the baby into the laps of her parents!—and rushes madly off with him. It ended there and did not become tedious by describing the girl crawling back to her parents, as she eventually would have done. In reality one is unfortunately a little more trapped than that. The State takes a wearisome and romantic view about babies. So do Commanding Officers. But the story was very reminiscent of Evelyn and myself.

One thing certainly leads to another. Extraordinary, when one thinks about it, the way it does. If I hadn't sneezed in Cairo I would not have married Evelyn, met Bushell or encountered Olwen. Olwen can blame some tins of paint for her death, I wrote. Well, she can also blame a Dutch South-African girl named Bertha. I was enjoying the last of several evenings of a leave in Bertha's flat. I was neither the first nor the last to live with Bertha. She had come up to Cairo from Johannesburg, like many others, to acquire polish and poise and to enjoy herself. But the truth was, the girl was not very bright in the head. She was lumpy; voluptuous at the time, like a furtive drawing by Degas, but likely to put on weight and thus reveal her stupidity later. I wonder what the fool's doing now? Surrounded by the kids of some Afrikaner farmer, I expect. Good luck to him! He'll need it!

Anyway, the point was that Bertha's flat included a bath. Although I was an officer, a bath was a luxury out there. Shortly before I left Bertha I used the bath, and being refreshed, made love to her afterwards. As a result I was sneezing long before I reached my aerodrome, and after breakfast I felt bad enough to see the Medical Officer.

My crew were killed that day. The sneezes saved my life. I was lying in the station hospital talking to a nurse when some Wellington bombers took off. The nurse and I were fooling about when the fourth kite came roaring towards the hospital (a typical wartime layout!). Its engines were making a laboured, rasping, unhealthy racket. There came a few startled cries from other wards; the nurse's eyes went wider and wider open; the kite skimmed over the hospital, and then there was a great slam of noise. Silence for a few seconds, in which the nurse (like Olwen) said, 'Oh, my God, I beseech You——' and then the well-known, almightier woof as the petrol blew up. The nurse, making a strange, screaming noise, was galvanized abruptly into action, and I was left alone in the small ward with the obscure certainty that it was my crew who had perished. Laughter swelled in my throat; I wanted to roar with it—the joke being that I had avoided death—and I could scarcely keep a straight face when the Adjutant, pale and trembling, and pitifully polite although he loathed me, came in to confirm my guess.

I wrote beautiful letters (another of my talents!) to the parents and widows, and packed small parcels to be sent to England. In the navigator's locker was a gold wrist-watch. I was damnably in debt—women like Bertha light their fires with pound notes, I think—and felt I should have the watch. If I could flog it I should be in the clear. The boys would understand, and if they didn't, weren't alive to argue about it. Not many days later my Commanding Officer said, 'I'm posting you to England. It seems there's a battle going on over Germany—I don't know what the hell they think *we* are doing—and they want bomber pilots.' It was a terrific relief. I didn't need to flog the watch now. In fact, I could run up a few more debts before I departed (I believe I used 'Harrison' then); for no one's going to pursue half-way round the world for a few quid. Then I found someone had posted the parcels, so I kept the watch as a souvenir of those days. It's still absolutely reliable.

Back in England, I found that there really was a battle going on over Germany. It was far, far worse than the solitary, isolated sort of raids we'd been making over the Mediterranean. Pilots were getting killed by the hundred. It was painfully obvious that I should be killed, too, but I wasn't scared. It was good to be back in England, to see girls by the thousand: painted legs, scarves over their heads and a knowing exhaustion under their eyes. I would have died for them willingly if I hadn't been sent on this Kiel suicide.

It was for this purpose that I was posted to the aerodrome at Little Over. This was in Lincolnshire, in the flat, wet, foggy bomber country, over which one could see Lincoln Cathedral and the Boston Stump on an immensely distant horizon. There were W.A.A.Fs. doing the ground-to-air control, cool and poised officers, efficient as though they'd been in the war for years—they were running it and *I* was the stranger, the amateur. A few were sweet, but the majority thought it fine to have casualties; you just couldn't be killed quickly enough for them; in this crack squadron their vicarious courage was supreme. I didn't admire their attitude, but I did the usual murderous night operations willingly and efficiently. Over Germany, despite flying in new four-engine jobs at a great altitude, the air would be dotted with bullets; fighters even laid corridors of flares; the searchlights probed the sky in hundreds; the whole night sky for hundreds of miles was like an artificial, illuminated, glaring day. It shook me, I can tell you, after the desert, but I would have continued with it if it hadn't been for the Kiel business.

Eighteen kites flew on that raid in broad daylight over ten-tenths defended territory to lay mines—they have to be laid while flying very slowly just above the water. This heroic and futile gesture was made to contain two battleships in Kiel while an important convoy came down from Murmansk. In short, we were expendable. Of the eighteen kites I saw five shot down in the sea and two blow up as flak hit their mines. Another five didn't come back, so that only six out of eighteen returned; and in those six were a number of wounded and dead. I didn't like being expendable. This was late enough in the war for the Navy and Fleet Air Arm to look after themselves. I suddenly saw the whole war for what it was. To hell with it, I decided. Patriotism is more than enough. On the way back I had a brainwave. If I crashed on landing, it would add to the impression of glory and sacrifice. It would also offer me an excuse to commence symptoms which would get me out of the suicide of Bomber Command.

My engineer had been killed, so when I spluttered my two port engines the rest of the crew presumed we'd been hit in them and stood by to bale out. But I struggled back to base, and as we approached it said my stuff with brave calm to the poised, efficient, unknowing W.A.A.Fs. They allowed me a runway to myself. I overshot it deliberately and piled up in a wood beyond. It was a bad, frightening moment although there was little petrol left to start a serious fire. While my crew were rescuing each other heroically, I kicked a few more lumps out of the fuselage and smashed the instrument boards. We were, in any case, embedded in this wood, and the aircraft would clearly have to be broken up piece by piece to be extricated.

Everybody was very pleased with me and I understood I was to have a gong (or medal). I shared a room with a flight-lieutenant and for the next few days I did some muttering. I'd 'wake up' waving my arms and shouting. When the other officer became anxious and sympathetic, I asked him not to mention my 'turns' to anyone, and explained that I'd had them in the Middle East. But naturally he wouldn't allow a good type such as myself to carry on in a distraught condition and kill myself and a crew. A few days later I found the Medical Officer sitting by me at lunch, apparently by accident. I spilled a glass of water for his benefit, but evaded his inquiries about operational flying and my health. Eventually I allowed him to talk me into an examination, and at the examination, under protest, I admitted the 'nightmares', 'tiredness', forgetfulness about details, and so on. After about an hour I let him talk me into being transferred, following a long leave, to flying training.

I was transferred to a flying training school not a hundred miles from home. I never volunteered for operations again. The whole 'crack' squadron carried on without me, killing its numbers two or three times over. My second crew went on with another pilot and engineer, lasted nearly a year, and then were killed. I never rose higher than flying officer during the remainder of the war; somebody must have smelt a rat, for I never heard any more about the medal. At the training school I was very conscientious: very few of my pupils killed themselves: they all went on eagerly to other commands so that the Germans could do it. I spent my days stooging quietly round in Tiger Moths and Harvards; wandering round the nearby village; or visiting the two pubs and a rather genteel café which were among the few buildings in the village. The local beer and cider were very good; there was a town about seven miles away; my leaves were frequent; the girls proved amiable; oh, I soon learned that the non-operational side of war can be very attractive. . . .

It was here that I met Bushell. He was a medium-sized man, plump, getting towards middle age even in 1943; cheerful, fond of the beer, shrewd despite his blatant humour. He had been reckless once as a pre-war flying instructor at a club. Apparently, great things had been expected of him early in the war, but he'd had the sense to go into flying training. Nevertheless, it was on his conscience, and if I talked of operational flying he would squirm. Bushell, I found, liked to talk. He regarded the war as already won and was in his shrewdness making his plans for the peace. I found that by listening to him I got on well, and when I learned what he intended I made my peace plans with him.

One evening, sipping bitter at a village saloon bar with him, we watched the entry of a young woman who came in with two

Army officers. She had a lot to say to them, and the laughter at the other end of the bar was tantalizing; I longed to join in; we tended to be quiet in its presence. 'Who's the bag?' I asked.

Bushell said, 'She's not for you. She's the vicar's daughter.'

It seemed so unlikely that I laughed, but as the girl and the officers went out I observed that one man was a padre, and this seemed to confirm it. The young woman was dressed expensively. She was quite tall, perhaps a little too slim, but it was an attractive slimness, tense, quick and excited. Her head was small and her face probably too long; but the face, too, with its large, sullen mouth, arrogant blue eyes and her snobbish, pointed nose, was far too much of this world to belong to the quietness of a country vicarage. That young woman did not hear a word I said to Bushell. Because Bushell was with me, I tended not to stare at her. She did not seem to notice me at all, and yet as she went out with her companions her quick glance in the direction of the flying officer in the corner of the bar made a split-second challenge of awareness. No doubt my returning stare, equally instant and as quickly removed, had the same stimulating effect. I knew that outside in the darkness her words would be to others, but her thoughts would be about me, as my thoughts within the bar concerned her. The beginning of each battle is always fascinating. I knew that if I met her in the village on the next day and made an outrageously impertinent remark she would not stare through me and walk on, but would stop to talk as if we'd known each other for years. This awareness, which needs no details or names, is something all the pious text-books and magistrates' courts in the world cannot stop: it is beyond parental and moral control: it is something that pertains only to the young and the completely alive. The tedious and the tired and the narrow-minded do not understand it and therefore condemn it.

On my afternoon off later that week I borrowed a bicycle and cycled to the other side of the village. Parking the bicycle outside its porch, I walked slowly into the village church.

It was stale inside with a sweet atmosphere of its own, and unbearably quiet. Nobody was about and I stepped on the graves of the long-dead locals, looking at the pious pictures of such deplorable, sickly taste and the equally sentimental stained-glass windows with their Technicolour glare. All that stuff means nothing to me: I belong to radar and aerodynamics and psychiatry and mathematics and contraceptives: yet it began to affect me as the avoidance of some superstitious act will trouble the supposedly non-superstitious:

and I longed to light a cigarette. The dates on the stone—1647, 1731, 1849, 1890, 1913—began to annoy me. The dead were dead —they had been the same as myself once and had no right to stare in accusation. It was as if they questioned my intentions regarding the girl when I had not decided the intentions myself. The silence was absolute, spatial, and therefore unfamiliar. We are not used to silence and we do not belong to it. Noise is carried by air, and this planet of ours is unique in possessing air. We were not meant for silence: we are animals who talk and make music: the fact that spoken words are the only expression and communication of the humans in this world seems to me another proof that there can be nothing beyond it. I was awed by that silence because it belonged to the dead wastes of the universe, and any man who can stare into the night and not be a little afraid is made of suet. But after an hour I was not awed; I was weary. I was about to move off and cycle into the town, to pick up something real and human and fleshy and noisy, when a priest entered the church. He was about the right age to be the girl's father: once again my stratagem had succeeded.

'Hallo,' he said. 'Having a look round?'

'I've been admiring the stained-glass windows.'

'They are pleasant, aren't they?' the vicar said. He smiled. 'But there's nothing special about them. Are you interested in windows?'

'Yes,' I said. It was a perfect example of comparative truth: I had been interested in them for three days because they might lead me to the dark, modelesque young woman who was, Bushell had said, this man's daughter. 'It's nice to return to these things,' I added sententiously.

'You have been abroad?'

'To Egypt.'

'The one good thing about the war,' he said. 'The young can travel. I talk every Sunday about the Egyptians, but I've never seen any. What are they like?'

'Not especially nice,' I said. 'Poverty makes them commercially minded.' I thought briefly of how commercially minded the Egyptians had been: of the woman in the officers' brothel who wouldn't accept cheques: and enjoyed the irony of the conversation.

After being carefully manœuvred into it, the vicar asked me to tea. 'You must meet Brian,' he said. 'He's keen on glass.'

Brian, the Army padre, was also keen on the dark girl; he was sitting with her in the Vicarage library when we entered. I had a nasty feeling that perhaps they were engaged, but didn't worry unduly: the pilot's wings, some charm and the modest admission of a few heroisms would draw that girl away from her country backwater.

The vicar introduced us. 'This is my daughter Evelyn.' He smiled rather firmly. 'One of the Philistines, I'm afraid.'

'Oh, Daddy,' she said. 'Just because I only come to one service a week.'

We all laughed. Good for you, I thought, and shook her small, cool hand.

'And this is Brian.'

It was not explained who Brian was. He was beefy, pleasant, with a naïve face, and had a strong, dry grip.

'The Flying Officer is interested in stained glass,' said the vicar.

'Ah!' said Brian with dreadful heartiness. 'And what do you think of St. Mary's?'

'I like it very much.'

'How do you think it compares with the Swiss?'

'I know nothing of the Swiss,' I said, 'apart from their rolls.'

They all laughed. Brian would have proceeded with the stained-glass business, but the girl said, 'Are you from the aerodrome?'

The change of subject was a relief. I made sure we didn't return to the glass. I was introduced to the vicar's wife, tall like her daughter, but parochial, tedious, unbearably full of good works.

During tea I managed to convey the impression I desired. After that I felt I had done enough for one day. Evelyn saw me to the front porch.

She held out her hand, rather unnecessarily. 'I hope I'll see you again,' I said.

'I expect you'll try,' she said. 'You're not very expert at the stained glass, are you, Flying Officer?' Her eyes mocked me: the remarks were outrageous, following a polite, two-hour acquaintance, but it was as I'd thought: she knew I had not arrived by any accident.

'I'm not very good at anything,' I said carefully. She knew what I meant! 'But don't tell anybody, will you?'

'I won't,' she said. 'I'm on your side in the matter.'

But that wasn't quite true: it took weeks of persuasion before she would share the ultimate excitement of my side of the world.

On the Sunday there was no flying and I came into the village to the morning service. Evelyn was there with her mother and

Brian, and she smiled cautiously. After the service, outside the church, the girl said, 'I have a little petrol and we're going for a run this afternoon. Why don't you come?'

I chose to ignore the pain and entreaty on Brian's face and to accept eagerly. It was the last day of Brian's leave and I marred it for him. Not that it was exciting: mere conversation: but before the afternoon ended Evelyn was calling me 'Roy'.

Evelyn and I met again, more and more frequently, following telephone calls to, and later from, the Vicarage. When I knew her well enough to be sure she wasn't concerned about anything except enjoyment—she went to church as a formality and was desperate to leave that village—I began to obtain petrol for her from the aerodrome. Then we were able to drive beyond the confines of the village.

She explained this desire to get out of the village one evening when we had driven out of it. Everyone in the village knew her and acknowledged her, of course, and she was confined there emotionally as well as physically. 'I want to get out,' she said. 'It's impossible to have even the mildest excitement and enjoyment here—a little too much laughter with a young man at the garden party and the whole village stares. They're talking about you and me now, I suppose: why, she's practically engaged to Brian, and as soon as his back's turned . . . You know. I'm horribly trapped here. Other girls are living wonderful lives at the moment, going abroad, taking risks, meeting people. . . . I wish I could fly, but since I can't, then I wish I could stay out late, dance all night, make men jealous of each other, flirt a bit. . . . I'm allowed to wear attractive clothes, but not to attract with them. . . . Oh, my parents are kind enough, but I have to remember who and what they are.'

'Why don't you join up?'

'Father's a pacifist, of course. Brian's my only hope.'

'Are you going to marry him?'

'He loves me,' she said. 'I like him. If it's the only way out, I'll take it. But that will be tedious too. He thinks it's terribly broad-minded to have a sherry in the saloon.'

'Perhaps,' I said, 'you'll marry someone else.'

'Don't hint, darling,' she said. 'You don't want to marry me: you want the vicar's daughter to do things she didn't oughta.' But her eyes shone and I knew she'd like me to talk marriage.

'You have a low opinion of me,' I said.

'Brian said something about a waitress in the village café.'

'I abandoned her the moment I saw you,' I said. 'I'm no saint, Evelyn, but you're not likely to have fun with a saint.' I kissed her on the mouth. 'Let's go back in the car,' she said. 'It's no fun kissing against a gate.'

In the car she leaned heavily in my arms. I could feel the warmth of her glowing through her dress, and the wild, frightened beat of her heart. Like Olwen, she was having a mental struggle to find excuses to pass from her world to mine. She moved about in fear of my touches.

'Roy, I don't think we should,' she said.

'Darling,' I whispered, 'aren't you on the side of enjoyment?'

'Is enjoyment necessarily sin?'

'But you don't really believe in anything.'

'I do when I'm scared.'

'Then why not let me——?'

She was like a small girl despite her smart clothes and model's height and expression. 'I'm scared now,' she said. 'Don't think I've never been naughty,' she went on quickly, apologetically—they always apologize for their virginity! 'When I was at boarding school I went about with another girl. We went to dances with her brothers, and after one of them Michael—well, you know, loved me with his hands. . . . I was too young to understand really. . . .'

'I'll take you out of here,' I said. 'I'll show you——'

'Oh, darling,' Evelyn whispered. 'I'd love to let you, but how could I face them afterwards? My mother likes you. . . .'

'We could say we're engaged.'

'But we're not.'

'We could be.'

'But, darling,' she said, 'you're no saint and you might break it off.'

That was exactly what I'd intended to do. Evelyn was no fool. I saw that then, but even so, underestimated her determination. That night, in the car, she surrendered to me, not finding it particularly enjoyable. The subsequent love-making was much better and we enjoyed that summer very much.

One autumn afternoon she came to me, bright-eyed and near to tears, the taut look of panic on her face. Before I could greet her at all she burst out hysterically: 'Roy, I'm scared. I think I'm going to have a baby.' I stared at her, equally horrified, and she rushed on: 'If you want to ditch me, Roy, tell me now. Say you had a good time but don't like the responsibility. Don't tell me a lot of lies and then go away. Be honest with *me*, so that I'm left with a reasonably pleasant memory of you.'

Her gallant words belied the cunning she had shown. She was scared now because she knew she had trapped me. If she was prepared to forgive her own pregnancy, others would not be. Her father would quite certainly see my Commanding Officer, and that gentleman, who didn't like me, might offer me the choice of Bomber Command or the resignation of my commission (and *that* would have meant call-up as a soldier in the ranks). Oh, I was trapped all right. We would have to be married in a hurry. Evelyn would escape from her village all right. The bright glitter of the summer had gone. Purchased fruit is never so enjoyable as stolen, and I looked at Evelyn in something like terror. You'll suffer for this, I thought. Nobody traps me. On the other hand, Evelyn had money coming to her; she was smart; no doubt she could cook; socially she might prove an asset. I didn't like it at all, but I had to swallow the insult and put a good face on it. 'You're a bloody good sort,' I said. 'Why all the fuss?'

'You mean you won't ditch me?'

'We're engaged, aren't we?' I said. 'We'll be married.'

She wept now. 'I'm a fool,' she said through her tears. 'I'm only a woman. I thought you'd ditch me.'

'Not you,' I said.

'I'm so glad,' she said tremulously. 'I thought you would. Ha!' she laughed. 'My parents won't be glad. Registrar's wedding for the vicar's daughter.'

'Do they have to know?'

'I told my mother,' she admitted. 'I was so scared, Roy.'

The old man was indeed quite ferocious when I did see him. 'I suppose you thought you were extremely clever worming your way into our hearts via blasphemy and sin,' he said. I wasn't worried: clergymen, like women, rarely offer violence, and this one was a shrivelled-up little thing. I said, 'Save it for the pulpit. I don't believe in any of that fraud any more than I care about stained-glass windows.' He went very pale and quiet, but whether from anger or shock I don't know. He'd managed to lure Evelyn into his study to browbeat her, and she'd emerged very white and trembling; he had no mercy on his victim, so I didn't pull any punches either. At least it had the good result that I've never been plagued by my in-laws.

I wrote to my mother, saying that I was to be married, but that Evelyn's people were snobs who didn't approve of me. I advised her not to come to the wedding because we were, I said, experiencing heavy air raids. I knew that would keep both my parents away: some air attacks on Birlchester in the previous year had rattled them badly. My mother wrote back, giving sixteen reasons why nobody need be a snob in front of her son, and, more to the point, enclosed a cheque for two hundred pounds.

Much to my relief, the cause of all this emotion and activity was born dead a few months later. Evelyn was upset for a while and said it was a punishment.

IV

JULY 30th. A quiet Saturday morning. I only had two calls to make, and then I was free to complete this record. I've quite enjoyed composing it. It occurred to me yesterday that I've not told you about the most vital day of all: when Olwen died, and why. It will take time to describe it all, and I cannot resist including two irrelevant matters, both associated with the same person. This morning I spoke to someone about the murder; in a humorous manner, I said I had done it; and she simply refused to believe me!

This was when I decided to have my eleven o'clock cup of coffee. On chance, I entered the café I visited the other day. It was practically full—middle-aged ladies treading on Pekineses and fighting ruthlessly for biscuits! There were only a few single seats available and, glancing rapidly about, I was astounded to see doe-eyes and her children. Admittedly I only entered that café because I had seen her there previously, but I hardly anticipated such extravagant luck. To find her there and at the same time own a legitimate excuse to sit opposite her pointed, arrogant, foolish face! She has rather a beak nose and when her big, firm mouth opens she reveals too many teeth; but the general effect is attractive. Her dress sense is excellent. I found out that her name is Mrs. Ransome, and that I was right about the husband: he really is in the Civil Service. I was very tempted to go on recklessly and inquire whether he was going bald, was serious and easily shocked by passion; but she is the easily-shocked type herself.

I approached the vacant seat, faced her, and said, 'Excuse me, but is this seat available?'

Doe-eyes glanced up and blushed scarlet instantly. No doubt as to whether she remembered me or not! She spoke in her station-announcer's twang: 'Actually, yes. I mean, I believe so.'

'Would you mind if I shared your table?'

'Not at all. I mean, by all means.'

Her dialogue seemed confused, so I continued carefully, 'It seems very crowded, but it's rather a nice place.'

It was then that doe-eyes dropped her extraordinary hint: 'Yes, it is actually. I come here quite often.'

The waitress arrived and I said, 'May I have the pleasure? Perhaps the children would like some cakes?'

The girl said, 'Mummy said we shouldn't have cakes before dinner.'

'Well,' I said, smiling at doe-eyes, 'perhaps we can persuade Mummy to change her mind.'

I gave an order, and doe-eyes said, 'It's terribly nice of you, you know, but you really shouldn't. . . .'

Her vocabulary appeared limited. I patted my briefcase and said, 'Never mind. I can always put it down to expenses.'

'Are you in the Civil Service?' she asked.

'No,' I said purposely. 'Something much more exciting than that.' A pause, in which I affected to be shocked. 'I'm sorry. Is your husband——?'

She laughed. 'I'm afraid he is.'

'I apologize. I really know nothing about the Civil Service beyond the forms they send me.'

'It's really quite interesting.' She mocked me with a glance. 'They don't have time for cakes and coffee on a Saturday morning.'

'A pity,' I said. 'I'm all in favour of freedom, aren't you?'

The waitress arrived before doe-eyes could offer me her views on freedom. I said to the little horror, who had begun to spread chocolate wafer all over his face, 'What's your name?'

'I'm Peter Ransome,' he said, pausing with reluctance.

'I'm Angela,' the girl said.

'And I'm Roy Harrison,' I said, laughing. 'Now we really know each other. . . . Are they at school?' I asked.

Doe-eyes twisted her mouth in a grimace. 'They don't return until September, I'm afraid.' She made it obvious that she was at least looking forward to freedom from her children, anyway; and I made a mental note that the affair with Brenda could be over by September.

There were occasional awkward pauses in our conversation; she had to be careful in front of her kids, I suppose. To cover one of these pauses, I looked down at a paper I'd been carrying. I commented now: 'They haven't caught the murderer of that redhead yet.'

Doe-eyes said, 'Do you think they will?'

'No,' I said. 'As a matter of fact, I've followed the case closely and it looks as if he's going to get away with it.'

'My husband says the man must be mad.'

'Rubbish!' I said. 'Damnably sane, I should have said. He seems to have left no tracks.'

'A pity for the poor girl,' doe-eyes said.

'Oh, I don't know. She asked for trouble, don't you think?'

'She was in trouble, certainly. But you can't kill girls just because they're—well, you know——'

'I hope your "you" was not singular,' I said, smiling.

'It was a generalization,' doe-eyes said. 'I know *you* wouldn't do anything like that.'

'How do you know?'

'Well,' she said, waving her hands about slightly, 'I mean, you're a civil servant——'

'But I'm not,' I said. 'I'm a traveller and they're looking for a traveller. . . .'

'Are they?'

'It says so in the papers.'

'Not in mine.'

'Well, in one of them. You see, Mrs. Ransome, you presume you're quite safe, but as a matter of fact I'm a man who goes around seducing girls and then killing them.' I looked into her face and then at her silk-covered, strap-controlled breasts so that she would know that part of what I said was true. The two kids carried on eating chocolate wafers. Doe-eyes went red in the face, wriggled uncomfortably on her seat, and explained, 'You're just teasing me because you know I don't understand these things. But you know I'm really right, don't you?'

'Of course you're right,' I said quickly. 'I'm a perfectly normal representative. I sell soap. A very dreary occupation, although quite well paid.' I smiled my gentlest smile at her and with difficulty resisted the urge to pat her hand. 'We both live dreary, respectable lives,' I said.

'What else is there to do?'

'Nothing really,' I said. 'But supposing one fell in love or something like that. Should one stick to the dreary respectability or should one give oneself wildly to life?'

'I just don't know,' said doe-eyes, 'because it's never happened to me.'

'Perhaps it will.'

Doe-eyes stood up. 'Until it does,' she said with another attractive, rueful grimace, 'I'm stuck with dreary respectability. . . . It was terribly nice of you, Mr. Harrison, to buy us our cakes and coffee, but we're late and must fly now. . . .'

'It was a privilege,' I said. 'Perhaps I'll have the pleasure of seeing you again.'

'Maybe,' she said, and gave a careful smile. Then she made her kids thank me, and drifted towards the door, scared to death, I think, of some friend coming in to find us. She had high heels on to-day, which, adding to her height, made her wide hips more sensuous. A girl with wide hips should always be tall. If she is, it adds to her desirability; if she isn't, wide hips subtract from it. Furthermore, high heels gave doe-eyes an improved walk. She turned at the door, as her kids shot beyond it, and offered a final smile and a nod.

She was absolutely correct about the newspapers. I read about the case in three of them, and there was certainly no mention of any traveller being sought. However, doe-eyes is hardly likely to check on that. The *Gazette*, which gives the fullest report, no doubt because it's the local rag, says that the Yard man has been to several places in connexion with the death of Olwen Hughes. I don't know what else they expect him to do! He's been following up all the false information and has visited places I've never heard of. It's a pleasure to learn of him making such a fool of himself, and not only himself, but all the men under his direction. He hasn't abandoned the chase yet, but the vague reports make it clear that he doesn't know what happened. Obviously, without wasting further time, I must tell you and, through you, him—or, rather, his successors. . . .

I met Olwen for the last time on Tuesday, waiting in my car in Clifford Avenue, parked cautiously under the heavy shadows of some plane trees. I sat sleepily on the warm leather seat, looking through smoked glasses towards the hairdresser's shop a few hundred yards away, but on this day she did not arrive from that direction.

'Roy!' she said from the other side of the car.

I turned quickly, startled, thinking for a brief moment that it was some other woman who knew me. But the smoked glasses hid any shock from Olwen. 'My dear,' I said. 'Where did you spring from?'

She leaned on the car, gripping it with her hands, her perfect left hip jutting out. Her lips seemed petulant and there was something about her eyes that suggested a nearness to tears. There was a kind of sadness about her—almost as if she knew the future—and she said, apparently in relief, 'Oh, Roy, darling, I *am* glad to see you.'

'Well,' I said, looking at her, 'that does sound pleasant.'

Olwen was wearing her bottle-green costume and a pale green blouse. Her breasts seemed to swell inside the blouse; the skirt fitted tightly round her hips; on this day she was as desirable as she had ever been. Her hair hung limply as if it were damp; it was copper-coloured and shone in the sun at her every gesture. With a slow silky movement she climbed into the car and sat as though she were tired. Pouting slightly, she said, 'I've had a horrible morning.'

I started to drive. 'You're in safe hands now,' I said. 'Tell me what happened.'

'I more or less had the sack.'

'Why? Whatever for?'

'She found out something.'

'About you?'

'Yes,' Olwen said. 'About me.'

I laughed and commented: 'Surely there's nothing to find out about you?'

She looked at me seriously. 'It's not funny to me.'

I put a hand on her shoulder for a moment. 'It was just that I couldn't imagine you doing anything wrong.'

She stared at me again and moistened her lips. 'Can't you?'

'What we've done was not wrong,' I said, but blushing a little at her intensity.

'No,' said Olwen coldly. 'Because it gave us pleasure.' She looked out of the window and commented acidly, 'That's the main thing, isn't it? To have pleasure. Although I understand that Freud, who started this sort of justification, was a bitterly unhappy man. So were his wife and mistress, I understand. But no doubt there's an explanation for that in his own works.'

Hello, I thought, what's this? Has she got fed-up before me? This sounds like Myrel. This presages something. This seems like woman about to make her demands, to exact her toll of misery. 'Olwen,' I said. 'Don't be unhappy with me. You said you were glad to see me. The world may think we've done wrong, but we know we haven't. . . .'

'Take no notice of me,' she said. 'I just had a moment of panic, that's all. A few weeks ago I quarrelled with a friend because of you. . . . Now I've left my employment. . . . I feel trapped.'

'You're not alone,' I said. 'You're with me. If your friend despises you, you can make a new one. It's a question of time, that's all. . . . Tell me what happened this morning.'

'Not now,' she said, hesitating. 'Later I will. Darling, it's only fair to tell you that now I've left work I'll need some money. . . .'

'Dearest,' I said. 'Was that all you were worrying about? Tell me how much you need.'

'Later,' she said. 'Let's have lunch first. You might think I want a lot. Perhaps I'm not worth that much. You mustn't quarrel with me. Promise you won't quarrel with me. Does it say anything in Freud about whether one is permitted to quarrel about money? Do you think I made a good whore?' She started to cry.

'Olwen,' I pleaded, 'what is all this?'

'All this,' said Olwen in slight hysteria, 'is known as the survival of the fittest. The hot war or the cold war. Or something. I'm not being very gay, am I? Would you like me to give an imitation of a young woman being gay?'

'You sound so unhappy,' I said, but relieved because she was just having the usual moan about conscience. 'You've no cause to be unhappy.'

'I will tell you,' she said. 'Who is going to tell you if I don't? What is this thing called love? Do I sing well? Tell me the definition. Answer the song. Do you think love is a physical thing? Tell me, how do people manage to love God if it is? Did you say I've no cause to be unhappy? Then we must make a cause. It would be terrible for two people to be happy. Somebody might notice. Do you love me very much?'

We were turning into the car park at the Dragon. There were very few people about: a man too far off to observe: a double-decker bus a quarter of a mile away. I leaned Olwen backwards on to the seats, kissed her fervently to damp her bitterness, and explored with one hand quickly to her swollen nipples. 'I love you very much,' I said.

'Yes, but how much? Oh, Roy, do you love me like that man— what was his name?—like Peter Abelard loved?—so much that you could go on liking me after they'd castrated you?'

'I could,' I said, shocked at these sort of words from Olwen. 'But why should I?'

'I haven't the faintest idea,' Olwen said. 'It was just a thought.

I'm slightly hysterical. After lunch I will give a little lecture—not about God this time—but on the causes of hysteria in women. Oh, Roy, I'm tired and I hate being a woman sometimes. . . . Let's have about fourteen sherries so that I can be as brave as you. . . .'

She had three sherries before her lunch, and for a time they seemed to calm her. 'Where are we going?' she asked during the meal.

'Almond Vale,' I said. 'We'll have tea somewhere there. I haven't brought anything.'

'Let's walk along the river bank to find that island,' Olwen said.

'Which island?'

'Don't you have any memories of me?' she asked, moody again. 'Aren't you starting to collect them against the day when I'm sweating fat with child, or thin and bent with old age, or the day you find I'm cheating on the housekeeping? How do people love when they're old, Roy? Eternity's a long time—will the memory of my breasts last you that long? Don't you think you ought to commence collecting other sorts of memories? My silly words or my laughter or something we endured together. There's no guarantee with my body,' she said in anguish. 'It may last a long time for you. But there's absolutely no guarantee. A road accident or a machine-gun bullet or some childbearing could ruin my legs for you. I can't guarantee my breasts against cancer. They'd take them away and put them in a jar, and I'd scream until pain made my face ugly too. You should think of these things. I wish you'd try to believe in God, because that sort of love covers all situations, I understand. Even if it's a lie——'

'I remember the island,' I said calmly, not reminding her that some of her words applied to Evelyn. 'It was that day you surrendered to me on the train. I rowed up the river and there was a large island, with steps down to the river and two swans. . . . I'm sorry if I seemed slow recalling it, but such a lot has happened since then.'

'Too much has happened,' Olwen said.

'I wonder what that means?'

She smiled without humour, stretching an arm across the table to touch me. 'I'll tell you later. Another lecture: the facts of life and love.'

We left the Dragon just before closing time and were in Almond Vale before three. I averaged fifty, which wasn't bad. Almond Vale is really a main road that slopes slightly. It's the surrounding country-side that has given it some slight fame: the blossom on the fruit trees and, of course, the well-known jam factory farther down the river. The town itself is the one main, half-asleep road and the surrounding network of dwelling-houses. At the top of the slope is a cross-roads, a cinema, a church, the police station from where this Maddocks and Superintendent MacIndoe are operating. To reach the river one turns left (turn right for Worcester, straight on for the jam factory); one walks along wide pavements, under flower baskets and past the rather snobby horsy and tweedy shops until a grass square is reached. This square is by the river bank—a sort of official point—and it is here that one can hire boats. Because there is a weir upstream there is a tendency among boaters to move the other way, following the downward slope of the town. That was the way we'd boated previously; it was the way to the island, but I persuaded Olwen to explore the other way. I expect it has saved my life.

I parked the car on the cinema park (to avoid any official payment: another thing that leaves me anonymous) and we walked along the river bank. A boatman spoke to us, but it was Olwen he stared at. He won't remember me, and if he does he didn't seem the type who would be on good terms with the police. It was a very warm day: one of those that are warm even when the sun is hidden. Very few people were about (it was a working day, of course) and what few there were did not pass close enough to recognize or remember features. There was nowhere private enough for love-making, and we had to walk nearly two miles altogether before we were at a safe distance from everyone and there was a screen of bushes.

I found a hollow and examined it. Olwen stood a short distance away and said unexpectedly, 'Let me take your photograph.'

She was carrying a satchel. 'Is that what that thing contains?' I asked, laughing. 'I thought it was food.'

'Stand still,' she commanded. 'I want to have a picture of you so that I shall always remember you.'

'Why?' I asked. 'Are you thinking of leaving me?'

'I may have to leave you.'

'But why?'

'With no job, I must go back to Wales.'

'You'll obtain another,' I said, 'and I'll tide you over until you do.'

'Don't look so concerned,' she said. 'Stand still and smile or you'll spoil the picture.'

I stood there with my hands in my pockets and grinned. 'Now let me take one of you,' I said.

131

'What for?'

'I'd like one,' I said. 'If I have to start collecting memories . . . You look so lovely to-day.'

'I don't believe that. I don't feel lovely.'

'Put the camera down.'

'Take the picture first.'

I did this and then put the camera on the ground by her handbag. Smiling knowingly, Olwen stood still. She affected surprise when I embraced her. Standing on a tuft of grass she was awkwardly balanced and gradually leaned on to me so that we both sagged to the ground. In my embrace Olwen sighed and seemed to groan. 'Whatever's the matter to-day, Olwen?' I said. 'You're so determined to be unhappy.'

'Do you really love me?' she said. I started to explore, but she protested, 'No. I don't mean that sort of love. Would you love me if we were in trouble? Would you help me?'

'Of course I would. Why should you doubt it?' I was aching to love her. 'Don't torture me, Olwen.'

'Don't touch my body,' she pleaded. 'It belongs to somebody else. Roy, Roy, I'm going to have a baby.'

That was it. The trap. The oldest female trick in the book. We lay there in the sun talking about it. 'Is it mine?' I asked.

'I don't love anybody but you, Roy. Surely by now you know that.'

'It makes things rather different,' I said.

'Of course!' she groaned. 'I knew it would. Now you won't want to marry me. Loving me is one thing, but the arrival of a baby is rather sordid, isn't it? Even the baby isn't allowed to be grateful. He has to cry.'

'Don't rush to conclusions,' I said. 'We'll get married.' My mind was working like radar, sending out impulses, hearing echoes, exploring distance.

'When will we be married?'

'When we can.'

'When's that?'

'Eventually.'

'Why not now?'

'Haven't you forgotten Evelyn?'

'You haven't. I see that.'

'What do you want me to do? Commit bigamy? We *have* to wait.'

'I suppose you don't believe me. You want to see me swell to make sure. You're really frightened, aren't you? You should have had more sherry. Are all bomber heroes frightened of birth? Is it only death they're brave about?'

'Don't quarrel with me,' I begged. 'I understand how you feel. Is this what Mrs. Harper found out and sacked you for?'

'She didn't sack me. I told her I was leaving, that's all.'

'Then you lied to me.'

'I was confused. I *had* to leave, Roy, because of the baby. I'm ill every day.'

'I'll give you some money to pay your board.'

'How much money?'

'As much as you require.'

'I've got to go through the shame and the agony. A man can boast about it. It's rather funny for him, and quite a convincing proof of potency.'

'We'll get married.'

'I don't want to get married now. You don't love me.'

'What do you want, Olwen?'

'I don't know. I loved you so much, Roy.'

'I'll give you fifty quid.'

'Is that all my virtue was worth?'

'It's all I've got. You've cost me a packet.'

'Wasn't I worth it?'

'I'm trying to be reasonable,' I said. 'I will marry you when I can, and in the meantime I'll give you all the money I can.'

'Why not see your Mr. Bushell and ask for a rise?'

She was determined to quarrel. I got hold of her and shook her. She wasn't nice to look upon now. They say redheads have tempers and in her case it was true. She was disappointed about something and spitting mad with it. 'How do you know about Bushell?' I asked.

Olwen sneered. 'I bet he'd like to hear about what his traveller does.'

'Then he hasn't heard?'

'No,' she said. 'But he could.' She stood up and collected the camera. 'Why, I even have pictorial proof.'

'You needn't threaten me,' I said. 'Women don't threaten me.'

'Women?' she said. 'So there have been others who might have threatened you. I phoned Mr. Bushell and he said Harrison was in Sheffield. That's the sort of fool you took me for. What's your real name, Roy? Tell it me so that the baby may at least know who his mother ought to have married.'

I told her my name. She went very pale. All her silly dreams collapsed and she knew now that she had surrendered her everything to someone she didn't know at all. She thought she'd understood me inside out, but now she realized she was just another victim. 'I shall go to see your Mr. Bushell,' she said. 'He ought to know what's going on. Perhaps the others didn't have that much courage, but I have.'

I grinned. It was true that she had courage; but no brains, of course; they never have brains. 'You've no proofs,' I said.

'I've got a letter here that talks about marriage,' Olwen said.

The exploring mind had touched the word 'victim', and I knew what I had to do. I'd had enough. It wasn't the sort of quarrel which could possibly have any reconciliation. It had become too ugly. It was time to look after Number One. 'Got them here, have you?' I said.

Olwen had made a mistake admitting that, and she knew it. Her knees trembled. 'They're at home,' she said.

'They're here,' I said; 'same as that picture you've just taken.'

'You can't frighten me,' she said.

She was running to where she'd dropped her handbag. The camera lay near. I had no alternative now but to bring thought into reality. She had been the victim all along; it was her part in the game, and it was how the game must end. Olwen caught the bag and camera and would have run onwards, screaming revenge, but her foot caught on the tuft of grass and she fell on to her face. No scratches, I thought; she can't scratch in that position. They always look for a man with scratches on his face.

I was on top of her and, knowing the inevitable, she struggled madly. Like all of the others, she pleaded at the end. I'd had no wish to harm her twenty minutes before, but the mind, dealing with the permutation of possibilities, found only one solution. It saw the whole sequence of events: those anonymous meetings; the lack of witnesses; I'd never met her friends or her employers or her relations; here at hand was the only written evidence that could have damned me; the false name. . . . It required physical courage to kill, but I have that. It required a kind of moral courage, too, even when, like myself, you've abandoned the hereditary law, order and religion. In a way it had all ended rather beautifully. She would never grow old or ugly. We would never become tired of each other in the frustration of marriage. We would never be ordinary. She would never become fat, or thin, or be in a road accident, or have cancer, or see me grown old. . . . The good die young, and in a way they're lucky.

When I released my grip, her body fell limply, grotesquely, almost suggestively, but I knew that this abandonment belonged to death. I'd seen the queer, crumpled attitude of the dead before and there was no mistaking it.

Then I became conscious of the tremendous silence. It was almost a physical presence weighing down on me. I felt that we had been shouting for the whole world to hear, although my reason told me that the sound would not have carried beyond the surrounding bushes. There was nobody within half a mile, I knew, and yet eyes seemed to stare out of every bush. I knew the urgent need to run. But there were things to do first, and if I did them I would escape. This was the real battle; not Kiel or Hanover, but the very real, personal, dead Olwen; and having won, I had to survive.

I looked around and was surprised. We had not fought, but it was like a battlefield. Things were scattered about for twenty yards. I searched through the handbag, found the letter I had written to Olwen, and stuffed it into my pocket. There was another letter there and a postcard. They seemed harmless. The letter was from her parents and they seemed anxious. Surely that might indicate that she wasn't writing because she had something to be ashamed of. In view of what they would establish medically, it might indicate she had been a whore. The police don't worry about whores much. I left the letter in her handbag. At last I resisted the terror of her dead body. I looked at it and it was just a dead body. I was relieved by I don't know what. I looked at the twisted body and hips, at the legs which would dance no more, covered by the stockings I had given her to arouse my own desire, and for a moment knew regret. I had gone on for too long, that was the trouble; the thought of her auburn hair and innocent face; the ecstasy of seducing that reluctant body time after time had brought me back months after the initial satisfaction. That was when I should have left her alone; but no, I had to win the same battle over and over again. I wiped the silver of the handbag after closing it, and threw the bag near the body. *They* mustn't attach importance to it. *They* must presume that she had been picked up, and while resisting, killed, or attacked by a madman. . . .

The urge to depart was terrifying. It handicapped all thought. The thing to do, I decided, was to climb a tree and get an idea of the layout, see if anyone was near, and if not, clear out. I climbed a small tree and, although it was not as high as others, from a branch I could see the spires of Almond Vale. They seemed damnably close, but on the other hand there was nobody along the river path. A mile off, on the other bank, there seemed to be a cricket match being played by schoolboys; even from that distance I thought I could hear the thin, reedy voices. On this bank there was nobody. I did not want to return the same way nevertheless, and I could see that if I went another way, ignoring the public footpaths altogether, I would reach a field and then the main road. In this way I could avoid the boatman, people who might have noticed Olwen's hair, and children. Children especially, I thought. The way would take me three times as long to reach my car, but it was safer. I would never come to this bloody town again. Nor the Dragon, I thought. Nor anywhere near her lodgings. Sales would not be affected much. I covered the whole suburb on a Tuesday morning; it was how I had met her each Tuesday afternoon. I could even do some of my work by post and telephone. Better, I decided, to keep out of the way for a long time. A year at least; I'll mark a calendar.

I had walked five hundred yards when with a great slam of fright, which set my heart thudding and started a violent headache, I remembered the camera. She had taken a picture of me! It was the one thing I had forgotten, and the most fatal. What a gift for the Middleshire Police! I was sweating, justifiably, with nerves but had to go back. In a panic, I could not at first find the spot. When I did it was quite a surprise to find the scene exactly the same: the auburn hair and the lines down the uncovered legs. I ripped the back off the camera, wiped it, and threw it into the sunlight in my fear. The sun would soon finish *that* off. . . .

The headache was insidious and the strain beginning to tell. I was very tired and panted as I walked and occasionally trotted away. As far as possible I kept near to trees, ready to hide if necessary. But no one was about and I reached the main road safely half a mile out of the town. A few cars passed, but I knew they would not notice me; they would tear straight through Almond Vale; it was beneath their notice. . . .

My head hurt so badly that I longed to relieve it before I drove away. As I neared the town I came to small cottages and then a rather grubby café. Although it was empty, I would have passed it had I not seen a sign: 'Aspirins.' A bell jangled as I entered. Inside, there were a few tables and chairs, a tea urn and bottles of sweets. A chalked notice bespoke of meat pies, bacon sandwiches and other edibles; the thought of them made me queasy. On a wall, as if to mock me, was an advertisement for cigarettes: an auburn-haired girl whose body seemed swathed in tightly-fitting

136

coloured gauze. At any other time it would have promoted desire, but now it only reminded me of danger.

The waitress who attended to me might also, on another day and in another place, have aroused concupiscence. She had large breasts and swayed wide hips as she walked.

'Cup of tea, please,' I said.

'Nice day,' the waitress said.

'Lovely,' I said bitterly.

'On holiday?'

'No,' I said. 'Just passing through.'

'A pity,' she said boldly.

I made no comment until she said, 'Twopence halfpenny, please.'

'Got any aspirins?'

'How many?'

'A small packet.'

'Got a hangover?'

I smiled feebly. 'Yes; that's it.'

'I know just how you feel. Shilling, please.'

I paid her and sat down with my back to concupiscence. The waitress hovered near, but I decided not to pay my usual witty attentions. I took three of the aspirins with my tea and within five minutes was on the pavement again.

The car was still there. It started at once, and I drove slowly and unnoticeably through the town in the wrong direction. If anyone does remember a red sports car at about 4 p.m. and its direction, the direction at least will give a false impression. I had to drive in a thirty-mile triangle to correct this, and arrived home at about five o'clock.

I was very tired and went to my bedroom to lie down. I drew the curtains and sprawled on my bed, waiting for the headache to go. But first I read the letter, trembled at what it might have told the police, and then burned it. I recognized that to-day I was afraid and exhausted. It was natural enough. There was not really a great deal to worry about. To-morrow, I knew, I would see things more clearly and my nerve would be restored.

And that is what happened. I've written everything down here, and although it will all be over and done with when you read it, you will quickly appreciate the situation as it seemed to me on that day of the killing.

Olwen had telephoned Bushell, and I worried badly because her vague telephone call might have made Bushell suspect *something*— he knows me of old. But I'd forgotten that her call was made to a Mr. Harrison, and no doubt Bushell told her that Harrison was in Sheffield. In any case, that anxiety was relieved when I saw Bushell yesterday. The barman at the Dragon has seen Olwen and me often, but he can only give a physical description. He knows no names or addresses, and I shall not go near the place again. If he saw the car he may describe it, but he knows no number, and now my car is a black saloon. Olwen's friends, Hazel and Peggy, and perhaps her landlady, Mrs. Wilson, no doubt know of my existence, but little more than that. If they know a name, it will be the one Olwen knew, the false one, and they didn't see the car, because I never drove her home. Olwen's parents have no knowledge of me; the letter I left in the handbag confirmed what she'd said herself.

There are other details, but I've accounted for them all. The main things are in my favour—the letter and film I destroyed; the false name and the lack of witnesses, not only of the deed, but of all our association. There is no 'external' evidence, as the police say, and no circumstantial: i.e. no one who knows me saw me in Almond Vale that day, and no one has any letters, fingerprints, etc. The Middleshire Police aren't stupid, and if they are, the Yard man isn't. But they've almost nothing to go on. I am an unknown, dark, tall man who is wanted for murder. But what the novelists and newspapers never mention is the high percentage of unsolved crimes, the near-impossibility of finding such a person, and then proving him guilty.

PART THREE
POLICE

I

THE man standing on Platform Two stared at the shimmering horizon, watching for the smoke of the overdue express. He yawned and for a moment his sunburnt jowl slackened; he became just a middle-aged man who had stepped out of bed early on the final morning of his holiday. It had been a pleasant ten days, and he stood now on the concrete platform, aware that it was over. Like other middle-aged men, he left the seaside with reluctance. He knew that in twenty-four hours the reluctance would have been swallowed up in work; the very holiday would begin to seem unreal. But at this moment he felt nostalgic. If only one could live in this quiet town all the time! Peace was what everyone wanted. Everybody made plans for peace, prayed for it, argued for it, but waited for and expected noise, confusion, violence, enmity. . . .

Not many people moved about—Saturdays and Sundays were the busy days, and this was a Tuesday. A faint breeze moved from the sea; there was a smell of salt, but already it was mixed with that of railway engines. It presaged normality. A bell rang somewhere and the man heard the distant clonk noise as a signal fell. One or two people hovered at the bookstall. The man read indecision in their faces: whether, being still on holiday, to surrender to the pornography, or to buy the alarming literature of normality: the problems of the day. The bright glare over everything faded slightly at the first fine, high cloud spreading across the sky. It will be stifling in London, the man thought, and as he thought it the technical voice above his head mouthed enormously the destination of the overdue express: Paddington. The man said suddenly, 'I'll get a paper.'

A boy of about ten said, 'Daddy, can I have a comic?' and the plea was taken up by a girl of about eight, his sister, 'And me, Daddy.'

'Will ye hurry up?' their mother said. 'Ye've been standing there for twenty minutes——'

The man grinned. 'Wouldn't ye like to miss the train?'

The woman said, 'Ye know very well——' but the man was already five long strides away. The children, still in sandals, clanked buckets and spades restlessly, impatient for the joy of travel. 'Oo, Daddy, the train is coming.' Round a slight bend thundered into sight the express for Paddington. It seemed to be sweating in its exhaustion. It hissed in creaking protest as its engine went by, so that the two children stepped slightly away. The woman's tension eased as coach after coach passed by and each proved nearly empty. The twenty or so people on the platform walked leisurely in the two directions, taking a mild pleasure in this unexpected ease of entry on to a train: the last pleasure of the holiday.

A crowd of people seemed to spring from nowhere. Milk-churns were trundled along the platform. A girl wheeled a wagon, offering tea and ices and unexpected sorts of food. An old lady, escorted by three porters and a small dog, moved anxiously towards a first-class compartment. Similarly, a red-faced, vaguely military man shot out of the refreshment-room, porters rushing madly at his every decision. Some overloaded soldiers, having stepped off the train, made a gesture of forming a straight line, but, seeing the refreshment-room and the adjacent pornography, began to dump their kitbags recklessly. A porter approached the man, his wife and children. He touched his cap in a futile salute. 'Porter, sir?'

The man declined. He picked up two heavy cases, apparently without effort, and led the way to a compartment. His wife relaxed into a corner at once. Anyone could see that she had accepted normality already. She welcomed it. It was strangeness and new-ness that worried her. From this could be deduced the probability that she was not worldly.

Inside the compartment the man seemed larger. He seemed too big for it. You sensed that he was more powerful than the first glance had indicated, and you wondered who and what he was. On the platform he had seemed like a businessman—big, heavy, somewhat dumpy. In the compartment you saw that his shoulders and chest were too good, too physical for an office. Perhaps he was a military man, but that did not seem probable because of his pallor. Certainly his face was tanned now, but it was easily recognizable as a face that was normally pale in colour and rough in texture. In spite of his size, you did not think the man was a police-man. You expected policemen to be rather young, and this man was within middle age.

Nevertheless, he was a policeman. His name was Andrew MacIndoe and he was a Detective Superintendent from the C.1

Branch of the C.O. (Commissioner's Office), New Scotland Yard; a branch which is known as the Murder Squad. He was forty-eight years old, going bald, weighed fifteen stone and, perhaps because of his width, did not give an impression of being particularly tall. Also, of course, he no longer wore a uniform or helmet. We are perhaps inclined to forget that detectives are policemen whose powers are no greater than those of a constable. These powers had been explained to MacIndoe soon after he had been nominated, taken the oath before a Chief Constable, had received his appointment, a warrant card, a truncheon, a whistle, his instruction book, and had set out on a beat as his father had done before him.

As well as learning what were his powers of arrest and detainment under reasonable suspicion, MacIndoe had slowly understood a great deal more: what to do in the event of a road accident; how to keep fairly dry in eight hours of pouring rain; what to do with drunken persons; how to collect useful friends (milkmen, postmen, doormen, liftmen, ex-policemen, informers); how to keep order at a football match and at the same time watch it; what to do with suspicious parcels and natural deaths; how to settle quarrels; how to find dogs; how to control crossing streams of three thousand vehicles an hour; how to stand about at elections without yawning; how to grab a quick smoke in a doorway or a public lavatory; how to control political meetings; how to handle rich motorists who presumed that their social importance granted them immunity; how to deal with crowds at processions and strikes; and above all, how to remain calm when others were flustered. All these and other things were learned in uniform, but after three years on a beat MacIndoe had become an *aide* to the C.I.D. of his locality. He had been confirmed in this appointment and had risen through the ranks of police constable, C.I.D., detective sergeant second- and then first-class, detective inspector with a division, to that of chief inspector. For two years he had held his present rank. He could even now quote the Traffic Regulations and suchlike matters, but, of course, they were no longer his to attend to. Rather he sought now for tyre-marks and oil leakages, signs of forcing and entry, shreds of fabric, the shape of bloodstains, footprints and their direction, the possibility of fingerprints, blood-stained clothing and laundry-marks, debris from rivers, entries in hotel and other registers, letters and diaries—in fact, all the patient and rather wearisome accumulation of what is known as external evidence.

MacIndoe's method was to complete the chain of external evidence (i.e. the facts and non-personal materials), so that the cross-examination of a suspected person was scarcely necessary. When it did become necessary, his usual method was to talk round the most vital subject—shunning the word 'murder' or 'robbery' or whatever it was—and before he approached it he would drop hints: 'It's always best to tell the truth. Then you know where you are. It looks bad if the court is convinced you're lying. Besides, perjury is a punishable offence. . . .' His attitude was sympathetic and the sympathy often genuine. 'You tell me the truth,' he seemed to say, 'and I'll give you the best advice I can.' And when the wretched, messy truth had been revealed he would say, 'A pity. I don't think there's much we can do about that. It seems you'll have to go to prison. . . .' This may seem an unfair, mildly hypocritical technique, but the people he dealt with had to be tricked in some degree. They consisted of liars, scoundrels, fools, robbers, lunatics, perverts, murderers—every one of them eager for any loophole, any sympathy that could be exploited, any information that could be twisted to their advantage. MacIndoe could not really afford to be absolutely sympathetic to either criminal or victim. To be sympathetic is to be prejudiced, and to be prejudiced destroys the technical advantage of impartiality. Yet in general MacIndoe was a kindly, humane man who rarely raised his voice, much less indulged in violence. His brain and his dour persistence pursued the criminal, and then his sympathy made him wish the pursuit had not succeeded. But it was as well for society that it usually did.

A high percentage of C.1 officers are Scots, and terrible orgies on the Embankment are reputed each New Year's Eve. But, like many Scots, MacIndoe had a strong moral and religious sense, an attachment and devotion to both work and his home. The work he did was arduous and its hours even more irregular than other police officers'; because of it, he placed a high value on his home life. His greatest pleasure was to watch his wife Janet and their two children, Andrew Junior and Mary; just to listen to their nonsense as he sat smoking his pipe. Younger than he, Janet was still now, as she had been when they met, of a shy, silent, somewhat obstinate disposition. There was nothing glamorous about her, but she was attractive in person, generating a kindliness and gentility which are more hard-wearing than physical beauty. She had not the shrewdness of her husband—in fact, she sometimes described him as a 'cunning one'—and would have been quite content if he had never become more than constable. She was not curious about criminals and knew little of the dirty side of life. MacIndoe told her the main facts of each case, but never mentioned the small vilenesses, the perversions and cruelties which formed or caused it. Janet was not the sort of person who would listen with satisfaction to such details. In any case, it was her husband's wish to keep her innocent. She was the person to whom he could return after weeks of living near the sordid—he could return to her and know that *she* represented normality. It was not, as in disappointment and disgust he sometimes nearly believed, a world in which the evil predominate, but a world in which the average try to maintain their standards despite the uproar created by the others.

II

OUTSIDE there was a flash and it was followed almost at once by the deafening crash of thunder. MacIndoe stirred in bed. As he had expected, it was stiflingly hot in London. 'I'm glad we reached home before the weather changed,' he said, knowing that Janet was awake.

A girl's voice said from another room, 'Mum-eee, I'm frightened.'

'What's the time?' Janet asked.

MacIndoe stretched an arm out of bed and looked at his luminous wristwatch. 'Half-past one,' he said. In the distance thunder rumbled: another part of the storm. MacIndoe started slightly, not at the thunder, but at the telephone extension by his bedside. As it shrilled he said, 'Make a note of it,' and laughed wryly. From the other bedroom Mary's voice came again, 'Mum-eee, I'm frightened.' Then Andrew Junior's voice, in exasperating contrast, said, 'It's ever so good—just like a bomb.'

MacIndoe grunted affirmatives into the telephone: 'Whereabouts? —Is Tony coming?—Yes, yes, verra nice—Good weather too— I've plenty of petrol—No, we never use it on holiday; Janet gets travel sick—No, that's all right; I was awake anyway—and the kids—Good—All right—Goodbye.'

Mary had come shamefacedly into the room. MacIndoe looked at her in tenderness. 'What's the matter, chicken? Afraid of the noise?'

'I wanna come in with Mummy.'

'All right. Daddy's going to work, anyway.'

Janet said, 'Was it serious?'

MacIndoe looked quickly at Mary and answered cautiously, 'Yes, they've found a girl. I have to hurry. It's a long way and I must be there ahead of this rain.'

'Where have you to go to?'

'A place called Almond Vale.'

'What a pretty name. Where is it?'

'A small town in Middleshire.'

Janet stepped out of bed. 'Then you'll be driving all night and you'll be without breakfast. I know you. I'll make some sandwiches and coffee.'

'Och, it doesn't matter.'

'Why can't the Yard phone at a reasonable hour?' But she knew the answer to that question before it was given.

MacIndoe said, 'I was at the top of the rota from midnight. I've had a free hour and a half. Ye mustna grumble.' He felt slightly distant already, involved in the technicalities and tears of others. He thought vaguely of the sea; imaginary seagulls fluted in his mind and he grinned. 'Never mind,' he said, touching his wife. 'It was a nice holiday.' The tension was not altogether unpleasant. It might be an easy one. It was the possibility of the unsolved crime that worried him: failure at work. There had been thirty murders during MacIndoe's police career, and of these he had been the chief investigating officer of seven. They had all been solved.

'Did they say what sort of a girl she was?'

'They know very little.'

Mary said, 'Has she been a naughty girl?'

'I don't think so.'

MacIndoe dressed quickly and then packed pyjamas, shaving kit, soap, a tooth- and a hair-brush (he was inclined to baldness, but still used one). Before going downstairs he said, 'Kiss Daddy,' and Mary's warm, sleep-softened face touched his gently. 'Mummy'll be upstairs in a minute or two.' From his own MacIndoe went to his son's bedroom. The boy was looking out of the window at the storm. Rain lashed the glass. MacIndoe said, 'Hey, back in bed, m'lad.' He tousled Andrew's hair and kissed him on the neck without request. 'Bye, bye, son.'

Downstairs he donned a belted raincoat and slammed a bowler hat on his head. As he backed his car out of the garage a police car turned into the cul-de-sac where he lived. A young man in plain clothes stepped out, thanked the uniformed driver, and strode up to MacIndoe while the vehicle departed.

'Hello, Tony,' said MacIndoe.

'Had a nice holiday, sir?'

'I've got my strength back. Are we ready?'

'Absolutely. Shall I drive?'

'All right,' said MacIndoe. 'You take her as far as Oxford and then I'll take over.'

A bar of light spread from the front door. Janet had opened it and was standing there. The two men approached her and stood in the porch out of the rain.

'Hello, Sergeant Baker.'

'Good morning, Mrs. MacIndoe,' said Tony. 'They picked a fine night for it.'

She passed the small parcel of sandwiches and a thermos flask. 'See that he eats some, won't you?'

MacIndoe said, almost shyly, 'I'm too heavy already.' He kissed her. 'G'bye, m'dear. Don't ye worry.' He was thinking, as she was, of the last case but one, when someone had fired a revolver at point-blank range and had only missed because a revolver is not really an accurate weapon.

There was very little traffic about and the two men were more or less silent as the miles receded. Long before they passed Oxford, still driving in a north-westerly direction, the thunderstorms and rain had been left behind, and they travelled in the same hot, sultry weather that London had experienced not many hours previously.

Before sunrise they reached Almond Vale. The police station there happened to be the county station, but it was, nevertheless, not large. Outside, under the blue light of the street lamp, were notices about Civil Defence, the Colorado beetle, the Royal Navy, the number killed and mutilated by vehicles during a recent month, a charity dance (tickets six shillings, dress optional) and two photographs of a man, incredibly ugly, who was wanted for armed robbery. Inside, the Enquiries Room was of the usual large institutional sort, with some of its green paint flaking from the walls. In the centre of the room was a very solid, antique-dealer's sort of desk covered with books and forms. Against the far wall was a longer desk with three telephones on it. On the walls were many notices: a framed picture showing the varieties of thoroughbred dogs; a notice about bicycles; a large map of Middleshire and a smaller one of Almond Vale; a Notice to Prisoners; some yellowing papers on files—Case Summaries, Police Orders, Crime Information and Special Crime Information. (What, one wondered, was the difference between crimes and special crimes? Was a special crime a sin against the Holy Ghost?) Along another wall was a board from which keys hung from pegs. Two red fire buckets stood near the doorway, full of stagnant water. Despite the sultry weather, a small fire was burning in the enormous grate. In front of it stood the inevitable constable warming his back. Facing him was an old man in a boiler suit, sitting down. Both were drinking tea.

'Good morning,' MacIndoe said. 'I am Superintendent MacIndoe and this is Detective Sergeant Baker.'

The man in the boiler suit said with enormous tact, 'I'll be away,' and slid out of the room. The constable put down his tea urgently and said, 'Good morning, sir. The Deputy Chief Constable is waiting for you.'

The two detectives were led into his room, a less institutional one, where the Deputy Chief Constable of Middleshire greeted them. He explained that the Chief Constable did not live in Almond Vale, but would be along presently. 'I expect you'd like to meet Maddocks,' he said after a while, and took them to the C.I.D. room.

Detective Inspector Maddocks was a tall, wiry man, forty-ish, with a fresh complexion and an alert, sensitive sort of face. His dark skin and hair and his lean frame contrasted with Baker's blond, pudding bulkiness. After some introductory remarks the Deputy Chief Constable left the three men alone; they, after all, were the men who were about to investigate the crime.

Maddocks said, 'Would you like a cup of tea to start with?' The two others assented and Maddocks telephoned an instruction. 'We thought we'd call you in straight away,' he began to explain. 'I'm knee-deep in a fraud case.' He waved a hand at the papers on his desk. 'I shall be in court most of this morning. Also,' he added with a smile, 'the Chief Constable decided that as I hadn't had a murder yet—we're so damn' respectable round here, y'know. Poaching and that. Not used to anything worse. In fact, damn' glad to see you. . . .'

A constable entered with a tray. 'Have you ever noticed,' MacIndoe asked, 'how quickly a constable can make a pot of tea?'

Maddocks smiled. 'I believe it forms part of their training.'

The constable grinned. 'Well, sir, we have to have a pot ready in case of shock.'

They all laughed, still in the introductory politeness; but MacIndoe already knew that he was going to like Maddocks. The Inspector said, 'Will you have one of the cars ready? We'll be going to the scene in a few minutes, I expect.' He looked at MacIndoe in inquiry, and the Superintendent nodded.

'Well, let's have this tea,' said Maddocks, 'and I'll tell you what I can.'

They all sat on the hard, official chairs and sipped tea. 'The victim is a young woman,' said Maddocks. 'She's lying on her face and we haven't moved her yet. She seems to be—well, rather beautiful. Her hair is an unusual auburn. I don't think she was a local girl—not that I notice all the local girls,' he added, 'but this girl's hair is so distinctive that I think it would be remembered. . . . None of the constables had seen her before. She seems to be more or less fully dressed, but her clothes are disarranged. There must have been assault of some kind before she was killed.' Maddocks looked down into his cup and continued, 'I'm damned if I can understand the destruction of beauty. I always thought that murder was the sudden release of some unbearable tension, with both the victim and the killer needing almost equal sympathy because of their ugliness. . . .'

MacIndoe said, 'It usually is like that. They stand there pitifully and say, "I don't know why I did it." '

'There are marks on her throat,' said Maddocks. 'I expect she was strangled. There'll be no scratches on the face of the criminal. She was found last night by a young couple out walking. They didn't know her. There are a number of things lying about—a handbag, a sort of satchel and a camera with its back taken off.'

'Was it light enough for our own pictures?'

'Yes,' said Maddocks. 'It was quite light and we took several photographs.'

The constable re-entered. 'Car's ready, sir.'

'Thank you, Constable.' Maddocks took his raincoat from a hatstand and put it on. 'Perhaps we'd better go now before the rain arrives. Will you explain that to the Chief Constable—that we've left to examine the body and the scene, as there is a probability of rain?'

The constable acknowledged that he would.

The sky in the east was spreading pale, dull silver as the men came down the four steps to the pavement and the waiting police car. Maddocks pointed down the hill. 'This is High Street. It starts at the other end, at the bottom of the slope. We've booked you rooms at the George. It's not far down the road. It's pretty full up in summer, so we were lucky. I didn't think you'd want to go the dozen miles into Birlchester. Food and beer's quite good,' he concluded. 'We have the Christmas party there.'

'The George will suit me very well,' said MacIndoe. 'Thank you. Perhaps we'll have a party before Christmas.'

'I'm sure we will,' Maddocks agreed.

The police car moved off. The streets were deserted. Even in this essentially agricultural district it was too early to expect activity. The car crossed over a bridge—MacIndoe saw a river gleaming coldly below—turned left and after a mile's further drive stopped.

MacIndoe stepped out, looked back at the slope of the town and heard the faint murmur of the river where it dropped in a small waterfall somewhere. He realized with satisfaction that it was a very small town. He could cover, almost individually, every café, garage, boarding-house, hotel—everywhere needing the routine part of an investigation could be examined in hours, or, at most, a few days.

They walked past a few huts, stacks of deck-chairs, lines of rowing boats, flower beds and official trees to the river bank itself. 'It's a pretty town,' commented Baker. 'It smells of holiday—sort of fresh,' he explained. 'Perhaps the girl came here as a holiday-maker.'

'The camera suggests it,' Maddocks said. 'The couple who found her are almost sure they visited the same spot on the previous night, which may mean that the girl was there alive yesterday.'

'A camera presupposes the victim had company,' MacIndoe said. 'So do the sexual indications. Suppose she did walk with someone she knew—would they be likely to walk this way?'

'If they didn't know Almond Vale, it is a sort of natural and obvious way to come for a walk out of the town,' said Maddocks. 'Not that it goes anywhere.'

'It doesn't lead to any beauty spot?'

'No,' said Maddocks. 'If the river hadn't been so low they wouldn't have reached as far as they did.'

It had become much lighter, and about two hundred yards away two constables could be seen on guard before bushes. The path ended and the three detectives had to walk on the caked mud.

'If it had rained before eight o'clock last night,' Maddocks said in something like horror, 'she might not have been found before next summer.'

MacIndoe grunted. 'Let's not worry about what might have happened. What did may prove difficult enough to deal with.'

They were by now quite near to the uniformed police, and Maddocks called a greeting. He explained who MacIndoe and Baker were, and asked if the pathologist had arrived. He had not.

Moving on into the bushes, they came to where another constable stood talking to a sergeant. There were more greetings and introductions; the sergeant explained with dry humour that a lot of people had come to have a look at the scene on the previous evening, but for some ·eason had left quickly at dusk. The sergeant was an old sweat; not impressed by death, he said without concern, 'Shall I uncover the body, sir?'

'Yes,' said Maddocks.

The sergeant removed the covering material very gently, and in the sultry light of early morning MacIndoe and Baker saw, statuesque in her death agonies, the body of a young woman. As Maddocks had said, her hair was of a fine texture and the colour of amber. It was still quite neatly arranged. Her arms were twisted backwards—she lay face downwards—and one leg was limp over the other. The shoe had dropped off the right foot and lay a few yards away in line with the legs. The girl's dark green skirt had rolled as high as her hips—whether as a result of her fall or even, MacIndoe realized grimly, prior to it, he could not yet say. The matching green jacket lay neatly a short distance off near a handbag. All stocking attachments had come undone—at the stocking end—as though one terrible frenzied kick had snapped them free. It suggested violence held in check by greater violence—someone strong. It was impossible not to know that the girl had graceful young legs. Above her waist she was covered by a blouse of paler green than the jacket. This was undamaged at the back, but whether or not it was unfastened or torn at the front MacIndoe did not intend to find out before an examination by the pathologist.

MacIndoe saw all this in one glance. The first thought beyond the technicalities, his first opinion of the girl herself was that she was innocent. He was a man who had seen a great deal of personal violence and he knew that whether to be the victim of it or to inflict it causes an alteration of character and physique; it throws a strain on the body to live violently or quickly or without moderation. People who rush both times round the clock whittle themselves down; they become taut in face and thinned in body. This girl did not look as if she had been weaned on gin; she had a sort of schoolroom plumpness, a physical innocence. He could not see her eyes, but her face seemed soft and rounded also. From her physical appearance alone one could hazard the probability that the girl had been essentially innocent. MacIndoe retained a Scottish dourness concerning sophistication in women. He did not like women who drawled witticisms; he did not value or understand them; to talk in an amoral fashion, he considered, implied maturity of the wrong kind. But the body before him was that of a school-girl—the clothes were suburban, the girl's face and nails unpainted, the hair style quite simple, the eyebrows thick and natural. MacIndoe was stirred to pity. 'Poor lassie,' he said gently—only in moments of emotional intensity did he reveal any Scottish accent. 'Ye must ha'e known some bad moments yesterday. . . .'

This was obvious and disturbing even to an experienced police-man. If policemen are participating in a battle, as far as violence is concerned the battle has to be one-sided. Policemen cannot fight back; they do not become calloused by themselves killing, as sol-diers do. They can only collect evidence for someone else to punish by killing. And the evidence of the girl's death frenzy was not nice to look upon. Someone had perhaps tripped her as she had struggled to get away and, having got her down, had kept her down in brutal callousness or panic. Perhaps someone she had been fond of had taken her there, pleaded for physical love, and, living on physical terms alone—that is, unable to wish the loved one well and leave her alone without them—had inflicted physical death when the love had been refused.

MacIndoe wondered in a brief moment of detachment whether he would hold such a generous opinion of the victim at the end of the case and beyond. The trouble with human beings is that every one is the exception. . . . He could be completely wrong. It would be difficult for him ever really to know. The girl would never speak to him. Everything about her would be learned from others. He would hear opinions the girl herself had never heard. They will all be prejudiced, he thought. Some will love you, others despise you, yet others remain apathetic; and the only means I shall have of evaluating their opinions will be to relate them to what kind of a person offers them. Which in turn means that my eventual opinion of you will be formed by my own prejudiced opinions of others. What a pity I couldn't have met you. I think I'd have liked ye.

'She was running,' he said, 'and she might have got away, but she tripped or was tripped—see the way the one shoe's dropped off?—and he—och, what's the use of pretending it's not a man?—he jumped on top of her and killed her. I only hope he wasn't a madman. . . .'

He sighed (he was travel weary too), and sighed with justifica-tion. If the girl had been killed by a man whose mental balance hovered between sanity and madness, a man of perverted instincts

—then they were in for difficulties that might prove insoluble. Every parent of a daughter fears these people. They form only a very small percentage of the population, and fewer still commit murder. But it is their tendency to hover where children like to play: they expose themselves or commit assaults in parks or along lonely paths. Not all of these assaults are rape, but the wounds and types of assaults are sexual in character; they are terrifying and painful, being nearer to sadism than pleasure as it is usually regarded in sexual matters. Police officers know most of these people in their district, but can do nothing until an offence has been committed, and not a great deal then. But exposure is merely the beginning of the tendency, and the tendency leads to rape, assault or murder; and, being unknown to the girl victim's friends prior to the outrage, the persons are extremely hard to track down. It is the repetition of the outrage—the habit of it—which brings them to justice. Even so, an alarmingly high percentage of child- and women-killers are *not* brought to justice, and MacIndoe dreaded this type of murder. One could not even have the pleasure of anger, for how could one morally assess the insane? He sighed now and asked Maddocks, 'Any recent assaults on girls or children in the district?'

Maddocks said, 'No; nothing recently.'

'When was the last?'

'A year ago. He went to prison.'

'For how long?'

'I don't know. We'll look it up.'

'We'll ask the City of Birlchester Police too,' said MacIndoe, adding wearily, 'They'll know of thousands. . . .'

'Shall we search the ground?' Baker suggested.

'We did have a brief look-round before dark,' said Maddocks, 'but there only seemed to be the camera, the satchel and the hand-bag.'

With great care, these were put into special boxes. 'We'll have them all tried for prints,' MacIndoe said. 'I don't suppose *he* has a record, but if prints are there it would be a pleasant confirmation when we get him.'

There was an obvious truth in his comment. Fingerprints are kept of all known criminals; but there is no such thing as a known habitual murderer, and habitual criminals for the most part do not intend to commit murder even if it would complete their escape or prevent their detention. Unless it be the obvious one of assassination or the killing of a night watchman prior to robbery, which in itself would explain a motive and even indicate the killer, murder is a crime in isolation and without precedent. All the fingerprints of a murderer would do is confirm the deductions of the detective after he had made an arrest via other evidence. The truth still is that, in a murder case, all the detectives can do is identify the victim and question her friends and acquaintances, especially people known to be in her company immediately prior to her death. It is a question of elimination in terms of time and place, although such circumstantial evidence needs the assisting proof and confirmation by science before a conviction is secured. Fingerprints can also be taken from the hands of the victim—for the purposes of elimination and identification. Victims cannot always be identified easily; if relatives and friends cannot do it, it may still be done satisfactorily through the examination of clothes and laundry-marks, teeth, objects in the pockets, blood-grouping. . . .

The policemen searched for about twenty minutes, but found only old cigarette cartons and a broken thermos flask in the bushes. They would have continued but for the arrival of some constables with a stretcher, a tall, gaunt man in plain clothes, and the Chief Constable. The gaunt man was the Home Office pathologist, Dr. Baxter. Too tall, apparently, for his own strength, knobbly at all joints, having pale skin and pale green eyes in a hollowed, intellectual head, the pathologist looked like a caricature of his own scientific type. To a lesser extent, so did the Chief Constable, who was enormous and broad, very upright, red-faced and with militant blue eyes.

There were introductions, and then MacIndoe, who already knew the pathologist, asked him, 'What happened to you? I heard you'd started before us.'

'A puncture,' the pathologist said. 'Miles from anywhere and the rain doing its damnedest. I was nearly struck by lightning. I wish you gentlemen would find your bodies at reasonable hours.'

The Chief Constable smiled grimly and said, 'It's not done to a time-table, Doctor.'

'Doctors and policemen,' Dr. Baxter went on, 'lead a dog's life— or, rather, a cat's. Did you ever hear of a woman having a baby during the daytime? I never did. Well, let me have a look at this poor devil.'

The same sergeant removed the material once more, and the pathologist, taking a clinical thermometer in one hand, bent down to examine the young woman with red hair. 'What do you know about her?' he asked.

Maddocks said, 'She was found yesterday evening at eight-fifteen by a courting couple. They think they passed the same spot on the previous evening. There's a camera here that suggests a daytime visit. All of which indicates that she died some time yesterday.'

'She did,' said the pathologist. 'Conditions indicate between three and four yesterday afternoon. Sorry I can't be more exact than that. The poor girl was strangled. Big hands, I think, MacIndoe. She's not a virgin, your girl isn't. By which I don't mean she was raped. Nothing took place yesterday, although it's obvious something was attempted.'

'Then it's someone she knew,' said MacIndoe. 'We shall find him.' He felt an unreasonable disappointment in the girl because she had not been a virgin. . . . I'm a sentimental fool, he thought. There was bound to be something. And what's it got to do with me? I'm not her judge or her avenger. But he still felt disappointed. The first impression of the sprawled girl had suggested innocence, which was a quality he admired. . . .

Some way off lightning flashed, and it was followed soon after by a long roll of thunder. 'I'm going to get wet again,' complained the pathologist. He turned the body and it rolled heavily on to its back. The girl lay now completely relaxed in death; the doctor had destroyed the previous posture of violence. The girl had a beautiful face. Despite his conclusions concerning her, MacIndoe was quite startled. It was the face of a sad, wise child; it contained more than mere innocence; it had integrity, which implied a successful struggle. And yet her blouse was undone at the front—not torn—and this confirmed the pathologist's statement that she had not been attacked. To some extent she must have surrendered. The simplest and most obvious explanation occurred to him: she was not a virgin because she was married. It was curious, but even in these atheistic times, a woman could surrender her body in marriage and retain her expression of innocence, yet when it was yielded out of marriage the expression changed subtly, imperceptibly, to guilt or at least awareness. He looked at the girl's left fingers and saw no wedding ring. It must be something complicated; there is a story here, he thought. Perhaps someone has tricked her. Knowing that faces do not indicate more than the main characteristics, MacIndoe still could not help believing what the girl's face conveyed to him. It was too gentle a face to be resisted.

Something like this must have been passing through the doctor's mind also, for he commented, 'She had a good body and a pretty, honest sort of face. She doesn't look like a whore to me, but like a healthy young thing who should have been bearing babies.'

'Perhaps she was,' the Chief Constable said. 'We know nothing about her. She may be married—anything.'

The rain came suddenly and tropically. 'Doctors and policemen,' the pathologist commented again, 'need to be in good condition so that they can do the work which would exhaust and kill anyone else. . . . Come on. Let's get out of here. I'll do the rest in a laboratory. . . . There isn't anything else, is there?'

The Chief Constable glanced at MacIndoe, who said, 'No. Not at present.' The Chief Constable signalled to the waiting constables, who arranged the body on the stretcher, covered it, and followed the small procession back to the cars and ambulance. In the pouring rain the party tended to hurry. The dead girl was to be taken eventually, without her own permission, to a laboratory in the city of Birlchester. The policemen were driven to a breakfast of sausages and bacon.

III

THE contents of the handbag had been examined and the probable identity of the victim established. In the handbag had been found a compact and lipstick tube (although there was no make-up on the dead face); a comb retaining a few strands of auburn hair; a packet of cigarettes with five of the original ten remaining; some hair-grips; a box of matches; a pair of green woollen gloves; two handkerchiefs (no laundry-mark on either); a photograph of a middle-aged man and woman inscribed by a feminine hand 'Mama and Dada, 1953'; a postcard with a view of Weston-super-Mare on its glossy side; and, finally, a letter.

The letter and the postcard were both addressed to the same person: a Miss O. Hughes, care of a Mrs. Wilson at an address in south-west Birlchester. On the postcard was simply the message or plea, *My love, I'm sorry. Peggy.* It had been posted in Weston on July 18th, more than a week earlier. There was no address on the letter, only the day, 'Sunday.' It began 'Olwen dearest,' which told MacIndoe what Miss O. Hughes's Christian name was. The letter was from Mama and was affectionate but anxious. Apparently Olwen had not written for ten days and her mother wondered if she was ill. Someone named Tom (the Olwen's brother, perhaps)

154

had met a girl, but if Olwen came home for the Bank Holiday she was requested to say nothing about it. The letter was posted on July 25th, two days earlier, and the county was distinguishable as Merionethshire. If Miss Olwen Hughes was the victim—and it was at least strongly probable that she was—it seemed clear that she had been alive on Tuesday morning to receive a letter.

MacIndoe and Baker were now travelling through the pouring rain, guided by a map loaned by Maddocks, to see Mrs. Wilson. Maddocks himself had gone to the local Almond Vale magistrates' court. The rain lashed at the windscreen faster than an instrument could clear it, and after a silence of some time MacIndoe said, 'I'm glad we have an excuse to avoid that copse for a while, Tony. Let the reporters get wet. They deserve to more than we. They represent morbid curiosity while we—what do we represent, eh, Tony?'

'I don't know,' said Baker. 'Justice perhaps.' He recognized that MacIndoe was in a good mood; no doubt the result of finding the letter; it was always irritating to a detective if he had to devote time to finding who a victim was before carrying on to inquire why. 'Justice or revenge.' He sensed that MacIndoe wanted to talk; this was rather unusual.

'We're not seeking revenge,' MacIndoe said. 'I certainly am not. And I'm not sure justice belongs to prejudiced people like us. Justice is indivisible, m'lad, and belongs to God. No, Tony, I think we are the representatives of civil law—and civil law, not liking murder, says that anyone who commits it must hang as a warning and example to others.' A pause. 'What's your impression of the victim?'

Baker was slightly startled. 'The victim. Well, I think I would have liked her very much.'

'Do you believe in ghosts?'

Baker laughed. 'No, sir.'

'Neither do I particularly,' said MacIndoe. 'Yet I thought the same as you without much reason to do so. Look for a cinema on your side, Tony. We should be about there.'

A few minutes later Baker said, 'Here's the cinema: the Rialto.'

'Now we turn right, third left and then right again,' said MacIndoe. 'We find No. 37 and have all our impressions wiped away.'

'Perhaps,' said Baker, voicing his thoughts, 'the murderer will answer the door.'

MacIndoe shook with amusement. 'It's not happened to me yet.'

The thunder had stopped an hour earlier, but the rain was just as heavy as it had been in the copse. The two men huddled in the porch of No. 37, an Edwardian house—one of a long line—and waited for someone to answer the door. A puddle had formed in the small front garden; the hedges glistened in cleanliness in the rain; a tradesman's van passed by; an old man walking slowly stared from across the road. Hell, MacIndoe thought impatiently, what's she gone out in the rain for? Is it early-closing day in Birlchester? I forgot to ask Maddocks. There was an alteration in the pattern of light beyond the frosted glass of the front door. Someone was coming slowly down a long hall. A woman. She said, 'Half a minute.'

The woman who answered the door was elderly, stout, tidily dressed except that her sleeves had been rolled up and there was soapy foam on her plump arms. MacIndoe's thoughts formed an opinion telegraphically: lower middle class; widow; too pale to be in good health; kindly and even cheerful; doesn't know we're police officers; we shall get the truth if she knows it; opinion of the Olwen girl will be favourable, possibly prejudicially so. The woman said, 'Hello. Lovely day for the match.'

'The match?'

'The cricket match.'

'Oh, yes. Perfect. We would like to speak to Mrs. Wilson.'

'I am Mrs. Wilson. Will you come in? You'll get drowned out there.' The policemen stepped into the hall. 'Let's go in here,' said the woman.

They entered the front room, which had the appearance and smell of a parlour: overcrowded with photographs, ugly china dogs, the furniture and the fabrics too dark, it left an impression of being available rather than used. 'We are police officers,' said MacIndoe.

She was visibly shocked. 'I thought you'd come for rooms. Perhaps you have.'

'I'm afraid not, Mrs. Wilson,' MacIndoe said. 'We came to inquire if you know an auburn-haired girl, probably with the name Olwen Hughes.'

Mrs. Wilson sat down quickly on one of her own chairs. 'Yes, I know Olwen.'

'Are you a friend of hers?'

'She'd never do anything wrong——'

'She hasn't done anything,' MacIndoe said gently. 'I'm afraid I have bad news of her, Mrs. Wilson.'

'She's been hurt?'

156

'I'm sorry to say that she has been killed.'

The pale, fat face lost its apathy; suffering seemed to colour it from inside. The murderer had claimed another victim. This woman —who did not yet even know that it was murder—would never be quite the same again. She was trembling now so that she could scarcely breathe. She was old; she would never recover; there would always be a nervous tic, a fear of answering the front door. . . . Mrs. Wilson said in a sort of protest, 'But she was always so careful.'

'Careful?'

'On the roads.'

'Did Miss Hughes have fine, dark red hair?'

'Yes.'

'Then there's no doubt.'

'Is she hurt—bad?'

'It wasn't a road accident, Mrs. Wilson. She was killed.'

'Killed? Then what with?'

'I mean she was murdered.'

A pause in a tremendous silence, then the tears streaming. 'Excuse me. I can't help it.' MacIndoe said, 'It doesn't matter. I only wish——' Her emotion reached him and he did not even know what to wish. Another silence. Mrs. Wilson's sniffs. The pouring rain outside. The woman said in a foolish, smashed, defeated voice, 'What would anyone want to kill her for? She was a nice kid.' I knew it, MacIndoe thought, in something like elation.

'We don't know yet,' he said. 'Do you think you could identify Miss Hughes for us? It would help us greatly. I can't start my inquiries until that's been done. And it may save her parents a little of their distress.' They'll be the third and fourth victims, he thought in depression. The brother Tom will be the fifth. And so it will go on, the one act of destruction spreading suffering to everyone the girl knew. And if I catch him, MacIndoe thought bitterly, they'll say he wasn't quite adjusted to his environment. He just needed to kill girls to make him feel good. How hard they all tried to give sin another name!

'She's not—cut or anything?'

'No,' said MacIndoe. He added nothing about the way the girl had died.

'I suppose I'll have to come. Where do I go?'

'She's at Almond Vale,' said MacIndoe. Mrs. Wilson seemed surprised. 'We'll bring you back afterwards,' he concluded.

In the car Mrs. Wilson was almost silent. She was obviously

frightened, and MacIndoe forbore from questioning her before she had seen the body. At the entrance to the police station she hesitated. 'I've never seen anyone—killed,' she said.

'Olwen looks quite—peaceful,' MacIndoe said.

'All right; but if I feel ill or anything——'

'You'll be all right.'

But when she had seen the dead face Mrs. Wilson could not speak. She nodded through a stream of tears. MacIndoe guided her into Maddocks's office and gave her a drink of tea—for shock, as the constable had said earlier.

Ten minutes later she felt much better. The ordeal being past, she was garrulous. 'She was a nice kid, Inspector. Don't you get the idea that because—I mean, it shows she resisted, doesn't it? Who was it, Inspector? Some madman?'

'I don't think it was a madman,' said MacIndoe. 'It must have been someone she knew.'

'Then it was this man—this married man. She wouldn't bring him to see us because she was ashamed of him,' Mrs. Wilson said in slight bitterness. 'Or else she was ashamed of us.'

'Who is this man?'

'She never said anything much,' said Mrs. Wilson. 'Didn't like being teased about it. I wouldn't have known of his existence if Hazel hadn't told me.'

'Is Hazel a relation?'

'Hazel and Olwen shared a room,' the woman said. 'I've got a spare room, you see—well, you *know*. I have to have two in because I haven't got a man at the back of me. My husband's been dead twelve years. The bombing. He would go—at his age. I haven't even got a pension. It's mean, you know. He'd been there twenty-four years. That's a long time, Inspector.'

'Indeed it is,' murmured MacIndoe. 'Can you tell me the name of this man?'

'Oh, no. I've never seen him. Hazel will know all about it.'

'How long had Miss Hughes been with you?'

'Three years at least. She came from the sanatorium. She was a nurse there for a long time. Lost her boy friend there. . . . She's got a friend there still——'

'A boy friend?'

'No. A nurse. Peggy. She used to come a lot, but we haven't seen her lately. Except the once—about six weeks ago—when I think they quarrelled.'

'Do you know what about?'

'I think it was about this man. Peggy didn't like Olwen knocking about with a married man.'

'Can you tell me any more about her affair with the married man? When did it begin?'

'I don't know much. Hazel will tell you. She met him every Tuesday on her half-day. Poor Olwen. She used to go out dressed so nicely and when she came back her eyes would be shining in wonder. Except lately. She's got a cynical touch lately. A few weeks back she said, "Do you think there's any love that's not selfish except a mother's?" It wasn't the sort of thing she usually said.'

'What sort of a girl was she, Mrs. Wilson? Was she vain, kindly, unselfish, callous—or what? What sort of things did she normally say?'

'She says to me once—I'll never forget it—"You're the salt of the earth, Mrs. Wilson," she says, and blushed because she hadn't meant to say it. Then she said—about Albert—"Do you miss him so that you have to relive every little moment you can remember to prevent yourself going mad?" Well, there was a time——'

'Did she have any men friends?'

'No. One or two in the years she's been with me. Nobody at all for twelve months except this man.'

'Did she mention anyone who was fond of her? I mean, someone whose affection she might not have reciprocated.'

'She wasn't bothered whether she had a boy or not,' Mrs. Wilson explained. 'She'd always lived in a feminine world—nursing and then the hairdressing—and she was kind of innocent. Now, Hazel——'

'Did she work at a hairdresser's?'

'Yes. Olga Harper's on the main road.'

'How long had she been there?'

'Ever since she left the hospital.'

'She's only had the two jobs?'

'I don't know what she did before she came from Wales.'

'Can you give me the address of her parents?'

'Yes. It's going to upset them, Inspector.'

'There's no way out of it,' MacIndoe said. 'Have you a photograph of Miss Hughes which you would be prepared to lend me?'

'I've got a few snapshots.'

'It would help us. We'd let you have them back. Will ye try to answer some questions about time now, Mrs. Wilson? When did you last see Olwen?'

'Tuesday morning,' said Mrs. Wilson. 'She always gives me a cheerio.'

'As far as you know she went to work as she usually did?'

'Yes; at about half-past eight yesterday. And she was togged up like I told you. Oh, I know what you're going to ask me,' Mrs. Wilson said. 'What did I think when she didn't come back last night? You know what I thought. I thought she'd gone with this man. I was hurt, but I would have forgiven her. I loved the kid.'

'You've been very kind,' said MacIndoe. 'Very brave too. I'll take you back home now and then we'll see Olwen's employer. We'd like to see the other young lady—Hazel. When will she be in?'

'Well, if she does the same as yesterday and Monday, she'll come home at about three. She's on early this week, see?'

'Will you tell her not to touch anything in the room they shared?' MacIndoe asked. 'We'll be along at about three o'clock.'

He drove back through the still-pouring rain to Birlchester. Mrs. Wilson supplied him with the address of Olwen's parents and two photographs of the dead girl. One of these was very clear and MacIndoe knew that the photographic department would be able to enlarge it considerably. The honest, straightforward face, with the wide eyes staring at the camera and the straight, good mouth slightly nervous, would soon be known to every detective constable in the county, and perhaps to the whole nation.

From Mrs. Wilson's the Superintendent drove to the nearest kiosk to telephone the Almond Vale police. Maddocks had not returned; another officer took the address of the victim's parents, and MacIndoe knew that within the hour they, like Mrs. Wilson, would be suffering. But it was a duty he could not avoid, and for them to learn the dreadful news from some newspaper would be inexcusable callousness. . . . While he was in the box he looked for Mrs. Olga Harper's address in the telephone directory. It was described as a hairdressing establishment. Within two minutes he and Baker had reached it.

Inside the shop the air was warm and sickly sweet. There were the usual pictures on the walls of girls with various coiffures, the discreet advertisements for personal hygiene; by the cash desk stood an electrical contraption that looked like a hatstand. There were three cubicles, each screened by wood and frosted glass. Nobody could be seen, but a voice, suggesting plumpness, said, 'It was second degree burns. Poor little mite. They oughta done something when I told 'em. . . .' A girl's voice said, 'Yes. Excuse me a minute.'

A dark, plump girl with a pale, wide face emerged from a cubicle.

'Good morning,' said MacIndoe. 'We would like to see Mrs. Olga Harper.'

'Just a minute,' the girl said. Her life seemed to be spent apologizing for minutes. She entered a second cubicle and there ensued some fierce muttering inside: 'What do they want?'—'I don't know'—'Well, ask, you fool'—'They asked for you'—'Everybody asks for me. Tell them to come back in an hour.' The girl came out, no longer pale but a radiant pink, and said, 'Could you come back in an hour? She's very busy with a client.'

MacIndoe smiled dourly. 'Explain that we are police officers,' he said.

The girl returned inside the cubicle and the muttering recommenced: 'Oh, my God, *now* what?'—'They're police officers'— 'What am I supposed to do? I haven't done anything wrong'— (You mean illegal, MacIndoe thought. You're doing wrong now) —'Well, I thought'—'*You* thought. That's likely, I'm sure. All right, get on with your work'—'Yes, Mrs. Harper.'

There was a flurry of white as the girl hurried past the two men. Then a short, thick-set woman, middle-aged, with carefully over-coiffured blonde hair, hard eyes and scarcely any lips, stepped reluctantly out of a cubicle and confronted the two detectives angrily. 'Look here,' she complained. 'You ought to telephone before coming to see me. Everyone else has to—why not you?'

'Mrs. Olga Harper?'

'Of course I'm Mrs. Harper.'

'We're police officers investigating a murder,' said MacIndoe. 'We've only this minute obtained your address so an appointment was impossible. We wish to ask you about a girl named Olwen Hughes.'

Mrs. Harper had produced a nail file from a pocket and rasped away at the nails of her left hand. No pause in the battle for (or was it against?) beauty. Occasionally she lifted the fingers to her mouth and blew; it was as if she were working on a splendid piece of furniture. She only seemed to hear MacIndoe's last two words, and her response was an increase in indignation. 'It's no good coming to me about that young woman,' she said harshly. 'If she's got any complaint, she can come to make it herself. She wanted to go and I gave her a week's money. We didn't kiss bye-bye. What's she moaning about, anyway?'

MacIndoe said, returning the harshness, 'Miss Hughes has been murdered.'

The taut, painted face sagged momentarily, its innumerable lines seemed to slacken, and for a moment a new expression appeared: generosity, grief, or bewilderment. (Where, along the line that brought me to this moment, did I go astray?) But the compassion was resisted. To yield to it would mean analysis. Better stick to safety, to the steam and the gadgets, the cash register and the copies of *Vogue*. She was not strong enough to surrender. 'Well, well, what a thing to happen! Miss look-down-her-nose has got involved in something unpleasant. I always said she was too quiet. Still waters run deep, I said of that one.'

'You say you gave her a week's money and she went,' MacIndoe queried. 'Why?'

'God knows. She just wanted to go home. They're all the same. Just do what they like. Damn you, I'm all right—that's the motto.'

'When was this?'

'Yesterday.'

'She was killed yesterday afternoon in a copse,' said MacIndoe. 'Now, it's very important that we establish as far as possible what Miss Hughes did; the times of her every movement and conversation.'

'We were having our ten o'clock cuppa,' Mrs. Harper explained. 'She said she wanted to talk to me privately. She said she wanted to go home.'

'Did she mean to her local home or to Wales?'

'You tell me. I didn't ask. They think their every little affair is more important. "I'll work until the holiday," she said. Like hell you will, I thought, and gave her a week's money.'

'At what time did she leave? Ten o'clock?'

'Well, say between a quarter and half-past.'

'Why didn't she stay until the end of the day?'

'It was her half-day. She insisted on having it—said she'd got something *important* to do. Good God——'

'Do you know what it was she had to do?'

'No.'

'Did she say anything about it at all?'

'No. Only about it being important.'

'Would any of the girls know?'

'I doubt it. They weren't especially friendly.'

'Do you know why?'

'She worked too hard for 'em. They like to sit about talking.'

'She worked hard?'

'Well, yes. . . .'

'Why were you so willing to lose her, then?'

'She wanted to go. I'm not going to plead with them.'

'What was her behaviour like?'

'How should I know?'

'I mean her behaviour here.'

'It was good. She worked hard. Why not? She was a big, strong girl.'

'Yes, but apart from her work.'

'I never saw her socially. I've got my own life to lead.'

'Didn't she talk to you?'

'She hadn't much to say.'

'How long had she been with you?'

'About three years or so.'

'She just came to work and went home? Didn't she talk at all?'

'Sometimes.'

'Well, then, what about?'

'What d'you want to know about *her* for? I thought you said she was dead.'

'Did she talk about her private affairs?'

'They wouldn't be private if she did, would they?'

'Didn't she confide in you at all?'

'She'd talk sometimes about flowers, or the work, or her home, or an occasional film.'

'Did she have any men friends?'

'She never mentioned them.'

'Did any ever call for her?'

'Never. Some of the travellers liked her, but only because she was intelligent.'

'Intelligent?'

'I mean she attended to them properly.'

'Did any of them ever take her out?'

'No. Good God, they're all middle-aged men with families.'

'It was a married man she met each Tuesday.'

'I didn't know she met anyone—Tuesdays or not.'

'Did anyone ever telephone her?'

'I don't allow private calls. They'd be on all the time.'

'Have you seen Miss Hughes since she left this establishment?'

'No.'

'I'd like to see the assistants,' said MacIndoe. 'They might remember something. How many are there?'

'Only two. I haven't replaced Olwen yet. You'd better come in the office. This looks as if it's going on all morning.'

The office was another partitioned section. In its confined space were a desk, two chairs, an old typewriter, a telephone and, on the wall, a calendar. 'I'll go and get on with my work,' Mrs. Harper said.

'Quite the duchess, isn't she?' Baker commented.

MacIndoe grunted. 'Leaving out her opinions, the rest's quite useful.' He would have said more, but the pale, plump girl entered with a brown-haired, tall, thin, bespectacled girl who looked alert enough to merit questioning. Both girls seemed shocked; the plump one was obviously quite nervous, but their apprehension was due to the impending interrogation. Through the nervousness of the spectacled girl MacIndoe discerned fascination; he did not think either girl had any mental picture of Olwen's sprawled, twisted body and its surrounding litter.

'I'm Superintendent MacIndoe,' he said. 'I expect you've heard what has happened?'

'We heard you talking,' the taller girl said.

'What we want to establish are who Miss Hughes's friends and acquaintances were,' explained MacIndoe gently. 'Then we can ask them all when they last saw her and who with, and that sort of thing. What are your names?'

'I'm Miss Barber,' the plump one said.

'Sheila Simson,' the taller girl said.

'Right,' said MacIndoe. 'Let's establish first what happened yesterday morning. Suppose you tell me, Miss Simson.'

'Well, everything seemed the same as usual,' the girl said, beginning nervously and then gaining confidence. 'But when we were having tea Olwen—that's Miss Hughes—said to Mrs. Harper, "Can I have a word with you?" or something like that. Anyway, they came in *here* and we could hear them speaking angrily.'

'Didn't you hear anything at all?'

'Well, just before Olwen came out I *did* hear Mrs. Harper say, "And don't come back." Olwen said, "I won't," and she walked straight out of the shop.'

'Is that what you heard, Miss Barber?'

'Yes,' the plump girl said. 'Then Mrs. Harper came and said she'd sacked her.'

'Did she say why?'

'No.'

'Has she explained subsequently?'

'No.'

'Did she say anything about wanting to go home?'

They both stared in negative silence.

164

'Did Miss Hughes ever bring any of her friends here?'

'The girl she lives with—Miss Murphy—came in now and again,' said Miss Simson.

'No one else?'

They thought about it. 'No.'

'Do you know where Miss Hughes went when she left the shop?'

'No.'

'Did she say anything at all?'

'No. I think she was crying.'

'Do you know any of Miss Hughes's friends?'

'Only Hazel—that's Miss Murphy.'

'Did either of you associate with Miss Hughes—outside of here, I mean?'

Miss Barber said, 'I've been to the cinema a few times with her.'

'What were her interests? Did she talk to you at all?'

Miss Simson said, 'I don't know. I'd never really asked.'

Miss Barber said, 'She wasn't fast or anything. I can't think why——'

'What sort of a girl would you say she was?'

Miss Simson said, 'She was always nice to me, but I didn't know her well enough——' The explanation tailed off.

The mouse-like Miss Barber, scarlet and near to tears, said, 'You'd think she ought to be conceited, she was that beautiful. But she wasn't. Mrs. Harper treated her like a servant, but Olwen never got angry. "Her work is her only happiness," she said to me once. "Why spoil it?" It wasn't sarcasm.'

'Did either of you meet her boy friends?'

'I don't think she had any,' Miss Simson said.

'Oh, she must have,' the plump girl said, 'because I saw her get into a car.'

MacIndoe said, 'Did you? When was this?'

'A few months ago,' said Miss Barber. 'It was her half-day—she had Tuesdays—and I happened to go across the road to the Post Office for Mrs. Harper. I thought I saw Olwen at the cross-roads—by the lights—getting into a car.'

'What sort of a car?'

'A red one.'

'What sort of red?'

'Scarlet.'

'A saloon?'

'No. A little two-seater. It had the hood down. The driver was a man—that's why I thought—but perhaps it wasn't her.'

'At what time of the day was this?'

'One o'clock. I'd just come back from dinner and Olwen had just gone for hers. That's what made me think——'

'Did you see the driver?'

'It was too far to see clearly,' Miss Barber said. 'I think he was young. He had dark hair. Anyway, he was tall.'

'How do you know that if he was in a car?'

'Well, Olwen was quite tall, and when she sat in the car—if it was her—this man was a head taller.'

That makes him as tall as myself, MacIndoe thought. He asked aloud, 'Did you mention it to Miss Hughes—that you'd seen her?'

'No. I forgot all about it until just now.'

'Do you know anything about the car or its driver?'

'No, sir,' the girl said. 'I'm sorry.'

'That's all right,' said MacIndoe. 'Do you know if any of the travellers who call here have red cars?'

'No.'

'They don't,' confirmed Miss Simson. 'I've never seen one.'

'Do you know how Miss Hughes spent her half-days?'

'No,' they both said. 'I haven't been out with her for several months,' added Miss Barber.

'All right,' said MacIndoe. 'We'll leave it at that. If it becomes necessary I'll come to talk to you again. You've both been very helpful. If you do recall any behaviour of Miss Hughes's which was abnormal—and by that I don't mean startling; I mean slightly different from the day-to-day routine—then let me know. I'm at the Almond Vale police station, but you can go into your local place any time.'

He and Baker took their leave of the two girls and Mrs. Harper. 'What's the time?' MacIndoe asked outside on the pavement.

'One o'clock,' said Baker.

'Let's have some lunch. Where can we go?'

'I saw a pub a few miles back,' said Baker. 'Shall we try it? It's called the Dragon.'

IV

THE bicycle plunged down the steep hill into what seemed darkness. The constable put the gear into top and worked up as great a momentum as he could, for beyond the plunge the road climbed upwards again. The wheels hissed through puddles under the dark trees, the grey bulk of the Vicarage on the right. A quick impression of two cows with mild expressions over the hedge on the left. Mr. Dowell's. In bottom gear now, then standing on the pedals; finally, the necessity to get off and walk. The saddle would get wet. The rain was driving parallel to the sea. The constable looked up, saw the grey patches scudding along the hillside. Bright yellow clusters of gorse stood out on a very dark blob where last autumn there had been a hillside fire. Some boys. He had caught them. At the top of the hill he reached the road that ran along the foot of the mountain; he turned right, mounting the bicycle again. Some English holiday-makers stood outside the pub, not knowing quite what to do with themselves. They must be waiting for the toast-rack bus to take them down a mile to the shore (where they'd get really wet, the constable thought). The two middle-aged women were obviously wishing they were indoors by a fire, but the men drank beer and were enjoying themselves like naughty boys. (Not a bad little place this. Must be twelve months since I had a drink.) The women sipped short drinks with visible self-disapproval. One of the men called out, 'Hello, Constable. After a murderer?'

The constable started slightly and did not answer. He did not feel equal to answering. The weather was bad enough—it had penetrated most of his clothing—but his duty was even more uncomfortable. He had just received an instruction by telephone from the divisional police station at Bar Quay. A girl had been found strangled in Almond Vale—scores of miles away in England—and *he* had to request her parents to go through the pouring rain to the station and be informed. He did not have to inform them himself; which was a great relief. He did not know how he would remain expressionless—as if he had no knowledge—but he knew he would manage it. He had to. It would have to be another case of the mysterious *they*. *They* did not explain to me. . . .

Now the constable turned left and dismounted to push his machine up a steep lane. Under the comparative shelter of a lamp-post and wide trees he lit a cigarette. He puffed the damp tobacco a few times and then threw the stub away. Mustn't be indecisive, he thought. Must help the poor devils if you can. But he was still scared, knowing how much suffering he might inflict.

It was only a small place, called Wood Cottage, not because it was made of wood but because it was surrounded by trees. Behind it was the slope of the mountain. It was as dark as evening. The constable had passed the place scores of times before—poachers, peepers, and courting couples went this way up the hillside—but he had never been inside. Here goes, he thought. God be kind to them.

A young man answered his gentle knock. 'Hello, Constable. What can we do for you?'

'I have a message for Mr. William Hughes.'

'You're lucky. Dad's in. We're all having lunch, but come in, man; you're wet enough as it is.'

The constable entered, taking off his helmet. 'Go in there,' said the young man, opening a door.

'Perhaps,' said the constable, 'you'd all better hear the message.'

The young man stared. 'Okay. I'll fetch Mama and Dad.'

The room was quite small and the eye was caught by pictures. A large oil painting, so dark that one had to stare at it for some time before one realized that it portrayed a human being, not a landscape. A clock ticked in the rain-enclosed silence of the room. It was on a marble mantelpiece. A girl's portrait stared from alongside. Time like an ever-rolling stream bears—— No, the constable thought, it can't be you. His mind refused to admit the probability. There must be another daughter besides this one, who looked as beautiful as an advertisement. He looked more closely at the photograph and saw the embossed sign, 'Swift, Birlchester.' Jesu, he thought in horror, this is worse than the war.

They trooped in silently, in awe of his size and uniform. The parents were middle-aged, the man, rather tall and gaunt, carried quite a youthful air; the wife looked older, tired, as if other disasters had reached her first. The young man said, 'This is my father and mother.'

'I am sorry to interrupt your meal,' the constable said. 'I've been sent with a message for Mr. William Hughes.'

Dark eyes stared directly at him. Like *hers*, the constable thought, but not the same colour. 'I am Hughes,' the man said. They were all standing although the woman had made a gesture, an invitation to sit, with her hands. 'What is the message?'

'It was from the station at Bar Quay. They would like you to go there, see?'

'The railway station?'

'No. The police.'

'What's up? What have I done?'

'It's nothing like that. They would like to see you.' The constable turned his helmet round in his hands. I wonder what these things are made of? Damn' silly anyway, turning me bald. 'It's about your daughter.' If there were two they would ask now, 'Which one?'

They didn't speak at all for long moments. From the other room a technical voice could be heard saying, 'Speaking to-day at Newcastle, he said that before negotiations could be resumed there had to be mutual trust, and he did not feel that at the present time such trust existed or could exist——' The other game went on.

The father said, 'Has *she* done anything?'

The constable looked up from his helmet. 'No. It's just that *they* have to inform you. As far as I know—I mean, I understand—well, see, she's been—hurt.'

He had done it. The rest was evasion.

'What's happened to Olwen?' the woman said, breathing with obvious difficulty. 'Which hospital is she in? Is she—dead?'

'Be calm, Mama,' the young man said. 'Was it an accident? Can you tell us anything?'

'I think it would be better for you to go to the station,' the constable said. 'They have all the information, see?'

'Yes, we'll do that. That's the best thing,' said Mr. Hughes. He was slightly dazed, but endeavouring to be sensible and calm.

The young man said in irritation, 'Why can't you tell us? She's my sister. You *know*, don't you? Why didn't they give you all the information?'

The constable remained calm. He had done his duty; nothing they said could irritate him, he pitied them so much. Anger, anxiety, the pursuing of details—these were normal tendencies and he could deal with them. 'Believe me,' he said, 'it's best for you to go to the station. I don't know everything. Have your dinners first, and when you get there ask for Inspector Prosser.' You won't eat another meal for days, he thought.

Mrs. Hughes said, 'We'll go now. I can't eat. Let's get it over with.' She was eager to be hurt on Olwen's behalf, to share her disaster.

'It's useless going now,' Hughes said. 'There's no bus for half an hour. Let's have a drink of tea.'

'There's no hurry,' said the constable. 'Mr. Prosser will be in all afternoon. I'd better be on my way. I am sorry to be the one who——'

'It's all right,' said Mr. Hughes. 'Tom, boy, show the constable to the door.'

At the front door Tom said, 'Listen. Is it very bad?'

The constable whispered, 'Yes.'

'How bad is it?'

'As bad as it can be.'

The young man said, 'Oh. . . . Thank you.'

He returned to his parents, who were discussing the implication of the constable's every word. They were trying to ignore the numb despair that told them Olwen was dead. Optimistically they decided she had lost her money. It was, of course, even remotely possible that she had done something wrong; unintentionally though, they did not doubt. The very worst thing any of them could imagine—even Tom, who knew his sister must be dead— was that she had been involved in an accident. She was all right, of course, the parents decided—and Tom could not bear to be the one who told them otherwise—but why all this fuss? Red tape. You had to have things done legal like when the police were involved. In some obscure respect for authority, Mrs. Hughes insisted on changing into her best dress. They drank their tea and in the end had to hurry to catch the small bus which Hughes drove himself sometimes.

The driver, accepting their fares, said, 'Hello, Hughes. Going to the market?' but Hughes merely said, 'Hello, Parry,' and his wife and son, obviously in distress, said nothing at all. There were no other passengers in the vehicle; it hissed through the rain until they approached Bar Quay, when Hughes said to the driver, 'Put us off at the police station, will you?'

'The police station?' the man echoed. 'Anything wrong, man?'

'I don't know.'

The driver watched in morbid curiosity as the three persons stepped from his bus and walked with terrible slowness—ignoring the rain—along the pavements. They were soon lost in a jostling crowd of holiday-makers who poured out of Woolworth's sucking pink ice-cream and screeching enjoyment. He saw the three figures mounting the steps into the police station when the traffic lights ahead of him changed and he had reluctantly to drive on.

Inside the police station all was unfamiliar. A constable was typing. Another was on the telephone, shouting into the mouthpiece as though the person at the other end of the line could only hear the machine. A middle-aged holiday-maker, with time on his hands and a straw hat on his head, talked to another constable who was writing. 'No, it isn't the same now. You can't get them. I can remember thirty years ago when you could get a first-class one, hand made by a craftsman, for five shillings. It's not a lie. Five shillings.' The constable yawned, but the voice went on. It seemed as if no one was going to take any notice. They would have to go out and make another entry. They were too afraid and tired to protest. Their eyes looked unseeingly at the unfamiliar notices on the walls, the books and a hard gleam of metal on a desk: a revolver. Please, constable, can you tell me if my daughter is dead? All in good time, my man. This is not the post office. We have crime to attend to. Anybody know anything about this man's daughter? It was market day and already a few drunks had been captured. Somewhere a man was singing a hymn; he stopped, groaned for some time and then began to be sick. Someone was upbraiding him in Welsh. Please, constable, can you tell me if my daughter is dead? Don't hurry it, my good man. You are approaching your own destruction. Dead? did you ask. You look upset. Death is so easy. It comes in so many forms. Anybody know how this man's daughter died? Did it come in an attractive form? Was there much pain? Oh, she was killed by the man she loved? Unusual, that. Not so protracted as death by boredom, death by exhaustion, death by cancer, tuberculosis, marriage, child-bearing, napalm bomb, food-poisoning, blood pressure, starvation, old age, bayonet thrust, road accident. But when you learn how she died you will curse God for not letting her live another five, ten or forty years to die another way. Anybody know why the man this man's daughter loved should kill her? No. Sorry, I'm afraid we don't know that. There's a man called MacIndoe working on it now. Perhaps he'll find out. He's quite a good fellow—the best we have.

The constable replaced the old-fashioned receiver on its cradle and came to attend to Mr. Hughes. 'And what can I do for you?' he asked.

'I'm Hughes. The constable called. I have to see Inspector Prosser.'

Jocularity was replaced by caution—caution and courtesy. The courtesy was so marked that it could only presage disaster. Inexperienced as the three of them were, they recognized this. The courtesy was based on pity. They were that official inconvenience, the next-of-kin. No sooner had chairs been fetched for them than the same constable walked—with such delicacy as to seem to be tiptoeing—over to them to say that the inspector would see them now.

They were ushered into his room—it was an office, but with comfortable chairs. The constable was waved away and there was silence. It was like a three-guinea consultation. An operation would almost certainly be advised.

The uniformed inspector was a large, dark, rather handsome man. He viewed his three visitors carefully and said, 'You are Mr. and Mrs. Hughes?'

They sat in discomfort on the edges of the comfortable chairs, hands on knees, eager to show politeness. 'Yes,' they said, and added, 'This is Tom, our son.'

The inspector said with a calmness that was almost detached, 'It is my duty to offer you some unpleasant information. I would particularly ask for your co-operation. What I mean by that is that we may need your help—in fact, we would be glad of it. What is done is past and we cannot undo it—I only wish we could. The information concerns your daughter, Olwen Hughes. . . .'

The mother was already weeping, quietly, endlessly, not concerned with suffering silently or keeping a stiff upper lip; her emotion was total and excluded room for analysis, etiquette, or thought of others beyond Olwen. Mr. Hughes said, 'What has happened to Olwen?'

'Would you first tell me where your daughter was living?'

'At Birlchester.'

'With a Mrs. Wilson?'

'Yes.'

'Would you describe her—briefly?'

'She's got red hair,' said Tom. He knew the tense was wrong, but could not help using it; besides, there was half a minute to go before she was made officially dead.

The inspector paused, hoping for words like soothing ointment, but not finding any. There had been the tiny hope that Miss Hughes had not had red hair, and some other inspector would have had to inform some other parents. 'I have to-day received a communication from Almond Vale, which is near Birlchester,' he said, knowing it had to come slowly. They had been ready for disaster since the constable had called, but even now one could not blurt it out: murder, strangulation, the body not properly attired. . . . He said, as MacIndoe had said to Mrs. Wilson four hours earlier, 'She has been killed.'

The mother went on weeping, shaking her head from side to side. Hughes gasped 'Ooh' slowly. Tom, instead of paling, coloured slightly, and said, 'Oh, God, God, why couldn't You look after her? She was one of Yours.'

'I am so sorry,' the inspector said. 'Believe me, if there had been anything at all—any way—I'm afraid I have few particulars.' They said nothing. 'I have to have a few details. Routine.'

'Yes, yes, of course,' said Hughes.

'How old was Miss Hughes?'

'Twenty-six.'

'Has she always lived at the address with Mrs. Wilson?'

'Since she left the sanatorium.'

'She was in a sanatorium?'

'As a nurse. Then she left, see, a few years ago and went in this hairdresser's shop.'

'I'd better have the address.'

Mr. Hughes gave it.

'And was that when she went to live with Mrs. Wilson?'

'Yes.'

The inspector pressed a button on his desk and almost at once the jocular constable appeared. 'Make some tea,' said the inspector. It was brought immediately and was a small but real comfort. When they were sipping tea—the inspector deliberately leaving his untouched in a queer token of sympathy—he approached the final half of the disaster. The loss of the daughter was terrible enough, but they had to be told how she had died. The girl's integrity had to be smashed before their faces. Inspector Prosser said—as nobody was going to ask; they were too stunned—'We have reason to suppose that Miss Hughes was killed by a man— probably a young man.'

'Killed by a man?' echoed Tom. 'You mean by a car?'

'I'm afraid not,' the inspector said. 'She was killed—deliberately.'

Silence. Their faces changing from those of the bereaved to the more pitiful faces of victims. Hughes said, 'Do you mean that she was *killed*?'

'Yes,' the inspector said. 'It was not an accident or anything like that.'

Hughes, white as death, said, 'Oh, no, God, no, not my little Olwen. . . .' Tom whispered, 'Surely you don't mean murdered?' The inspector nodded. Mrs. Hughes, who had been near-silent in her tears, lifted a dreadful face and said suddenly, 'That damn' Peggy. Why couldn't she stay at home? Why couldn't it be her?

She deserved it. I'll never set foot in church again. Olwen. . . .'
She was unable to say any more.

Inspector Prosser said, 'Perhaps you'd prefer to have another talk with me later. There are a few other questions—just a few. We have to make inquiries.'

'What's the use?' Hughes said. 'What do you want to know?'

'Had your daughter any male friends? Did she mention them? Their names. . . .'

'No,' said Hughes. 'None at all.'

'She would have told me,' Mrs. Hughes said. 'She was my daughter.'

'Yes,' the inspector said. 'I didn't mean——'

'There was Stephen,' said Tom.

'Stephen?' said Hughes. 'Who was he?'

'She told me about him,' said Tom. 'He was a patient at the sanatorium. He died, of course,' he concluded bitterly.

'Did she mention anyone else? Even distantly. In another connexion perhaps. . . .'

'No. Nobody,' said the mother. 'I would know. I'll read all her letters again, but I know. Her boy was Joe, who was killed in Normandy.'

'I think that will be sufficient,' the inspector said. He pressed the button again. 'I'm dreadfully sorry about all this, Mr. and Mrs. Hughes.'

Hughes said, still polite, 'It can't be helped.'

'I'm going to order a car. It will take you home.' The constable entered and the order was given. 'Please call me—about anything,' Inspector Prosser said to Hughes. 'I'll come to see you when I have any further news.'

As they were going out, Mrs. Hughes said abruptly, 'What about Olwen? The funeral——'

The inspector tensed—it had been an ordeal for him too, despite his calmness. 'It can take place normally,' he said, stressing the last word, 'after the autopsy and the Coroner's inquest. . . . You can attend that, of course, if you wish. . . .'

His words conveyed the last ounce of reality. They—more than anyone else; more even than the doctors, the newspapers, the witnesses, the police—above all *they* could picture the scene and imagine Olwen's agony. She was going to be cut up by doctors. Why? Why? Why? What had happened to her? She would be treated like so much tripe for analysis; perhaps someone would laugh. Perhaps there would be students there who might say,

'Gosh, she's young. A bit of all right, eh?' Then she would be patched together (or would she?) and they could have her to bury. A train would have to bring the coffin. Complicated arrangements would have to be made with unknown, indifferent people. 'What kind of freight do you wish to send?'—'To take the body out of the United Kingdom you must have the consent of the Coroner and the Registrar'—'We can't do it for less than fifty quid, madam. Sorry.' Tom, who had been thinking a little romantically about revenge, knew that *he* would exact no revenge; knew also that he might be discreetly dropped by the girl he had recently met. He was as innocent as his sister, but in a murder there is a stigma of horror which makes even the innocent seem as though they have played some dreadful part.

They all walked into a sort of courtyard to the waiting car. Seagulls flapped overhead; heads peered cautiously out of windows; there would never be privacy again. They walked to the unknown and as yet not experienced misery of being the family of a girl murdered in sin because of sin; were driven to the horrors of the cynical, besieging newspaper reporters, the Sunday paper that doubled all other offers for the exclusive biography; the crime specialists who would later want details for some special book about trials or unsolved crimes; to the whispers and the silences and the stares; to the sympathy of friends, neighbours and tradesmen, all tinged with curiosity; to the questionings, the sadness, the analyses, the self-reproaches, the letters and communications, the curious at the funeral, to the death of all silence.

V

BAKER hovered in the huge dining-room of the Dragon. It was half-past two, but a few men were still eating; there was the crunch of biscuits and the rustle of *Telegraphs*. The Dragon had a dining-room like an airport or the Customs and Excise office at a major port. The whole place was too large for mere eating and drinking; how did they manage to make a profit? He saw MacIndoe come through swing doors from another part of the building. He didn't look like a policeman at all, Baker thought, remembering many senior officers who looked the part: beak noses, stern faces, a military walk and heads held well back. You might believe him to be a rate-collector or a bailiff, but even that was difficult. He had a face that was too kindly. Why doesn't he get a new raincoat? That one's absolutely filthy. I bet the Chief Constable thinks we're a couple of scruffs. Mac even walks like a grizzly bear.

MacIndoe ambled across the room. 'The manager's looked it up and there's a bus due from Almond Vale at two forty-three. We'd better wait at the bus stop outside.'

Outside, the rain had slowed down to a drizzle. It still dripped heavily from trees and the edges of buildings, but was obviously going to stop altogether within the hour. The buildings looked clean and fine; the gutters drank away all the black filth; the city had had its face washed.

They stood at a bus stop on the main road, leaving MacIndoe's car parked on the tarmac that surrounded the Dragon. They both yawned now and again; it had been a good lunch. After a few minutes a red bus appeared along the straight road. 'This'll be it,' said MacIndoe.

The bus overshot the stop and did not cease moving altogether. Maddocks jumped lightly to the pavement and turned to meet the two London detectives. He grinned. 'There must be a regulation about that.'

They all walked to MacIndoe's car. 'We've had too much to eat,' confessed MacIndoe. 'What sort of morning have you had?'

'Lousy,' said Maddocks, grimacing.

'No conviction?'

'Oh, they were convicted. I meant the court. It smells of dust and old gentlemen.'

'They all do.'

'What about you? Is it all over?'

'No,' said MacIndoe. 'Still, we had quite a useful morning.' He detailed the events of the morning to Maddocks. Maddocks then said, 'The Murphy girl may be able to confirm what Miss Barber had to say about a red car. She may even have this married man's name. Then, I suppose, it's a question of having a look at him and seeing what he's got to say.'

'Yes,' said MacIndoe. 'It may be as simple as that. And if his prints are on the camera that will be the end of that—bar the shouting.'

In MacIndoe's car they drove back along the main road towards Birlchester, reached the cinema and zigzagged the few roads to Mrs. Wilson's house. Someone moved away quickly from the ground-floor window as they approached.

Mrs. Wilson answered the door at once and led the three officers into the same parlour. She had gone to the trouble of lighting a fire in the room. In a leather armchair a girl sat uncomfortably. Dark-haired, pale-faced, wearing a black bus-conductress's uniform that fitted too tightly round her plump body; shoes dirty; rough, friendly hands. . . . She sat looking resentful, clutching a tin box, tickets and satchel. It was evident that the girl had only recently arrived, that the two females had been talking about the death of Olwen, and that this girl had been crying. Jolly, simple, kind-hearted, easy-going, MacIndoe thought; a girl who will laugh or cry easily and for anyone; likes a drink (probably of beer—she's getting fat); too generous and impulsive and careless to be a virgin; a close friend, probably, of the victim; certainly not an enemy. Her enmity would be reserved for the stuffed shirts of her world: the manager who said she was lazy, the passenger who complained of impertinence, the traffic inspector who found her arithmetic wrong; and at the first laugh she would forgive these. . . .

'This is Hazel,' said Mrs. Wilson. 'I've just been telling her what's happened.'

'What's your other name?' MacIndoe asked.

'Murphy.'

'And you live here?'

'Yes.'

'We'd like to ask you some questions,' said MacIndoe. 'There's nothing now anyone can do to help your friend Olwen, but your assistance may save some other girl.'

The girl opened her mouth but said nothing. Mrs. Wilson said, 'They've got to find him anyway; it stands to reason.'

MacIndoe ignored her words and said, 'Was Olwen a friend of yours?'

'Yes, she was.'

'How long had you known her?'

Hazel cleared her throat. 'Three years about. She was here when I came.'

'She shared accommodation with you?'

'We've got a room upstairs.'

'It's the biggest room in the house,' interrupted Mrs. Wilson.

'What sort of a girl was Olwen?'

'She was nice. Just because she was—it doesn't mean you can—but I don't suppose you'll believe me.'

'I shall believe you,' said MacIndoe gently. 'I haven't come here to criticize Olwen—you know that, don't you, Mrs. Wilson?'

'Of course,' said Mrs. Wilson. 'He's just got his job to do.'

'Well, I meant that just because she did the same sort of things as anyone else it doesn't mean that she was like—well, like me.'

'You were friendly?'

'Yes.'

'Did you go about together out of working hours?'

'When we could. She worked different hours sometimes. And then we might be too tired to go out, so we'd stay listening to the wireless.'

'Where did you go together?'

'When I finished early we'd go shopping together, or to the pictures; have some chips; once she took me to church. . . .'

'She went to church?'

'Yes.'

'By herself?'

'Yes. I only went once.'

'Did you go dancing?'

'Sometimes.'

'Olwen also?'

'No, not Olwen. I couldn't get her to go.'

'Why not? Didn't she dance? Or perhaps she didn't drink. Was that it?'

'She wouldn't drink in a pub. I like to dance and I like to meet the chaps and have a beer. Olwen—she didn't mix easily. Like I told you—she was nice—better than me.'

'Do you mean she was shy? She thought the chaps were—rough?'

'Something like that.'

'Didn't she have a boy friend?'

'She hadn't had one for ages.'

'Until when?'

'Until March 17th.'

'What makes you remember that date?'

'I'm Irish,' said Hazel. 'It's St. Patrick's Day, and I remember on that day Olwen came home and said she'd met someone.'

'Whom had she met?'

'I don't know. She wouldn't tell me.'

'But you know now, don't you?'

'No.'

'She met him in March and it's now July. Oh, come, Miss Murphy, you're more feminine than that.'

'I only know it was Roy.'

'Didn't she tell you his surname?'

'She didn't tell me anything.'

'How did you find out?'

'She'd put it in her diary.'

'*What* did she put in her diary?'

'Something about how she'd met "R.", and that he was a traveller.'

'He was a traveller?'

'Yes.'

'For whom?'

'I don't know.'

'Did you look in the diary?'

The girl blushed. 'Yes.'

MacIndoe smiled. 'I'm glad you did. Tell us about this "R."'

'I don't know his surname. But it *can't* be him. Olwen said he was going to marry her.'

'You didn't read it in the diary?'

'I don't know.'

'I mean, she did talk a bit about him, didn't she? What did she say?'

'She said weeks ago that he wanted to marry her, and would when his wife died. . . .'

'When his wife *what*?'

There was a shocked silence as the girl realized the implication of her own words. 'Oh, but he didn't mean anything like that. His wife was insane, Olwen said, and had been for over a year. I said he ought to get a divorce—you know, because his wife was nuts—but Olwen said No, she was ill and would die.'

'Did she die?'

'I don't know. Olwen never said.'

'What was the wife's name?'

'I don't know.'

'Her address?'

'No. I don't know that.'

'Which asylum was she in?'

'Olwen never talked about it.'

'Where does this Roy work?'

'I don't know.'

'Wasn't that in the diary?'

'No. Except that he was a traveller.'

'Did he ever come here?'

'No.'

'Has he a car?'

'Yes.'

'What colour?'

'Red. It's a sports car.'

'Have you ever seen it?'

'No; but Olwen told me.'

'What did she say about it?'

'I can't remember. I know she told me. They went for picnics sometimes on her half-day off.'

'On Tuesdays?'

'Yes.'

'They always met on Tuesdays?'

'Nearly always. I think she sometimes met him on a Sunday. He had to see his wife at the asylum then. She'd stopped going to church.'

'Do you know why?'

'I can guess.'

'Did she ever tell you?'

'No.'

'Why do you think she stopped?'

'It's not up to me to say.'

'What were Olwen's relations with this Roy?'

'I don't know,' Hazel said excitedly. 'It's not fair. She's dead. You mustn't——'

Maddocks said, 'She was in love with him?'

'She must have been.'

'They were going to get married?'

'Yes.'

'Do you know where?'

'No. Birlchester somewhere.'

'Then he lives in Birlchester?'

'He must do.'

'Why do you say that?'

'If he visited his wife . . .'

Maddocks said with gentleness, 'What did you read in the diary? Don't be ashamed to tell us. We realize that Miss Hughes was—tricked.'

'It said a lot about God and forgiveness. She was religious. There was something about temporal love and eternity. I didn't understand. You see, I've never loved—— And then there was some poetry—about breasts.'

'When were these entries made?'

'Oh, about May and June. I haven't seen it for at least six weeks.

She locked it up in her case. Besides, after that, I didn't like to look. It wasn't like—a bit of fun.'

Maddocks said, 'Is this house on the telephone?'

Mrs. Wilson said, 'No.'

'Did Miss Hughes receive letters?'

'Quite often.'

'Where did they come from?'

'They came from Wales.'

'All of them?'

'I don't know,' said Hazel.

'She had some from Birlchester,' Mrs. Wilson said.

'From Peggy,' Hazel suggested.

'Some were typed,' said Mrs. Wilson.

Maddocks said, 'Were the envelopes from any company or society or anything like that?'

'I think they were just plain envelopes,' said Mrs. Wilson, 'but they *were* typed.'

'How many of these typed letters were there?'

'I can only remember one or two.'

'Did either of you see the contents? Please be honest—it would help.'

'No,' said Hazel. 'I didn't even know——'

'I saw one once,' said Mrs. Wilson. 'It was lying on the dressing-table. As it was typed, I thought it must be for me. But there was nothing in it.'

'The envelope was empty?'

'No. I mean it just said, "I can't come on Tuesday. I've got to go to Bristol," and it was signed "R."'

'What was his address?'

'There wasn't one.'

'Not even the town?'

'No. Just the day. Friday. It was ten weeks ago at least. . . .'

MacIndoe said, 'Did Miss Hughes ever describe the man?'

Hazel stared. 'Do you mean you don't know anything about him?'

'No. Why should we? Who is going to tell us if you don't? Mrs. Harper doesn't know him; the girls in her shop do not; Mrs. Wilson here has never seen him——'

'Well, I have,' said Hazel.

'You've met him? She introduced him?'

'No. Not exactly that. They were in a cinema and when the lights came on I saw Olwen with him.'

'Was that the only time you ever saw him?' In a poor light, thought MacIndoe, but better that than nothing.

'Yes,' said Hazel. 'He was talking to Olwen. I didn't like to interrupt—they seemed so happy.'

'What did the man look like?'

'Well, that's what I mean. I can't believe—because he looked really nice—a gentleman. Even the way he sat was sort of—distinguished. And his clothes.'

'What was he wearing?'

'He'd still got his overcoat on—it was a long time ago,' explained Hazel. 'It was a brown tweed—heavy and expensive.'

'How tall was he?'

'A head taller than Olwen.'

'Was he as young as she?'

'No. Over thirty, I should say.'

'What colour eyes?'

'Brown, I think. His hair was brown.'

'Was his complexion good?'

'How do you mean?'

'Was it fresh? Had he a good colour? A smooth skin? Or did he have skin trouble of any sort? Blotches or pimples?'

'He had a brownish complexion—sallow, d'you call it?'

'What was his build?'

'I don't know. He'd got his overcoat on. I don't think he was fat. Of course, I was some rows off, but naturally I was curious because Olwen had said it might be serious. I couldn't blame her.' Hazel's voice faltered. 'If only——'

'What about his facial expression?'

'His expression?'

'Had he any jowls, heavy creases, birthmarks, large lips or deformities?'

Hazel smiled wanly. 'I only saw him side-faced. He'd rather a small face—wedge-shaped. There were sort of hollows under each cheekbone. He hadn't got any marks or anything.'

'What shaped ears?'

'I don't know. Does it matter? Big ones, I think.'

'Every detail matters if we've no name, Miss Murphy. What about his nose?'

'Sort of beakish. Aristocratic.'

'Did he have any characteristic walk or gestures?'

'I didn't see him walk. He waved his hands about a lot—rather slowly.'

Mrs. Wilson said, 'Good Lord. All these questions after a day's work. Give the kid a break.'

MacIndoe smiled. 'I'm sorry. We were rather going it. Would you like to show us now which were Olwen's things?'

'All right,' said Hazel nervously. It was obvious she hadn't yet visited the room she'd shared with the dead girl.

'I'll put a kettle on,' said Mrs. Wilson. 'You come and have a cup of tea while they're having a look.'

As the detectives mounted the stairs behind the girl MacIndoe said, 'Ye've been a fine help, Miss Murphy. Are ye quite sure now that your friend did not have any *other* male friends?'

'No; none at all.'

'Did she ever say she had been followed by anybody?'

'No.'

'Did she ever receive threats from any man? Did she jilt anyone?'

'No. I'm sure nothing like that happened. Honestly, she treated everyone the same—with kindness.'

'Yes. I believe you.'

They had reached the landing, and the girl fumbled nervously at the particular door, her mouth open in protest. The room they entered was, as Mrs. Wilson had said, quite large; it was threadbare, but clean. There was a large, faded pink carpet on the floor, an old dressing-table and chest of drawers, an electric fire, a gasring, a cumbersome old wardrobe and two single beds. On the chest of drawers were some books, including the New Testament. That's hers, MacIndoe thought, meaning Olwen's. The books were a mixed lot: a nurse's dictionary, *Pride and Prejudice*, *Gone With the Wind*, the poems of Shelley, the poems of St. John of the Cross, some romantic novels and some pocket mystery books. The windows were closed and the room was musty. A few saucepans were stacked inside each other by the gas-ring and there was some cutlery by the chest of drawers.

'Where were Olwen's things kept?'

'She had the chest of drawers.'

'You have the dressing-table?'

'Yes.'

'How about the wardrobe?'

'We shared it.'

'Would ye mind getting her things out of the wardrobe?'

The girl opened the wardrobe and withdrew three frocks, a spring overcoat, three pairs of shoes, some undies and some dirty handkerchiefs. These she laid across one of the two beds. 'Her bed?'

MacIndoe queried, and Hazel was only able to nod. From the top of the wardrobe she pulled down a yellow suitcase. 'This was hers too. It's locked.'

'One other thing,' said MacIndoe. 'Have a skim through your own stuff to see if ye've by accident got any of hers—ye know, letters, bills, photographs. . . . Then we can be sure. . . .'

While the girl did this MacIndoe watched her. The two other officers stood about awkwardly, Baker gazing through the window to the road below, Maddocks examining the ceiling. Hazel said, 'There's nothing.' A pause while she blew her nose. 'Shall I wait?'

'No,' said MacIndoe. 'You have your tea, lassie.' The girl sniffed. 'And try not to be upset. Think of it this way: Olwen's disillusion-ment didn't last long—only a few minutes of terrible unhappiness —it probably seemed quite unreal.'

As soon as the girl had left the three officers became busy. They looked through the chest of drawers, examined the pockets of the clothes, and even stripped the late girl's bed in case anything had been put under the mattress. In the chest of drawers was a box which had originally contained stationery. Inside it MacIndoe found a bundle of letters tied up with pink ribbon. Some other letters were also there, not tied up and having different handwritings on the envelopes. As well as the letters the box contained a regimental cap badge, a cheap, tarnished brooch in the shape of a lighthouse, some lavender and a few sea-shells. Inside the books was the name Olwen Hughes and the year each had been bought: she had pur-chased *Pride and Prejudice* in 1949, *Gone With the Wind* in 1953, and the New Testament had the same rounded feminine hand-writing, only younger, the year being 1944. Inside the works of Shelley was the inscription *He says it so much better than I can, Stephen*, and the year, 1950.

MacIndoe moved the frocks and sat suddenly on the bed. 'This is a damn' long day,' he explained. 'Ye mustn't think I'm callous. I'm awful tired.' He stretched his feet along the bed and settled down to read the letters.

Baker said, 'The case is locked.'

'Ye have my full permission to open it.'

MacIndoe untied the ribbon and examined the letters. He saw in disappointment that they were postmarked in 1944 and had been sent to the address in Wales which he had already been given. The first one was written from a military camp in Bar Quay and read:

Baker said in excitement, 'The girl was right about March 17th, sir. The man's a traveller who called when "Mrs. H." was out. Later she mentions the red car, the mad wife; they even had lunch at the Dragon.'

'Oh, no, this is too easy,' protested MacIndoe. 'That was where we went. We must go again, obviously. Let me read my last letter, Tony, and then we'll sort through the diary.'

The letter had been written in January, 1945, and seemed more formal than the others:

DEAR MISS OLWEN,

I am sorry I have not wrote before, but it has taken me weeks to get the address. And what I have to give you is bad news, which you may have had already.

It is with regret that I have to tell you that Joe has been lost. I nearly had it myself as you can see by the address. [MacIndoe looked—the letter came from a German prisoner-of-war camp.] We was on patrol ahead of the others when a Tiger come out of a yard. Joe was killed instant. I ran for it but some of 'em on motor-bikes caught me and two more blokes. We was lucky not to be killed.

It's not bad here. I hope this letter reaches you safe, even censored, because it is only right that you should know. I always remember that night of the dance, you and Joe scared to death. He was very fond of you, you know, quite different from your friend and me. (Give her my regards, won't you?) Chin up, Miss Olwen, because Joe never knew nothing. No pain and that. And I suppose it was you he did it for. He had no folks. He was a good kid, but the good die young as they say. The older ones have got more sense.

Believe me, I am,

Yours Very Faithfully,

HARRY COXHAM

The Tiger tank and the marked passages of Shelley. 'She says to me—I'll never forget it—"You're the salt of the earth, Mrs. Wilson," and blushed because she hadn't meant to say it.' She bought the New Testament in 1944 when the boy died. It was one of war's little jokes that one should be inveigled into believing that one had found something perfect and perhaps immortal, only to be shown that in the face of chemical and exploding steel it was not. 'Did they say what sort of a girl she was?' No, they had not explained that. They were unaware that she was exceptional beyond the statistically remarkable fact of the way she had died. They said they were sorry to do this, but your name was at the top of the rota. They had an idea that the case would be difficult and sordid; it might prove to be interesting; but it was not within their experience that it should be beautiful. 'Don't you know about yourself? Hasn't anyone ever told you? Why aren't you conceited?' Yes, why weren't you conceited? You would have lived if you had been. If you had been conceited you would have been aware that a beautiful girl is always a protagonist in a battle for her own destruction; and you would have fought with your brain while you made surrenders with your heart. 'The good die young. The older ones have got more sense.' Sense meaning cunning, of course. Cunning is not beautiful; it knows nothing of tenderness or passion or humility or even anger; but it makes sure of the contraceptives; it has solicitors; it wants to know particulars of addresses and salaries and wives who are in asylums. . . . I must find this man, MacIndoe thought. It's an affront to all those things I believe in that I should allow the possibility of his meeting another innocent girl without conceit and destroying her in a similar fashion.

The diary was a larger volume than MacIndoe had anticipated. Each page measured about a foot in length and was nine inches in width. It was too large to be carried in a handbag, which no doubt explained why it had neither passed into the possession of the murderer nor been found at the copse. It also explained why there were no diaries for the previous years: this one was the New Year's gift (no doubt to Mrs. Harper's business) of a chemical company. It could have been a gift from the murderer—although he didn't seem to like the written word—who might have been a traveller of that company, but MacIndoe knew that it was not, for the entries began, not on March 17th, but on the first day of the year. The early entries were short and trivial—letters from home, films she'd seen, meetings with Peggy and others with Hazel. From the day she had met the traveller the entries were lengthier; the ones for each Tuesday were so long that they tended to overflow into the spaces for Wednesdays. MacIndoe studied the entries with care. Everyone the girl knew would be questioned closely, and it did not follow that this Roy was the murderer, but MacIndoe certainly wished to interview him.

The advantage of the diary was that it recorded the events, irrespective of their distortion. The girl was not used to deception;

she'd got to put down the truth somewhere, and here it all was. Even if ninety per cent. of what the man had said was untrue, the girl did not lie: she put it all down in love and good faith so that it disturbed one to read it, knowing what it led to. In addition, she put down the small, hard facts that policemen can work on. MacIndoe noted every tiny, available one. The man had lied from the very first moment—the story was too familiar to doubt that— but he couldn't lie in a vacuum. He'd told his lies in the Dragon, at the Priory Tea Rooms, in a 'small inn in Brownhill', in a red sports car, in the 'Queen's in the city', somewhere where they went dancing—and all these places could be visited. It only needed one single person who knew him to have seen him once with the red-haired girl as they travelled about, ate in restaurants, danced or walked. The man had cunning. He'd been aware of the necessity of being anonymous from the start. Mrs. Wilson had never seen the man: 'She was ashamed of him, or ashamed of *us*'—whichever it was you could be sure the man had agreed readily to Olwen's arrangements that she wasn't taken home. In addition to physical places the man had mentioned, he had had to give some account of himself. No doubt in her love the girl had longed for details. He had a wife called Evelyn who was in an accident and insane. That had a ring of truth, or why should he have admitted to being married at all? He said he had been a pilot who had dropped mines in the Kiel Canal. He'd obtained an order for 150 gross (what of? soap?) from Birrell's. That might give him away. 'R. had to go to Bristol to-day.' That tiny fact might eventually prove some-thing. Olwen kept talking about the twelve months they were to wait. What twelve months? Has the wife only that long to live— until next March? After her last visit to Wales the girl had written, 'I had to be on guard against those who, loving me possessively, wished to hear about my every activity.' So her parents don't know about Roy even now. What bitter news for them. And no informa-tion for *me* from the Welsh police. 'R. is funny—he makes me use typed, addressed envelopes.' Why? I wonder. As Olwen said, who would the landlady make trouble with if she did open a letter, since the wife is mad? I've got a feeling that there is no wife; she was there as an excuse ready for when he decided to abandon Olwen. Perhaps Olwen began to plead for marriage and he ex-plained (very skilfully, no doubt: he'd had previous experience of explanations) that they couldn't be married because the (non-existent) mad wife showed signs of recovery or at least of survival. Then comes the day when Olwen, with the fluttering gift of new life inside her, says that a decision must be made. She explains why and repeats what she put down in the diary, that she did not wish to kill the baby. And so he kills both of them.

'Like I told you—she was nice—better than me.' Hazel appreciated that your love had a quality different to her own. Joe felt the same sort of awe: 'I feel ugly and afraid beside you.' And you were only sixteen then, Olwen. He must have looked at your serious, virtuous face and realized that it wasn't the same as others he'd known or wanted to know. 'I'm glad you stopped me loving you'—but he hadn't stopped loving you; on the contrary, his love had developed. When you were a child Leslie wrote: 'Nothing will ever be the same.' He was wrong, for you kept his brooch for more than twelve years. You had the quality of compassion and they were all in awe of it—except R. You must have been a good nurse with your pity, the sort who continued her kindnesses off duty. Like you did for Stephen. You didn't really love him, did you? You wanted to show mercy to him, the compassion that in a beautiful girl leads to disaster if someone abuses it. Saints and nurses shouldn't be beautiful. Stephen couldn't help noticing that. 'You don't use lipstick and your lips have little lines, like the grains in wood. . . . No doubt your shoulders and legs have the same perfection.' Aye. Even I couldn't help seeing that you'd been a bonny girl.

I like ye verra much, Olwen. I'm glad I met ye in the first person, and didn't collect all my opinions from others. Tony says he thinks he would have liked ye too. I wish ye could have met him. He's a fine boy. He's a big, blond, honest-looking lad, about your age, and he didn't eat very much breakfast after he'd seen your lithe, dead body. He's still young enough to believe beautiful people can never be killed. Like you, Olwen, although ye had pity for the ugly also. When Tony reads your diary he's going to be angry. It's not a good thing for a policeman to be angry; he loses his impartiality; but I shan't blame him. Ye musta been a fine girl, Olwen, but ye were foolish. Ye shouldn't have read *Gone With the Wind*. It makes romance out of something that more probably wouldn't have been romantic. Ye should have read your own diary before ye went out of the house that day. Don't ye see, it conveys the story of your own destruction? Notice how lightheartedly and with what tenderness ye started out, and with what despair ye ended. Notice that when it's written down one sees all too clearly that it's a trick; the man's intentions become obvious quite quickly. 'I go about sighing and smiling to myself; I have to lower my gaze in buses and pretend to take an interest in hair styles for fat ladies. And all the time I think of him.' I know what ye thought— all tenderness and gentility. I have a wife who's still like that. She's forty-six years old and still shy. She would have liked ye. 'I had to slap R.'s face!' Ye thought in your charity that he was just being foolish and excited. 'He said something about how the war and Evelyn's illness had destroyed all his religion.' Ye should have known then. A man's religion is not destroyed by adversity; on the contrary, he clings to it all the more tightly. Didn't he ever go to church to pray for this wife of his? On the train a few weeks later ye lose your control over him. He insists and ye can't stop him. 'It's a marvel I wasn't scared, but then, despite his eagerness, I trust him.' Oh, lassie, didn't ye know what the sherry and the first-class compartment were for? But I suppose all lovers, innocent as well as guilty, want privacy. 'He longs to possess me and is even showing slight impatience at my arguments.' What arguments? Were ye still going to church at the time? 'I had the feeling I would have had to quarrel to stop him.' He was very impatient, wasn't he? But only for your body, Olwen, not for your love. He already had that. And so ye went on to surrender and the diary begins to record your unhappiness. 'I sometimes cry, but heaven knows what about.' He wasn't unhappy, though, was he? He always had his own way after that. I'm afraid your friend Peggy was right. If it was a thing ye couldn't tell your mother about ye must have known it was wrong. Did ye know, I wonder?—did ye begin to see that if one half is ugly the whole cannot be made beautiful?

Ye will have to excuse me reading your letters and diary. Ye needn't be embarrassed. Ye won't see me—policemen don't go to Heaven—they're not needed there. Ye have been a great help to me. Ye see, this description ye have given me of the man ye loved tells me what sort of a man he was. I play the record in reverse and the music is no longer sweet: it comes out bitter and discordant. Ye know now he was exactly the reverse of what he persuaded ye to believe. Ye see that? Ye see the trick? His enormous advantage was that he looked the lie. Your friend Hazel confirms that. He looked distinguished. They don't usually. Ugliness comes into their faces when they're granted the surrender they seek. Ye were very unlucky. But why didn't ye put down the name of his company, Olwen, or his surname, or the number of his car? Anything. Ye can't love an initial. Ye see, he may even get away with it. Hazel's given a good physical description: he has to move about, and so does his red car; and we'll be looking for him. But it's possible he may evade us. I am a pretty good detective, but partly because the average man does not want to commit murder. He does it in a rage and grief and without premeditation, and even if his nerves don't make him surrender, he leaves evidence behind for us. . . . But this man from the very first moment he met ye was deceiving ye, and through ye, me. I don't like it, Olwen. It suggests callousness, premeditation. But I may be wrong. Ye will know now. Ye know the very best and worst of him. Perhaps he is suffering acutely now. Perhaps he has already surrendered, thrown himself on our mercy. In any case, my estimation of ye is that ye will have forgiven him. But I can't do that, Olwen. I am not supposed to have any opinion; I only have to find him; and that I still intend to do.

VI

AT Mrs. Harper's. Women hanging about, mouths open, one of them weeping. Resentful stares—as though the police were responsible for the crime. Both assistants looking absolutely exhausted. Mrs. Harper chain-smoking: the over-sweet atmosphere as thick as that in a pursued submarine. 'Oh, God,' she protested. 'You again.' No signs of compassion at all. All that pushed out of the way. The resentment genuine now. (Oh, God, in whom I unfortunately have not the emotional capacity to believe, why did You let this girl be killed and cause all this inconvenience to *me*?)

MacIndoe said, 'We have reason to believe Miss Hughes knew a man who was a traveller.' He waved a hand to stop Mrs. Harper's impending protest. 'He must have called *here*, because it happened on March 17th, which was a Thursday. In other words, he called on what I take it—correct me if I'm mistaken—was for Miss Hughes a working day. In addition, we understand he's about thirty, probably more, has a red sports car, is tall and rather dark, gives an impression of being perhaps upper middle-class, has the Christian name Roy. . . .'

Mrs. Harper took two aspirins. 'I've got a headache. I can't think about anything. You do it. I'm tired. Who told you all that?'

'We can't go into that. The point is, do you know him?'

'No,' said Mrs. Harper. 'I've been thinking—when they've let me—about travellers. They're all middle-aged. None of them use sports cars.'

'You are referring to regular callers, I presume,' MacIndoe pointed out. 'What about men who have called and had their stuff rejected? This man certainly seems to have only made the one call.'

'It's possible,' said Mrs. Harper. 'But the only young man I can remember in months was a blond boy, about twenty-five, cheeky, came in a black Ford. I soon threw him out.'

'Who else would attend to travellers? Olwen?'

'Whoever it was would have referred them to me,' Mrs. Harper explained. 'None of my staff can turn away a traveller—they all see me.'

Bowler back on head, back through the small crowd. 'All right. We'll leave you to brood on it.'

'I shan't be able to do much else, shall I? It'll be wonderful for business—everybody'll be in. My God, she wasn't worth this much fuss.'

At Birrell's. The smell of bacon and cheese. A machine slicing the bacon. A child eating a biscuit. Four or five women waiting about, shoulders sagging. One of them pretty and very upright. Pregnant. She'll be sagging soon. A man saying, like a ritual, 'How about sauces? We've Worcester, tomato, brown, sweet pickle——'

A man wearing glasses, white face heavily creased, exhausted after the years of selling things for the stomach. The manager.

'Good afternoon.'

'Good afternoon. We're police officers investigating a murder.'

The inevitable, unbearable silence. Heads turning. Only the child, too young to know the word, continuing to eat. 'Oh,' said the manager, while behind him every one of his staff looked and listened without pretence. The customers could wait and did so willingly. The pregnant girl's eyes widened in horror. Like Olwen's, MacIndoe thought. 'We are anxious to interview a man who is a traveller. He is known to have called here on Tuesday, March 22nd, and obtained an order for a hundred and fifty gross—I do not know what of.'

'I see,' said the manager slowly. Raising his voice, 'Fetch the books for March, and stop gaping.'

The man who had been slicing bacon left the machine and presently approached with two heavy books. 'Soon tell you,' the manager said. 'We keep a record of everything. Damned income tax and auditors and ministries—you have to know where you are. March 22nd, did you say?'

'Yes, March 22nd.'

'I'm sorry. We didn't give any orders on March 22nd.'

'Nothing at all?'

'No. Are you sure about the day?'

'Absolutely sure.' (I can trust Olwen.) 'It was a Tuesday.'

The manager thumbed a calendar. 'Yes, Tuesday it was.'

'Have you other branches?'

'No.'

It didn't make sense. Olwen had written it down, and not an hour ago Hazel had told them, before they left Mrs. Wilson's house, that it was the place where she had obtained her groceries. She wasn't likely to forget that. MacIndoe bit a thumb-nail. The customers and staff waited to hear what he would say.

'Just possibly,' he said, 'the traveller didn't obtain an order, or the witness was misinformed. This man we wish to interview has a red sports car. He is tall, darkish, well-dressed, about thirty-five, probably good-looking.'

'I don't know him. I've never heard of a man using a sports car for *work*.'

A girl approached. About twenty, tall, a heavy, rounded body, long, slow-moving limbs, full breasts. Her face very pale, but not without sensuality. 'Excuse me, Mr. Belcher.'

'What is it, Miss Young?'

'A man did come to see you in a red sports car. It was several months ago.'

She was acutely uncomfortable. MacIndoe wondered why. Perhaps she didn't like to admit recalling such a man: it would imply that she had carried the thought of him for months. That might be an act of disloyalty to someone. MacIndoe looked at the girl. It was easy to imagine 'R.' staring at her in admiration, not caring for the moment about Olwen in the car outside. Perhaps 'R.' couldn't resist using his charm on every attractive face. He would soon find out.

'In March?' he asked.

'It might have been.'

'Did you see his car?'

'Yes, out of the window, like we can see yours.'

'What colour was it?'

'Scarlet.'

'Was there a girl inside it?'

'I couldn't see. I think it was raining that day, and there were yellow sort of windows—celluloid, I think—as well as the hood.'

196

'You didn't observe the number?'
'Oh, I didn't notice anything like that.'
'What made you notice at all?'
She blushed.
'Was he good-looking?'
'Yes,' she whispered.
'Did he speak to you?'
'Only for a minute.'
'What did he say?'
'Something cheeky.'
'What was it he said?'
'Oh, "Hello, beautiful," or something like that. Then something about peaches.'
'He sold tinned fruit?'
'No. He never said what he sold. I was stacking tins of peaches and he said something about one peach looking after the others.'
'I see.' (And you've carried the memory of that for four months and five days.) 'What happened then?'
'He saw Mr. Riley.'
'Is Mr. Riley here?'
'Not now. He's dead.'
'He retired,' said the manager, 'and died soon afterwards.'
'Did the man give any indication of what he was selling?'
'Not to me.'
'Has he ever been again?'
'No.'
'Have you ever seen him again?'
A sigh. 'No.'

At the Priory Tea Rooms. Built in 1928, it gave the impression of having been erected three hundred years earlier. Black and white outside; more pseudo-beams inside. A pitiful attempt at antiquity: little horse-brasses above the fireplace, crossed swords and a shield on one wall, a nineteenth-century oil of Shakespeare on another. Sea-shells and oil lamps: the centuries incredibly confused. (Stratford-on-Avon was in an adjacent county. Small plates celebrated this fact expensively. There was always the possibility that Americans, exhausted after innumerable traffic jams, would seek the black-and-white café before moving on to the hotel bars in Birlchester.) At the moment rather crowded, mostly with ladies of the middle age and class. The absolute certainty that they would not be provided with a solid meal. Nevertheless, it was after five o'clock and the three detectives decided to stay. It was a relief to sit down. People had a tendency to keep police officers standing, and as these inquiries went on all day it meant tired feet and backs.

There was only one waitress. Middle-aged, dignified, slightly harassed and thrown into a panic when, after tea, MacIndoe said, 'We'd like to speak to the manageress.'

The old parchment face blushed in resentment. People looked round. Even Shakespeare appeared perturbed. 'Wasn't the tea satisfactory?'

'Quite satisfactory. We are police officers.'

'Oh, dear,' said the waitress, all of a tremble. 'Oh, dear.' She went away and they could hear her calling, 'Gertrude, are you there?' She returned to the table, viewed the detectives with horror, and said, 'My sister will see you now. Will you come?'

Behind the café the rooms did not dispute their lack of antiquity. They were all very much twentieth-century: ovens, typewriters, a telephone, chairs that stacked into each other's laps, a potato-chipping machine, steam, gas, electricity and dirt. Behind a desk in one room sat the waitress's sister, Gertrude. Tall, angular, bony, she gave an impression of intelligence, almost of scholarship. 'You wished to see me?'

'Yes,' said MacIndoe, 'and possibly your sister also.'

The waitress hovered reluctantly. MacIndoe produced the photographs of Olwen Hughes and passed them to the bony sister. 'Have you ever seen this girl?'

She put on a pair of spectacles. 'Yes, I think I have.'

'Where have you seen her?'

She thought for a moment. 'I remember. She works at a hairdresser's along the road. She did my hair once. A pleasant girl.'

'Have you ever seen her in here?'

'Oh, no, definitely not, because I don't see the customers. I do the ordering, the cooking and—organizing.'

'Perhaps your sister?'

The waitress examined the photographs. 'She had auburn hair,' MacIndoe said.

She didn't want anything to do with it. 'No. I mean, we're respectable people. We've never been involved with the—— Besides, why can't you ask the girl herself?'

'She's dead.'

They both said, '*Dead!*'

'She was murdered,' said MacIndoe. 'Are ye sure——?'

The waitress stared at the photographs for some time. 'I can't

be sure. It's such a long time ago. You say she had red hair?'
'Yes. Fine red—auburn.'
'I believe she did come in for tea once. But it was a long time ago.'
'Who was with her?'
'A man with a case. How funny. I remember *that* quite clearly.
He had a leather briefcase—thick and with a gold-coloured lock.
It got in the way of my feet.'
'Were there any initials on it?'
'I don't know.'
'Did you see the contents?'
'Papers. It was thick with them.'
'What sort of papers?'
'I can't say. Just papers. Like a file. I remember—the case had
compartments and these were labelled alphabetically.'
'You're doing very well. Anything else?'
'No. I'm sorry. It was a shiny case—very expensive, I should
think.'
'Do you know who the man was?'
'No.'
'Had you seen him before—or since?'
'No.'
'Can you describe him?'
'Not very well. He was young and well-dressed. Tall, I believe.
Very talkative—you know—excitable.'
'Did he come in a car?'
'We can't see the street from the café.'
'You can see the main road.'
'Yes; but they can't park there. They have to go down Clifford
Avenue.'
'*We've* parked there.'
'Well, you shouldn't. The police . . .' She giggled nervously.
'We'd better move on, then,' said MacIndoe. 'Thank you for
your help. We may ask you to identify this man later.' A few
female voices were complaining, 'Waitress, waitress!' MacIndoe
said, 'I'm sorry to have come when you're busy.'
He was walking away with Baker and Maddocks when the
woman pleaded faintly, 'The bill!'

At the Birlchester Mental Hospital. Twelve miles from the Priory
Tea Rooms. It had been until recently more or less in the country-
side. Now industrial Birlchester encroached. A long line of houses
being built on the other side of the road—probably for the staff.

In the distance a crane operating. Pipes laid along the lane—it was still a lane—ready for the installation of sewage or water. An old man lighting a fire on an allotment. He yawned. The realization by MacIndoe that he, too, was tired. The afternoon was warm in its collapse. Constable clouds moving majestically across a light blue sky. The asylum itself and its surrounding wall of ugly red brick slightly mellowed by dirt and age. Surrounded and darkened by many tall trees. Not altogether unpleasant. Formalities at the gate. A uniformed man approaching the car. 'Who d'you want?' —'We are police officers'—'You wanna see the Superintendent?'— 'Yes'—'Will you park over there? I'll get someone to attend to you.'

Led by another uniformed man along asphalt paths, through gates and doors—keys to unlock and relock all the way—past dustbins, parked bicycles and two cars, across a courtyard. Nobody about. 'It's very quiet,' commented Baker. The man shrugged—a suggestion of insolence. (What d'y'want 'em to be doing? Pastoral dances?) He said, 'Recreation time. They like to read the magazines and play draughts same as the patients in any other hospital.'

In the Superintendent's office. Everything very solid—the woodwork, the chairs, the desk, the stone window frames, even the Superintendent himself, an enormous man. The man who had brought them said, 'Shall I wait, sir?' A faint smile on the Superintendent's face. 'No, don't wait, Evans. I'll ring.'

Introductions by MacIndoe. 'Three of you,' the large man said. 'It must be very serious.'

'It is,' said MacIndoe. 'It is a case of murder.'

The other Superintendent pulled a pipe from a pocket and bit on it like a bulldog. 'Then I don't think it's us. I really don't. Of course, many patients who have their freedom are still not strong in the head. But nobody violent has been released, and nobody has escaped. . . .'

'It's nothing like that,' said MacIndoe. 'We're anxious to interview a man, but we don't know his name. What we *do* know is that his wife, who has the Christian name Evelyn, is insane as the result of an accident about two years ago. She may also be physically ill in another way.'

'Then she won't be here,' said the Superintendent. 'But I know you'll want to have our Evelyns checked.'

Twenty minutes later all the patients had been accounted for. 'I'm sorry,' the Superintendent said. 'I would have liked to have helped.'

MacIndoe grimaced wryly. 'I appreciate what you have done. You have helped—by elimination.'

'There are other hospitals you should approach, of course,' the large man said. 'Apart from private premises, she may be at St. Catherine's or an in-patient at the Nerve Hospital. Do you know where they are?'

'I do,' said Maddocks.

The Superintendent rang a bell and soon the uniformed man appeared. 'I hope you find her—and him,' said the Superintendent. 'Murder's a terrible thing. I shall be anxious until the case is concluded.'

Another wry smile. 'We shall too,' MacIndoe commented.

At St. Catherine's Hospital. Another journey of seven miles to reach it. It was an enormous, impressive, recently built, pink-stoned building—like a skyscraper placed sideways. The drive was a quarter of a mile long—so long that at two intervals were shelters and seats for the old and the tired. (The blind visited the blind, the half-dead the almost dead. They always are old and tired, MacIndoe thought. Old and tired, but never embittered so long as someone is kind enough to listen to their stories. The same applied to their relatives inside.) There was a great deal of grass—everything made attractive, but you could not hide the fact that it was a hospital and a busy one. Nearer the large buildings lines of cream ambulances waited, a few men smoked cigarettes. A crowd of nurses came streaming off duty. Glaring white uniforms in the sun, with a blood-red cross on each chest. They all talked excitedly and in their laughter showed the vitality of youth. They all had honest, straightforward faces—like *hers*, MacIndoe thought, although not so extraordinarily beautiful. I like nurses, he decided. They work hard and have a strong sense of duty. I like all the people in the world who do the worthwhile things.

All the entrances were enormous—one could have laid a railway through each—except the one the detectives sought. The door labelled 'Inquiries' was ridiculously small and inconspicuous—MacIndoe could well imagine the about-to-be-bereaved making inquiry after inquiry at the wrong entrances, exhaustion and panic accumulating. It's a silly entrance for visitors, he thought; an afterthought, where they put the cat out each night. A porter listened to what MacIndoe had to say and directed him along a corridor—it seemed to stretch to infinity. Coloured lights flickered above his head as he walked along the shiny, polished floor: it was like an airport or a heliograph training school. Stairs led off at each side to various wards, X-ray rooms, operating theatres. . . . Half-way along the polished corridor some men in pyjamas sat at a counter drinking tea and talking with the wild excitement that indicates nervous relief.

The almoner's office was quite small and comfortable. She was not available, so the three detectives sat down to wait while her secretary signalled all over the hospital. She was reached eventually in a surgical ward, and soon afterwards appeared in her own office armed with papers and books. The almoner was a woman in her early thirties—intelligent, courteous, shrewd, but with a Giotto-innocent face. She listened to what MacIndoe said and was willing to help him. But the system defeated her. There was no quick way of finding Evelyns.

'No categorization by type of illness?' queried MacIndoe.

'I'm afraid not. Alphabetical order—surnames only. Of course,' said the almoner, 'we could visit the Mental Wards; but the chances are they won't remember the Christian name.'

'Well, can you let me know to-morrow?'

'Why not wait?' she said. 'If you're prepared to wait, we'll look the names up for you.'

They waited an hour. At the end of this period the almoner announced, 'One only. The other two Evelyns I discovered were maternity. The one in Mental was Evelyn Chloe St. Erskine.'

'*Was?*' queried MacIndoe.

'Removed to a private asylum in Worcestershire,' quoted the almoner. 'She left in August last year.'

'Who's her next-of-kin?'

'Her parents.'

'No husband?'

'No.'

'Thank you for wasting your time,' said MacIndoe. 'I'm afraid you did, although even elimination helps. We're going to the Nerve Hospital now.'

'They might know,' said the almoner. 'Ask for Miss Burrows. I know!' she added excitedly. 'I'll 'phone her now and ask her to find out for you—it would save time, wouldn't it? You look tired,' she concluded sympathetically.

'I *am* tired,' said MacIndoe. 'I'm like the psychiatrists—I can think of nothing but the unconscious.'

But at the Nerve Hospital, a smaller building, dirt-encrusted, surrounded by the demolition work of the *Luftwaffe* and the Birlchester Corporation, the detectives, still following the 'mad Evelyn' of Olwen's diary, obtained no information. 'Do you know what I think?' MacIndoe said to Maddocks. 'I think that either the Evelyn or her madness, or both, are figments of Roy's imagination. A depressing thought. Perhaps we'd better go to the Dragon and have a drink.'

At the Dragon. More crowded now than it had been at lunch time. Cars parked on the tarmac. At the back a sort of rustic garden and car park. Drinks served through a window. A small queue waiting with tongues hanging out. All the frail tables crowded. Children running about or eating crisps. A sheep-dog rushing excitedly up and down, barking at anybody. Some youths talking tough and shoving each other in the shoulder. Their girls waiting patiently at a table. The inevitable old solitaries, drinking and staring into space. Watch and pray, watch and pray. But more likely stunned into incapability. All eyes turning to watch a young man and girl dismount from a tandem. They don't belong, and know it. The girl's mouth petulant because male eyes stare at her legs. The youths talk even tougher, they snigger, eyes ache with resentment because they know the girl is still intact. The girls waiting at the table sneer as the lovers pass. They sense something they'll never know: love in isolation, love with words, love without the need of bludgeoning the senses, love without giggles, love in seriousness. . . . The young man orders cider. Nobody notices the bulky man in a shabby raincoat, yawning as he steps from a car. He goes into the saloon bar.

Inside the saloon bar it is more impressive than at lunch-time. A large man, forty-ish, talks intently to an overdressed blonde, thirty-fivish, about cars. Both talk with the pedantic, slight overemphasis of the slightly drunk. Some men in white flannels talk about cricket. Two men pay attention to a woman, strikingly beautiful, who keeps crossing her legs and saying, 'My dear, I'm simply too tired.' Another woman, quite plain, sits by her in resentment, ignored. Trouble for somebody later. A middle-aged man, too much body, too much money, tells the barman what is wrong with the world. (Too much sympathy in the world. Going soft. I know a man. Wouldn't happen in business. I'm not selfish but . . . Nothing would be wrong with the world if everybody was like *me*.) The barman cannot look him in the eye; he polishes glasses. He knows. . . .

He was the man who had waited on MacIndoe and Baker at lunch-time. He moved down the bar with relief.

MacIndoe said, 'Three beers.' The noise of conversation was loud enough to cover their own words. MacIndoe said, accepting his change, 'What's your name?'

'I'm Robert, sir.'

'We're police officers, Robert, investigating a murder. Do you recognize this girl?'

The barman looked quickly round the bar and then at the photograph of Olwen Hughes. 'Got ginger hair, has she?'

'That's the one.'

'Um. I seen her now and again.'

'Think hard about it, Robert. It's very important.'

The barman said, 'She was in here yesterday. She come in with a bloke.'

'What time?'

'Oh, about one, say. They been in before.'

'Often?'

'About once a week. I remember her 'cause of her ginger hair. She seems a nice kid, not used to boozers. He always gets her coked up for it on sherries, see? Funny, that—it made me notice. They usually have gin. . . . They only come in for lunch. I never seen 'em in here at night.'

'Who did she come in with?'

'Now you're askin'. He's a big 'un. Speaks posh.' The barman grinned and in an exaggerated high tone imitated the man he had seen: ' "May God, you don't rally say so." He talks like that. Officer class.'

'Do you know this man?'

'No.'

'Where he lives or works?'

'No. Shouldn't think he does work. He used to bring her for lunch on a weekday—Tuesdays was usual, now I come to think of it—and stay for an hour and a half. And even then I heard him say once as they left: "Where now, may dear?" '

'Did you see his car at all?'

'No. When I'm on duty I don't go out.'

'Has he been here before with anyone else?'

'I don't think so.'

'What I mean is, does anyone here know him? Did he speak to any of the other diners, for instance?'

'No. Always had a corner table and tried to keep others away.'

204

'If I send a man here to-morrow at one o'clock, will you point out the regulars? Somebody might know something.'

'Yes, sir, of course. Will you speak to the manager about it?'

'I will. I shall see him, anyway, and the others of the staff. What was this man wearing yesterday?'

'Flannels and sports coat. You know how hot it was.'

'What colour flannels and coat?'

'The flannels were a pale brown. Beige, do you call it? The coat was a tweed. It had a lot of colours running through it. He's worn it before. Looked brown from a distance, but when y'get close y'can see grey, red and blue running through as well.'

Maddocks said, 'What sort of tie did he wear? Birlchester School or University or anything you could recognize?'

'He did wear a school tie sometimes, but I don't know which. Not Birlchester. Nor St. Alban's. Nor the Rovers. Nor the cricket club. I know all *them*.'

'Can you tell us the colours?'

'Red, white and blue, I think. Or maybe just red and blue. Oh, hell.'

'Perhaps it was a regimental tie. Have a look at an outfitters when you go into the city,' urged Maddocks. 'You might help us there. Can you give us a physical description?'

'A physical description?'

'What he looked like.'

'Um. Tall, brown hair, about thirty-five. Educated like. Small head shaped like a parsnip. Beak nose.'

'What about his complexion?'

'Yella. Like he'd been in the Pacific and got malaria. Well, not quite as bad as that, but like he'd been on his holidays.'

'Did he have any characteristic gesture or walk?'

'He waved his arms about—you know, like the bloody Poles and Wogs used to do.'

'Has he ever been in with any other woman?'

'No. I've only seen him with the one. I bet he has her on a line. She laps it all up. Seems a shame really—he isn't new to the game, but she is—well, you know, she'd stare at me all shy like. Still, y'can't blame him. Someone's got to give her the chop; she's a lovely bit of stuff. Hey, what about the girl? Suppose she comes in.'

'She won't. She's been killed.'

The barman winced, took a long drink, and said, 'Jesus, that's rough. She was *nice*. Hell, that's going too far.'

MacIndoe said, 'Listen, Robert. You must have waited on them many times. Did you ever hear what they talked about? Did they discuss places or mention names?'

The barman said, 'She was *killed*. I can't believe it. If he comes in here again I'll—— Look. I heard something yesterday. Maybe you can make sense out of it.'

'Something he said?'

'No. Something she said. They was on edge yesterday, I think. I brings the lamb, see, and instead of stopping talking she goes on, queer, all unhappy-like.' The barman looked down at a puddle of beer. 'It doesn't make sense to me and yet it sort of made me uncomfortable. She says, "Don't you remember anything at all? Aren't you starting to collect memories against the day I'm sweating fat with child, or old and thin? (or something like that). There's absolutely no guarantee with my body (I think she said body: it didn't make sense). It may last a long time for you. But there's absolutely no guarantee." I went away then. Was it poetry, d'you think?'

'Yes,' said MacIndoe. 'I believe it was.' (What a day ye had, what a terrible day. I didn't know it was as bad as that.) 'Did you hear anything else?'

'No.'

'What about your pal? Let's talk to him.'

They talked to two other barmen and the landlord. Only one new detail emerged: 'R.' wore a thick gold ring on a finger of his left hand. It didn't seem much.

Travelling back to Almond Vale, Baker driving, MacIndoe sitting in the rear of the car. Occasionally they discussed a point with Maddocks, but in truth MacIndoe was too tired to talk. He still had duties to perform at the police station, the Chief Constable to see, inquiries to set in motion. It was about eight-fifteen at night, but with the deceptive appearance of afternoon, because still light; he had been on duty for nineteen hours. Plenty of cars and buses were still on the move, couples strolled along with the slowness of their own infinity, sagging into each other's sides.

People. How many, MacIndoe thought, have I met to-day? How many almoners did I question? Was it two or three? It was three hospitals, anyway. How will all these people spend the evening? What are Mrs. Wilson and Miss Murphy doing? How did one spend the hours when one's friend had been killed? That's a part of my profession I shall never know. Sooner or later, feeling guilty, they will have to eat. The blood must circulate, the bowels move, there must be an obedience to the cursed flesh which had been the cause of this problem. It was such a busy day I remember them all but vaguely. *She* was the most real of them all. Alive, I would never have known her. At the most I could have said, 'She has an honest face.' Dead, I know her as well as do her parents. Better perhaps. With most people one knows the ordinary actions and opinions, but never the secret thoughts that matter. With Olwen it has been largely the other way round. One wondered sometimes what the dead poets would say about the biographies others have written about them. The opinions, memories and letters were collected and made into a chronological pattern, and assumptions and deductions made as a result. But correctly? Hardly. Not that the poet's own opinions and recollections would necessarily be more truthful than the accumulation of third-person evidence. They could only be a part of the whole evidence. It was a proof that each human being is too complicated to be completely known. And if no one person can be known by himself or others, wasn't it presumption to conclude anything at all? Leave it to God. What are you trying to say, MacIndoe? Nothing. I'm tired. It's just that I can't help making conclusions, and I like the girl. Perhaps what I want to say is that damnation has spread from that man's one act. It has spread resentment, despair, anger, fear, and cynicism: all bad qualities. It isn't just murder the man has committed. Damage would be done to the parents, the brother, the landlady, the friends, the employer; and it would spread to others—it was impossible that the act could cause anything that was good. Did *he* know that, I wonder? Did he know that the girl's life had impinged on so many others? They were all benefited as a result of meeting her. As far as one knew, that is. One must make the qualifying remark. But *he* didn't bother to analyse her like that. He thought to himself: Here's an ordinary sort of girl—nothing's ever happened to her, but she's got good legs and unusual hair. I must have them. Nothing will be changed if I seduce her. She herself will be grateful and will see that I, R., the tall, dark man who has been a bomber pilot, am a more worthy person than she. I must move freely through the world having what I require. I must not be repressed. It's written in a book somewhere. But you—you're only a shopgirl. You're just a fool with a body that I want. (There are a thousand million women in the world; all of them are fools; I've proved it.) You know nothing of moral emancipations, scientific proofs, significant modern literature, political trends. Don't you know that the world of intelligence has proved that you only exist for me? And, since for some reason I am careless and you have become pregnant, you must be killed. You must be discarded a little more permanently than your predecessors. It's all quite obvious and unimportant. There's nothing more to be said. Don't you read the intelligent books and papers? Surely you understand it's all a question of glands and things. There are no things of the emotion and the spirit; merely movements and rearrangements of the flesh; what you think is a touching faith in God is merely your hydraulics out of order. (Of course, you could be pedantic and insist that your God made the glands and hydraulics to create the emotions, but that hardly vouches for life beyond the grave, does it?) The old sins have new labels, my dear. It's you who are sentimental, not the God you believe in. The joke, once you've undone the buttons, is on you.

Maddocks, sitting by Baker and guiding him as he drove, said in astonishment, 'Good heavens! What's going on here?'

They were in Almond Vale High Street, and outside the police station hovered about a dozen men and two women. MacIndoe thought bitterly: here they are; the world has arrived; here's an end to all of Olwen's integrity. 'Hell,' he said. 'I'd forgotten *them*. The gentlemen of the Press.'

As he stepped out of his car they crowded round. Someone said, 'It's MacIndoe of the Yard.' A battery of questions began at once:

'Caught anybody?'

'Was it rape?'

'Was she on the stage?'

'Can we have a picture?'

'Not of me,' said MacIndoe. As he said it someone took one.

'Of the girl.'

'Probably. I'll see the Chief Constable.'

'Good God! Have they got a Chief Constable in this dump?'

'Do you expect to arrest anybody soon?'

'Is it the work of a madman?'

'Is this chap a prisoner?'

'Don't be silly. That's Inspector Maddocks.'

'Who's the other b——?'

'Where did the girl live?'

'Who are her parents?'

'Where did she work?'

'I'll have all the available information provided for you,' said

MacIndoe. 'But lay off for ten minutes, will you? I'm tired and I would like——'

'*You're* tired. Christ, I had to come to this dump by *train*. It took years.'

Someone said something vulgar about the victim, and a woman reporter said, 'I'm sure I don't know what *that* means.'

'You give me ten minutes while I see the Chief Constable,' said MacIndoe. 'You've got hours before you go to press,' he added with some small satisfaction.

'This is going to go on all bloody night,' said one reporter. 'I wish to God I worked for *The Times*. Let's go and have a drink.'

Forty minutes later MacIndoe was able to have dinner with Baker and Maddocks at the George Hotel. They were the last persons to eat, but the waiters did not seem to resent it. They had found out who MacIndoe was, and they too asked questions. At about ten o'clock MacIndoe retired in relief to his bedroom. It was still quite light, but he could scarcely keep awake. He wrote a letter to Janet. She hated telephone calls; they frightened her; besides, a letter was something permanent; it could be enjoyed again. In bed MacIndoe realized that he had not said any prayers. He was too overwhelmed by exhaustion to climb out again. 'Oh, God,' he prayed, 'look after her'; but whom he meant he did not specify. It was intended to be Janet, but as he fell asleep, the prayer unfinished, he realized that it included Olwen.

VII

DAY Two began in Maddocks's office. They sat about on hard chairs, reading letters, making decisions, waiting to proceed to the Coroner's inquest. People were beginning to come in with scraps of information and to telephone. Olwen Hughes's photograph had appeared in the local morning papers and in a few national dailies as well. A detective constable would shortly be proceeding to the Dragon. Even at this moment uniformed constables and plain-clothes detectives—every man available—were calling on chemists' shops, garages, cafés, and would later visit Almond Vale's few pubs with photographs of Olwen to ask if she had been seen, if the man with her had been seen, if his red car had been seen, the direction in which they had been moving (and whether on foot or in the car) when they were seen, and so on. A woman named Penelope Johnson, waitress at a café called the Choc-Box, 1658 Almond Vale Road, Birlchester, had telephoned to say that Olwen had been in that café some time on Tuesday morning; she believed it had been between ten-thirty and ten forty-five. No, the girl hadn't said anything. On the contrary, she'd seemed very quiet. Subdued? No, well, she wouldn't say that. What would she say? Well, sad. Honestly, she wasn't making it up after the event—the girl had appeared sad. . . . Similarly, a Mr. William Benson, chemist, 1253 Almond Vale Road, had telephoned to inform that Olwen Hughes had bought a camera (Veronica Mark I) on Tuesday morning. She had also purchased a 127 film which he had inserted for her. The satchel he had given her—she had seemed nice; now, he'd seen in the papers that—— The time was about twelve-fifteen, and he'd never seen her before. It all confirmed what the pathologist had decided—that the girl had died in the afternoon.

The 127 film had been developed. Most of it had been destroyed by exposure to sunlight, but something interesting had remained. The girl had evidently taken the first photograph and it had been of her male companion. She had wound on the film, and the part that had rolled round the spool into darkness, although pale, had not been beyond development. Only half of the picture was available—and it was the wrong, lower half: no face, but the lower half of a tweed jacket, a pair of flannels, and his shoes which had buckle fastenings. They were not black shoes. In view of the fact that R. dressed well, they were hardly likely to be yellow; MacIndoe was quite certain that they would prove to be brown. In addition, as a confirmation which could also become evidence, the girl's handbag was in the picture. The copse itself was not identifiable as such.

One of the two telephones on Maddocks's desk shrilled suddenly. The inspector picked up the instrument at once, speaking his own name so quickly that he turned it into one syllable.

The gaunt doctor sat on a chair, using a toothpick on a back tooth. He had been telling MacIndoe about the autopsy, and now sat listening to what MacIndoe had to say. 'It took about six weeks to seduce her,' explained MacIndoe. 'He eventually talked marriage—marriage when a sick wife was dead. It was only talk, of course. There was no wife—I'm damned if I can understand that part of the man's story. The girl was asked to keep quiet about their association, not to write, or, at any rate, only to send letters in envelopes provided by *him*. Then she found herself with child.

It took her some time to pluck up courage enough to tell him—that's significant, I think—and the rest you know. What worries me is that he may have intended to kill her from the very beginning. So many lies from the very start—what were they for?'

'He lied because he wanted to possess the girl,' said Dr. Baxter. 'Now, I've told you that there's nothing more to be said about the girl, physically, beyond her pregnancy and that she died by strangulation. But I have a kind of proof that the man's intentions were physical. He isn't mad, but he is passionate. Among the marks on the girl's throat are some made, not by his hands, but by his teeth. These are so deep that we've been able to make an impression for you. Find your man, MacIndoe, and ask him who is his dentist.'

'Good,' said MacIndoe. 'That's the sort of evidence I can go to court with.'

Maddocks said in some excitement, 'Someone to see us. Wants to make a confession.'

The others stared in astonishment. MacIndoe said calmly, 'Well, let's see him.'

'I'm getting out of here,' said the pathologist.

Two constables entered as the doctor left. Between them walked a man of about thirty-five, unshaven, tall, thin in tension, trembling now in a condition of considerable excitement. 'Are you the Chief Constable?' he asked.

'No. I am Superintendent MacIndoe.'

'I've got to see the Chief Constable.'

'What about?'

'The murder of this girl.'

'What about the murder of the girl?'

'I did it.'

'You'd better tell me,' said MacIndoe. 'I'm the officer who's investigating the crime.'

'Oh, it's not a crime.'

'Well, let's say that it's a crime technically,' said MacIndoe. 'What's your name?'

The man gave it.

'And your address?'

It was a local one.

'When did you kill the girl?'

'Tuesday afternoon.'

'Why did you kill her?'

'She tempted me.'

'Tempted to kill?'

'No, no, nothing like that,' the man said, waving his arms about. 'She tempted me with her apple.'

'With an apple? How?'

'Bold looks, leers, nakedness. . . . It was right to kill her. If thy body doth affront thee, destroy it. See what I mean?'

'Where did you kill her?'

'Where she was found.'

'And where was that?'

'Don't you know?'

'Oh, I know,' MacIndoe said, 'but I want *your* statement.'

'It was in a copse along the river; the left bank.'

'Tell us what happened.'

'Are you going to caution me?'

'The constable is taking it all down,' said MacIndoe. The man turned his head and noted this with apparent approval. 'Then we'll have it typed, and before you sign it I will caution you.'

'I was walking up High Street,' said the man. 'It was after dinner. This girl jumped off a moving bus and nearly knocked me down. "I've hurt my ankle," she said, and stood in a doorway tempting me with her flesh. "Couldn't you walk?" I said. "Not unless there was something to walk for," she said. It was obvious that she was a strumpet. I said, "Will you come a walk with me?" (so that I could kill her), and she was able to walk then.'

'Where did you walk to?'

'Along the river bank.'

'Did anyone see you?'

'I don't think so. It wasn't long after dinner.'

'What happened then?'

'We walked to this place where she was found. She said her name was Temptation and asked if I thought her hair was beautiful. I said, "Do you tempt men?" and she undid her blouse to prove it and to destroy me by temptation. So I killed her.'

'You resisted the other temptation?'

'What other temptation?'

'The temptation of her beauty.'

'Of course I resisted! Is not a woman's beauty the means of damnation?'

'What did you do afterwards?'

'I dunno. I had an ice-cream at Joe's café and took one home to Mum.'

'What time was this?'

'About four o'clock.'

'What did you do later? Read the paper?'

'I went to the pictures.'

'Had you ever met the girl before?'

'No. She jumped off the bus from Birlchester.'

MacIndoe said in weary pity, 'What did you do with the rope and knife? We can't find them.'

The man grinned broadly. 'I dropped 'em in the river.'

'What was the title of the film you saw?'

The man's brow puckered. 'It was *Devil Maniac's Conspiracy*. It was real good.'

'All right,' said MacIndoe gently. 'You can go now. Oh, wait a minute. What's the name of your doctor?'

The man became truculent in fright. 'What do you wanna know for?'

'You've done this before, haven't you?'

'I haven't! I haven't!'

'Do you want to go back to the asylum?'

'I shan't go back. I'm all right.'

'Of course you're all right,' said MacIndoe quietly. 'But you mustn't come in here talking nonsense. There was no rope or knife. The girl was comparatively innocent. She never spoke to you, did she?'

'It says in the papers——'

'I know it does. But they stress the wrong things in the wrong way. The police have a very difficult job to do, and you've wasted our time.'

The man became completely abject, desperately humble. 'Yes, sir. I'm sorry, sir. I only wanted to help. I picked the wrong girl, sir.'

He was ushered out by a constable. The constable said soothingly, 'Come on, Charlie. Home to Mum. Don't do it again.'

Maddocks said, 'I suppose that often happens.'

MacIndoe said, 'Yes. Nearly always. He'll probably be upset for weeks. Retarded progress.' He concluded bitterly, 'Another of R.'s victims.'

In the Coroner's Court. Dark, heavy wood, a suggestion of permanency. (You may be murdered, or become mutilated by a vehicle, or drowned in a pond, or gored by a bull, or take your life because you are unhappy, but in the finality of your death we do not admit permanency. Only we, authority, exist to have permanency.) The windows of stained glass. Something about the arrangement of the seating, and a musty, incense-like smell that in any case suggests the church. Except that this building is crowded. What kind of people come to hear about the death of a girl? Impossible to say. Coming to the court seems, by appearances, to be their only common characteristic. There are burly men who must be farmers, middle-aged women who look as if they're waiting for a train, the sallow faces of the gentlemen of the Press, young, nervous men who appear to be bank clerks, two pretty girls who might have come in for a giggle, but seem scared now in the presence of silence and tension. On the far wall which most persons present are facing is a huge clock; beside it, a calendar. Time is the final authority worshipped here. It is eleven-thirty on the morning of the twenty-eighth day of July in the year of Our Lord (the One still used for this purpose) one thousand, nine hundred and fifty-something. Olwen Hughes is about to be murdered officially.

It is done with comparative dignity.

The Coroner arrived punctually and glared with courageous contempt at the morbidly curious. He was a man of medium height, bulky, extraordinarily clean and tidy. At his direction the windows were opened and the proceedings began.

Mr. Reginald Meredith, twenty-two, thirteen stone, vaguely agricultural, tall and with large, nervous red hands, explained that he and his girl had been walking along the river bank on the Tuesday evening and, desiring the privacy of bushes, encountered what they at first thought was another couple. Questioned by the Coroner as to whether another couple was present, Mr. Meredith said, 'No'; and when questioned, quite reasonably, as to why he thought so in the first place, Mr. Meredith, very red and confused indeed, let slip his explanation, which was that he could see a girl's legs. Mr. Meredith, obviously a long way indeed from the bar of the George, in which he had been heard to boast of the advantages of rubber goods and the technicalities of the artificial insemination of cows, had the one consolation that his girl was not present in the court. Indeed, with the eyes of the whole court upon him, and even the simplest, most rural mind knowing exactly what he meant, Mr. Meredith was very glad that his own integrity was not in question.

If the original dignity of the court was slightly infringed by Mr. Meredith's account and the nervous titters of the two girls, it was restored by a Mrs. Harriet Wilson, sixty-one, widow, who was dressed completely in black, so that many persons in court presumed her to be a relative of the girl she had identified. In a whisper she explained that she had known the girl years, had believed her to be a very fine young woman, and had seen her dead body (or, rather, face) in the Almond Vale police station on Wednesday. Quite suddenly the memory of that moment wounded again and Mrs. Wilson wept. There was an electric silence of sympathy in the court as Mrs. Wilson was led away to a seat.

The Coroner afterwards proceeded to the medical evidence. Dr. Baxter explained in technical detail that Olwen had been strangled. The cervical vertebrae was snapped at its fifth member; the hyoid bone was fractured; the brain was congested; there were also indications of asphyxia in the eyes, nose, ears, lips and the tips of the fingers. All these were symptomatic of death by asphyxia by throttling, and very probably by manual strangulation.

There was a gasp in court, a mass inhalation of breath, as the pathologist, having told how the girl died, went on to explain (to whom it may concern and hurt, if anybody did care and could be hurt, and no doubt there must be somebody) that the girl was nearly three months pregnant. He offered also the information—equally vital and fascinating for tired, incapable minds—that her stomach had contained undigested meat, probably lamb, and some alcohol, probably sherry; and that there was a mark on her throat which, if it did not indicate a madman (he did not believe the mark had been made by a madman), at least indicated a person of excitable and perhaps badly controlled physical characteristics.

MacIndoe, sitting by the Chief Constable, waiting with slight irritation to proceed with his work, thought: The extraordinary thing is that they do care. The shock of the words 'three months pregnant' was still physically present. Why? Why did sex still shock this supposedly most sordid of generations? Surely they were so saturated with it that nothing could shock, or scarcely interest them. They had come to this court for a laugh or a thrill, for a bit of what they'd call Good Theatre. Yet here were these people, including a number of that most cynical of professions, the Press, tense on behalf of the dead Olwen. They did not yet despise her. Here, in this court, in the assault of the moment their emotions were restored to a natural humanity and they felt hurt with her. No doubt the atmosphere of the court had helped to give dignity; no doubt the tears of Mrs. Wilson had conveyed a reality; no doubt in their own world later on, nerves restored by ordinariness, they would laugh or smack their lips at Olwen, but here and now was a moment of truth. I am glad of it, MacIndoe thought. While people care there is always hope; it is a kind of proof of some ultimate standard.

Detective Inspector Maddocks was then called, and gave evidence of having been telephoned at eight twenty-six and proceeding with other available officers to as near the scene as a car would take them. Mr. Meredith and Miss Best (in a distraught condition) were waiting by the telephone booth from which they had called. The officers were led to the hollow where there lay the body of the deceased girl (Maddocks described her as a girl, not a woman —he had seen her), face downwards, with her clothes somewhat disarranged and indications on her throat (so far as he was able to judge: Mr. Coroner had now heard the medical opinion) that she had died by violence.

The Coroner: 'Have inquiries been made?'

Detective Inspector Maddocks: 'They have. The local police are being assisted by two officers from Scotland Yard.'

The Coroner: 'What are the results of the inquiries?'

Detective Inspector Maddocks: 'It is probably not in the interests of justice that these should at present be revealed. . . .'

The Coroner then adjourned the inquest for three weeks, until August 18th. He spoke of the brutality of the crime, hoped there would be no repetition, and urged the public to assist the police in their difficult inquiries.

Coming out of the stuffy darkness of the court into the warm, excited light of the High Street, MacIndoe sighed, yawned and decided he was hungry. Then he thought: Lord, I'm callous too. I listened to all that, untouched myself, hardened by years of it to the extent of being impatient if people didn't speak up properly or comprehend quickly enough, and then I'm quite prepared to go and eat the best meal the George can provide. I'm sorry, Olwen, my dear child, but the truth is that I must have strength to pursue this enemy of ours; in short, I must proceed to luncheon. . . .

At the sanatorium. Cumulus clouds moving slowly over a brick horizon; a backcloth to Wagner; warm in the shafts of sunlight; a sleepy, comfortable feeling of afternoon. A bus service passed the sanatorium grounds. (It was not in the countryside—fifty thousand people lived in the suburb.) From the top decks of the buses one could see every private agony, every humiliation. The air was city air, but the rows of huts, or chalets as they were called, were surrounded by lawns and rockeries. The medical blocks and that part of the premises which housed the staff were of brick; more permanent structures than the chalets; after all, it was the patients who were the impermanent things. Concrete paths along the front of each row of chalets. Some of the beds outside. Pale heads on paler sheets and blood-red top blankets. Faces looking up from magazines as the detectives passed: the fear of doctors in a few eyes. A man in a dressing-gown, thirty-ish, incredibly thin, a cadaver, sat on a wicker chair, shoulders bowed, skeleton arms and wrists moving with incredible slow feebleness, polishing a shoe. A taut, hollowed, pale, intellectual face smiled at the police officers. Brown eyes in the hollowed head pleaded like a spaniel's. Please, I'm normal. It's true that I may die disgustingly later but at this moment I'm normal and wish to be treated as such. 'Good afternoon.' (A deep voice despite the Belsen face and body.) 'Were you looking for a patient?'

'No. We're police officers.' (Give him that titbit.) 'We're looking for Matron's office.'

'Over there.' The skeleton arm revealed, as it lifted to point, the sleeve of the dressing-gown falling away. 'Has the old devil robbed a bank?'

'Quite probably. Thank you.'

Round the corner indicated, they seemed to walk into the female section. An ambulance drew up. The driver and a nurse came from their two seats at the front to unlock the back of the ambulance. Some girls stepped out carefully. Quite an impression of prettiness. One girl in fact was extremely pretty: quite plump, lovely, bonny arms, ash-blonde hair, a rounded pink face, blue eyes rimmed pink. The pink face became too pink and excitable in chatter. How long? MacIndoe wondered. How long? Another girl began to be sick. She continued for several seconds, recovered, and then said to the driver, 'You drove too quick.'

The nurse led the one girl away, the others following. Another girl said over her shoulder, 'Well, you did.'

Matron was a small, innocent-seeming woman; apparently old and as frail as a rabbit, she nevertheless took the word 'murder' in her stride. It was as if anything that happened outside the sanatorium, her world, was unreal, and could be discussed dispassionately, theoretically. MacIndoe and Baker found her in her office, a room as comfortable as a drawing-room. Maddocks had remained in Almond Vale to supervise the visits of police to garages, cafés, shops and the railway station; and to be available to callers.

'You're from Almond Vale?' queried Matron.

'We're from Scotland Yard,' said MacIndoe, 'but we're operating from Almond Vale.'

'We had one of your officers here,' said Matron. She was in no hurry. 'What was his name now? What *was* it? Ah, Roberts, that was it.'

'Is he still here?'

'Oh, no. He died.'

MacIndoe continued his explanation and Matron, tapping her nose with her spectacles, said, 'You're probably after Davis. She's from Wales.'

'Christian name Peggy?'

'I don't know.' Matron smiled at the idea. 'We'll ask her.'

It was soon apparent that Matron was the only member of the staff unaware of Olwen's death and not discussing it. As Peggy Davis came into the room she said excitedly, 'I know you're police officers. I was going to come to see you to-night.'

'Dear me!' said Matron, slightly perturbed. 'What about?'

'Well, I saw Olwen a few weeks ago.'

'You'd better sit down,' said Matron, pointing to a chair. 'I expect this will go on for some time.' It occurred to MacIndoe that she was, despite appearances, interested.

He said, 'You were a friend of Olwen's?'

'Yes,' said Peggy.

'She used to work here?'

'Yes; but I knew her before that. We came from the same village. I know her parents and everything.'

'We have Olwen's diary, Miss Davis, and in it is mentioned your last visit to her. You had a sort of quarrel, didn't you?'

'Yes; we did.'

'Is that why you subsequently sent a postcard from Weston-super-Mare saying, "My dearest, I'm sorry," or something like that?'

'Oh, I'm glad I sent that,' Peggy said. 'I should hate her to have died thinking—— But I was right. I must have been right.'

'About what, Miss Davis?'

'Well, to have quarrelled. I was always very fond of Olwen because—well, because she was sort of—I know it sounds silly—sort of pure.'

MacIndoe looked at Peggy Davis. She was a big, healthy girl. There was a tension about her face which suggested that she worked and played hard. She was too fleshy to be innocent. The type of girl who would be known as a 'good sport'; after hours of hard work she would go on to dance, drink gin and perhaps end up sprawled in somebody's car. She would know next morning that it hadn't really been a good time, but would be unable to resist the next invitation. ('There's nothing else to do.') Olwen would represent something unattainable—a girl who never surrendered to the wrong sort of invitations, a girl who went to church, and yet a girl who was strikingly beautiful. Naturally, Peggy would not wish Olwen to be finally humiliated by someone unworthy.

MacIndoe said, 'What was it you quarrelled about?'

'This man she was going with.'

'You didn't like him?'

'No.'

'Then you'd met him?'

'No.'

'Why should you dislike him?'

'I knew he was tricking her. She was a nice girl, but already he'd persuaded her to—well, you know—to love him.'

'You taxed her with this?'

'Yes.'

'What did she say?'

'It was hopeless. She was in love with him. She was ready to believe him before anybody.'

'Did she tell you about him?'

'How do you mean?'

'I mean from our point of view. What is his name?'

'His name's Harrison—Roy Harrison.'

'D'ye know where he lives?'

'No; but it's locally.'

'Where he works?'

'He's a traveller.'

'For whom?'

'I don't know; but he called at the place where Olwen worked. They would know.'

'They don't,' said MacIndoe bitterly.

'Why don't they know?' Peggy asked. 'Surely they *must* know. Oh. Perhaps it was because *she* attended to him.'

'According to her employer, Mrs. Harper, she would still have to refer him to her.'

'Well, she didn't this time. He started his lies from the first moment. . . . Well, you know his name now.'

'He's told such a lot of lies, Miss Davis, that I suspect the name is false too.'

'Oh, God, yes.' (They always gave a false name, if they gave one at all. They had a horror of affiliation orders.)

'Did Miss Hughes have any other male friends or acquaintances?'

'Not that I know of.'

'Did she mention anything else about this man Harrison? His address, his car, his employers, his wife——'

'He had a wife,' said Peggy. 'She was in an asylum, Olwen said.'

'That was a trick to get what he wanted,' explained MacIndoe. 'I don't think there was a wife at all.'

'Then why should he mention one?'

'To postpone their own wedding, of course. According to her diary, the wedding was twelve months off—that was when the wife was to die.'

'It's absolutely horrible,' said Peggy. 'I can't bear to think of such a terrible thing happening to Olwen. All those lies to obtain —and she such an innocent sort of person. I'll try to think of every single thing she said that day. I'll write it down—but if it was all lies anyway——'

'People lie in their own terms,' said MacIndoe. 'He may have mentioned things and places familiar to himself. We could visit them.'

At the Queen's Hotel in the city of Birlchester. Smoke-encrusted, antique before its time, a façade of stone and gleaming windows at its front, cheaper bricks, the ugliness of piping and the noise of a railway station at its rear. A strictly utilitarian building, ugly outside and too much plush inside. Outside the small, pillared front porch a doorman, an old man looking like a monkey because he's recently had his teeth out. On his uniformed chest the row of medals. (Why? Did one have to go through the bloody filth of Passchendaele to prove one could operate a lift or open the door of a car?) Inside, a more bulky warrior who tended to be bumptious. He knew his stuff: MacIndoe's dirty raincoat didn't belong in here. This was a part of the world that still believed in property.

'We are police officers,' said MacIndoe. 'Will you tell the manager we wish to see him?'

The doorman said, 'The manager is not available.' He turned away in arrogant satisfaction—as if he had a personal hatred of the police—and called to a woman, 'Miss Bartlett, Sir Norman 'phoned. . . .' The woman said, 'How many will be coming?' The doorman said, 'About a dozen.'

MacIndoe tapped the man's chest. 'Do you always obstruct the police?'

'My duty is to the hotel. I can't have people asking for the manager whenever they feel like it.'

'Obstruct me again,' said MacIndoe with a smile that took the sting out of his words, 'and I'll run you in for it. Now stop playing ceremonials and get on the blower. Tell the manager that we're from Scotland Yard and we're investigating a murder. . . .'

'I see,' said the doorman, dropping the ceremonials instantly. 'I thought you was on about the cars outside. They're always on about it.'

The manager approached at once, a trembling figure in black and white, a portrait in nervous sweat. 'What's all this about? A murder? It can't possibly have anything to do with us.'

I don't see why not, MacIndoe thought. If adultery and theft can take place here, why not murder? But let us be hypocritical: the results will be obtained more quickly. He said, 'I'm sure it hasn't. The problem is this. A man came here to dinner with a girl on March 29th. They may have been again—that I don't know. The girl is dead. Who was the man?'

'It's a long time ago.'

'Here is a photograph of the girl.'

'Ah,' said the manager. 'It was in this morning's paper.'

'Do you remember her?'

'No. But, then, I don't always appear in the dining-room. Charlie here has a good memory for faces—it goes with the job.' He called the bumptious doorman over and showed the photograph to him. 'Remember her?'

The doorman said at once, 'Yes. A redhead. Nervous 'cause she wasn't used to hotels. Is she——'

'Yes,' said MacIndoe. 'She's dead. Who came with her?'

'Tall, thin, darkish fella. Officer type. Probably ex-Air Force,' said the doorman, ' 'cause he had that sorta shirt on—you know, pale blue.' He grinned. 'Course, he coulda been a policeman. . . . He's been in before.'

'With the girl?'

'With women.'

'What sort of women?'

The manager said hastily, 'I assure you, I didn't know. . . . We try to maintain the standards of——'

'You know the sort,' said the doorman. 'Good-looking, good manners, politely contemptuous, don't know what a day's work's like, never seen the inside of a bus. . . . Oh, he could pick 'em.'

'Have you seen any of these women here lately? Not necessarily with him.'

'No, sir, I haven't.'

'Do you know this man's name?'

'No.'

'Where he works?'

'Sorry.'

'Do you know of any of the women's names?'

'I'll have to think about it, sir, but I'm doubtful.'

'I want you to keep an eye open for him,' said MacIndoe. 'I want a talk with that young Romeo.' He turned to the manager. 'I'll have to see everybody else he might have encountered when he brought her to dinner. I know it's a nuisance. . . .'

It was more than a nuisance. It took over an hour and was a waste of time.

They had just had their tea. 'I'd like to examine the copse again,' MacIndoe said. 'I don't mean search it. I just wish to visit it the way he did—go for a walk, in fact. Will you come?'

'Of course!' Baker and Maddocks said. It was agreeable to both officers to have orders issued as requests which, they felt, could quite easily be refused.

A few minutes later they were standing in Almond Vale High Street outside the police station.

MacIndoe pointed down the hill. 'Let us presume he came in his car. From Birlchester he enters the town up this hill. He doesn't park the vehicle in the one official car park—at any rate, they don't remember the car or the girl—and he cannot park it in High Street without being pinched. Correct?'

'Yes,' said Maddocks.

'Therefore,' said MacIndoe, 'he parked it in one of the side streets. He then walked with Olwen to the top of the town and along the river bank to the place where she was later found. Now, looking at your map, it would seem that, no matter if he went straight up High Street or if he turned left along a side street and later turned right to reach the river that way—whichever he did he would emerge by the square or whatever it's called. The date of your map, I noticed, was 1936. Do you know of any short-cuts made subsequently which would permit him to avoid the square?'

'No,' said Maddocks. 'He was bound to emerge by the huts where people hire the boats.'

'And from there,' said MacIndoe, 'he must have proceeded along the river bank. Let us do the same.'

The three detectives walked straight up High Street and turned left towards the square. Most of the shops had closed; a few constables were still visiting premises to inquire about the traveller with the red car. The air, warm and dry once more, had dried the pavements; people moved slowly in the evening heat, carrying their raincoats. At the river's edge old people sat in silence, youths were hiring the boats, a child with bread searched for swans to feed, while his mother leaned in tiredness on the handle of his push-chair. It was a typical evening following rain, a peaceful aftermath in the wake of yesterday's storm: smoke rose in slow, straight columns and there was excellent visibility.

They soon reached the stacked deck-chairs, the concrete ornamentation and the lines of boats. MacIndoe pointed to the huts at which the boats were hired. 'Have inquiries been made there?' he asked.

'I don't know,' Maddocks said. 'Let's make them now.'

Inside the hut a man of about thirty in vaguely maritime attire was sitting on an oil-drum looking at a pornographic magazine. He will have noticed her, MacIndoe thought, remembering Olwen's straight young legs.

'Oh, it's you, Carter,' said Maddocks.

'What if it is?' the man said. 'You've got nothing on me.'

'We want your help.'

'Ha! After being inside.'

'A girl has been murdered.'

'So they tell me. Are you going to pin that on me?'

'We've never pinned anything on to you,' said Maddocks. 'If you steal things, we have to send you to prison.'

'Coppers!' said the man Carter. 'Lot of bloody saints they are.'

'If a policeman steals he goes to prison too. Some of them do.'

'I'm pleased to hear it.'

'What about this girl, Carter? She didn't steal anything. She was innocent.'

'I'll bet she was. Three months. D'you think what she done was better than stealing?'

'She was tricked.'

'What kind of talk is that? A woman doesn't have to drop her skirt. They do it 'cause they like it.'

'She was innocent, Carter.'

'So you say. I suppose she went to church and believed in fairies.'

The world, thought MacIndoe. The world is always with us. Whatever you did, the world could convert your motives into dirt or conceit or the condition of your body. The world is a cynical old man, satiated himself, who watches closely, eager to see failure, and, when it came, certain that it had been caused by the same old dirty motives that had once actuated himself. The world is an old man whose arteries have hardened, who does not wish to forgive, does not want even to have reason to forgive; who does not desire redemption for others for he is beyond it himself. I'm cynical, too, MacIndoe realized, but bless you, Olwen, I know you didn't really fail.

Maddocks said, 'Did you see her on Tuesday afternoon?'

'How do I know? I see dozens of 'em walking about.'

'She had auburn hair.'

'What d'y'mean, auburn? I heard that in the boozer. Auburn. What kind of a disease is that?'

'It's a colour. Red.'

'She had red hair?'

'Yes, Carter.'

'Then I did see her. Why don't they say what they mean?'

'Didn't you see her picture in the paper?'

'I only get the sports edition.'

Maddocks produced a photograph. 'Is this her?'

The man was startled out of his hostility. 'D'you mean to tell me them two walked past me and he killed her in them bushes?'

'Yes, Carter.'

'But I'd have heard the screams.'

'She was throttled, Carter. She couldn't scream.'

'What d'e want to kill her for?'

'He wanted to dump her. Who is he, Carter?'

'Oh, Crise, I'd know him all right. But who is he? I don't know that.'

'Ever seen him before?'

'No. He don't live in Almond Vale.'

'What was he wearing?'

'Grey flannels and a brown sorta jacket. I asked him if he wanted a boat. He turned to the girl and said, "Do you?" She said, "No." I thought, You bitch you; you're in a hurry for it.'

'What time was it?'

'Just after three.'

'Did he come back alone?'

'He didn't come back at all.'

'We shall get this man, Carter, and we shall want you to come and identify him. . . .'

'I might have known it.'

'And we'll want a statement,' said Maddocks.

'I can't write.'

'We'll write it for you.'

'There's no way out then, is there?'

'Don't you *want* to do it?'

'She asked for it, di'n't she?'

The police officers walked on. Not many people were about— an old man walking with a dog; some old ladies peered from seats; half a dozen children fished with string and jam-jars; a young man and woman walked in nervous silence, and a solitary boat on the river was being propelled with precise, sure strokes by a sailor. There were no persons near the murder scene: the novelty had worn off: the entertainment was over. The earth beyond the public footpath was drying, but had not yet rehardened, and the officers stepped with care over the mud. In the copse the distant sounds were quite abruptly cut off and replaced by the nearer murmur of insects. MacIndoe had a sudden apprehension of how alone Olwen Hughes must have felt in the last moments.

He examined the copse and its surrounding trees. 'Whether he came by train or by car,' he said, 'he had to return into Almond Vale—the station and the only parking places are there. Yet he didn't return the way he came. How did he know which way to go? Answer: he climbed a tree.' MacIndoe selected a tree and commenced to climb. 'Don't ever tell anyone you've seen a portly gentleman from the Yard doing this,' he said. 'It would end our reputation.' He ceased talking as climbing and breathing became more difficult. 'Ah, yes, he could get back to the main road *that* way.'

Baker had already climbed a more difficult tree; Maddocks rose behind MacIndoe. 'It's very probable,' said Maddocks. 'But what does it indicate?'

'Nothing,' said MacIndoe, 'but we'll walk there too and see what it feels like.'

They all did this, but reached a stile and the main road without finding anything. Walking back towards the town they soon reached a small café and some cottages. MacIndoe asked, 'Have inquiries been made here?'

'Yes,' said Maddocks.

'How about the cottages?'

'No. We've only dealt with cafés and garages.'

There were three cottages, and at the third a child remembered a man coming by himself over the stile on the Tuesday afternoon about an hour before tea-time. The child's description fitted the wanted man; in addition, she had seen him enter the café.

In the café were the usual chalked notices about sandwiches; a tea urn; bottles of fizzy lemonade; marble-topped tables; wooden stools, and a lurid advertisement for cigarettes. This showed an auburn-haired girl swathed in highly inflammable coloured gauze. That, thought MacIndoe, was how R. must have visualized Olwen.

A heavy, good-looking girl of about twenty-seven attended to them. 'We're police officers,' said MacIndoe.

'What, again?' said the girl. 'What is all this, anyway? I told them I hadn't seen a dark, tall man with a redhead.'

MacIndoe said, 'Did you see a dark, tall man without a redhead?'

The waitress frowned. 'Are you kidding?'

'No. I believe the man we wish to meet may have passed here on Tuesday after he'd left the redhead.'

'They didn't ask me that.'

'I'm asking you.'

'Tuesday afternoon?'

'Yes.'

'Was that before the storm?'

'Yes; the day before.'

'A tall, dark man of about thirty-four came in about four—no, a bit earlier. He bought a drink of tea and some aspirins. Sat there taking them one after the other. Said he had a hangover.'

'Do you know him?'

'I'd recognize him.'

'Did he seem agitated?'

'No. He was silent. He wouldn't speak.'

'Why should he?'

'Well, he was the sort who would.'

'You mean he was attractive to women?'

'You could put it that way. I asked him if he was on holiday, but he said he was just passing through.'

'Did he say anything else?'

'Only that he had a headache.'

'What was he wearing?'

The waitress's description of the man's flannels and sports coat was similar to that provided by the barman at the Dragon. She added, 'He wore brown shoes—very soft leather, I remember, and they had a fastening like a woman's.'

MacIndoe remembered the photograph in Olwen's camera. 'A buckle fastening?'

'Yes. I couldn't think of the word.'

Maddocks said, 'What sort of a tie did he wear? Birlchester Grammar?'

'No.' The girl looked from Maddocks to MacIndoe and then to Baker. She pointed to the detective sergeant. 'It was almost exactly like that gentleman's,' she said.

'R.A.F.,' said Baker in some excitement.

'Are you sure?' asked Maddocks.

'Well, it wasn't quite the same. *His* had sort of notches.'

'Like Vs?' queried Baker.

'That's right.'

'She means the R.A.F.V.R.,' Baker said triumphantly.

MacIndoe frowned. 'Why didn't the waiter at the Dragon recognize your tie? We asked him about ties.'

'I wasn't wearing this one yesterday.'

MacIndoe laughed. 'The vanity of youth! He comes down here for a short time and brings a load of ties!'

Baker said in embarrassment, 'Well, I'm not married, like you two.'

MacIndoe said, 'I don't know what that's got to do with it.' The girl stared in confusion. After the laughter MacIndoe asked her, 'Which way did the man go when he left here?'

'He went round the back to the cinema.'

'How do you know?'

The girl blushed. 'I went to look at the back. He turned the corner.' She hesitated and then admitted, 'Well, he was good-looking. He went to fetch his sports car from the cinema car park.'

MacIndoe glanced at Maddocks. 'Ah, he did! How clever of him. We hadn't thought of that. Did he drive down the hill towards Birlchester?'

'No. Uphill through the town.'

'Could you identify this man if we found him?'

'Has he done something wrong?'

'I believe he has,' said MacIndoe.

'What a pity,' said the girl. 'A handsome man like that.'

'And when you've finished your duties will you come to the station and make a statement? Just what you've told me.'

'They won't put him in gaol if I do?'

'Not for long,' said MacIndoe evasively.

As they walked up the High Street, MacIndoe said, 'What's the implication of the tie, Tony?'

'He could be in the R.A.F.V.R.'

'If he was in the wartime R.A.F. would he automatically retain his commission?'

'Almost certainly.'

'Is there a local squadron?' MacIndoe asked Maddocks.

'Yes,' said Maddocks. 'The County of Middleshire. They're on manœuvres.'

'In England?'

'Oh, yes, locally. They're at Greenridge. It sounds hopeful, doesn't it?' Maddocks gave a slight groan. 'Hell. I've just thought. They've been there since last Saturday.'

'Perhaps they didn't all go on Saturday,' said MacIndoe. 'Perhaps at least one officer turned up on Wednesday. Tony, m'lad, you know all about aeroplanes, and I want you to handle this. Another thing for you: the R.A.F. has something to do with this Harrison. The barman at the Dragon described him as "officer type". The doorman at the Queen's said he wore a pale blue shirt of the type R.A.F. officers wear. Olwen herself wrote that he was a pilot at Little Over during the war and went on a big raid to lay mines in the Kiel Canal. Get everything you can about that raid and that squadron. I've written to the Air Ministry already, but I'd like the personal aspect.'

Baker said, 'I was on fighters, but a pal knows all about bombers. I'll contact him.'

'Yes; do that,' MacIndoe said. 'Send him express messages, telegrams, pigeons if you like—I've got a feeling that Mr. Harrison likes to boast.'

Returning to Almond Vale police station, they found that there was no Mr. Harrison—or at least none fitting Hazel's description. A message had arrived from the City of Birlchester police. There were three men in that city with the name Roy Harrison. They were twenty-one, forty-nine and sixty-seven years of age respectively; they were all able to account for their movements on the Tuesday afternoon; the oldest one possessed a car, but it was a saloon; not one of them was a commercial traveller (two, in fact, had been working in offices at the particular time); the older two had wives who were alive and well and didn't answer to the name Evelyn; none of them had served in the Royal Air Force.

'Tony, m'lad,' said MacIndoe in depression, 'we're approaching the stage at which I shall be forced to use intuition.'

At the Greenridge R.A.F.V.R. station an hour later. Beyond

the village of Greenridge ran a private road flush with the surface of the aerodrome. An enormous expanse of grass—at least a mile long—with a wide concrete strip running from south-west to north-east. A long way off two blue lorries crossing the field, brown dust rising high behind them. A few airmen walking past huts with mugs in their hands. The faint sound of a piano. Round the edges of the aerodrome fighter aircraft parked haphazardly. A few concrete buildings on the aerodrome itself, a wind-sock hanging limp, all the other buildings on the side near the village. The faint hum of a solitary aircraft. One of ours.

At the main gate—a surprisingly flimsy barbed-wire trestle—the sentry was thrown into some confusion. He didn't know what to do with detectives; but a sergeant of the R.A.F. police—apparently under the impression that he, too, served justice—eventually fetched the Orderly Officer. The Orderly Officer telephoned the Commanding Officer, and that young man, having just finished a considerable dinner and one and a half pints of beer, and therefore being loth to move from his chair, suggested that the detectives be brought to the officers' mess.

In here MacIndoe and Baker were greeted in some amusement by several officers. A slim, blond moustachioed squadron leader said, 'I'm the C.O. I say, are you johnnies really detectives, or is it that you're off duty?'

Baker said, 'I'm afraid we're on duty.'

'Have a drink?'

'Don't,' said a pilot. 'It's all poisoned.' All the young men found this remark exquisitely funny.

Baker said, 'What sort of kites have you got?'

'*Kites?*' protested the squadron leader. 'You'll be asking us about our balloons next. We fly jets, old man. Arrows.'

'I was on Spitfires during the war,' said Baker.

'Lord bless you!' said the squadron leader. 'How *old* you must be. These bloody Arrows *stall* at about four hundred. Have another drink?'

'I haven't had one yet,' said Baker.

'Lord, how *slow* you are,' the squadron leader said. Some drinks were brought. 'Does your Dad drink too?'

Baker said in protest, 'That's Superintendent MacIndoe.'

'I say,' another officer said. 'I've just thought. Perhaps they're from Scotland Yard.'

There was more laughter. 'We are,' said Baker. There were at once cries of, 'Line! Line!'

'Are you looking for a body?'

Baker said, 'We've found the body.'

The laughter ceased. Everyone stared in shock at Baker. The squadron leader said, 'Have you come about Harris? It was an accident. Surely the less said——'

'What happened to Harris?'

'He was killed yesterday. It happened forty miles off. Went straight into the deck. The funeral's to-morrow.'

'I'm sorry,' said Baker. 'I'm afraid our inquiry is about something equally unpleasant.'

'Perhaps,' said the squadron leader, 'we'd all better have another drink.'

'We may have to abuse your hospitality.'

'Well!' said someone. 'They suspect one of *us*.'

There was a slight renewal of the laughter.

'Do you?' queried the squadron leader.

'No,' said Baker. 'At least——'

'You'd better tell us. What is it? A hit-and-run motorist?'

'Anybody here named Harrison?'

'No. We had Harris, of course.'

'Christian name Roy?'

'No; it was John. I say, damn it, the fellow's dead. . . .'

MacIndoe said, 'A girl is dead, too. She was strangled.'

They all turned to stare at him, their young faces full of horror. MacIndoe said, 'I'm sorry about Mr. Harris. I'm sure this is nothing to do with him.'

'It's all right,' said the squadron leader. 'All this is a bit vague, you know. I thought you Yard johnnies looked for men with gold teeth, bad breath, one finger missing—you know the sort of thing.'

'We have some details,' said MacIndoe. 'A name—Roy Harrison—which is probably false. He was a bomber pilot at Little Over in the war—although that may be false too. But he was wearing a R.A.F.V.R. tie on Tuesday afternoon. . . . He has a red sports car and is a traveller.'

'Tuesday, you say?' the squadron leader said. 'But we've all been *here* since Saturday. Tuesday afternoon we were flying. That rather settles it, doesn't it?'

Someone said, 'Wasn't George at Little Over in the war?'

'Was he?'

'Where *is* George?'

'Ah! Hiding! George, the master criminal!'

The Orderly Officer appeared at that moment. 'Come here,

George,' said the squadron leader. 'Weren't you at Little Over in the war?'

George nodded.

'Did you ever meet a Roy Harrison?' asked MacIndoe.

'Never met a Roy Harrison,' said the Orderly Officer. 'I knew an Eric Harrison. He was pranged.'

'Can you remember any Birlchester men who served as pilots?'

'There was Allday. He was pranged, too.'

'Some swine's going around shooting a line about it,' explained the squadron leader. 'He's killed a girl.'

'The redhead in the papers?'

MacIndoe nodded.

'Sorry,' said the Orderly Officer. 'I'm sure Bill Allday was the only one. Could he have been a sergeant pilot?'

'It's possible.'

Baker said, 'Were you there for the Kiel show? The mine-laying effort?'

'No. Before my time.'

'When did it take place?'

'I can tell you that. It was carried out in March, 1943. We lost about eighty men on that show.'

'You'd better get on to Records,' suggested the squadron leader. 'Even if George remembered someone, you'd have to approach them for the address.'

'I've already written to the Air Ministry,' said MacIndoe. 'I'm awaiting their reply.'

There was general laughter again. 'Oh, you wait *years*,' said the squadron leader. 'They never answer anything in less than three months.'

VIII

THE squadron leader was mistaken. A letter from the Air Ministry arrived on the following afternoon. It came with twenty other letters. There had been more than a hundred in the morning's post. The police at Almond Vale, including the visiting detectives, had by now had about three hundred doorstep interviews in the town, which was quite a lot for such a small force— sufficient to justify an index being made of the statements. The letters—and personal calls with similar information—did nothing beyond confirming that a redheaded girl had been seen in the town with a tall man. Arranged chronologically the information indicated the direction the two had taken; it all confirmed that the girl had been alive between three o'clock and three-thirty; the pathologist had said that she had died between three and four; someone would have to account for himself during every minute of that hour; the wearisome collection of information was strong, relentless circumstantial evidence.

The letter from the Air Ministry did not, on the face of it, add any relevant information; there was no mention of a man with the name Harrison.

SIRS,

The following were officers (pilots, observers or air-gunners) from the city of Birlchester and environs who served at the R.A.F. Station, Little Over, Lincolnshire, during the period of hostilities, 1939/1945:

Allday, William Laurence. b. 1917. R.A.F. 1938. Commissioned 1939. F/O 1940. Fl/Lt 1941. Sq/Ldr 1943. D.F.C. 1940, bar 1942. D.S.O. 1943. Killed in action November 1943. At Little Over May, 1943-November, 1943. Married, Birlchester, 1942. Two children. Address of next-of-kin (widow): Mrs. Myrtle Elizabeth Allday, 147, Blenheim Road, Iron Common, Birlchester 17.

Edwards, Charles Henry. b. 1916. R.A.F. 1935. Commissioned 1938. F/O 1939. Fl/Lt 1940. Sq/Ldr 1943. Wing Cmdr 1943. D.F.C. 1940, bar 1943. Prisoner of war September, 1943-April, 1945. At Little Over November, 1941-September, 1943. Married, London, 1941. One child. This officer is still serving in the R.A.F.

Ferguson, George Rodney. b. 1920. R.A.F. 1940. Commissioned 1941. F/O 1943. At Little Over March, 1944-December, 1944. Then transferred to Coastal Command Station at Rocksea. Married, Birlchester, 1940. Three children. Present address: 'The Hollies', Church Avenue, Paleside, Birlchester 22. This officer is serving in the R.A.F.V.R. (County of Middleshire Squadron).

Fortescue, Roy Marlborough. b. 1920. R.A.F. 1940. Commissioned 1940. F/O 1941. At Little Over April, 1943-May, 1943. Transferred to F.T.S. at Biggots Aybury as possible L.M.F., May, 1943. Address of next-of-kin (parents): Mr. and Mrs. H. V. Fortescue, 14 Cedars Avenue, Flowersworth, Birlchester 20.

Should you require information about non-commissioned officers, would you please give as much notice as possible, since such would need more time to ascertain.

I am, Sir,

Your Obedient Servant,

—— (illegible)

for Commanding Officer.

MacIndoe read the letter twice before passing it to Maddocks and Baker. 'I like the sound of Roy Marlborough Fortescue,' he commented, not altogether seriously. 'Tony, what does F.T.S. mean?'

'Flying Training School.'

MacIndoe considered it. 'He was transferred to a non-operational aerodrome, where he had time to look around and find a wife. How about L.M.F.?'

'It means low moral fibre.'

MacIndoe said in astonishment, 'I didn't know they worried about morality in the R.A.F.'

'It doesn't quite mean that,' explained Baker. 'It refers to morale rather than morals; and the fact that he wasn't discharged as L.M.F. means they didn't wish it; which in turn means he had a good record.'

'He won no medals.'

'That doesn't mean much.'

'But he's alive,' said Maddocks. 'And his name is Roy.'

'Why do they give the address of next-of-kin as parents if he's married?' MacIndoe said.

'It's the last address they would have,' said Baker. 'I expect that their information doesn't go beyond the date of demobilization. He must have returned with his wife to his parents—for a time, anyway.'

MacIndoe reached for his hat. 'I suggest we interview Mr. and Mrs. H. V. Fortescue,' he said. 'Of the names we have, one man is dead; one we've already seen: he was flying on Tuesday afternoon; another is still serving in the R.A.F. and presumably cannot be a traveller also; which leaves Mr. Fortescue, who has the attractive name Roy. I do like the sound of L.M.F. It's such a perfect description of the man we want.'

The three detectives reached 14 Cedars Avenue, Flowersworth, half an hour later. It was a large, detached house in a residential suburb of Birlchester. Hidden from the road by bushes and trees, it had lawns on three sides; on the fourth were two garages, a greenhouse, rainwater barrels, a shed and the tradesmen's entrance. Dogs began to bark as they walked along red gravel towards the front door. MacIndoe felt some misgivings. It seemed the wrong sort of house at which to inquire about murder. MacIndoe read occasional novels about murders at country mansions, but knew that in reality murder belongs with the rest of the world's miseries to the poor and the uneducated.

A maid answered the door. Beyond her in the hall MacIndoe saw a wooden chest, hundreds of years old, and on a wall, a drawing of a cathedral. The place stank of respectability. Ah, well, he was entitled to make his inquiry. 'Is Mr. Fortescue in?' he asked.

'No, sir. But Mrs. Fortescue is here. Do you wish to speak to her?'

'If we may.'

'What name is it?'

'We are police officers.'

'Oh.' The woman's mouth tautened: it was apparent that if she had known who they were, Mrs. Fortescue also would have been out. Her employers had to be defended against those who were not respectable: the maid knew that the police (no officer class) were included in this category. There's nothing quite like the English, MacIndoe thought. Just when you felt the whole lot of them were unbearable snobs and hypocrites one of them would laugh and you'd have to form an opinion all over again. But it was as well they laughed.

The maid returned to the door almost immediately. 'Will you come this way?'

The detectives were led into a lounge, where they were greeted rather coldly by a tall, middle-aged woman. She was well-dressed, alert and confident, with an expression of slightly hostile detachment; snobbish and confident, it was obvious that she had no reason to suppose their visit would be hostile. 'Did you wish to see me?' she asked, and her tone implied the question, 'How much money do you want?' In the end, everything came down to how much was to be paid.

'We really wish to speak to Mr. Fortescue.'

'He is at business.'

'I meant Mr. Fortescue junior.'

The woman's expression changed almost imperceptibly. 'What about my son?'

'We would like to interview him, but we haven't his address.'

'What about, may I ask?'

'I think we should discuss that with him.'

'Then why come here?'

'We'd like his address.'

'Do you suspect my son of some crime?'

'We have to satisfy ourselves that he was not concerned,' said MacIndoe. 'His name seems to occur in a diary, that's all. It's a question of tidying up everything appertaining to this particular crime, you see.'

The woman said, 'Oh, I think I can tidy up that part of your inquiry. I can satisfy you absolutely. My son is dead.' The astonishment of the detectives could not be quite hidden and the woman went on: 'You seem surprised.'

'We had just been informed that he survived the war,' said MacIndoe. 'It's a shock to hear of a young man dying in peacetime. I'm terribly sorry, Mrs. Fortescue. If we'd known——'

For the first time the woman smiled. 'You had to follow your clue, didn't you?' she said. 'What was the inquiry concerned with?'

'The murder of a girl.'

The woman turned away and reached a framed photograph from a table. 'This was my son,' she said.

MacIndoe thought in astonishment: Didn't she hear what I said? Doesn't the murder of a girl mean anything to her? Isn't she capable of shock or sympathy or even curiosity? Did she love her son so much that she's calloused to any other death? He stared long and carefully at the photograph of an officer with a pilot's wings. Dark hair, pointed nose, full lips, arrogant expression, large eyes —*He longs to possess me and is even showing slight impatience at my arguments.* It could be *him*, MacIndoe thought. But she says he's dead. 'He was a handsome youth,' he commented (the woman was not to know that the word 'handsome' was practically meaningless). 'I suppose he leaves a widow?'

'Yes.'

'Does she live with you?'

'No. We've rather lost touch.'

'What is her name?'

The woman looked into MacIndoe's eyes, but could not hold his gaze. She turned to one side in a slightly theatrical gesture and said, 'Does that matter now?' MacIndoe did not speak. She was forced to carry on and say, 'It is Margaret.'

'Was your son a commercial traveller?'

'Oh, no.'

Mrs. Fortescue was quite gay as she conducted the officers herself to the front door. 'You know, I really believe you suspected my son,' she said. 'Do you really think a boy from a home like this would commit such a crime?'

MacIndoe did not answer and it was left to Maddocks to say, 'Of course not.'

The three police officers walked slowly back along the red gravel. Once MacIndoe turned to look back at the house, and saw Mrs. Fortescue gazing from the bay window of a front room. Their interview had not taken place in that room, and the woman's action did nothing to abate the uneasiness in his mind. Not that she withdrew or appeared embarrassed—she is too subtle for that, MacIndoe thought—but merely opened a small window in an action that was too natural, too poised. The slightest embarrassment and MacIndoe would have put it down to curiosity—people were curious about detectives—but the stare, like all her other actions and words, had been too controlled.

By the car he said, 'Well, what did you think?'

Maddocks said, 'It wasn't very satisfactory, was it?'

'I'm not satisfied,' said MacIndoe. 'Did you see her face when I mentioned the word "murder"?'

'No,' said Maddocks. 'She turned away too quickly. She wasn't very interested in it, was she?'

'That's what worries me,' MacIndoe said. 'She was too disinterested. And yet I can't see why. It wasn't as if she had been expecting us or had anybody to shield. Did you notice how careful her dialogue was? She was able to find out why we had come before saying a word about her son.'

Baker said, 'But if he's dead, sir, it's not going to make any difference, anyway.'

MacIndoe sat in the driver's seat. 'She was lying about something.' He bit a thumbnail and sat in thought. 'Suppose he was alive. She didn't know about the murder, but we come along and mention a crime. She begins to lie to save her son from unpleasantness, and when she hears what the crime was continues the untruths because——'

'Because,' said Maddocks, 'she knows her son is capable of murder.'

'Exactly,' said MacIndoe.

Baker said, 'Aren't we presuming a lot from just a few gestures?'

MacIndoe smiled. 'Perhaps we are. She wouldn't know he was

236

likely to murder, but she would know if he was cruel to women. And she probably doesn't mind so long as she can still possess him. The doting mother. There were two photographs of him in that one room. The other was on the mantelshelf. She didn't seem very interested in her daughter-in-law and was completely apathetic about Olwen. . . .'

Baker said, 'You sound like a psychiatrist, sir.'

MacIndoe laughed and started to drive. 'Now I know I'm talking through my hat.'

Maddocks said, 'We could go back.'

'No,' said MacIndoe. 'If we shout at her or demand to see the grave—well, she would be very upset if we were wrong. . . .'

Ten minutes later, still driving, he said, 'You couldn't blame a woman if she protected her son—her only son. Women are not interested in the principle of justice at the expense of anyone they love. And I *know* the Air Force has something to do with this. It was almost the first thing *he* said to Olwen: I was a bomber pilot at Little Over. On the strength of that you must admire me. It's in character, Tony, with that face.'

Baker said nothing.

Maddocks said, 'Yes, I know, but——' and didn't conclude his sentence.

Five minutes afterwards MacIndoe said, 'I'm going down to that Biggots Aybury place. If her name was Margaret, I'll be satisfied. If it was Evelyn . . . The vicar will know.'

Baker said, 'You're not going *now?*'

'Is it far?'

'I think it's in Somerset.'

'I'll leave as soon as possible.'

'Shall I come with you?'

'No, Tony. One damn' fool will be enough. You join the Inspector in the search for the red car.' MacIndoe turned to Maddocks. 'When we've finished with Almond Vale, I'd like every chemist's and hairdresser's shop along Almond Vale Road visited. Say a mile each way from Olga Harper's shop. Someone must remember a traveller with a red sports car. If not, we'll try an appeal in the Press.'

MacIndoe was not able to leave Middleshire that day. Instead he started at dawn on the following day, a Saturday. It took four hours' fast driving to reach the village of Biggots Aybury. MacIndoe had no breakfast and stopped for a drink of coffee at the last large town on the route. Several times he had moments of panic, believing he was making a fool of himself, being too subtle, or that his inquiry could have been passed on to the local police, anyway. He reached the aerodrome at nine o'clock. It was almost deserted. The canvas flapped from the skeletons of hangars; sheep chewed where once rubber tyres had alighted; there were still Nissen huts and a brick control tower, but the aerodrome was clearly not in full usage. Along one side—near the road: available to anyone—were rows of gleaming silver parts: cylinders, bolts, unidentifiable engine parts, tins of paint, boxes of odd-shaped screws and rivets. The war had been over for more than a decade, but the mess was still being tidied up.

In the village the church was closed, and MacIndoe, relieved to be out of his car, walked to the large, tree-surrounded old house which must be the Vicarage.

An old lady answered his knock and informed him that the vicar was visiting a sick woman; there were two weddings that morning—twin sisters; yes, it was remarkable—could he call in the afternoon?

'I'd like to see him before then.'

'Is it something important?'

'Yes.'

The old woman pondered. She had a distant look; a kindly face which was no longer involved; it tried very hard, but was deep in some misery of its own. 'Why don't you wait in the church? He'll be along a good half-hour before the first wedding.'

'The church is closed.'

'No. It's never closed. Henry won't—— The door is shut, that's all.'

'Is there anywhere I can obtain breakfast?'

'Don't you live in the parish? I thought you were a—— There's a café in the village. I don't know whether they do breakfasts.'

MacIndoe discovered the café and was served with a breakfast of bacon and beans by a pleasant young woman. He ate the food and drank some coffee, watched by the woman's two children.

At ten o'clock MacIndoe turned the heavy door handle and entered St. Mary's Church. Outside there was the faint rustle of trees in the feeble wind, a pale blue sky with very little cloud, and, on the ground, everything defined sharply: the stone walls of the churchyard, the old gravestones, the splash of colour on the graves of the recently dead, the bark of the trees, the green fields stretching away to a hedge horizon. Every crack and mark in the stone church was revealed—the church is not faultless, MacIndoe thought as he saw the few chips and cracks and the splashes of bird-droppings. It was nevertheless a pleasant, square-towered little church. Inside was the smell of incense and wood and dead flowers and books. The light was softened except when one looked at the windows; then MacIndoe's travel-weary eyes felt burnt out by the force of the colours. There were no pretensions inside: no appeals to visitors to wipe their feet, or leave money, or pray for the relief of military victories; no flags; no references to novelists who had mentioned the district in their books; one was left free from hypocrisy and pomp to participate in the real battle if one chose; but one was not inveigled into doing so.

The atmosphere began to affect MacIndoe. He had been hurrying this day and on the previous few—*this* was stationary and eternal. I do not come often enough, he thought. I work on too many Sundays. It was absolutely quiet inside the church; it had been silent outside, but here the silence was a tangible presence; he was reached by it at once. The silence commenced to inflict its physical weight. Alone with it one was freed slowly from distractions. The things of the day and of the hour and of the moment passed, and one was left naked and forced to think. The mind thrashed about like a hooked fish, preferring the distractions, afraid of the silence. The distractions seemed safe, for they were by no means unreal: the world was full of the sound of men talking: in the courts justice and wisdom were dispensed like aspirin and one was left dissatisfied, as if that were not the end. In the silence one knew that it could not be the end: justice must be indivisible: it could not be the property of men with prejudices or poor eyesight or indigestion or a knowledge of books or an opinion of humanity formed from its dregs. In the silence one waited for the significant sound. One heard the protests of the arbitrarily condemned, the hissed respirations of the tortured, the self-satisfaction of the martyrs, the anger of the ignorant, the wails of the children. In the pressing silence one could hear the creak of wood and the laughter of the crowd at Golgotha. With sweat on the hands, one waited for another sound and eventually it came: from across the Channel on a night in the autumn of 1917: the rumble of guns. When I am a man I want to fight in a battle against wickedness. That war ended and before I became a man I knew it hadn't been a battle against evil; it had just been an economic stupidity. So against my father's wishes I joined the police. I wanted my battle to be real and physical; I wanted to pursue sin and hit it with

239

a truncheon, to sort out and expose the most complicated wickedness. But time and success had turned that ideal into the usual
policeman's battle against illegality. This was so complex that the
very procedure prevented one becoming involved oneself. The
criminals were pursued and sent to prison or hanged, not because
they had sinned, but because they had broken the law. You failed,
MacIndoe—even with your sympathy you failed. I know. I know.
Everybody fails. Whoever heard of an idealist whose ideals were
successful? We are all criminals. And what am I to do if I catch
this man R.? I am involved in this affair all right. I'm even making
a fool of myself. What am I to do if I win the legal battle? Am I to
preach at him? Should I give him her diary to read so that he may
know what he has destroyed? Shall I confront him with her
parents? But the truth is that I shall not be allowed by the law of
which I am part to do anything except ascertain and present the
proofs of his guilt. MacIndoe knelt down in perplexity to give the
problem to Another. In a fervent whisper that ended the silence
he mouthed part of that astonishing petition, the 119th Psalm:
'*I am small and of no reputation: yet do I not forget thy commandments.
Thy righteousness is an everlasting righteousness: and thy law is the
truth.*'

He heard the faint clatter of a light tread across the tiles and the
graves of the long-since dead. Someone was coming towards him
from the other end of the aisle. The detective rose to his feet to
meet another man. It was a priest who approached.

The priest was a small man and frail. His frailty seemed recent,
for his clothes hung limp on his body, a body that seemed more
bone than flesh. His face was as lined as a complicated etching.
In his whole dragged being only the eyes seemed to live, driven
on by a will that knew the truth despite what the eyes saw. He looks
ill, MacIndoe thought, sick with a prolonged illness that belonged
as much to the mind as to the body. The meek shall inherit the
earth. Yes, but only after humiliation and degradation had sickened
them of it. Was that it?

'Good morning,' the priest said. His face was quite different
when it smiled; one could see that it had laughed much once;
the garden parties and the baptisms and the teas had been an
accepted part of life then. 'Are you the best man?'

'Good morning,' said MacIndoe. 'No. I'm a stranger.'

'Welcome to our church.'

'I've come to see you.'

'I do not seem to know you.'

'I am a detective.'

'You've come from Taunton?'

'No. I'm from London, but I'm operating from Middleshire.'

'And you've come all the way to see me? Do you need some kind of—help?'

'Yes.'

The old man moved an arm in a faint gesture. 'I am here to help people.' The gesture was a bitter one. They did not want the help. They only desired the sanction of whatever it was they intended to do. They scrabbled in dirt for love and money and possession, and if you interfered they said you wanted power. You must not interfere unless asked to, and you should only reiterate their opinions when you did. God and His representatives had to understand that they were very busy these days on important matters—social and economic adjustments, legalized murder and fornication, the comprehension of art, the pursuit of politics, money, freedom and happiness. If God and His representatives did not remember their places, *they* would not enter church at all, not even every sixteenth Sunday, or for their daughters' weddings, or when a war was going badly; indeed, despite its difficulties, they would, if irritated sufficiently, begin to study science. And then where would God be?

MacIndoe said, 'What I have to ask is quite a simple question, but it is related to an extremely unpleasant matter. I think perhaps we should not discuss it here.'

'You'd like to move outside?'

'That is what I meant.'

'You are thoughtful.'

'Detectives go to church sometimes,' MacIndoe said. 'Not often, of course, because, like soldiers, they do not really understand the battle they're in.'

The priest stared at him. 'I see. Well, let's go outside.'

They walked to the door. Outside the heat struck them, ricocheting from the wall of the church. There returned to MacIndoe the noises of physical reality: the buzz of insects, the chirp of a thrush, the sighing of the wind, poultry somewhere clucking about their business, and some way off the roar of a vehicle in top gear.

The two men stood without words for several minutes, staring at the view, understanding each other. 'What I have to find out,' MacIndoe explained, 'is the name of a person who was married in this parish between May and December of 1943.'

'Do you know the name of one party?'

'I have the name of the man,' said MacIndoe, 'and want the name of the girl.'

'It means returning inside the church,' said the vicar. 'What is the name you have?'

'Flying Officer Roy Marlborough Fortescue.'

The clergyman gave a brief animal cry—a curious whelp of pain, misery or fright. 'What's the matter?' MacIndoe asked. 'Does the name mean something to you?'

Slowly the priest recovered. It had obviously been a tremendous shock; he was trembling still when he said, 'I can tell you the name of the girl.'

'Was it Margaret?'

'It was my daughter Evelyn.'

MacIndoe stared at him, appalled, feeling no exultation at all. The old man, dithering still in agitation, was to be wounded further; he had to learn what sort of a man his daughter had married. But perhaps he knew—the shock was obviously an unpleasant one.

The vicar looked at his watch. 'I've only a quarter of an hour before the first of to-day's weddings. Tell me as much as you can. Is my daughter involved in this extremely unpleasant matter you mentioned?'

'No. It's her husband.'

'I'm not surprised.'

'Is her husband alive?'

'Oh, yes. He's very much of the living.'

'Someone told us he was dead.'

'Who told you that?'

'His mother.'

'When did he die? How long ago?'

'I don't know. Some time back. She said she's lost touch with her daughter-in-law. . . .'

'Roy Fortescue was alive three weeks ago.'

'Then he's alive now.'

'I can't think why she should have lied to you. I never met her—I don't know what she's like. Is it possible that she misunderstood you?'

'No. She was lying. She lied twice, saying also that your daughter's name was Margaret.'

'What made you suspect?'

'She showed no sympathy for the victim of the crime——'

'There's been a crime?'

'Yes.'

'Does it affect my daughter?'

MacIndoe said cautiously, 'It will affect her. Tell me about your daughter.'

'What do you want to know?'

'When did you last see her?'

'I haven't seen her since she was married. She married against our wishes more than eleven years ago.'

'When did you last hear from her?'

'Three weeks ago.'

'Was she well?'

'Well? Yes, as far as I know.'

'Where did the letter come from?'

'It came from a block of flats in Birlchester.'

'She lives there with her husband?'

'Yes. I didn't read anything to the contrary. You see, this is the first letter we've ever had. It was as we thought—the marriage became a failure, a misery. I'll show you the letter. Will you wait? Another hour, but it will be worth it.'

'I'll wait. Was she married in your church?'

'Oh, dear me, no. He hates us, that young man does. No feelings at all. Just the body. There was a girl in the village—— What has he done?'

'He has killed a girl.'

The priest gasped. 'You have proof?'

'Not really,' said MacIndoe. 'We have circumstantial evidence, a few witnesses who saw him with the victim half an hour before. . . . And we have the girl's diary which exposes the whole trick. It's just possible—but myself I *know* he's guilty. He told the girl that he had a wife called Evelyn in a lunatic asylum. That's why I asked you——'

'That's his technique,' said the priest. 'That's typical of his cynicism. He has a sort of cunning charm—he deceived *us* for months during that year. Was this girl—a wicked one?'

'No,' said MacIndoe. 'A trifle foolish, perhaps, but she was in love with him. She was a religious girl. It took weeks of persuading and lying to——'

'You must not inform me,' said the priest quickly. 'So many unbearable things happen to the religious in our time that I am forced to wonder if the other side could win. We have taken it so much for granted that God's side is the stronger, must inevitably win. . . . And then, you see, if you tell me of the cruelty he inflicted on a foolish girl I shall, with my prejudiced, parental imagination, be able to picture with terrible clarity what Evelyn had to endure.'

MacIndoe said, 'But love, surely, can endure anything and survive?'

'It wasn't that kind of love,' explained the priest. 'Love?' He mused on the word. 'I am very tired of the misunderstanding of love, the deliberate misinterpretation by the world. I am sick of that kind of love. It confronts me on the hoardings and the newspapers; it jokes about its sanctity on the radio; it is in desperate pursuit of more energy, stronger soap, sweeter breath, more money, deeper sleep, and new, attractive means to stupefy and seduce; it is implied in implications within implications, so that one can scarcely hear a word or examine a paragraph without being led to sense abandonment and the grinding of bodies in a bed. The one thing it does not desire is sacrifice—the word is never mentioned. I sometimes wonder why they still come to us priests. Why do they continue to desire a holy bondage in this building they'll never visit again? Do you think we have stressed God's mercy so much that they have come to rely on it entirely? I talk to the young ones when they've seen the verger and fixed the details. Love is the world, I tell them, believing it still, and meaning *His* sort of love. But many of them snigger and their eyes are hot and they venture outside and say, "What an old fool," and then fondle each other in the bushes, and presume we do not know. . . . And when illness or death or unhappiness comes through their own mistakes and sins they complain and say God shouldn't allow it. . . . And I don't see them again. . . . Love, did you say? It is too large a thing for this most physical of generations. But never mind me—by their standards I am a sick old man.'

'Surely,' protested MacIndoe, 'you cannot be so bitter because of one man and one girl, even though the girl was your own daughter? I am a police officer and know of much suffering. Yet my impression is still that the vast majority of ordinary—let alone extraordinary—people are capable of great love and sacrifice for each other and others beyond themselves. . . . This is a generation that badly wants the truth. It has good qualities—a hatred of cruelty, for instance. Its own cynical humour frees it from the pomp of its predecessors. . . .'

The priest stared at MacIndoe again, a wan smile in the green, myopic eyes. 'Tell me,' he said. 'You are a man who presumably has seen much evil without it hurting you. Tell me, do you think a man like that can be made in the image of God?'

MacIndoe started in something like fear. '*You* ask *me* that?'

'Yes, yes. This is not a moment for polite conversation. I am an old man and I am hurt. I have worked hard all my life and I do not think my sincerity has penetrated a single soul. We seem all on our own in the end.'

'I suppose,' said MacIndoe, seeing in his mind the emotionless, proud, callous face of Mrs. Fortescue, 'that there were many moments before the world reached him. When he was a baby, a small child——'

'Will you see Evelyn?'

'I don't know.'

'Go to see her. She's a good girl. This man had to marry her—the baby died. Oh, what piteous, weak things humans are. How they crave someone to admire them. . . . They will sacrifice the universe. And knowing all the time that the man is evil. . . . It seemed such an unbearable affront to the compassion of God.'

'Shall I tell her to come home?'

'You will see her, won't you? We'd lost touch for years, and then this letter came. I thank God for it. Yes, tell her, persuade her to come home. My wife——'

'I will tell her.'

'And listen. You're a good man. (I saw you praying.) Try to convince *him* that it was wrong—not just legally mistaken, but *wrong*. I couldn't begin to penetrate him—he was in love with himself and evil.'

'It's very difficult. There are rules.'

'Yes, but try.'

'Do you think it would make a difference?'

'He's going to die, isn't he? Any small penitence might make a difference.'

MacIndoe read Evelyn Fortescue's letter an hour later. It was written from a block of flats in north-east Birlchester:

My Dearest Parents,

It is a long time since you have heard from me. I make no apology—we all know why it has been so. I have had a great deal of unhappiness during the years since I left you—you said I would—and would not have had the courage to write to you if that unhappiness had not become meaningless. And I have been thinking for weeks that there are still two persons in the world who love me and would wish to know that I have not forgotten them.

245

I was happy in my marriage for several years. I am sure you do not begrudge me that: it is every girl's wish. Then I found out that Roy had been unfaithful to me with a woman at our tennis club—a Mrs. Saunders; she was married too. We quarrelled, but I forgave Roy. Then I learned that unfaithfulness was a habit of his; his idea of sin was being found out. When I learned that only two years after our marriage he had been seducing airwomen—then my unhappiness began, for it meant that I had *never* meant anything to him. His letters to me at the time had been passionate and descriptive: I had thought they'd described *me*.

You can imagine the rest of it. I never knew before that one person—without violence or anger or indeed anything at all—could hurt another quite so much. I became ill and remained so for a long time. It took long years to find happiness in another way. I live now in a world he cannot damage: among books, music, a few friends and the Church. He is so absorbed in his own world—it includes other women, I know —that he can just about observe the day-to-day hypocrisy.

I want you to tell me that you forgive me. Dear father, was it a sin to love someone who is evil? I do not love him now, of course, but intend to stand by him. Some day he must become sick of himself and turn to me. Then I could try to undo all the evil. . . .

Please write. I am longing so much to hear that you are both well, and that you forgive

Your loving daughter,

EVELYN

MacIndoe, handing back the letter to the vicar, said, 'You must have been very glad to have received that letter.'

'We were.'

'It will still hurt her, of course. Some of her love probably remains.'

'Yes, yes, I see that. She has courage too. She would have stood by him and tried——'

'I shall tell her to come home,' said MacIndoe. 'It's too late to save him. This is where she belongs. Do you know where this man works?'

'He used to work for a shipping company.'

'Do you know which one?'

'I have all the details somewhere. You'll stay to lunch, of course. I'll tell you all I can.'

MacIndoe drove at great speed back to Middleshire. At the offices of the shipping company he learned that Roy Fortescue was no longer an employee. He also learned a number of other things about Fortescue.

At Almond Vale police station Baker and Maddocks were waiting in some excitement. 'We think we've got him,' Baker said. 'A chemist along Almond Vale Road says that a man—name unknown—from the Perfecta Soap Company calls in a red sports. Their place is closed on Saturday afternoons, but we've obtained the names of the directors and the district manager. We've been waiting an hour for you.'

MacIndoe smiled. 'Thank you. I've found out his name and address.'

'Was it the pilot?'

'Yes; it was.'

'He wasn't dead?'

MacIndoe detailed his journey and explained about the live, sane Evelyn. 'I'm not wasting any time about this. Other people may be in danger. Let's go and get him.'

'Are you going to arrest?'

'No; not straight away. It depends on him, really. We'll question him first. . . . Inspector, will you bring the impression Dr. Baxter made? If we should see the wife first, we'll obtain the name of his dentist, and perhaps you'd go straight there.'

They were driven the twenty miles to north-east Birlchester in an official police car. MacIndoe jumped to the pavement with surprising agility—as though seconds counted. A few passers-by stopped and stared in curiosity. In the main entrance hall was a list of the tenants. Fortescue's flat was on the second floor. MacIndoe operated the lift. They were silent, despite the absence of other passengers. Each felt the tension and was impatient with the slow movement of the lift.

The number of the flat was eleven and the name was in a small brass bracket: R. M. Fortescue. MacIndoe tapped lightly on the door.

A woman of about thirty, perhaps more, answered the knock quickly, as if she had been waiting for someone. The woman, who must be Evelyn Fortescue, did not answer to the mental picture MacIndoe had formed of her. She was good-looking in a taut, intense way, with an attractive, even arrogant face; she looked quite capable of looking after herself. She wore excellent clothes and shoes, adding to the impression of smartness. If he had not read her letter, MacIndoe would never have divined that she was an unhappy person or an unselfish one: she looked too worldly to be either. It was even possible that he might have disliked her.

She stared at the three detectives in frank curiosity, and MacIndoe's analytical pause was so prolonged that she said, 'Well?'

'Mrs. Fortescue?'

'Yes,' she said.

'We're police officers. Is your husband in?'

'No.'

'Where is he?'

'I'm not sure. I think he's playing tennis. Is there anything I can do for you?'

'You could give us some information.'

'Will you come in?'

Mrs. Fortescue led the three officers through a hall into a lounge. Everything was in what is known as good taste; but it's not a home to relax in, MacIndoe thought; it's an illustration from a glossy magazine. Mrs. Fortescue had evidently been writing a letter; she moved now to a small table and closed a writing pad. 'Do sit down,' she said, relaxing herself. The men remained standing. 'Is this something serious?' she asked when she noticed it.

'Mrs. Fortescue, do you know where your husband was on the afternoon of July 26th—that is, last Tuesday?'

'I'm afraid I don't.'

'Not at all?'

'You mean somewhere specific, don't you? He's a traveller, you see, and might be anywhere in Middleshire.'

'Did he come home for lunch that day?'

'He never comes home for lunch. Don't you think it would be a better idea to tell me what this is about and let me help you? I shan't try to trick you; and you can always tell when I lie, because I blush.'

'What time did he come home on that day?'

'Why don't you ask him?'

'He's not here.'

'It was about five. He was rather early for a Tuesday.'

'He's usually late on Tuesdays?'

'Are you asking me or telling me?'

'I was asking you, Mrs. Fortescue.'

'I'm sorry if I seem rude, but if you will treat me like a child——'

'Was he agitated at all when he came home?'

'No. Quite the contrary. He was exceptionally——'

'Exceptionally what?'

'This is a ridiculous conversation, or whatever you call these things. I was going to say he was exceptionally tender. Is that against the Traffic Regulations?'

'His behaviour was normal?'

'It was quite civilized. He asked me——' She stopped and then said, 'Oh, no. That was another day.'

'What did he ask you?'

'Well, if you must know such silly details, he wanted a bath.'

Maddocks said, 'Have you an immersion heater or central heating?'

'No. We're very primitive.'

'Then he asked you to light a fire?'

'You're too subtle for me. Anyway, the weather was too hot, so he didn't have a fire. As a matter of fact,' said Mrs. Fortescue brightly, 'he was a Boy Scout and can make his own fires.'

'Mrs. Fortescue,' said MacIndoe, 'we appreciate your loyalty, but we can't tell you what this is about. Quite frankly, it's so important that as police officers we simply have to retain the advantage of what information we have.'

The woman blanched. 'Then I'm not answering any more questions until my disadvantage is removed. It isn't really fair, is it? You're treating me like a guilty person.'

MacIndoe said as gently as possible, 'We know only too well, Mrs. Fortescue, that you are an innocent person—a victim even.'

She stood up, angry in apprehension. 'You'll probably find my husband at the Wellington Tennis Club. It's not far away. I'll leave you to find it yourselves, as you obviously enjoy playing detectives.'

'I'm not enjoying this, Mrs. Fortescue,' MacIndoe said truthfully. 'Has your husband ever mentioned the name Olwen Hughes?'

The young woman gripped the edge of the small table. One of her legs began to quiver. It trembled at a tremendous rate, while its partner remained quite still. Mrs. Fortescue said hoarsely, 'That's the girl——'

'Exactly.'

She said earnestly, as if pointing out a flaw in an argument, 'But you asked what Roy was doing on Tuesday. . . . Surely you don't think——' She gave a brief, hysterical laugh. '*Well, do you?*'

MacIndoe said, 'I'm terribly sorry, Mrs. Fortescue, but we do.'

Evelyn had become very pale. Her one calf still fluttered at intervals, occasionally stopping altogether as if she had regained control of the muscle, although she was probably completely unaware of the fluctuation. Her mouth was too rigid for her to speak naturally; it was as if she had become acutely aware of it so that each word was formed with difficulty. 'He's never mentioned her name,' she said.

'Has he ever mentioned any of their names?'

'I don't know what you mean.'

'I mean, has your husband ever mentioned the names of the women he's been with?'

'Do you want to gossip about my husband? Is that it? And do you expect *me* to join in?'

'Mrs. Fortescue, a girl has been murdered. She mentioned your husband's name in her diary in a way that gives foundation for something more than gossip. She said——'

'I don't want to hear what some shopgirl said.'

'It wasn't the real name, of course, but the false one. She wrote down in pitiful sincerity that this Roy Harrison, commercial traveller with a red sports car, ex-bomber pilot at Little Over Aerodrome, wanted to marry her; and that he would when his wife Evelyn died in the asylum in which she had resided for the last year or two. What are we to think of that? Should we dismiss it as gossip? What do *you* think, Mrs. Fortescue? How far do you think you should carry your loyalty?'

Evelyn sat down again and stared abstractedly at the grate. 'Tell me, Inspector—or whatever you are: I expect you're quite high up in the hierarchy—tell me, would you betray *your* wife if someone came round to question you?'

MacIndoe said, 'If she were ill, I would get a doctor.'

'That wasn't what I asked.'

'Well, no, Mrs. Fortescue, I suppose I wouldn't; I'd try to persuade her to walk to the nearest police station of her own accord. I'd suffer badly until she did.'

'And if she didn't?'

'I'd wait until they came to fetch her.'

'Suppose they didn't?'

'That doesn't arise in your own case, does it? We have only to wait here and Mr. Fortescue will come home. Or we can go now to the tennis club you mentioned—the Wellington, was it?'

Tears were trickling down Evelyn's face, but, apparently unaware of them, she said, 'You mustn't ask me any more questions about him. If you know so much you don't need any betrayal.'

'All right,' said MacIndoe. 'May I ask about yourself? You're not ill, are you? Ye never were mentally ill, were you?'

'Yes,' said Evelyn, turning to him. (She has a nice face after all, MacIndoe decided, once the proud façade has crumbled.) 'I was ill for quite a long time. I had a sickness that started on the day I met *him*. But it was a very pleasant illness at first. Then there was a crisis. We had defied my parents, you see, and we had defied God, and I thought, We're doing fine: the rest of the world can look after itself. Nothing matters. If anything seemed to, then he would point out the flaws in it and I'd laugh. I was only twenty-three and it was nice to conquer the world with him. Until I found that I wasn't exclusive; I was part of the world he despised; if he could have an affair with a W.A.A.F.—and two years after our marriage he did—he would do so without concern for *me*. I should have known when the baby died. . . . I did know. . . . God is not mocked. He waits and forgives for a long time because the young must be expected to be foolish for a while; and with some people you think they're going to get away with it altogether. But they don't. Someone they value dies; illness comes; or loneliness; or fear; they have to learn humility or fail. . . . If only the child had lived. . . .'

Evelyn stopped talking to struggle against the tears. The detectives stood absolutely motionless in the presence of her suffering. After a while she resumed: 'I had a nervous breakdown. My two worlds met and clashed: while he loved me and talked my mind was crucified by the knowledge of the others. When I'd recovered I came home from the hospital. I looked so well I could read the desire in his eyes. The clash occurred again. I went to my doctor and he found me organically sound—thought me a self-pitying fool, I suppose. I proceeded to a psychiatrist—after all, they were invented in conjunction with sexual freedom, weren't they? I told him about it and said, "You see, even while I was away in hospital Roy was having an affair" (such a mature word, don't you think, Inspector?). He said, "Well, of course, the thing to do is combat his technique. Enjoy yourself. Have an affair too. You're not one of the Christians, are you?" It was then that I knew with unshakable conviction that Roy's half of the world was evil. "Yes, I am," I said, and walked out of his consulting room. I made a very good recovery.'

'Does he know that you know?'

'That I know what?'

'That you—recovered?'

'Until you told me what that poor thing had put in her diary, I didn't realize that Roy was so aware. One thing about Roy: he has a splendid sense of irony.' Evelyn's tone changed and she said in an agony that made the others squirm: 'It's rather amusing really. Terribly theatrical. His attitude is so careless that, without a word ever being spoken about it, he informs me all too clearly about the others. Sometimes we look at each other, both knowing, and I turn away in tears—I'm still convalescent, you see—recovery is not easy—after all, we conquered the world together. And then he's scared—not of me, of course, but of his employer, Bushell. If I were to leave him, or if Bushell were to find out, then Roy would be sacked and his fantasy would be over. . . . In an asylum, did the girl think I was? Here in this very room I've been in hell for years. . . . I do feel awful after all this repertory. Would you mind if I had a small glass of sherry? One thing about Roy—plenty of booze. All contingencies catered for—if trouble rears its ugly head, bludgeon the senses. Simple, isn't it, and so effective that quite soon there is no sensibility left to bludgeon—one can look at the misery of the world and think of how to extract the next pound of flesh.' She walked across to a cabinet. 'Perhaps you'll have one too?'

'No, thank you.'

'Of course. You're on duty. All this for you is *work*.'

Evelyn sipped the sherry; her hands trembled all the time.

MacIndoe said, 'It's too late to go back, Mrs. Fortescue. We can only move forward. I have to proceed with this, although I scarcely want to. Has your husband a briefcase?'

'Yes; it's in the other room.'

'Could we have it?'

'I can't stop you.'

Baker went to fetch it. The briefcase had alphabetical compartments as the waitress at the Priory Tea Rooms had said. 'We'd better take this,' said MacIndoe.

Evelyn protested, 'Now, wait a minute——'

'You said we could have it. Who's your dentist, Mrs. Fortescue?'

'My dentist?'

'That is what I asked.'

'It's Mr. Wiggins.'

'His address?'

Evelyn gave it.

'Is he your husband's dentist too?'

'Yes. Why?'

'It was just a point.'

Maddocks said, 'Shall I go now?' and MacIndoe nodded.

Evelyn said, 'Where's he going?' but MacIndoe, instead of answering, asked, 'Is your husband wearing white flannels?'

'Yes.'

'Are his other clothes here?'

'I suppose so.'

'Would you show me his wardrobe?'

'His wardrobe?'

'The contents.'

'All right. If it makes you happy.'

The bedroom was an adjoining room. MacIndoe opened the man's wardrobe and sorted through the suits and coats until he found the flannels and the sports coat with the blue, red and brown zigzag. 'I'll take these,' he said grimly. (There would be soil or dust or grass or something in the turn-ups.) 'These may be evidence.' The shoes with the buckle fastenings were in a compartment. 'And these.'

Evelyn was weeping again, but without hysteria. It was a deep, despairing cry, almost like a cough: the release of a long-pent-up flow of tears: the despair of more than a decade of disastrous, one-sided marriage. 'No, no,' she pleaded. 'Please don't do that. I won't tell him, I promise, but don't take them away. It would mean that *I* had done it. . . .'

Her tears and loyalty moved even MacIndoe, who had much experience of tears and despair. He touched her shoulder. 'No, lassie,' he said. 'Ye mustn't refuse me. This is permanent, this is beyond repair. His behaviour is normal, isn't it? He's gone to play tennis, hasn't he? With a girl, d'ye think? The dead shopgirl doesn't mean a thing to him. He imagines he's immune, beyond reproach. . . . Ye don't need to be a Christian to see that that can't be allowed. It's against humanity. She was alive and with child and in love with him, but he killed her. It's not something ye can dismiss with an explanation by Freud. It's beyond repair.'

Evelyn shuddered. 'I didn't know it was as bad as that.'

'What good would he be to ye now? Ye've done all ye could, and ye must abandon him if ye can. Ye've got your own life to repair. Ye're an innocent person.'

'I'm not!' she cried. 'I'm not! I knew what I was doing. Oh, God, how I wish I was.'

'Ye know he's done it, don't ye?'

253

She said quietly, 'Yes.'

'Ye know without any proofs. His mother knew too, and lied to us, pretending he was dead. Ye both know he's guilty without hearing a word. *Why?* Because ye both know he's rotten.'

Evelyn said desperately, 'It's not going to be easy. I thought I'd stopped loving him years ago, but it seems I haven't.'

'Aye. But it's over. Go home, Mrs. Fortescue. I've been to Biggots Aybury and your parents are longing to see you.'

Evelyn wept now without words, without awareness of their presence. She was deep in her own bitterness. MacIndoe became concerned. 'Will ye be all right? We've got to leave ye.'

'Will I see him again?'

'Not here.'

'What shall I do?'

'Go home as soon as ye can. Don't do anything silly, will ye? You're only a girl really—there's a lot of life left yet.'

She said hopelessly, 'Be gentle, won't you? I mean——'

'I know what ye mean. Ye won't use that telephone in the hall, will ye? It wouldn't help him.'

'You're going now?'

'Yes.'

'I didn't betray him, did I?'

'No.'

'Will you tell him that?'

'I will.'

MacIndoe went down the steps two at a time; he didn't even wait for the lift; and he was yards ahead of Baker. The driver of the police car knew the whereabouts of the Wellington Tennis Club, and drove the vehicle furiously along the few roads to its gates. He turned the car round on the car park so that it was ready to depart without hindrance. There was no red sports car in the park.

The two detectives walked along an asphalt path, leaving the driver standing by the car. The less fuss the better, they felt. A few people in white were standing by a pavilion talking; a number of women sat in deck-chairs watching the play; the six courts were all in use. MacIndoe felt shabby and mean among so much whiteness. I must have this raincoat cleaned, he thought in a moment of detachment. Janet has told me about it at least three times. A few people stared but most carried on talking in nasal, middle-class voices.

'He must be in the pavilion,' said MacIndoe.

As they went up the few wooden steps someone said, 'I say, are you members?' but MacIndoe took no notice.

There were very few persons inside the pavilion. All the tables were laid for tea, but only three of them were occupied. A middle-aged man ate salad with two young women; his daughters perhaps. Two young men sat with two pretty girls; they laughed eagerly and their cutlery clattered. MacIndoe, in an acute state of intensity, had time to think: There is nothing that hurts God so much as the destruction of a child's innocence. Then he felt a small tumult of emotion as he saw the wedge-shaped face of the mother's photograph. Fortescue was sitting at a table talking to a girl in white shorts. The girl had shapely legs and embarrassingly good breasts. She was only about nineteen and her eyes, facing MacIndoe, shone in naïve reverence. You look innocent, MacIndoe thought. I hope to God you still are. Fortescue was doing the talking; he's flattering her, MacIndoe decided, seeing the girl blush and wriggle in pleasure and self-deception. Olwen, MacIndoe thought, are you here too? D'ye see him now? D'ye understand now? He's too handsome, lassie, to be beyond himself. They only love themselves, these do. The rest of us, staring into our mirrors and realizing our ugliness, are grateful for the love we are offered. We know only too well that we are fallible and imperfect. Still capable of detachment, he thought of Fortescue: I bet you don't know I've seen your parents-in-law this morning.

He and Baker were right by the table before the eagerly talking man and girl looked up. Fortescue's eyes shone with fear. He knew what they were.

'Mr. Fortescue?' MacIndoe asked.

He could not lie because the girl was with him. 'Can't you see I'm engaged?'

'Are you Mr. Fortescue?'

'Yes, yes. What is it?' The man waved his left hand in nervous irritation, and MacIndoe noted the thick gold ring on one finger.

'We are police officers,' he said. The silence was suffocating, unbearable, so that even MacIndoe wanted to smash it. It was not the silence of St. Mary's Church, but a destructive silence. Something is different, something has ended, MacIndoe realized. It worried him. What was it? Had a clock stopped? He realized then that it was the noise of the cutlery; everybody had stopped eating to listen. 'We'd like you to accompany us to Almond Vale police station.'

The girl tittered. 'What a long way. Twenty miles.'

Fortescue said, 'What on earth for?' It still isn't real, MacIndoe thought. He still imagines that with words he can escape it. Words have never failed before.

'I think we'd better discuss that when we reach there.'

'Can't it wait until after tea?'

'No.'

'What about my attire? I can't come in flannels.'

'That doesn't matter.'

'What's it all about, anyway?'

'The death of a girl named Olwen Hughes.'

The girl in shorts blinked heavily in shock and her mouth fell open. MacIndoe could hear her uneven breathing. Fortescue said, 'Who's Olwen Hughes?'

MacIndoe said with weary humour, 'If you don't know, the matter will soon be cleared up.'

Fortescue stood up. Vanity or courage? MacIndoe wondered. 'I suppose that you'll only say I'm obstructing the police if I refuse,' Fortescue said. 'Who's going to bring me back?'

MacIndoe said, 'I'll bring you back myself if it's possible.'

Fortescue said to the girl, 'I say, this may be rather fun. Why don't you come?'

The girl replied quickly—she wasn't that naïve—'I can't because I'm on in the semi-final.'

'Wait for me,' Fortescue said. 'We'll have a drink.'

'Yes,' she said.

The men began to walk away. Everybody at table looked down at their food; the agitation of the cutlery suddenly recommenced. Baker lingered, smiled at the girl, and said, 'I shouldn't wait. These things take a long time.'

Fortescue heard the words; his mouth opened to protest, but instead he walked on to the waiting car with MacIndoe.

IX

IN the moving car the police officers sat in silence. There was a crackle from the radio until MacIndoe turned the set off. The driver drove with great efficiency and speed, and only Fortescue wanted to talk. At intervals the quiet was too much for him; it was condemnatory and therefore unbearable; he was in a world without women; these were real men, not in awe of his size or his words or his amatory successes; not interested in dirty jokes; not open to persuasion by the purchase of drinks; at last he was alone, and occasionally in the face of their unspoken contempt he made remarks. 'Oh, boy, are you going to look a fool!' he said, but nobody really was under the illusion that MacIndoe was a fool. Then Fortescue said, 'No wonder the rates are high. Two detectives, a car and a driver just to get one man—and that the wrong one.' But the driver just looked ahead, concerned solely with reaching Almond Vale quickly; Baker, sitting by Fortescue, yawned; MacIndoe himself was thinking about his children. Little rogues, he thought. God, how I love them. When no comment was forthcoming from the police officers, Fortescue said, 'How did you find me, anyway?'

MacIndoe said over his shoulder, 'Ye've a number of habits.'

Fortescue seemed quite put out. 'I have not,' he protested. 'That's the one thing I haven't got—set habits. What are they, then?'

MacIndoe did not answer aloud, and Fortescue said like a child, 'You can't tell me, because you don't know.' I know all right, MacIndoe thought, but I'm not giving you any advantages; you didn't allow Olwen any. And this is going to be difficult enough as it is. Fortescue's habits, he knew, were telling untruths, seducing women, and boasting in semi-lies. He's not a fool, MacIndoe thought. His technical advantages were his callousness and his conceit. It was obvious that his thoughts now were all about himself: evasion; how far to lie; remorse was not touching him at all; it was not there to unnerve him. I'll have to go all round it and try to trip him up. We shan't obtain many direct answers until we've shown him we have brains, too, and not even then unless we put the fear of God into him. MacIndoe was thinking of his impending cross-examination. Although he had a number of proofs that Fortescue had associated with Olwen Hughes, he had nothing, unless the dentist could provide it, which would say to a jury, 'This man was in the copse when Olwen died.' (There had not been any fingerprints found on the camera.) He had a number of proofs (not yet tried out, though) which could be given to the director of prosecutions—the most fatal of them being Carter and the waitress in Almond Vale—but even then a jury might acquit Fortescue by virtue of insufficient evidence. One was not permitted to tell the jury about the mother's lies, or the tears of Fortescue's wife, or the unhappiness of the priest, or the cruelty revealed in Olwen's diary which had also stared at him from the photograph in the living-room; and one was not allowed to explain one's own emotions and conviction that this was the man. One had to answer in the non-opinionated legal 'yes' and 'no' language; in the end justice was operated by those with the gift of dialogic manœuvrability. One had to present proofs and admissions, and even then a good counsel for the defence could do damage to them. It was impartial; it was fair; yet it was not always satisfactory. Sometimes one decided that justice had no relationship to truth, but was evolved by trickery, coincidence and the payment of fees. One had the feeling that the machine was only good and usable because it was operated by honourable men.

However, all that belonged to other people. As a detective, *his* job was to obtain evidence, witnesses and the accused person; and he could cross-examine that accused person providing he used no persuasion, violence, threats, maltreatment by exhaustion—in fact, providing he treated him all the time as though the wrong person had been captured, as though he was innocent.

His cross-examination began shortly after the arrival in Almond Vale. Baker and two constables were also present; Maddocks had not yet returned. Fortescue sat in a chair at the other side of Maddocks's desk. He leaned back in exaggerated confidence, crossed one leg over the other and put both hands in his pockets.

MacIndoe said, 'What is your name?'

Fortescue said, 'Don't you know? You asked me once.'

MacIndoe said quite patiently, 'Don't waste time on facetiousness. Many of my questions will seem irrelevant. For your own sake, just answer them. It will save your breath. Now, let's have your full name.'

'Roy Marlborough Fortescue.'

'What is your job?'

'I'm a representative.'

'When you say representative, do you mean a traveller or some other kind of representative?'

'A traveller.'

'Who are your employers?'

'The Perfecta Soap Company.'

'How long have they employed you?'

'Since 1946.'

'Which area do you cover for them?'

'Middleshire.'

'All of it?'

'Yes.'

'How long have you been doing this particular job?'
'Since I joined them.'
'Do you know the county well?'
'Naturally.'
'Do you travel to Almond Vale?'
'I have to.'
'Who are your customers there?'
'A chemist in High Street and a hairdresser by the bridge.'
'When did you last call?'
'Oh, I can't remember.'
'Was it last Tuesday?'
'No; before that.'
'How long before?'
'Weeks. I call about once a month.'
'You don't go there often?'
'No.'
'Can you cover other small towns and villages on the same day?'
'Yes. That's what I do.'
'You don't spend much time on small towns?'
'No. I can do several in a day.'
'Where do you spend the major part of your efforts? Large towns?'
'Yes.'
'And the city of Birlchester?'
'Naturally.'
'You know Birlchester well?'
'Of course. I live there too.'
'If a new shop is opened, you would notice it and make a call?'
'Of course.'
'And if one was repainted?'
'I suppose so.'
'Do you cover south-west Birlchester?'
'I told you: all of it.'
'Have you ever called at Swan's of 57 Clifford Avenue?'
'Yes. I often go there.'
'How often?'
'Once a fortnight.'
'On what day?'
'Tuesdays usually.'
'Have you ever called at Birrell's, two doors away?'
'I don't think so.'
'It's only two doors away.'

'It's not a chemist's shop.'

'How do you know?'

'I've passed it.'

'Did you ever call there? Did you call there on March 22nd?'

'I don't think I've ever called.'

'What makes you sure?'

'It's a grocer's shop.'

'You don't bother with grocers?'

'I do, but not as much as the others.'

'What others?'

'Chemists.'

'You said others. That's plural. Who else besides chemists? Do you call at hairdressers?'

'Yes.'

'A few of them or many?'

'A lot of them.'

'As many as possible?'

'Yes.'

'Have you ever called at 1227 Almond Vale Road?'

'It doesn't strike a chord.'

'It's round the corner from Swan's and Birrell's. You remembered *them.*'

'I don't remember it.'

'The proprietress is Mrs. Harper. The shop is called Olga's.'

'I've never been there.'

'It's been there years. It's not a new shop, although they repainted it not long ago. It's on the main road. You've been calling in the district for years. You call at every shop, you say, but not at that one. *Why not?*'

'Perhaps I did and they rejected my stuff.'

'Are you incompetent at your work?'

'I'm not infallible.'

'Then why didn't you call there?'

'I don't know. Perhaps I did.'

'Make up your mind.'

'It's a long time ago. I——'

'*What was a long time ago?*'

Fortescue stammered. 'When I first covered that suburb.'

'If you were rebuffed then, wouldn't you have called again?'

'If I had time.'

'Surely you would make time. Isn't that the whole point of your job—to expand the business of your employers?'

Fortescue did not answer, and MacIndoe proceeded: 'What are the names of the products you might sell to hairdressers?'

Fortescue gave the names.

'Those are household words,' said MacIndoe. 'Wouldn't a hairdresser actually need them?'

'A good one would.'

'And wouldn't one who failed to purchase them be liable to lose customers?'

'Yes.'

'Knowing that, wouldn't you be eager to call again?'

'Unless they'd been unpleasant.'

'But they hadn't, had they? You would have remembered it, wouldn't you?'

'Not necessarily.'

'Who served you when you made your first call at Olga Harper's?'

'I can't remember.'

'Can you remember when you called?'

'I don't think I did call.'

'Did you see Mrs. Harper?'

'I don't know.'

'Perhaps she will know.'

'She won't.'

'*Why won't she?*'

Fortescue's lips trembled; he could see that even with care one could be trapped. 'Why should she?'

'Don't pither,' said MacIndoe in an enormous voice. 'You make a definite statement: Mrs. Harper will not know if you have called. *Why?*'

'I didn't go there.'

'Then she would know if you had called, wouldn't she? Don't be evasive, Mr. Fortescue. Why won't Mrs. Harper recognize you?'

'I didn't see her.'

'Whom did you see?'

'One of her staff.'

'Which one?'

'I don't know. Perhaps it was Mrs. Harper, but she seemed too young to be the proprietress.'

'Then you remember her?'

'Only that she was young.'

'Was she pretty?'

'How should I know?'

'Don't you notice pretty girls?'

'No. I'm married.'

'Did you ever know a woman named Myrel Burgess?'

Fortescue stared. 'It does seem a familiar name.'

'Were you her lover in 1940?'

'I was only a kid.'

'Was *she* married?'

'Yes.'

'I don't understand your principles, Mr. Fortescue. Would you like to explain them to me?'

'I don't know what you mean.'

'I mean that in 1940 you, a single man, a kid as you call yourself, go through the business of love-making with a married woman, but now that you're married you say you never look at girls—implying that it's because you're married. I just wondered at the logic of it, that's all.'

'I don't see what that's got to do with it. All that was before I was married.'

'You've changed your outlook since you married? You appreciate the sanctity of marriage now—is that it?'

'If you like to put it that way.'

'Do you know a Mrs. Saunders?'

Fortescue said excitedly, 'Good God, what bloody silly questions. It all goes back years. Trust the police to dig that up. She was at the tennis club. She wanted an affair with someone badly—it didn't matter who—and I fell for such easy meat.'

'Then you must have looked at the woman,' said MacIndoe. 'In other words, you *do* notice pretty girls. But perhaps Mrs. Saunders was ugly. What was the girl like—the one at Mrs. Harper's? Was she fat?'

'I don't think so.'

'Did she wear spectacles?'

'No.'

'Then it must have been the third girl,' said MacIndoe. 'It must have been the auburn-haired girl whose name was Olwen Hughes. Have a look at this photograph—was it *her*?'

Fortescue did not look at the proffered picture. He said, almost in anger, 'Just because I knew her, doesn't mean anything. Why don't you ask me what you want to know and let me get back to the tennis match?'

'Nobody's said that knowing Olwen Hughes implied anything,' MacIndoe said. 'It's just that there's an acute shortage of people who knew her—I'm sure I don't know why—and that we need

262

the help of those who did. Don't be anxious about the time, Mr.
Fortescue. We mustn't hurry this; we have to be very accurate and
sure of ourselves; justice is not quite the same as selling soap.
Perhaps you'd like a drink of tea?' He smiled, the irony still there.
'Let's *all* have a drink of tea. The constable will prepare one. . . .'

A constable put his head out of the door and bellowed, 'Tea
up!'

Fortescue sat motionless, a great deal of his confidence still there.
He was quite unaware that he had in any way committed himself;
he did not realize that there were implications in MacIndoe's questions; or that his obvious lies had been examined and where necessary disposed of. It seemed to MacIndoe that Fortescue had not
in any way prepared a story; he had not, in anticipation of questioning, evolved lies that overlapped each other; so confident was
he that he just dealt with each question as it came along, truthfully
if possible and untruthfully if not.

'So you knew Olwen Hughes?' MacIndoe commented, glancing
at Baker as if to point out that all his questioning had been to arrive
at this one important fact, as indeed it had. 'Why didn't you say
so in the first place?'

'I know you people,' said Fortescue. 'If anyone's associated with
a hot woman you think he's killed her.'

'Oh, no, nothing of the sort,' said MacIndoe. 'If anyone's mixed
with a dead woman we want to find out if he *could* have killed her.
We'd be silly not to, wouldn't we? What was your relationship
with Miss Hughes?' He sipped his tea as if the matter was academic
and of scarcely any interest.

The door opened and Fortescue turned quickly in his chair as
if half expecting to find someone he didn't wish to see: a barman
or waitress or boatman. Instead, it was another detective.

Maddocks, who was the detective who had entered, nodded to
MacIndoe and said, 'He's prepared to swear in a court of law that
those particular ones would make that particular impression.'

'Good,' said MacIndoe, while Fortescue stared anxiously. 'Thank
you, Inspector. That's something we can really use without much
dispute. This is Mr. Fortescue.'

'Yes, I know,' said Maddocks. 'Good afternoon.'

Fortescue seemed a little startled. Then he said, 'I suppose you're
Maddocks.'

'That's right,' said MacIndoe. 'I wonder how you knew that.
Perhaps you've been reading the papers.' A pause while he let the
implication of that sink in, then he said, 'Mr. Fortescue says he

knew Olwen Hughes.' He turned directly to Fortescue. 'You were about to explain your relations with Miss Hughes.'

Fortescue said, 'Well, she was just an ordinary pick-up.'

'How did you pick her up?'

'She gave me the eye in the shop and then came for a ride in my car.'

'You asked her?'

'I suppose so.'

'Where did you go in the car?'

'Oh, just driving around.'

'Anywhere in particular?'

'I don't think so.'

'Whose car was it? The company's?'

'No. Mine.'

'What sort of car was it?'

'A saloon. Black.'

'What's the number?'

'The number?'

'Yes, that's what I asked.'

'I can't remember.'

'How long have you had it?'

'Oh, months.'

'And you can't remember the number?'

'Not at the moment. I can look it up.'

'Did you ever possess a red sports car?'

'No.'

'Have you ever borrowed one?'

'I don't think so.'

'Where did you go with her?'

'I told you: nowhere in particular.'

'Did she mean that little to you?'

'She was only a pick-up.'

'Do you often pick women up?'

Fortescue hesitated. 'No.'

'Then where did you take this one to obtain privacy?'

'We parked in lanes and places.'

'What for?'

'The usual.'

'Did she demand payments?'

'No; she just hinted.'

'Did you give her any money?'

'Sometimes.'

'What for?'

'For a present.'

'You need not have done?'

'No.'

'Why did you, since she was only a pick-up?'

'She might have gone to someone else.'

'Would that have mattered?'

'I don't like women dumping me.'

'You like to dump them?'

'Naturally.'

'You are successful with women?'

'I can get the skirt I want.'

'Women don't usually dump you?'

'No fear. I dump them.'

'Did you dump Olwen Hughes?'

'No,' said Fortescue quickly.

'Did she dump you?'

'No'—in equal haste.

'You were still on friendly terms with her at the time of her death?'

'I hadn't seen her for some time.'

'Quite. But you were still friendly?'

'I liked her.'

'Has her death upset you?'

'Yes.'

'Why?'

'Well, because we were friends.'

'You were friends?'

'Yes.'

'She was something more than a pick-up?'

'I suppose she was.'

'Were you fond of her?'

'She had what it takes.'

'How do you mean?'

'She'd got a good body.'

'I asked if you were fond of her.'

'Well, yes, I suppose so.'

'Was she fond of you?'

'Yes.'

'Was she in love with you?'

'She liked it.'

'I asked if she was in love with you.'

'She might have been.'

'Good God! Don't you know when a woman is in love with you? Was she or wasn't she?'

'She must have been.'

'Why all this doubt? You'd had previous experience of people being in love with you, hadn't you? Was Olwen?'

Fortescue smirked. 'She was.'

'Was she satisfied with the pick-up relationship?'

'She must have been.'

'Did she ever talk about marriage?'

'They *always* talk about marriage.'

'What did Olwen Hughes say about it?'

'She'd drop hints.'

'What about?'

'About how nice it would be to be married.'

'To you?'

'To anybody.'

'But she was in love with you.' Fortescue made no comment, and MacIndoe proceeded: 'She wanted to be married to you?'

Fortescue waved a hand in a gesture of contempt. 'They all do.'

'Did you wish to marry her?'

'No.'

'Why not?'

'I'm already married.'

'Happily married?'

'Within the limitations of marriage.'

'If you are happily married, why pick up women at all?'

Fortescue said callously, 'Why not? I don't go to church.'

'Yes; but doesn't your wife mind?'

'God knows. She doesn't know anything. She's ill, anyway.'

'What sort of illness?'

'Psychological, I suppose.'

'Mental, d'you mean?'

'Not quite that.'

'Why not get divorced?'

Fortescue shrugged. 'What for? She's a good cook.'

'Then you could marry someone else.'

'I wouldn't be that stupid.'

'Would you have married Olwen Hughes?'

'How do I know?'

'If you were in love with her, you would know.'

'I wasn't mushy about her.'

'Did you tell her that you were married?'

Fortescue hesitated. 'Yes.'

'What did she say about that?'

'She wasn't worried.'

'She didn't mind the fact of your being married?'

'No, no; she just wanted what she could get.'

'It amounts to this, then,' said MacIndoe. 'You become friendly with a girl, you seduce her, allowing her to talk marriage without rebuffing her. She falls in love with you and gives you all that a woman in love can. At the same time you are not in love with her. You are married and explain this to her, telling her that your wife is ill. . . .'

Fortescue glanced up in pure fright at the last words, which must have seemed to come from the very grave. 'I didn't kill her. You can't blame me if I pick up a good-looking woman who's giving it away. She was bound to meet someone unpleasant sooner or later. I expect she's given herself to one of these mad bastards who get excited and kill people.'

MacIndoe knew now, from the mouth of the man who had destroyed Olwen's innocence (unless the diary was a fantasy, all lies, and there had been others before Fortescue), that, although she had had frequent intercourse with Fortescue, her motives had been comparatively innocent. This had little value in any legal proof of guilt; but MacIndoe wished to bring the realization to Fortescue that, irrespective of murder, he had done an evil thing. It was not just that MacIndoe intended to do what the priest wished. The dead Olwen had affected him personally more than had any previous victim. Only somebody of extraordinary evil could do what had been done and then talk about the girl as if she were rubbish, of no account, as Fortescue was doing. Even if Fortescue had not committed murder, his dialogue showed an exceptional callousness. Evelyn, another victim, had said, 'I don't want to hear what some shopgirl said.' Perhaps she had been tainted by her husband; perhaps she had merely flinched from the words of the shopgirl; but in any case the attitude was mistaken. It was as if each stood as a symbol—the girl of goodness and the man of evil. The words of the good were feeble; they showed no results or dividends; held out promises only of suffering and endeavour and at most peace. The words of the evil seemed more subtle and persuasive; they proceeded more logically; they held out proofs and possession and enjoyment, at any rate until death. In the face of distance and time, the bleatings of the good about life after death, the reward of a particular type of behaviour against all instincts, seemed absurd. The Fortescues of the world knew that the churches were empty except for those whose fear and feebleness made enjoyment for them impossible in any case; those who could not indulge and enjoy protested at those who did; it was the reverse side of the acceptance of instincts. This was the attitude MacIndoe had to defeat, and he knew in dejection that he was making no progress.

It would, of course, have been necessary to find out Fortescue's exact relationship with the girl apart from the moral sense. Since Fortescue had admittedly been sexually involved with her, from the police point of view it remained to be established when he first became involved with her (if, in fact, he could have caused her pregnancy), and when he was last involved with her. It was obvious that he, as a person intimate with a girl who had on the day of her death allowed a degree of intimacy (the undone blouse) —and allowed it willingly—would have to account very precisely for his movements on that day. The fact that MacIndoe was quite certain of Fortescue's guilt did not make such questioning unnecessary.

He asked, 'When did you first meet her?'

'In the spring.'

'In March?'

'Could be.'

'How often did you meet her?'

'Once a week.'

'Any particular day?'

'Usually on Tuesdays.'

'Why that particular day?'

'She had her half-day then.'

'Did you ever meet her on any other day?'

'Once or twice on a Sunday.'

'How were you able to meet her on what was for you a working day?'

'I used to hurry up my work so's I could see her.'

'At what time on the Tuesdays did you meet her?'

'When she finished work.'

'What time was that?'

'One o'clock.'

'Where?'

'At the cross-roads.'

'In Clifford Avenue?'

'Yes.'

'After lunch?'
'Sometimes before.'
'Then you took her to lunch?'
'Sometimes.'
'Where did you take her to lunch?'
'Anywhere handy.'
'Where in particular?'
'I can't remember.'
'Did you ever go to the Priory Tea Rooms?'
'We may have done.'
'To the Dragon Hotel?'
'No, not the Dragon.'
'You can't remember where you went, but you can remember
where you didn't. Do you know where the Dragon is?'
'No.'
'You might have been there.'
'No. It's a boozer. Olwen didn't drink.'
'She didn't have to drink.'
'Well, we didn't, anyway.'
'On how many Tuesdays did you take Miss Hughes to lunch?'
'Nearly every time I met her.'
'You met her often?'
'Yes.'
'Every Tuesday?'
'Well, almost.'
'Miss Hughes has been seen in the Dragon.'
'Not with me.'
'She's been in there with a man for lunch—always on a Tuesday.'
'I didn't meet her every Tuesday.'
'You met her almost every Tuesday.'
'We didn't go in the Dragon. It was probably another redhead.'
'No, no,' said MacIndoe. 'The barman and the waiter identified
her at once from a photograph. It was *they* who said she had red hair.'
'Then it shows you—she was anybody's pick-up.'
'It was always the same man.'
'It wasn't me.'
'Where did you go to lunch with Olwen?'
'We once went to the Castle at Brownhill.'
'Is that a licensed hotel?'
'Yes.'
'Miss Hughes didn't want to go in the Dragon, but she didn't
mind the Castle?'

'Well, they've done it up to look like a castle.'

'Did she have anything to drink?'

'She sometimes had a sherry.'

'*Sometimes*—when you only went once?'

'I brought it in the car sometimes.'

'Why, since she didn't drink?'

'She didn't at first.'

'You persuaded her to?'

'It was the same with everything: she'd pretend to be goody-goody until she'd been talked into it: then she was the same as the others.'

'You had to talk her into things?'

'Yes.'

'Did you talk her into love-making?'

'Why else would I go with her?'

'Is that how you deal with other people?'

'I don't know what you mean.'

'Has anybody ever talked you into anything, Mr. Fortescue?'

'I don't think so.'

'How would you feel if someone talked you into doing something you knew was wrong? Would you love them?'

'No.'

'Olwen Hughes loved you. Can you imagine why?'

'Because she was a fool.'

'Do you think all pretty girls are fools?'

'Most of them.'

'What about the ugly ones?'

'What about them?'

'Are they fools too? What are their qualities?'

'They're just damn' unlucky.'

'Why do you think people are created, Mr. Fortescue?'

'Because their parents went to bed.'

It was useless. He was impenetrable. MacIndoe said in something like despair, 'What do you think of your mother? Are you fond of her?'

'You bet. She's got the cash.'

Perhaps, thought MacIndoe, he will see it if we can break him the other way. He proceeded: 'Where did you take Miss Hughes in your car?'

'Usually for a drive in the countryside. We've been to the pictures a few times.'

'To dances?'

'One or two.'

'And always on a Tuesday?'

'Nearly always.'

'What did you do last Tuesday?'

'I worked.'

'Whereabouts?'

'In Birlchester.'

'Which part?'

'All over.'

'Including the south-west?'

'No; not that part.'

'Why not?'

'I'd no cause to go there.'

'Do you have a routine of any sort?'

'Not specially.'

'You just go to places when you feel like it?'

'I go when I've got to.'

'That's no answer. You have already told us that you visited that part on a Tuesday. Am I right, Constable?'

The constable turned back the sheets of his note-book. He said, 'You said to him, "Have you ever called at Swan's of 57 Clifford Avenue?"—"Yes. I often go there"—"How often?"—"Once a fortnight"—"On what day?"—"Tuesday usually"—Then just now you said to him, "How often did you meet her?"—"Once a week" —"Any particular day?"—"Usually on Tuesdays." '

Fortescue, sweating slightly, said quickly, 'Well, it wasn't as hard and fast as all that. I tried to get there on Tuesdays when I wanted to meet Olwen.'

'Did you meet her on Tuesday?'

'No. I'd stopped meeting her.'

'When was this?'

'For several weeks.'

'Had you dumped her?'

'Yes.'

'Why?'

'She was mushy.'

'You have already denied dumping her,' said MacIndoe. 'Also that she dumped you. Suppose you tell us what did happen.'

'She said that she'd met another man, and that we mustn't meet again.'

'So she did dump you?'

'It was mutual.'

'Did she say who the other man was?'

There was the ghost of a smile on Fortescue's face as he said, 'His name was Harrison.'

'We've been trying to find Mr. Harrison,' said MacIndoe. 'The only information we had was that he had a mad wife called Evelyn. You're married, aren't you, Mr. Fortescue?'

'Yes.'

'What's your wife's name?'

'She's not mad. . . .'

'I didn't ask that. Her name?'

'Evelyn Margaret.'

'Which do you call her?'

'I call her Evelyn.'

'And she has a psychological illness, hasn't she?' MacIndoe said. 'Your mother calls her Margaret. Can you suggest why?'

Fortescue was at last startled. 'My mother——?'

'Answer the question!'

'I can't.'

'Have you seen your mother lately?'

'Ten days ago.'

'Can you suggest any reason why she should think you were dead?'

'Think I was dead?'

'Yes. She thinks you're dead, Mr. Fortescue. I wonder why.'

'I don't understand all this.'

'I think I do. I don't believe in coincidences, not when there are four, five and a dozen of them. Did you ever know a man named Guy Lester?'

'No.'

'Have you ever heard of him?'

'No. What's his line?'

'He's dead.'

'I don't know any dead people.'

'You don't think much about death, do you, Mr. Fortescue?'

'I'm not scared of it.'

'Do you ever think about old age?'

'I'll worry about that when I reach it.'

'And if you reach it, Mr. Fortescue. A lot of people die young these days. What will you do if you reach old age? Will you, in the absence of physical potency, read dirty books? You'll have to do something, won't you, Mr. Fortescue? Perhaps you'll start to think.'

'I'm under no obligation to listen to this tripe. Have you run out of questions? You're not allowed to threaten me.'

'There was another subject I'd like to talk about. I see you're wearing a Royal Air Force tie. Are you a member of the R.A.F.?'

'No.'

'I understand the Mr. Harrison we're seeking may be a member of the R.A.F.V.R. Are you in any Air Force reserve, Mr. Fortescue?'

'No. I've more sense.'

'Why do you wear the tie?'

'I was in during the war.'

'Were you really? Sergeant Baker here was on fighters. Whirl-winds, was it, Sergeant?'

'Spitfires,' said Baker.

'Were you on fighters, Mr. Fortescue? You look the type.'

'I was on bombers.'

'I had a cousin at Mildenhall,' said MacIndoe. 'He was on radar. Perhaps you met him.'

'No. I was at Little Over.'

'The name strikes a chord. Didn't something special happen there?'

'We did the Kiel show from there. Dropping mines in ten-tenths flak. Only a few got back.'

'Did you go on that show?'

'You bet.'

'Did I ask you about a man called Guy Lester, Mr. Fortescue?'

'Yes. I've never heard of him.'

MacIndoe said in a hard, official voice, 'Wing Commander Guy Lester led the Kiel show, Mr. Fortescue. He was killed. You didn't fly on that raid, did you? You don't know any dead people, do you? I think you know one named Olwen Hughes very well.'

Fortescue's hands writhed. 'There were other raids on Kiel. I thought you meant——'

'We know where you went,' said MacIndoe. Fortescue flinched before the power of his voice. 'You were at Little Over in April and May of 1943. After that you proceeded to Biggots Aybury, where you met your wife.'

Fortescue said in fear, 'It doesn't prove anything.'

'You say Olwen left you for a man named Harrison?'

'Yes. It must have been——'

'Do you know Harrison's Christian name?'

'She didn't say.'

'A friend has told us that it was Roy.'

'I can't help that. My surname's Fortescue.'

MacIndoe slammed the desk with the palm of his right hand. It was a movement of tremendous strength, so suggestive of physical power that even Baker and Maddocks were quite startled. 'Mr. Roy Harrison was a pilot at Little Over in the war,' he said in an immense voice. 'He was a commercial traveller. He took Olwen Hughes to the Castle at Brownhill. He coked her up on sherries in his car. He had a mad wife called Evelyn. What kind of fools d'ye think we are? Did ye kill Olwen?'

Fortescue's mouth, scarcely under control, the jaw slack and the teeth chattering, said in a feeble, childish voice, 'You're saying all that because you know I was all those things. . . .'

'Harrison said them.'

'I don't know Harrison.'

'Olwen Hughes did.'

'If you know Harrison said them to her, you must know Harrison. . . . He must have told you.'

'He told her, and she told us.'

'She's dead. How could she?'

'In her diary.'

Almost inaudibly Fortescue said, 'Oh, Christ, oh, Christ.' (Oh, Christ, in whom I, Roy Fortescue, do not believe, save me now from the justice of these men who will kill me, so that I may again have the privilege of not acknowledging You.)

Death, the thing he had mocked at as trivial and defeasible a few minutes before, looked at him from across the desk. Death was a middle-aged man in a cheap, dirty raincoat. Fortescue looked at him in fear: he had not seemed an important opponent: even now he did not look like a man who won intellectual arguments. Death was a tubby man who had left his tea to grow cold. He was a man with a rounded, benign, sunburnt face, going bald so that the top front of his head was browned also, like the sort of egg housewives prefer. His brown eyes stared at you in sadness. He did not seem to mind the fact of your death: he had some other bee in his bonnet about Olwen: whether you had loved her and a lot of curious questions about morality: as though, if you said, 'Yes, I know I did wrong,' he would smile and say, 'Well, that's all right then, and we can both have a clear conscience about your death.' They all moralize when they are old, but make sure of their pleasures first. Donne's famous sermon had the title, 'Remember now thy Creator in the days of thy youth'; but Donne had been as bawdy as the rest of the youth of his time. What he had done to Olwen was no worse than what Donne had done to many a girl in *his* youth. Olwen had asked for it, hadn't she? Was it that he, Fortescue, was married? Was it the fact of Olwen's pregnancy? Death had said nothing about that, although he must be aware of it since every newspaper in the land had mentioned it. Fortescue, so frightened that he could scarcely hold his water, and without the strength to stand upright and walk, was yet able to think. He made no surrenders or apologies yet, and his only acknowledgement had been negative and selfish, but thoughts beyond himself were beginning to enter his head.

MacIndoe, seeing that his agony included something else besides fear, aware that at last something had penetrated, said quietly and even reluctantly, 'Are these your shoes, coat and flannels?'

Fortescue said confusedly, not knowing what he ought to say, still longing to escape, 'No.'

'The coat has your name on it.'

'It isn't mine.'

'We fetched it from your home.'

Fortescue gasped, 'From my home!'

MacIndoe nodded. 'Yes, of course. Where else? Your wife didn't want to let us have them.'

'You saw my wife?'

'Yes. She knows all about you, Mr. Fortescue.'

What it was Evelyn knew Fortescue dared not ask. He said, 'Then they must be my clothes.'

'Quite,' said MacIndoe. 'And is this not a photograph of you wearing them?'

'It's not a very good photo.'

'No. It was exposed a little to sunlight.'

Fortescue shouted in fear, 'It's not me. . . . I wasn't there.'

'You weren't where?'

Fortescue leaped frantically over the trap. 'It's not me,' he said. 'Anybody could be wearing those sort of clothes. The jacket may be another shade of colours.'

'Who is your dentist?'

'My dentist?'

'Yes, your dentist.'

'It's Mr. Wiggins.'

'His address?'

'Somewhere in Flowersworth.'

'At 49 High Street?'

'I expect so.'

'Have you been to him often?'

'Since I was a kid.'

'Do you think he is competent?'

'I would trust him.'

'So would I,' said MacIndoe. 'And he says that the teeth marks in Olwen's throat are yours. He is prepared to say so on oath in a court of law.'

Fortescue seemed scarcely able to breathe, let alone speak. In an uneven voice he said, 'He's a liar. He must be. He can't know I did a thing like that.'

'You did do it, didn't you?'

Faintly Fortescue said, 'Yes.'

'You killed her, didn't you?'

Even more faintly—'Yes.'

'Why did you kill her?'

'I put her in the family way, see? She intended to open her mouth. It would have ruined everything—my job, my wife. . . .'

'But you're an old hand at the game,' persisted MacIndoe. 'What happened to this one?'

'I couldn't use precautions,' said Fortescue. 'If she'd known I carried things around with me, she'd have known there'd been other women.'

'You mean she was an innocent girl?'

Fortescue was dazed; he had lost track; it was all he could do to survive each moment. 'I don't know why you keep bothering about that.'

'Don't you think it matters?'

'No. It's like religion. It never meant anything to me. People always do the things they want to. They go to church because they're made that way.'

'Olwen Hughes went to church before she met you.'

'She came out with me quickly enough. She did it willingly enough. Perhaps she was fed up with church.'

'She'd had opportunities before she met you. She'd loved other people. How did you persuade her to surrender?'

'I talked about marriage.'

'Did you persuade her to make love on the day you killed her?'

'I tried to, but she came out with all this stuff about a baby.'

'You knew you were going to kill her—and you tried to love her?'

'I didn't mean to kill her. I was scared. She shouldn't have threatened me.'

'She threatened *you*?'

'She intended to talk. To save others, she said, but it was revenge she wanted, of course.'

'I think that you are mistaken,' said MacIndoe. 'I think that, despite your successes, you don't know the first thing about the female character.'

Fortescue had begun to weep in great gulps. He was trying hard not to, but it was useless and his sobs came in great gasps of breath. 'I don't want to die. Don't let me die,' he pleaded in wet, loose ugliness.

'What are you afraid of if there's nothing on the other side of death?'

'I don't want to die,' Fortescue whined. Then to MacIndoe's astonishment he added, 'I don't want to see her. I can't. . . .'

'I think,' said MacIndoe, 'that if there is another side, the one person there who will have pity for you is Olwen. You must learn pity for her, and for the baby, and for her parents and her friends who've all suffered because of your vanity and self-love. Don't you feel sorry for what you've done?'

Fortescue's head was down on the desk, as were his hands, and the tears—or was it sweat?—ran in trickles towards the ink-marks: the liquids mixed and the clearer one muddied: it was the last spoliation he would ever cause. His words came in sobs: 'I can't! I can't! I've never been able to. . . .'

'Then for God's sake—and for yours—*try*,' MacIndoe pleaded. 'Believe me, you haven't much time.'

But he has a little, MacIndoe thought. He has weeks of suffering ahead of him yet: many humiliations to save him; many people to stare at him in horror and persuade him by their revulsion; and loneliness to eat at him; and the padre to convince him; and the cold, stern words of justice to be inflicted on him; and the common sense of the two men who would play cards in the death cell with him. And there would be the comradeship of pity: the small acts of kindness by those who were part of the machine to kill him; the cigarettes and the 'Cheer up, chum'; the wise books he could read if fear did not dement him. If there was a battle he had won part of it; but now he was a prisoner of war; and he must hope for more mercy than he had ever offered.

It was almost over. Less than three hours had passed since they had entered the tennis club. MacIndoe was very tired, but there was one more act. The official one. He said, 'I want you now to make a statement, Mr. Fortescue. But before you do I am going to caution you. . . .'

MACINDOE backed his car slowly into its garage and switched off the engine. He sat still on the leather seat for a moment. Silence was a relief; at times it was a pleasure. He yawned, thinking as he did, I'm always yawning these days, just as if I'd been on night duty.

He carried his front-door key in his left hand and his case in the other. The flowers had faded in the front garden; something had died; but someone had cut the lawn. The front door was open. Janet had seen, or perhaps heard, his approach, and was waiting in shyness just beyond it. She would not, he knew, embrace him anywhere which could be considered as in public, so he shut the door before he spoke a word. Words were difficult. It was like coming home from a battle. Everything was the same, but you were different. There was a weight of something like unhappiness inside you. The ones who had stayed behind wanted you back as you had gone away; that was how they had loved you. You could not explain with words about the battle: about the dead and the mutilated and the injured you could not help and the next-of-kin and the prisoners and the unbearable futility of the causes. He said gruffly, 'Well, I'm home.'

'I can see that.'

They held each other for a long moment, and MacIndoe touched the top of his wife's head. How small and frail women are, he thought. How clever they have to be—or how beautiful—to deal with men. How frail we all are: the human body is the softest part of any accident. He had a brief, terrible vision of the way Olwen Hughes had died and found it hard to dismiss from his mind. 'Are ye all right?' he asked.

'Do I look different or something?'

'No, thank God, ye look the same.'

'Ye mustna talk like that.'

'I meant it.'

'Well, you shouldna.'

'Away with ye. What's been happening while I've been away?'

'Nothing much. There's an invitation to the Horse Show and my sister's written. She's coming to London in a couple of weeks' time. She'll be staying with us.'

278

'Och, that's terrible news,' said MacIndoe. 'Policemen on horses and Edith coming.'

'Why don't ye like Edith?' Janet asked seriously. 'She's my twin sister, but ye've never liked her. Maybe ye don't like *me*. . . .'

MacIndoe pulled her head down on to his chest. 'The nonsense ye talk!'

'But she's just the same!'

'Rubbish! Her voice is different.'

'Is that all? Ye mean ye only like me for my voice? I never heard of such a thing! Did ye eat those sandwiches?'

'Aye.'

'And did ye give Mr. Baker some?'

'Yes, yes,' said MacIndoe. 'We ate them in Oxford.'

'Why in Oxford?'

'I don't know. It wasn't Oxford, anyway.'

'Ye shouldna lie.'

'It was Oxfordshire somewhere.'

'If ye can't be sure of the town, how can ye be sure of the county?'

'Stop your nattering. Ye're like a policewoman.'

'Thank ye for the card and the letter. It looks a pretty place.'

'It's nice enough.'

'Will ye be going back?'

'Aye. For the Assizes.'

'Shall I come with ye? Is it nice enough for a holiday?'

MacIndoe said quickly, 'No; ye'd better not come.'

She looked at him. 'Was it a bad one?'

'They're all bad.'

'Ye know what I mean.'

'It was pretty bad. I don't want to go there for any holiday. Not along the river.'

'It was only a thought.'

'It was where she died, ye see.'

'Ye caught him?'

'We did.'

'Was he a foolish one? He lost his head?'

'No. It was worse than that. He couldna face up to his responsibility. He didna mind who suffered. . . . He gave her a baby and then took fright.'

'He killed the two of them then? Oh, that's bad,' said Janet. 'Will they find him guilty?'

'They will.'

'Did they say anything at the magistrate's court?'

279

'No. They just committed him for trial at the Assizes.'

'What about his folk?'

'His wife's going back to her parents. The most extraordinary thing,' said MacIndoe, and it was indeed remarkable to him, 'was that he wrote about it in a book—ye know, an exercise book. We found it in his car. He wrote about that day and the words he put into her mouth were not the words she used on that day, but the sort of things she'd been saying for weeks. What he wrote down as her words was beautiful, and yet d'ye know why he wrote them? Because he thought they proved what a fool she was.'

'What a peculiar thing,' said Janet. But MacIndoe could see that she did not comprehend how extraordinary it was. One had to be a participant in the battle to understand the freak effects of war.

There was the sound of excited children's voices. A girl's voice cried, 'It's Daddy, it's Daddy!' MacIndoe's two children ran into the hall. The boy was taller and faster, and the girl gave a quick cry, tears not far off because she wanted to be the one who was loved first. MacIndoe hugged each one in turn; then he picked Mary up. She was the one who was full of laughter and tears, the one who needed love the more. Andréw, serious and quiet, was already moving out into a world of his own. MacIndoe said, 'And Daddy's brought something with him.'

'What?' she asked. 'Tell me.'

'Guess.'

'No. Tell me. A doll?'

'Almost right.'

'A teddy bear!'

She knew she had guessed correctly, because that was one of the things she wanted; and when one is eight years old one still has the things one wants; one is even entitled to them. 'Where is it, Daddy?'

'In the car.'

'Let me fetch it.'

From his raincoat pocket MacIndoe produced a small model which he handed to Andrew. 'Thank you,' the boy said. 'What's the red cross for?'

'It's an ambulance. I knew you hadn't one.'

'What's an ambulance for?'

'For when people get hurt.'

'Do people get hurt in your games?'

'Yes.'

'Which people get hurt?'

MacIndoe said, 'I think perhaps that all of them do.'